"I make for very dull company." There were things about her past that only a handful of people knew. Maggie had no desire for the viscount to learn her secrets. He might use them against her in some way. Compromise her. Or draw upon her weaknesses into a seduction.

That's what this was, wasn't it? An attempt at seduction? She couldn't imagine it being anything else. Especially the way he looked at her now, as if she were the only woman—the only person—in existence.

It was a heady, reckless feeling.

"I doubt that very much," he murmured. He stepped a little closer. So close she could feel the warmth of his body. But if she backed up, it would be ceding victory to him, and she needed to prove to him and herself that he had no power over her.

He continued, "Especially judging by your work. If we dined, we could talk long into the night about your writing. Or we needn't talk at all. There are so many other ways of . . . communicating."

By Eva Leigh

SCANDAL TAKES THE STAGE
FOREVER YOUR EARL

Coming Soon

TEMPTATIONS OF A WALLFLOWER

Eva Leigh

Scandal Takes the Stage

The Wicked Quills of London

AVONBOOKS

An Imprint of HarperCollinsPublishers

This is a work of fiction. Names, characters, places, and incidents are products of the author's imagination or are used fictitiously and are not to be construed as real. Any resemblance to actual events, locales, organizations, or persons, living or dead, is entirely coincidental.

AVON BOOKS
An Imprint of HarperCollins*Publishers*
195 Broadway
New York, New York 10007

Copyright © 2015 by Ami Silber
Excerpt from *Forever Your Earl* copyright © 2015 by Ami Silber
ISBN 978-0-06-235864-6
www.avonromance.com

First Avon Books mass market printing: November 2015

Avon Trademark Reg. U.S. Pat. Off. and in Other Countries, Marca Registrada, Hecho en U.S.A.
HarperCollins® is a registered trademark of HarperCollins Publishers.

Printed in the U.S.A.

10 9 8 7 6 5 4 3 2 1

To Zack, my source of endless inspiration.

Acknowledgments

Thank you to my agent, Kevan Lyon, for always being there, and to my editor, Nicole Fischer, who always has my back.

Chapter 1

Enter Phoebe, in country dress.
Phoebe: What a task I have set before me!

The Shattered Heart

London, 1816

The curtain at the Imperial Theater fell. The audience rose to its collective feet and applauded.

Standing in his theater box, adding his own applause, Cameron Chalton, Viscount of Marwood was filled with excitement. Much as Cam enjoyed the theater—he went practically every night, and often saw the same work over and over, enjoying it anew each time—half the pleasure came after the performances.

"What say you, Marwood?" drawled Lord Eberhart, one of Cam's companions for the evening. "Gaming at Donnegan's? Shall we away to the rout at Lord Larkin's? He's brought in a whole bevy of beauties from France just for the occasion."

"Why choose?" Cam answered with a laugh. "The night's in its infancy, and we can do anything at all."

"Good point." Eberhart grinned. He wasn't the

brightest star in the firmament, but ever since Cam's good friend Ashford had wed and settled into marital bliss, Cam couldn't afford to be as selective with his company. Besides, Eberhart was always up for a night's revelry. "Let's go."

"Not yet," Cam answered, watching the theater slowly empty.

The Imperial was smaller than the other popular theaters in London, with only three tiers for seats and boxes, plus a smaller pit and orchestra. Yet it wasn't shabby. The proprietors kept its appearance well. Painted plaster friezes depicting scenes from mythology adorned the fronts of the boxes, and blue velvet curtains draped the sides and top of the stage. Gas lamps provided lighting.

The boxes now released their occupants like tropical birds flying free of their cages. In the pit, the younger, wilder set laughed and boasted, jostling one another, flirting, arguing. Orange girls and women of fast reputation circulated freely among the young men.

Cam's status prevented him from sitting in the pit anymore, but he missed it. The energy, the rowdiness. Still, he couldn't complain, not when he'd just watched a performance of a work written by the celebrated and mysterious Mrs. Delamere. Not when the evening opened up for him like an endless banquet. One he would sample to his heart's content. But not quite at this moment.

"Tell you what, Eberhart," Cam continued, turning back to his companion. "I'll meet you at Donnegan's, then we'll sally forth from there onto Larkin's."

"Going to circulate?" Eberhart said with a grin.

"This is my kingdom," Cam replied with a wink. "I must inevitably tour my realm. Inspect its crops."

"Of actresses." His friend leered.

Cam tilted his head in acknowledgment. "Merely a part of my dominion."

"Enjoy, Your Highness." With a chuckle, Eberhart slipped from the box and out into the night.

Once his friend had gone, Cam took one last minute to enjoy the theater's house as patrons continued to leisurely make their way. The thrills from the performance still resonated in Cam's body, palpable as electricity crackling along his veins. Though he'd seen this particular work several times, it never lost its excitement—the soaring highs and resounding lows that came from watching characters' love and loss. He especially loved how the heroine thoroughly humiliated the aristocratic villain before gaining her tragic vengeance against him.

Not every work affected him as much. But for a reason he couldn't quite articulate, Mrs. Delamere's tragic burlettas stabbed him through as beautifully and cleanly as a jeweled knife. Her use of language, perhaps, was so much more articulate than other staged dramas. Or the relatable human longing and pain contained within in each work. Whatever caused it, Cam craved the next work from her the way a drunkard needed wine.

Still somewhat tipsy from the performance, he strode from the box. Almost at once, he ran into two young, red-faced lordlings, already listing from too much ale. A pretty courtesan snuggled between them.

"Marwood!" they exclaimed, practically tripping over themselves as they clumsily bowed.

"Gents," Cam answered, a little coolly. He didn't mind being a little disguised from drink, but it was a classic mistake of the young not to pace themselves.

"Come with us!" they cried. "We're going to Vaux-hall. Supposed to be quite a crush."

For a moment, Cam contemplated it. The pleasure garden always promised a good time, and delivered. Its theatricality and lurid beauty never failed to entertain, and more than once, he'd taken a female companion to the Dark Walk for an *al fresco* amorous encounter. There was something thrilling about being outside when engaged in carnal pursuits—the fresh air, the possibility of being caught.

The courtesan accompanying the two young men gave him a not very discreet looking over. Judging by the way her eyes brightened, she liked what she saw. Maybe she would be agreeable—if not enthusiastic—about the prospect of a trip to Vauxhall's Dark Walk.

However . . .

"Save me a slice of roast beef," Cam said. "I'll join you another time."

The two bucks looked somewhat crestfallen, but, after a quick exchange of further pleasantries, they and their female friend moved on.

Leaving Cam free to head toward his destination: backstage. That's where the real action took place.

As he slowly ambled toward his goal, he passed more and more friends and acquaintances. All of them hailed him. Dozens of invitations were issued. Some to sanctioned Society events, others to more daring, exclusive gatherings. Tempting, every one. He wished he had more than one self, so that he might partake of everything presented to him. Galas, private assemblies, midnight horse races. There was no shortage of amusements, no limit on the pleasures he might experience. Bold widows and bored wives offered their own wordless invitations with their provocative glances and heated gazes.

How could he resist? More often than not, he didn't.

Tonight, however, he had other plans. Specifically, the actress playing the ingénue.

After disentang'ling himself from another posse of aristocratic theater patrons, he headed down the stairs. Closer to his objective.

"What a perfectly dismal surprise," someone behind him said wryly.

Cam's heart rose. He knew that voice, almost as well as he knew his own. Now the night could truly begin! He turned to face the Earl of Ashford.

Standing beside Ashford was the earl's new wife, a very pretty blonde, and some of Cam's enthusiasm dampened. It wasn't that he disliked Lady Ashford. Far from it. But ever since she'd come into the earl's life, Cam's own world had been in a state of upheaval. It wasn't nearly as much fun running wild through the Town without Ashford.

"Now the evening's truly ruined," Cam answered.

Both Ashford and his wife were elegantly attired for a night out. Lady Ashford, in particular, glowed in blue. Though she was a countess, she prided herself on being a working woman. Yet Cam felt certain that the substantial sapphires around her neck and hanging from her earlobes were placating gestures to her husband. Ashford tried to spoil her at every turn.

The couple stood unfashionably close. Ashford had his hand on the small of his wife's back.

After kissing Lady Ashford's gloved knuckles and giving his old friend's hand a shake, Cam said wryly, "I'm older than I thought, since I'm certain that my eyes are failing. This can't be Lord and Lady Ashford actually leaving their home. Joining those of us who haven't found wedded bliss."

"It's not our fault that the female population of London considers you an irredeemable rogue," Ashford said.

His wife smiled warmly. "To women, his reputation acts as a lure, not a deterrent."

"And yet they'll find themselves sorely disappointed," Cam noted, clasping his hands behind his back. "Because this piece of beefsteak is not for sale at Smithfield market."

Ashford shook his head. "Don't tell your father. He comes to me almost once a fortnight, despairing of you ever finding a wife."

Cam rolled his eyes. His father was also Ashford's godfather, and ever since his friend had married, the efforts to see Cam settled and applying himself to the business of getting an heir had redoubled.

"So much labor," Cam said with mock sorrow, "and for so little an outcome."

"You are determined to remain a dedicated bachelor, then?" Lady Ashford pressed, ever the journalist. She used her matching blue fan to cool herself against the oppressive heat in the theater.

"I have a younger brother," Cam noted. "He has three qualities in his favor that I do not." Holding up his hand, he enumerated each aspect on his fingers. "One: he has already taken a bride of suitable lineage and fortune. Two: they have produced a child. And third: he has no compunction about assuming the role of Marquess of Allam should anything happen to me."

Shrugging, Cam said, "There are no obstacles to me

continuing to live my life as I so desire it. Free of entanglements." Free of disappointment.

His parents had a remarkably happy marriage. While they didn't show affection in public the way the Ashfords did, at home, it was another matter. His mother and father were devoted to each other, brushing hands, exchanging looks, even—God help him—sequestering themselves in the middle of the day in the bedchamber.

It hadn't been a love match, but it had become one, and Cam knew things like that occurred rarely. What had happened with a seasoned rake like Ashford was the exception, about as common as finding a pearl in an apple.

The only place where love happened consistently was on the stage. It wasn't meant for the real world. Not meant for him. He'd only find disenchantment if he tried for what couldn't be.

Which is why he always kept his amorous encounters temporary

Lady Ashford raised a brow. "You are quite convinced that you want no such 'entanglements.'"

"As convinced as you are that you must continue to work," he rejoined with a bow, "despite your new social standing."

She tipped her head in acknowledgment. "I yield—for now."

Ashford smiled. "Careful, Marwood. That only means she's taking a tactical retreat. When it comes to matters of significance, my wife is quite tenacious." He said this with obvious affection.

Cam couldn't begrudge his old friend this happiness. A new brightness and life shone in Ashford's eyes now, as if he'd discovered his purpose, the meaning of his existence.

After glancing around to make certain no one listened in, Cam leaned closer to Lady Ashford and said conspiratorially, "I saw a certain Lord V— deep in private conversation with Lord W—'s new wife."

Her smile was wise and knowing. "Already made note of it." Though she was a countess, she continued to own and run *The Hawk's Eye*, one of London's most popular scandal sheets. In fact, a series of articles in the paper about Ashford had actually brought the two together.

Cam bowed. "I see I cannot top you for intelligence, my lady."

"Few can," Ashford said with a grin.

Lady Ashford said, "It appears to this intelligent eye that we're detaining Lord Marwood from some objective. Perhaps he plans on paying a call on Miss Smith, who so delightfully played the role of the ingénue this evening."

Shaking his head, Cam had to admire the countess's shrewdness. "I admit nothing," he said instead.

"A good rake never does," she countered, though she smiled.

"Enjoy the hunt," Ashford chuckled.

"I will."

With that, Cam took his leave of his old friend. A bubble of melancholy settled in his chest at the thought of what he'd lost with Ashford's marriage, and that his friend had found love, when it was such a rare commodity. Given that lightning had struck twice so closely to Cam, it seemed even more unlikely that it would strike him. How much genuine love was there in the world? Very little. It was mostly contained within the proscenium arch of a theater.

He wasn't in search of love tonight. Only pleasure.

A tall, broad man stood guarding the backstage entrance. His thick arms crossed over his chest as half a dozen young men vied to be admitted behind the scenes—to the actresses' dressing rooms, most of all. Other theaters had a more lax policy regarding backstage visitors, but someone at the Imperial had years ago instituted a rule wherein all would-be suitors had to be vetted. Clearly, none of these bucks met the criteria.

"Come on, let me in," one lad whined. "She's expecting me."

"I've got a twenty-pound note with your name on it," another pled.

The mountain guarding backstage wouldn't be moved.

As Cam approached, the crowd parted. The noise died down. All the younger men stared at Cam with something like reverence. He tried not to preen. After all, he'd worked hard for his reputation as a hellraiser of the first water. It would be a shame if all that labor was for nothing.

"That's Marwood," one of the men whispered reverently to the other.

"Think he'll take us with him tonight?"

"Did you hear about the party he threw the other month? A masked ball the likes of which hasn't been seen since Ancient Rome."

"I say, Marwood—"

He ignored them. Instead, he stepped in front of the giant man.

"Lord Marwood?" the massive gent asked.

Cam inclined his head.

The man stepped to one side and waved him forward. "If you please, my lord."

Before he moved on, he turned to address all the panting, eager young chaps. "Never beg for anything," he said. "Makes you look desperate. No one respects a desperate man. Especially women."

With that, he strode backstage. All at once, the cacophony started up again. Sadly, it seemed none of the blokes took Cam's advice. Ah, well. They'd discover the truth of his words sooner or later.

Backstage, all was controlled chaos. Still in costume, performers of every stripe milled around—including acrobats, a dog act, a cloud of dancers, clowns, and the rouged, adorned actors and actresses from the final burletta. In addition to the performers were the stage crew, taking away painted flats, gathering up properties, and generally looking put out by the fact that they had to work in the middle of this bedlam.

Cam stopped in the wings and drew a deep breath. It wasn't a pleasant breath, thick as the air was with the scent of paint and sweat, but to Cam it still smelled as rich and heady as a fine perfume. This was the fragrance of the theater, of the magic of make-believe. It was slightly stale and very human. Precisely the reasons why he enjoyed it so much.

Many gazes landed on Cam as he paused in the wings. Within a moment, three actresses in their pretend silks and velvets gathered around him like painted butterflies. They batted their kohl-lined eyes at him, draping their soft ivory arms around his shoulders, and smiling with pretty little teeth. Beads of sweat that jeweled their hairlines only added to their appeal. Unlike the women of ballrooms and Society teas, these women had a realness about them, grounded as they were in the theater and its work. It was a paradox that, though they invested themselves in the realm of the pretend, they were more genuine to Cam than any debutante. He accepted his own contradictions.

"My lord," a brunette actress cooed. "A pleasure."

"Pleasure is my fondest pursuit," he answered with a grin.

The female performers giggled.

He was gratified to see that Miss Smith was among the actresses' numbers. Tall and willowy, with ash blond hair and gray eyes, she had the figure of a woodland sylph but a knowing gaze. And equally adept hands.

Those hands played across Cam's waistcoat, pressing against his chest. She would've made a lovely pickpocket. No man would have resisted getting fleeced by those pretty fingers.

"Oh, my lord," she sighed. "You're not soft like the other gents that come back here. You're hard all over."

"Indeed, I can be," he replied.

More titters arose from the women.

"Did you enjoy the performances tonight?" Miss Smith asked.

"Everyone was in rare form," he answered honestly. "Tears nearly rolled down my cheeks at the tragic conclusion of the final burletta. And I wasn't the only one in the audience who felt that way. We were all in a swoon." He spoke no exaggeration.

He didn't believe in false flattery. It was a cheap trick used by rogues and frauds who hadn't enough skill to win a woman through the truth.

"In fact," he went on, "I'd very much like to show my appreciation for such a performance by inviting all of you out for a private supper."

The actresses squealed with happiness. Miss Smith beamed at him, and her eyelashes batted so furiously, they nearly tangled. Cam realized that he'd told Eberhart that he'd meet him at the gaming hell in an hour, but he knew the other man wouldn't mind if Cam decided to entertain a small collection of actresses instead. A fellow had to have his priorities.

Cam was about to suggest to the women that they go change out of their costumes, when a movement in the corner of his eye caught his attention. Or rather, the absence of movement. In the sea of commotion, there was a small spot of stillness, and it drew his gaze.

A woman. Petite yet curvaceous, with a mass of nearly black hair piled atop her head, she read over a sheet of paper. Unlike the actresses and dancers, she wasn't in costume. She wore a simple russet woolen gown with a high neckline and long sleeves. Her face was tilted down as she examined the document in her hands, yet Cam could see that she had a small, pointed chin, nearly severe dark eyebrows, and a wide, lush mouth. Not precisely beautiful, but certainly striking.

Within the confines of her small, curvy body, she held a unique gravitas. A purpose and intent. She fairly burned with it. And damn him if that didn't appeal to Cam.

A sudden need to be near her blazed through him. She seemed familiar to him, somehow, yet he couldn't quite place her. Whoever she was, he wanted to smooth the crease between those arresting eyebrows. He needed to hear her voice—whether it was high and girlish, or low and husky. He wanted . . . he didn't know what he wanted. Only to be close by her side.

"Excuse me for a moment," he murmured distractedly, disentangling himself from Miss Smith and the other actresses. As if in a daze, he crossed the wings, barely seeing anything and anyone.

Only the mysterious woman before him.

Chapter 2

*Phoebe: Will anyone guess the secret of my
   identity? I pray not.*

   The Shattered Heart

Despite the swirl of controlled madness around her,
Margaret Delamere's focus remained solely on the document in her hand. The letter had been haunting her for
three days, ever since she had received it. And she was
no closer to answering the missive than she had been
when it was first delivered. But a reply was expected.
Nay, demanded.

She couldn't even enjoy the usual glow that followed
the conclusion of another successful performance of
one of her burlettas. All she could do was worry, anxiety a cold knot in her stomach.

As she reread the letter, Maggie became aware that
she wasn't alone.

Glancing up, she looked into one of the most handsome faces she'd ever seen. And immediately, silently,
cursed it.

Lord Marwood. Perfectly suited to one of Maggie's
own plays as the dashing, devilish rake, Marwood wore

his dark hair long, and it looked as though he'd spent several days apart from the company of his razor, given the stubble on his square jaw. He sported his phenomenally expensive clothing with dashing roguishness, his cravat barely tied. Though he wasn't exceptionally tall, he had a long, lean build, the kind well suited for all manner of athletic pursuits—including lovemaking.

Maggie immediately bristled. She didn't care for being interrupted, especially by *him*.

For a moment, he did nothing. Only stared at her. First with a look of pure male interest, then it slowly shifted. Into something much more subtle. Oh, damn it. He recognized her.

"Miss Delamere?"

"Mrs.," she answered.

"The author of my favorite theatrical works! *Love's Betrayal*, *What the Heavens Allow*, and—my Lord— *The Shattered Heart*." The viscount sounded as excited as if he was meeting Wellington himself. His dark eyes gleamed with enthusiasm.

"The same," she replied tersely. Though she ordinarily enjoyed meeting admirers of her work, the letter had put her in no mood to talk to anyone, especially a handsome, rakish aristocrat. Maggie knew all about him, given his reputation, and his frequency in attending the Imperial. It was a small world, the theater, and gossip and rumor spread faster than the ague.

Only last week, Maggie learned that Lord Marwood had been involved in a rather messy love triangle between a widow and an opera dancer. The awkward relationship had ended on rather . . . interesting terms. His list of lovers was the stuff of legend and speculation. And it seemed as though every wild party and private gathering required his presence. Not that Maggie ever went to such get-togethers, of course. Her blood remained steadfastly lowborn—a fact for which she was grateful. She'd no desire to rub elbows with High Society.

Bitter experience had taught her what happened when commoners and gentry mixed.

"If I'm not mistaken," the viscount continued, "you were also at Lord and Lady Ashford's wedding."

Damn and hell. She'd hoped he wouldn't recall that. But it appeared that, besides having an extraordinarily handsome face and virile body, Lord Marwood possessed an excellent memory.

"I was a guest, yes," she answered warily.

"You sat at the back of the church," he said. "Yet you didn't come to the wedding breakfast."

"There were matters at the theater that needed attending to." Which wasn't accurate. The truth of the matter was that, despite the fact that Eleanor, Lady Ashford, was Maggie's closest friend, even the prospect of friendship couldn't dim Maggie's acute unhappiness and discomfort in the presence of blue bloods. Maggie had slipped from the church the moment the vows had been exchanged, and retreated back to the safety of the theater. Thankfully, Eleanor had understood and sympathized. No ill will existed between her and Maggie.

Lord Marwood had been standing up with Lord Ashford, impossibly good looking in his formal clothing, his dark hair slicked back from his forehead, and the light streaming in from the stained glass windows falling in a multi-hued glow across the hard planes of his face. Between him and Lord Ashford, it was unlikely two more attractive men had ever stood before the church's congregation.

But Maggie had made sure to keep her gaze either on Eleanor or her hymnal. She'd kept far from Lord Ashford's aristocratic guests. And she'd tried not to attract anyone's attention, especially Lord Marwood.

Men like him were the very Devil. Handsome. Dangerous.

She didn't owe the viscount an explanation for her behavior. She barely knew the man.

"There were many people in attendance that day," she said. "Your vision must be very good, to spot me at the back of a crowded church."

"You're very easy to notice," he answered with a crooked smile. It shot straight between her ribs. What a weapon, that smile. Promising wickedness and pleasure. No wonder women all over London fell like cut flowers at his feet.

But she wouldn't be one of those flowers. She was a hardy little weed. Not showy, but tenacious.

"My lord," she said crisply, "you are a flatterer."

"Perhaps so," he replied with an easy shrug. "But I find compliments much easier to give when they are merited."

"And if the compliment is neither believed nor desired?"

His smile widened into a dazzling grin. "Then the challenge becomes all the greater, and I have discovered that I cannot resist a challenge."

"However," she went on, "the challenge can resist you."

He laughed, a rich, low sound. "Even better."

How infuriating. He likely took nothing seriously, least of all himself. Typical aristo. Given everything and denied nothing.

The viscount said with a low and seductive tone, "You and I should be friends."

"I am certain you have plenty of *friends*, my lord."

"A man like me can never have too many." Confidence radiated from him in alluring waves. "We have mutual acquaintances." His voice deepened. "Let's all dine together. Learn more about each other."

She could well imagine that to take a meal with him would lead to other kinds of feasts. A low flame kindled in her belly at the thought. But she had to extinguish that flame, for her own safety.

"I make for very dull company." There were things about her past that only a handful of people knew. Maggie had no desire for the viscount to learn her secrets. He might use them against her in some way. Compromise her. Or draw upon her weaknesses into a seduction.

That's what this was, wasn't it? An attempt at seduction? She couldn't imagine it being anything else. Especially the way he looked at her now, as if she were the only woman—the only person—in existence.

It was a heady, reckless feeling.

"I doubt that very much," he murmured. He stepped a little closer. So close she could feel the warmth of his body. But if she backed up, it would be ceding victory to him, and she needed to prove to him and herself that he had no power over her.

He continued, "Especially judging by your work. If we dined, we could talk long into the night about your writing. Or we needn't talk at all. There are so many other ways of . . . communicating."

"I have much to do," she answered, which was the truth.

A look of disappointment crossed his face. "Can you at least tell me when the sequel to *The Shattered Heart* will be performed?"

She stiffened. "I will tell you what I tell *everyone*: it will be ready at the speed of my quill."

"Can your quill move faster?"

She was saved the need for an acidic reply by the arrival of Miss Smith. The actress looked clearly put out by Lord Marwood's lack of attention, her lower lip poking out like a child's.

"I thought *we* were going to supper," she pouted.

The viscount started, as if he'd forgotten Miss Smith's existence. "Forgive me, my dear. I find myself in an odd humor tonight. I hardly know where I am, or who I keep company with."

"Well, Lord Frobisher has asked me to dinner with *him*," she tossed out.

"Oh, Frobisher is an excellent companion," Lord Marwood said with an easy smile. "By all means, join him."

Miss Smith huffed in displeasure, then flounced off.

"She didn't care for that at all," Maggie murmured.

"Ah, she'll forget me in moments," Lord Marwood answered, offhanded.

Somehow, Maggie doubted that.

"Can I not change your mind about tonight?" the viscount pressed.

"I am simply too busy," she said at once. "And I make it a policy never to dine with theater patrons."

"Do you dine with Lord and Lady Ashford?"

"They are friends of mine," she noted.

"Perhaps it's time to widen your circle of acquaintance," he said persuasively.

"I do not think so." They should have as little to do with each other as possible. Maggie would make sure of it. His kind were too alluring and too treacherous.

She suspected his main curiosity in her lay in the fact that his interest wasn't returned. That had to be novel for him. And aristos were always looking for the next novelty. But she was a human being, not a curiosity at a pleasure garden. She had the metaphorical scars to prove it.

"Please excuse me, my lord." Politeness demanded she give him a small curtsey, which she did, and then, quickly as she could, she walked away. Leaving him behind her, as she had to. For her own protection.

In contrast to the mayhem of several hours earlier, the Imperial now sat silent and quiet, empty of everyone. Except Maggie. And Mr. Pierre Kingston, a freeman and the theater's stage manager.

Sometimes Maggie liked to join the performers in their revels at local taverns following the evening's show. They would drink and comically toast one another, and themselves. If a performance went especially well, there might be dancing. Theatricals were a boisterous lot. Always had been, since the earliest performances in Ancient Greece. It was a hard life, marked often by poverty and drudgery, which meant they stole pleasure and merriment wherever they could.

For Maggie, tonight was not one of those nights. She simply hadn't the space in her mind to pretend to be happy, not when everything was on the verge of crumbling around her like so much plaster eaten through by dry rot.

Yet she couldn't quite be alone, either. Which was why she had taken a seat in Mr. Kingston's office as he sat at his desk and reviewed the night's tally. The room was cluttered with old playbills and *commedia dell'arte* masks.

"A good night tonight," he said in his Caribbean-accented baritone. "We can run *The Shattered Heart* a half a dozen times a week, and we nearly sell out every night."

"Nearly," Maggie remarked. "But not completely."

"Trust a writer to find the negative in that statement." A smile creased his dark brown face.

She shrugged. "We're fragile creatures, who live or die on a single word."

"I prefer to live on steak pie," he answered. "But I won't get any until I finish calculating these numbers. You needn't keep me company. They're all down at the Foxhead, getting, well, foxed."

"I like it here." She picked up one of the masks, this one with a very long nose and exaggerated angry eyebrows, and held it to her face. "That is, if you don't mind my presence."

"Good to have someone with me as I go about my labor. Makes it less lonely. That's a wonderful look for you, by the way," he added, waving at the mask. "Much more approachable."

"Bah." She set the mask. "I'm approachable."

"Clearly, the viscount thought so," Mr. Kingston said drily.

Oh, God. *That* man. He hadn't been far from her thoughts ever since they'd parted company. Where had he gone? Who had he gone with? And why should it matter to her?

She made a scoffing sound. "He's just like the rest of his class—good looking, useless, predatory."

"Yet awfully interested in you," the stage manager noted.

"He's interested in anything with skirts," she answered.

Mr. Kingston set his papers aside. "Not true. He could've easily found female company with Miss Smith, or any number of actresses or dancers. Once he saw you, he lost all awareness of anyone else."

Maggie made another dismissive sound. "I'm an oddity to him: a woman who can say no."

"Men don't look at oddities the way he looked at you," the stage manager argued gently. "Besides, all that business about the thrill of the hunt, that's just nonsense. Yes, men like a little bit of a challenge, but they prefer a sure thing."

"If there's anything I'm not, it's a sure thing."

"That is most definitely true." He rose, sighing. "Some damn fool didn't bring me the receipts for the second half. They likely left them in the box office." He started for the door. "Don't set anything on fire while I'm away," he warned her.

"Writers are compulsive thieves," she countered. "Not arsonists."

"Steal anything you like, then," he said with a wave. "It's all pasteboard, anyway." With that, he disappeared down the hallway.

Alone in his office, Maggie stood and began to pace. Mr. Kingston's comments about the viscount were part of the well-meaning badinage and gossip that belonged to theatrical life, yet how could he know that they stirred up thoughts and feelings Maggie didn't want?

She hadn't been able to stop thinking of Lord Marwood since they'd gone their separate ways after the performance. No denying that the man was handsome as hell, and wickedly seductive. She heard all about his reputation—not only for the number of his lovers, but the quality of his lovemaking. While some men studied science or politics, it seemed that Lord Marwood studied the art of bedsport.

Which was all the reason she needed to avoid him. He might give a woman pleasure, but it was a temporary pleasure. Men like him never stayed. They took what they wanted, and then moved on to the next triumph.

It might be temporary, but it would be fun.

She shook her head, dismissing the thought. *Fun* led to strife. She would *not* be added to his catalogue of lovers. "The lady writer," he'd likely call her when itemizing his conquests. She'd already experienced that kind of trouble, and had paid the price. And that's precisely what Lord Marwood was. Trouble in a pair of gleaming Hessians. No matter his dark good looks and alluring smile.

Besides, she had much greater problems to attend to besides one handsome viscount.

The letter burned in her pocket. Though she'd read and reread it, she pulled it out one more time to peruse its contents.

Dear Mrs. Delamere,

We hope this letter finds you in good health. As you have not responded to our last two missives, we can only conclude that either you are suffer-

ing from some ailment, or you are extremely busy working on the promised sequel to The Shattered Heart. *We sincerely hope that it is the latter.*

If, perchance, you did not receive our prior letters, or have yet to read them, let us reiterate our previous sentiments. The board of the Imperial Theater is exceedingly eager to produce the sequel. Given the tremendous success of The Shattered Heart, *we keenly seek to replicate that triumph at the earliest possible opportunity. The Imperial has been subsisting on the profits from this burletta, yet the surfeit of profits is now dwindling. The guaranteed means of replenishing them is with another success, which the sequel will most assuredly be.*

Please respond to our correspondence at the soonest chance with an estimation as to the completion of this work. We anticipate your answer.

Yours, &c.
The Board of Directors, Imperial Theater,
London

Maggie folded the letter. Then thought better of it, and crumpled it in her fist. Wise judgment got the better of her before she could throw the letter into the waste bin. Too many curious eyes could find the missive, and she had no desire to have anyone at the theater learn of her predicament.

Frantically, she paced the short length of Mr. Kingston's office. *Oh, God.* What was she to do? Everyone, from the board of directors to the Viscount of Marwood, wanted this blasted burletta. But she couldn't tell anyone her secret, an ugly truth lurking in the darkest recesses of her heart.

She couldn't write. She hadn't been able to pen a line for months, ever since she started *The Hidden Daughter's Return*, the sequel to her immensely popular *The Shattered Heart*.

No one was more anxious for the completed burletta's delivery than Maggie herself. Trouble was, she simply couldn't get any further. The words refused to come, like performers stubbornly waiting in the wings, leaving the stage empty and the audience hissing in derision.

She groaned aloud. What was the matter with her? She'd been able to produce at least fifteen full length burlettas and twice as many short pieces these past twelve years. Now, suddenly, nothing was coming out of her quill. Why?

God—maybe it had finally happened. Perhaps she had completely tapped her reserves of imagination, and the interior of her mind resembled a barren desert, wind-swept and empty.

If that was true . . .

An unmitigated disaster.

There had to be something she could do. Some way to flick the reins drawing the cart of her imagination, and set the whole damned thing into motion. Yet blankness only filled her mind. A vast stretch of nothingness.

Panic gnawed at her stomach. She would starve. The whole theatrical troupe relied on her for the majority of their income. They needed her. She couldn't let them down.

The more she pondered the bleakness of her situation, the worse her sense of doom became. She had to figure out something, and *soon*.

Perhaps she *should* have taken Lord Marwood up on his offer of company for the evening. A distraction could be just the thing she needed. It had been too long since she'd taken a lover. Was it merely a physical frustration that caused this block?

She shook her head. In Lord Marwood's case, the cure would be worse than the ailment. He was too handsome, too rich, too dissolute. Precisely the sort of man she avoided. At all costs.

Dropping into a waiting chair, Maggie couldn't help but recall how, despite the viscount's well-deserved reputation, he seemed genuinely interested in her work. Or perhaps he was so skilled as a seducer, that he knew precisely what to say to whom in order to lure a prospective lover into bed. Well, he would find that she wasn't so easily gulled.

Besides, she had much more pressing issues than the rakish Lord Marwood. *He* didn't have to worry about where his next meal was coming from. *He* didn't rely on his quill to put a roof over his head, or provide a means of living for nearly thirty men and women. She doubted he received demanding letters from an impatient board of directors, either. He could do precisely what he pleased, when he pleased.

She had no such freedom, trapped as she was in a prison of her own making.

Chapter 3

Phoebe: Though I have joys in abundance, I cannot help but feel an absence in my life.

The Shattered Heart

The following evening, Cam's carriage pulled up outside Allam House, his parents' residence on Mount Street. Gazing at it now as he alit from his carriage, Cam thought it a touch overdone. A bit too stuffy and formal for his tastes. But, then, he found his own family too stuffy, so it wasn't a surprise that their home followed suit. It was a striking, three-story structure whose numerous windows and columns presented an imposing façade to the world.

As the heir, he could live in his sumptuous suite of rooms at Allam House, but, given his wild lifestyle, it didn't seem quite suitable. Actresses and opera dancers under the same roof as his mother? He shuddered at the outlandish thought. He might be considered a rake, but even he had his limits.

He'd awakened this morning with the strongest urge to go to the theater to see Mrs. Delamere. Yet he knew that in the game of seduction, it was a tactical error to make himself too available, seem too willing, to his desired prize. So he would have to wait—though the thought strangely pained him.

Cam straightened his waistcoat and mentally prepared himself for the evening ahead. Perhaps if things concluded early, he might still make it to a gaming hell, and a ball after that. He checked his pocket watch and grumbled. Tonight's performance of Mrs. Delamere's *The Sorrows of Cassandra* was already underway and here he was, about to enter the lion's den of his parents' home for dinner. Not the way he wanted to spend his night, yet he had certain obligations that couldn't be ignored. Dinner with his family every fortnight was one of those unshakable obligations.

Today seemed to be filled with inescapable responsibilities. He'd spent most of the day with his man of business, reviewing his holdings, assets, and investments. It helped feed his admittedly extravagant way of life, so he readily invested in outside ventures. Technology was evolving at an astonishing rate. He glanced at the torches illuminating the front of Allam House. Someday, they might be replaced with gas lamps. Incredible.

He smiled wryly to himself. Likely few people—especially Mrs. Delamere—would suspect him of knowing anything about the latest advancements in technology, but if there was anything he'd vowed to himself, it was that he'd never be as old-fashioned as his father.

Speaking of which, the marquess wouldn't wait any longer. He was a man who enjoyed his timetables and schedules.

Drawing a deep breath as if readying for battle, Cam ascended the steps to Allam House.

"Good evening, my lord," the butler intoned, opening the door for him. He took Cam's hat, coat, and walking stick as Cam entered the vaulted foyer. "They await you in the drawing room."

"Marvelous," Cam muttered.

He proceeded down a long, richly carpeted corridor, passing portraits of men and women who looked like him. Cam didn't glance at the portrait of himself, painted just after he'd finished at Oxford and before he'd left for his Grand Tour. Studying one's own face was a tedious exercise in vanity. He'd lived with his visage for nearly thirty years. Why look at it anymore?

Voices sounded ahead, voices he knew better than his own.

"He's late," his father grumbled. Already irritated with him, despite the fact that Cam wasn't even in the room yet.

"Only by five minutes, dear." His mother. Her voice was soothing, but with that subtle steel beneath.

Someone exhaled in exasperation. Cam knew who it was before they said a word. His younger brother, Michael. "We always wait for him."

"It does seem unfair," agreed Michael's wife, Johanna, though her voice was soft and harder to hear from down the corridor.

"All my life, we've bent to Cam's will," Michael groused. "His whims, his predilections. Why? Because he's the heir." There was no small amount of bitterness in his words.

Cam took another breath and, for half a moment, considered turning around and simply leaving. There were dozens of ways in which he could spend this evening that were far more preferable than this. A night surrounded by perfumed, silken courtesans. Wagering outrageous sums at a gaming hell. A breakneck ride around London.

But if he did turn tail and flee, it would only confirm what his family—with the exception of his mother—thought of him. And while he usually enjoyed playing to their preconceptions, he now thought about the way in which Mrs. Delamere looked at him. As though, because of his reputation, he was unworthy of anyone's time. Especially hers.

Damn it—he could prove her wrong.

He stepped into the drawing room, ablaze with the glow of numerous candelabras. His mother had helped to decorate the chamber, so it was bright and modern, with several chaises and low chairs, and tables imported from Italy. His family standing in the drawing room was also quite fashionable. His father, standing by the hearth with a glass of sherry, wore his usual dark evening finery and his cane was close at hand. He glowered at Cam as he entered, and Cam had the distinct impression of looking into the future as he gazed at his father's face. But Cam suspected he wouldn't frown nearly as much as his father did now.

He wondered what Mrs. Delamere would make of this scene? How might she write it?

Enter the Prodigal.

"Don't worry, Michael," Cam said, stepping further into the room. "Maybe fortune will smile on you and I'll be killed when my phaeton overturns."

"Cameron Ezekiel Chalton," his mother chided, "there will be *no* talk of untimely deaths." But almost as soon as she scolded him, her anger seemed to dissolve. She glided toward him with a welcoming smile, then presented her cheek. "If you died doing something stupid, I'd murder you myself."

"A finer example of mothering couldn't be set by Medea herself," Cam murmured, kissing her soft, rounded cheek.

"She knew how to deal with unruly children," she said, tutting at him with her finger.

Moving away from his mother, he turned toward his brother and sister-in-law, both rising up from the settee.

"Michael," he said, extending his hand.

"Cameron," his brother answered, giving him a formal, stiff handshake.

Cam resisted the urge to sigh. It had always been this way between them. He'd been so excited to learn that he was to have a younger brother. Someone to get into scrapes with. Someone who loved mischief and trouble, too. He'd envisioned them playing pirates in the stream that ran through the upper northwest corner of their country estate, or unbuckling the vicar's shoes during Sunday school.

But instead, Michael had been a fussy child. He cried when he got dirt on his clothes. Disobeying his parents made him pale and short of breath. As he'd aged, he'd turned priggish, waiting up for Cam after a night's carousing then treating him to portentous silences and baleful looks, as if Cam had disappointed *him* somehow.

It was easier when they had little to do with each other. The disappointment they each bore didn't weigh as heavy.

Cam greeted Johanna, who have him a brittle smile as he bent over her hand. His brother had married well—a woman as humorless as himself, who agreed readily with everything her husband said. God, imagine what it must be like to be bound to such a woman for one's entire life. It wasn't love, but it was something that worked.

"Oliver takes after his uncle more and more," Johanna said with a small twist of her mouth.

"How desolate you must be," Cam answered.

The fleeting unhappy expression on her face proved just how right he was. If it was true, and little Oliver was turning out to be a hellion, he could think of no one better to eventually inherit the title.

Finally, Cam faced his father. They bowed at each other from across the room.

He thought of Mrs. Delamere again. *The Prodigal and the Patriarch greet each other like polite acquaintances.*

"Once a fortnight is all I ask," his father said, his brow low, "for you to be responsible for a change."

"Five minutes will not decide the fate of nations, Father," Cam answered. He accepted a glass of sherry offered to him by a footman. Taking a sip, he allowed himself a moment's pleasure to enjoy the liquor. They always stocked the finest at Allam House. At least there were some things that were enjoyable here.

Well, he did like spending time with his mother. She seemed to be the only one to tolerate him. Or perhaps that was a mother's obligation: to always accept her children as they were, rather than who she wanted them to be. That was the province of fathers.

"Tell that to Wellington," his father shot back.

"Dinner is not Waterloo," Cam said. Though this dinner could very well be *his* Waterloo. He finished his sherry and set his glass down on a nearby table.

Father clasped his hands behind his back. "A marquess or a viscount must consider all of their responsibilities as equal in importance."

"That's absurd," Cam said with a shake of his head. "I cannot give all of my energy and focus to everything. I cannot utilize a hundred percent on every endeavor. It's mathematically impossible." He gestured to the footman for more sherry.

His father continued to frown. "You quibble over details but neglect to consider the most important aspect of your duty as heir—"

"And so it begins," Cam muttered into his glass.

"Marriage."

Cam threw back his second sherry. "I wonder if it's humanly possible for us to be in the same room without you mentioning the topic."

"Not so long as you neglect your obligation," was his father's rejoinder.

"Ah, there's a romantic thought—marriage as an obligation." Cam needed to move, so he paced to the other side of the drawing room, and found himself staring at a painting depicting Marwood Park, his family's estate in Kent. It belonged to him now that he'd come of age. What he wouldn't give to be there now, with its rolling fields, its romantic ruin of a hermitage, and its blessed relief from parental pressure.

He thought again of what Mrs. Delamere might make of this scene between him and his parents. Would she find it tragic? Comical? She seemed to have already cast him in the role of wastrel. This might only prove her point further. Or perhaps, just perhaps, she might be sympathetic to his situation. He hadn't asked to be made heir, after all.

Michael, Johanna and his mother talked quietly amongst themselves as his father picked up his cane and crossed the drawing room and stood behind Cam.

"Your obsession with the theater has distorted your thinking," his father said darkly. "You believe that all unions should be based on love."

"Mother and you are in love," Cam said over his shoulder.

"We were fortunate to find it." His father's words were much warmer now, speaking of Cam's mother.

Cam turned to face his father. "And yet you expect me to enter into a permanent union based on what? Connections? Money? Her breeding capabilities?"

His father's brow creased. "Don't be crass, Cam."

"The heavens weep if I should speak plainly," he answered. He realized a moment too late that both he and his father were standing in the same pose, with their hands clasped behind their backs.

His father noticed, too. A corner of his mouth turned up in a wry smile. "Like it or not, you are the next in line for the title. The plain truth is that you do have a responsibility to fulfill. You need a wife, you need your own heir."

"Michael has that taken care of," Cam pointed out.

"I must show you the latest surveyor's report," his father said suddenly and rather loudly. "Come with me to the study."

Frowning, Cam followed his father out of the drawing room. His father's cane tapped softly on the carpeted floor as they walked. But before they reached the study, his father stopped him in the semidarkness of the corridor.

Leaning forward slightly, his father said quietly, "I'd rather everything went to you."

Cam's brows rose. This was the first he'd heard of this preference. Michael had always been the ideal son, whereas Cam had been the boy who couldn't be controlled, the wild one. The lost cause.

"Why?" he asked simply.

"Because . . ." His father cast a quick look down the corridor, toward the drawing room. "If you hadn't noticed, Michael's something of a fussbudget. A maiden aunt in the form of a young man."

Cam couldn't stop his surprised laugh. "He is, rather."

His father sighed. "I blame myself, really. Encouraged him to be too serious, when he ought to have allowed himself a little enjoyment in life. Some freedom from his perceived responsibilities." He gazed at Cam shrewdly. "Besides, I know you're a damn sight more intelligent and driven than you'd ever let anyone realize. You manage your properties and investments well. And all that interest you have in the theater—I can't claim to understand it, but it shows you're a man of thought, of feeling."

His voice gentling further, his father said, "You might not realize it, but you'd make a damned fine Marquess of Allam, and so would your son." He gestured toward a portrait of a solemn, dark-eyed ancestor from the previous century. The man wore a wide lace collar, and gazed out at the world with exceptional wisdom. "We've had poets, tacticians, and scholars who earned the ear of the court. I'd be"—he cleared his throat, glanced away—"proud to pass the title on to you."

What a night for revelations.

"How many sherries have you had?" Cam asked. Far easier to retreat into mocking humor than face what Father was actually saying. And he didn't want that obligation that someone's pride bestowed. It was simpler to play the scapegrace than actually live up to another's expectations.

"Cam." His father's tone was exasperated, something Cam was far more familiar with. Yet his annoyance only lasted a moment, his expression gentling. "I press duty and responsibility on you because, yes, you do have a duty as the heir to the title. But more than that . . ." He cleared his throat. "I worry for you. I tell you this now because you've been so out of control lately, wilder than usual. At the theater every night, then you don't come home until broad daylight. And the rumors about the company you keep . . ."

"Aren't rumors," Cam said, smarting that his father would keep so close a watch on him. He didn't mention, however, that instead of spending last night in the arms of a very pretty actress, after an hour at a private assembly, he'd actually gone home alone, to ponder a very pretty playwright.

His father huffed in frustration. "You need to know that you matter. That if something were to happen to you . . ." His voice trailed off, and he glanced away.

Cam didn't like the direction of this conversation at all. Where was his stern, admonishing father, the man he'd known his whole life? Where were their set, defined roles? How was he supposed to act, now that those roles had fallen away and left him and his father not as overbearing patriarch and willful scion, but concerned parent and uncertain child?

"My physician assures me I'm healthy as a ploughman," Cam said, seeking relief from all this unguarded emotion.

But his father wouldn't be distracted. "What's to

become of you when you're old?" he pressed gently. "Who will care for you then? Not your cronies. Not your opera dancers and courtesans." His gaze turned far off. "I see you alone, attended only by servants in your last hours." He shook his head, as if dispelling the image.

Cam felt a chill run along his neck and down his limbs.

"I'll have a bevy of French beauties weeping by my bedside," he said with a lightness he didn't feel.

"Because their source of income is dying," his father countered. "Not because they care."

Exasperated, Cam threw out his hands. "And what am I to the girls on the marriage mart, Father? They seek protection and financial security, too, only with them, the arrangement is permanent."

"Is that so terrible, permanence?"

"The girl and I could grow to hate each other," Cam said tightly. "Then we have a lifetime of resentment and disappointment to enjoy."

"Or it could turn into mutual esteem," his father countered. "Perhaps even . . . love."

Cam snorted. "You and Ashford were lucky with your wives, but that's the definition of luck. It seldom happens. Love exists on the stage, not very often in the world. I won't settle or be shackled to a woman I despise, or who despises me. I'll have love," he insisted, "or nothing at all."

His father looked disappointed. "So you are determined to be alone."

Cam forced a wide smile. "I'm seldom alone."

"That is debatable," his father replied.

Cam didn't know how to respond to that.

"Come," his father continued, "let us return to the others."

They walked silently down the hallway, heaviness in Cam's chest. He and his father reentered the drawing room. A moment later, the butler announced that dinner was ready. Yet Cam found, as he escorted Johanna in to dinner, that he had little appetite.

Chapter 4

Phoebe: How shall I ever proceed?

The Shattered Heart

Maggie sat in the property room at the Imperial, alone. Her current desk was an erstwhile banqueting table that had once hosted feasts for performances of King John and Richard II.

She and a blank sheet of paper now engaged in a staring contest, each daring the other to blink. Of course, the paper would never blink. Closing her eyes, Maggie dug her knuckles into her eye sockets, forcing back the headache that made its appearance every time she attempted to work on this burletta. It took place ten years after the events of *The Shattered Heart*.

The protagonist of *The Hidden Daughter's Return*, Alina, was no longer a little girl as she had been in the earlier play. And while Alina had had a difficult childhood—being torn from the arms of her mother—as an adult she was going to suffer a considerable amount more before she reached her happy ending.

Two floors above Maggie, footsteps clattered back and forth across the stage. Actors and actresses declaimed their lines as the orchestra played along—thus distinguishing it as a burletta rather than a play. Only Drury Lane and Covent Garden were licensed to perform spoken word works, both classic and new. That left the Imperial Theater and other smaller venues to stage "burlettas," which meant music must accompany any line said aloud by someone onstage. It was a particular mixture that been born of necessity—not unlike Maggie herself.

Hammers and saws also made a terrible din as stagehands and craftsmen assembled new sets. Mr. Kingston shouted above the chaos.

Maggie rubbed at her forehead. She hated working at home—it was too cramped, too lonely. As was her custom, she'd retreated to this dusty, seldom-used storage room in the bowels of the theater in order to let her creativity flow. With its props, its echoes of productions past, it reminded her of the vitality of the theater, how it was a living thing, full of imagination and magic and the sweat of honest labor. All things she prized.

Usually being here freed her thoughts and let her imagination take flight. Not today. And not for the past three weeks. The theater had opened at the end of August to prepare for the upcoming season. It was now the middle of September. In the whole of that time, she had written precisely three words. *Act Two. Enter.*

Enter who? What were they doing, whoever they were? What did they want? The more she asked these questions, the less the answers showed themselves.

All around her were props and bits of debris from other burlettas, including her own. There was the dagger that Count Le Cyr used to threaten poor villager Jacques into revealing Drucilla's hiding spot. Over there was a papier-mâché rock behind which the robber duke crouched as he waited to abduct Lena. Wild and melodramatic as those works had been, they had also been exceptionally popular. But to be surrounded by these props haunted her with the ghosts of her own successes, tormenting her.

The door to the storage room swung open with a bang. She spun around in her chair to firmly but gently admonish whomever had come in. Everyone in the company knew she was down here, and needed her seclusion. Only Mr. Kingston was allowed to come into this room. Everyone else knew they'd get the brunt of her ire if they disturbed her. Like the time that one pup of a strolling player, Barnstable, insisted he use the prop room as his own private rehearsal space. She'd written him a very unmemorable offstage death in *What the Heavens Allow*. Would she have to mete out the same fate for another unwise actor?

Words of reproof died on her tongue when she beheld the figure standing in the doorway.

Lord Marwood. Looking sharply handsome in his day clothing—including tall boots, and an ink blue coat that made his dark eyes gleam.

"This isn't the manager's office," he said dryly. He sauntered in, surveying the piles of detritus heaped upon the floor.

"Selective breeding has clearly benefited your powers of observation," she answered.

His deep brown eyes twinkled as he grinned. The sight was distressingly pleasing. "Never let it be said that my parents' efforts were in vain."

"I'll send them a note of congratulations." She knew she was being rude, but couldn't quite stop herself. This man made her hackles rise. His type was all too familiar to her—wealthy, privileged, handsome, idle. Utterly confident that he could have whatever—and *whomever*—he wanted. And he'd use his exceptional charm to beguile his chosen target. No one could stand a chance against the lethal combination of looks, money, and charisma.

She'd made that mistake with another man. Never again.

"Mrs. Delamere," he said, bowing.

"*Lord* Marwood." She stood.

As far as she was concerned, the most dangerous men in London weren't its footpads, but men like Marwood. Men who seduced as easily and often as they drank brandy. She had firsthand experience with being gulped down, swallowed whole. It had been nothing short of miraculous that she'd survived.

But if she wasn't careful around Marwood, she could easily fall victim again.

She pointed at the door. "The actresses' dressing rooms are two doors down."

Yet his teasing smile didn't fade, despite her coolness. "As I said, I'm looking for Mr. Kingston. I had a suggestion regarding the layout of the theater boxes."

She rolled her eyes. Naturally, a man of Marwood's status thought his opinion mattered—even regarding topics of which he had no real knowledge. One might attend a thousand plays, burlettas, and operas and never understand the subtleties and intricacies of how a theater was actually run. Typical aristo.

"He's upstairs," she said curtly.

Yet Marwood didn't move. He just continued to look at her with that provocative, mischievous light in his eyes, a half smile curving his lips. Her obvious dislike clearly amused him. Which only increased her sense of displeasure at his presence. She didn't like to be any-one's joke, especially not a man of his status. He could effectively erase all her hard-won accomplishments with a single grin or playful remark, reducing her to nothing but a mote.

But she was more than that, so much more. Alone and abandoned at a young age, she'd forged a path for herself when many other people would have given up and let despair overtake them. Now she had a good roof over her head, a bank account with *her* name on it, and audiences coming to see works created by her very own pen. That couldn't be dismissed by a wink or a smile.

"Is this the dagger that the terrible count used to intimidate Jacques?" he asked, the seductive tone of his voice turning suddenly youthful and excited. He picked up the very same weapon, then mirrored the gesture the actor had used in almost perfect recreation of the moment.

She was taken aback. "I think so," she muttered, gazing at a spot in the distance, but she knew the truth. It *was* the dagger, and the fact that he recognized it amazed her.

Setting down the dagger, he moved on to a painted vase. "And this adorned the bedchamber of innocent Lady Wilhelmina. Then it adorned the head of Prince Evernight when he tried to force his way into her bed."

Despite his evident interest in the props, there was a distinctly beguiling tone in his voice as he said the word "bed." It was clear he knew all the uses for a bed. An unwanted, unexpected heat rushed into her cheeks.

She tried to distract herself from her body's response to him. How did he know her work and the props used in it so well? Did he pay that close attention? He seemed eager, enthusiastic, almost boyish as he beheld props from countless burlettas and operettas.

It was a surprising enthusiasm.

Setting down the vase, his gaze fell on a few pieces of scrawled-over paper. Paper wasn't cheap. She'd had to write and rewrite over the sheets, crossing her lines. Despite the cost of the foolscap, Maggie had filled sheets with what amounted to utter rubbish. They scattered over the tabletop, and one had even slipped to the floor.

"I'm disturbing you at work," he said, sitting on the edge of the desk. He propped up one leg, so she was treated to a view of his thigh encased in tight buckskin, and a glimpse of the top of his tall, shiny boot.

Having him on her table that served as her desk brought him even closer. Reducing the distance between them. Damn him, at this range, she could smell his cologne—some unique, masculine blend of vetiver and cinnamon. It swept through her senses, tantalizing her with unbidden thoughts.

"Yes." Her answer was flat. He might be excited to see the theatrical properties, and he might be used to honeyed words from others, but Maggie was no one's crony, especially not a member of the gentry. And she had to work, not entertain a rich's man's fancy.

Worse than that, he was . . . appealing. A mixture between playful and alluring, giving just enough praise to flatter her writer's ego. She could not allow him to get close. She couldn't allow herself to invite him in.

He straightened. With a sleek movement, he bent down and swept up one of the sheets of discarded paper, then unfolded it. A seemingly involuntary sound of excitement escaped him.

"So you *are* working on the sequel to *The Shattered Heart!*" His eyes widened. Was that actual pleasure she saw there, not merely its mocking facsimile?

Indeed, his fingers tightened on the paper, as if it was something precious to him. But why?

"The Hidden Daughter's Return." She took a step toward him, though the table stood between them. "Return that, my lord," she said through clenched teeth.

"I've no intention of doing so," he answered distractedly, backing up and still looking at the paper.

"If you are a gentleman—"

"Ah, but therein lies the problem," he said smoothly, continuing to keep his gaze on what he held. "I have the status, but not the manners."

Her heart knocked angrily in her chest. "A fact of which I am becoming painfully aware."

He scanned the sheet. "Your handwriting is execrable."

So much for seduction. She planted her hands on her hips. "I must confirm that you have appalling manners, to point out my substandard penmanship."

He smiled brilliantly at her. "*Substandard* is a short, neat way of saying, *resembles the scratchings of a mentally disturbed chicken.*"

"This hen will not hesitate to peck you, my lord, if you do not return what belongs to me. Surely even a viscount with disgraceful deportment stops short at outright theft." She held out her hand.

He gave the paper another searching, hungry look. Thank God that she had deliberately cultivated poor handwriting so that none but her and one other well-trained woman could read the first draft of her work. Maggie paid Susan in Bedford Street to transcribe her writing into something far more legible. Some might consider such extreme actions to be unnecessary, but Maggie knew her competition—the playwrights who wrote original material for Covent Garden and Drury Lane—and they weren't above literally stealing from one another. A cutthroat world, the theater.

There was another benefit to encouraging bad penmanship, Maggie saw now. Marwood couldn't tell that all Maggie had written thus far was meaningless gibberish.

"Will this be Alina's story?" the viscount asked with anticipation.

It seemed that the world—or at least, much of England—wanted Alina's story. Including Marwood. And the board of directors. She had never known such pressure.

Why lie? There was nothing to hide. "Yes," she admitted, albeit reluctantly. She came around the table and again held out her hand for the paper.

Marwood backed up, pressing the paper to the center of his chest. As if . . . he was hoarding it and would not let it go. "When she was forced to leave her mother behind at the end of *The Shattered Heart*," he said thickly, his gaze cast upward, "not a single eye was bereft of tears. Including my own. Even now, I am on the verge of weeping, merely thinking about it."

She peered closely at him, looking for signs of deceit or insincerity. But, to her amazement, there was indeed a sheen of moisture in his dark eyes.

"You flatter me," she muttered.

His gaze locked on hers, rooting her to the spot. "When it comes to the theater, madam, I am always sincere."

She did see him in his private box nearly every night. No other member of the gentry came to the theater with such consistency. But she could not allow him anything, lest he become somehow more intriguing than he already was. "Does anything else merit your sincerity?"

A moment passed as he thought about it, a shadow fleetingly crossing his face. Then he winked. "Almost nothing."

How could she understand such a mercurial man? The answer was that she couldn't, and oughtn't try to, either. That way lay danger and possible madness. Still, she wasn't certain what to make of his reaction to her burletta. *The Shattered Heart* had been, thus far, her most commercially and critically popular work, with no fewer than seventeen consecutive performances last season, and even several offers to have it performed in Dublin, Edinburgh, Cheltenham and a handful of other regional theaters. Audiences could not seem to get enough of the tribulations of the wronged Phoebe, and they had been clamoring for the tale of Phoebe's daughter, Alina. Every day, Maggie was stopped in the street or received letters from eager audience members. Sometimes, they were polite and respectful, other times, excited. And then there were the angry ones who outright demanded to know what became of Alina. They staunchly refused to believe that, after Phoebe was forced to give up her daughter to secure her child a better future, Alina simply vanished into that place where all fictitious characters go when the curtain descended.

Which made the pressure of completing *The Hidden Daughter's Return* all the more onerous. Marwood's praise, while oddly pleasing and unexpected, only made the millstone around her neck heavier.

"So, when will Alina have her happy ending?" Marwood pressed—rather urgently.

Therein lay part of the trouble. Maggie seldom wrote

happy endings, but to give Alina anything less would potentially cause riots to break out. She didn't flatter herself. People who came to the theater were often deeply invested in the fates of the characters, and had been known in the past to tear up seats and rip down wall hangings if they were unsatisfied with what happened on the stage. Women and men frequently fainted with emotion at the end of *The Shattered Heart*.

As the author of the play, it was both thrilling and alarming for Maggie. She still couldn't quite believe that she, who'd once been in such disgrace with the world, and had been convinced she would die alone and unremarkable, could ever achieve such success. She would sometimes lie awake at night—in her admittedly tiny garret—for fear that to fall asleep meant to wake up, and all her accomplishments would vanish in the morning.

"When the burletta is finished," she answered.

"But *when*, madam? When?"

"When I deem it ready."

Finally, he handed her back the sheet of paper, and she snatched it away from him, clutching it in her fist.

Pressure built inside of her, threatening to explode. He couldn't possibly know how much his words heaped coal upon an already fiery situation. She could almost believe the board of directors had planted him to goad her into working faster.

"Then you are wasting precious time chattering away." He pointed to the seat she'd vacated earlier. "You need to get back to work, posthaste."

"That is precisely what I was attempting to do when I was interrupted by your lordship," she said tartly.

He shook his head. "For a woman of such immense talents, you are too easy to distract."

The audacity of this man! "It depends on the distraction. Some are more easy to ignore than others, who clamor for attention like colicky infants."

"I never had colic," he said with a wide smile. "Healthy as a farmer, I've always been."

She walked to the door and held it open. "It's time for you to locate a different field to plow. You'll find nothing but weeds and rocks here."

His laugh tumbled like poured wine. "Ah, but you're wrong. You're so very . . . fertile." He trailed a gaze over her, full of suggestion.

A rush of warmth followed wherever his gaze had lingered. It was a peculiar combination of anger and instinctive response. Any living woman would react to such a well-favored, vigorously healthy young man making their physical interest clear. Or so she told herself.

"My lord—"

"For stories and characters." He smiled like the devil himself. "They spring from your mind like Athena from Zeus's head."

Again with his enthusiasm for her writing. His words were far more enticing than any practiced seduction. If he'd complimented her looks or her figure, she could have readily dismissed him. But this . . . this was not what she had expected. Almost as if he thought about her as a human, rather than a conquest. Yet he also looked at her as if she was the most desirable woman in the word. What a heady combination.

"You over-compliment me," she grumbled.

"Perhaps a little." He shrugged his shoulders dismissively.

She scowled.

"You must admit that to compare a mortal to the father of the gods is a slight exaggeration." He chuckled softly as though her annoyance entertained him. "But come now, don't be angry. I repeat my invitation from the other night. Let us have dinner. There are many things that can be on the menu. We can be . . . friends. Very *good* friends."

Maggie's imagination flowered and spread like morning glory in spring. It was all too easy to visualize Marwood as a lover. The gleam of candlelight on his skin. The stroke of his hand along the back of her neck and between her shoulder blades. His voice, warm and deep, murmuring wicked encouragement. Her body warmed.

How long had it been since she'd had a lover? Judging by her physical reaction to him and her imagination, too much time had passed since she'd known the pull of physical pleasure, much as she craved it. She'd always been an innately physical person, a fact that had allowed her to be taken advantage of many years ago.

Never again would she be misled by intoxicating words or the lure of desire.

"My lord," she said, her voice brittle, "you are very kind for the offer. I am too busy at present to accept any requests to dine. While I appreciate your interest in my work"—strange as it was—"I now wish you good day."

"This is novel." He lifted his brows. "I don't recall ever being dismissed. Certainly not by . . ."

"By what?" she snapped, hands on her hips. "A woman? A person of low status?"

"By an artist," he answered. He paused, his brows lifting in surprise. "What? No acerbic rejoinder?"

In truth, she had nothing to say. No one had ever

called her an artist before. A scribbler—often. A writer—yes. But an *artist* . . . Never.

He straightened, backed up, then bowed, all courtly manners. "Good day, Mrs. Delamere. May your Muse fly swiftly. I shall be back to check on your progress. Now that I know that Alina's fate hangs in the balance, nothing can bar me from your door."

"What if the door is bricked over?" she asked, only partly under her breath.

He only smiled once more, then he strode out. His boots rapped sharply on the floorboards. The energy in the room seemed suddenly flat and still without him there, as though a raven had flown into a chamber, wheeled around the ceiling with its glittering ebony wings, and then flown out again.

She shut the door and leaned against it. Then exhaled.

Pray to the Lord she never spoke with him again, but she had the very strong, very unnerving feeling that their paths were going to be linked.

Now that he was gone, she felt something rising up in her. She quickly hurried to her makeshift desk and wrote a few lines. Then the inspiration dissipated. But she knew the feeling, craved it. That gleam of creativity and eagerness. It tried to come to life, but was held down by thick vines of expectation. In moments, the inspiration was gone again, burned out like a lamp.

Where had that inspiration come from, and where had it gone. Could it be . . . ? Marwood . . . inspired her. Just a hint.

Did he bring it out in her? God, she hoped not. She could ill afford to find her Muse in such a man.

Chapter 5

Phoebe: How I long for another life.

The Shattered Heart

Two nights after his last encounter with Mrs. Delamere, Cam sat in his theater box. Heat from hundreds of bodies and the countless smoky lights thickened the air. His companions joining him for the evening were Childers and Hudson, two young pups Cam didn't much care for, but good company was scarce ever since Ashford had married. Also in the box were two courtesans engaged for the night by the younger men, but unlike Cam, none of his cohorts tonight were at all interested in what was happening on the stage.

My God, when will they shut up?

Cam leaned forward in his seat, straining to hear the performers on stage above the combined noise from the crowd below and his companions in the theater box. The stage was only moderately brighter than the house, the audience almost as illuminated as the actors.

The piece being enacted wasn't one of Mrs. Delamere's—that would be after intermission in just a few minutes—but it was bloody annoying to come to the theater and not truly watch the damned acts.

Cam craved stories—any stories, though hers he hungered for most of all. The ups and downs. The tragedy and reversals. Love. Always love. He needed these tales the way drunkards needed wine.

Damn Ashford for falling in love, getting married and ruining everything. All their wild nights, two men of wealth and status let loose on the town. All gone. Leaving Cam to make do with the likes of Childers and Hudson, who were eager to learn the ways of the aristocratic libertine, but lacked any interest in the events transpiring onstage. The courtesans appeared amenable to just about anything.

Mrs. Delamere likely knew that he almost always came to the theater with members of the demimonde. The petite, dark-haired authoress probably knew a hell of a lot more about him than he did about her. Whatever information she had gathered, or whatever she believed, it obviously made her dislike him. Intensely. She had been barely civil, if not actually insolent, the other day. Almost no one spoke to him that way, and he usually had people clamoring for his attention. But he couldn't stop thinking about the woman.

She had an unusual, striking beauty. Strong features. Full lips. The slightest gap between her front teeth, which he found mysteriously erotic. And he couldn't help but respond to the generous curves of her body. He was a man, with a man's enjoyment of the earthy side of life. He appreciated Mrs. Delamere's form as well as her work and her talent. But he didn't know *her*.

Clearly, she was a widow, and a young one at that. No one ever talked about or saw *Mr.* Delamere. But when did he die? Had it been a happy marriage?

Had she taken any lovers since her late husband had passed away?

Mrs. Delamere's dislike proved a challenge. Challenges were rare for him. He could not stop himself from quizzing her, if only to see that heat and passion flare in her gaze, in her body.

He realized that once, months ago, he'd seen her circulating in the lobby of the theater. Her exotic looks had drawn his attention. She seemed so unlike the pallid English roses that adorned the theater. Then someone had pointed out that she was the authoress of his favorite works. Yet, despite his valiant efforts, he'd never been able to get close to her. She had always been elusive in receiving praise, and didn't linger long. Particularly, she seemed to avoid the gentry.

Then, a little while later, he'd observed her at Vauxhall in the company of Ashford's future wife. Cam had been intrigued by her—that unusual beauty, the way she held herself, proud and upright. He'd become determined to know her. In every way. How delicious she would be as a lover. So full of spirit and wit. The wedding between Ashford and his bride would have provided the perfect opportunity to get close to her.

But she'd disappeared before he'd gotten the chance.

So it had seemed like pure fortune to meet her backstage the other night. And then again a few days later. Cam hadn't wanted to neglect an opportunity.

The lovers onstage continued their prolonged exultations in being reunited after a long separation. *Just kiss and get on with it*, Cam thought. Social codes of decency would prevent the actors from actually kissing onstage, however, so instead they kept singing. And singing.

His body thrummed with memories of the verbal

sparring he'd enjoyed with Mrs. Delamere. On every front, she rebuffed him. Though at times he could sense her wavering, as if the blade of her wit lowered just slightly in their duel.

Cam knew how to play the long game when it came to seduction. She wasn't lost to him. Not by a mile. And now that he knew she was working on *The Hidden Daughter's Return*—a glow of excitement flared in him at the thought—he would find a way to get backstage more often.

"Did you see what Angleford wore to the Laphams' ball last night?" Childers half whispered, half shouted.

"That waistcoat!" crowed Hudson. "And the folds of his cravat! If the man doesn't sack his valet, then *I'll* do it as a public service."

Meanwhile, on the stage, two lovers sang their bitter joy.

"How alone I have been without you!" one trilled.

"Cold and so very alone," the other responded.

He winced at the clumsy lines. This one wasn't a particularly deft burletta, unlike Mrs. Delamere's clean, precise writing.

"Oh, my darling," sang an actress, *"what was life but an endless winter/ Without your arms to warm me."*

Not a good line, that, but it had a certain evocative quality. Perhaps—

"I warrant," Hudson went on, "that Angleford's valet could swing for murder. Murder of fashion!"

The courtesans giggled.

Cam swung around in his seat. "The lot of you," he growled. "Shut your mouths and watch the sodding stage, or get out of my theater box." He did have exclusive rights to it for the season, after all. And he didn't give a rot if he was being rude.

The courtesans, in their silks and rouge, gaped at him. Hudson and Childers did the same. The young men were perfect examples of rich, genteel bucks—lavishly dressed, meticulously groomed, flawlessly bred from generations of other aristocrats. And neither had a brain between them. Not even a crumb.

"I say, Marwood." Childers looked aghast. "Is that kind of talk necessary?"

"Yes," chorused Hudson, pressing a hand to his chest, "is it?"

Cam narrowed his eyes and dropped his voice. "My coffers are several pounds lighter every season because I pay for this theater box."

"You're not actually *paying attention* to that rubbish onstage, are you?" Childers' face was comical in its disbelief.

"When I carouse, I am the embodiment of Dionysus," Cam answered, planting his hands on his knees. "When I'm waltzing, I make sure my partner feels like she's flying. When I take a woman to bed," he added, flicking a glance toward the courtesans, "I give her the most intense pleasure she's ever known."

The courtesans fanned themselves.

"And when I go to the theater," he continued, leaning forward, "I *watch the sodding show.*"

His companions blinked woundedly at him. "But, Marwood," Childers exclaimed, "that's not the point of theatergoing. It's to see, and be seen." He gestured to the other boxes, where the audience spent more time talking to themselves and watching everyone else—with hardly a glance toward the stage. Though Mrs. Delamere's plays always commanded more attention.

Hudson nodded. "I never understand why we come to the Imperial, anyway. Everyone usually goes to the

Theater Royal, or Covent Garden. Or the Italian Opera. But not this *outré* place. Nobody likes it here."

Cam glanced toward the completely full house, then turned back to Hudson with one brow raised. "Yes, I can see that."

"It's so peculiar at the Imperial," Childers whined. He waved toward the stage. "I mean, these little farces are fine, but why must we watch those pieces by that female writer?"

An odd tension threaded itself up Cam's neck and tightened in his muscles. "You object to a woman writing."

Why were his hands knotting into fists? The woman had made it plainly clear that she didn't care a fig about him. Disliked him, even. And yet here he was, on the verge of knocking the innocuous Childers to the ground, causing a scene.

Which was a rather ridiculous concern. He never gave a damn about what other people thought of his behavior. His reputation was earned early, and he bore it proudly, like a medal of distinction. He showed up in *The Hawk's Eye* as "the scandalous Lord M—d" on many an occasion.

"Not too many females earning their coin by their quills," Childers stammered, seeing Cam's darkening look.

Cam kept silent about the fact that E. Hawke, the editor, owner of *The Hawk's Eye* was in fact, a woman and the wife of his very good friend.

"It isn't unheard of," he said flatly.

"Of course not!" Hudson gulped. "But why must she write about such . . . provocative subjects? You have to admit, Marwood, her works stir the embers of dissent between the classes. Haven't you noticed? None of the aristocrats she writes about come across well. They're almost always the villains, and the common folk are the heroes who punish the noblemen's wrongdoing."

"It's as if she wants what happened in France to happen here." Childers shuddered.

Maybe these two weren't as brainless as Cam had originally suspected.

"A few burlettas won't cause a blood-stained revolution," he noted wryly.

"Don't underestimate the power of someone's quill," said Hudson, who quickly flushed at his boldness.

"I never do," Cam answered. Books entertained him, but nothing captured him the way the theater did. And while the performances and stagecraft could entrance, he often found himself with his eyes closed, simply listening to the words and their meanings.

No recent writer's work spoke to him the way Mrs. Delamere's did. It was a strange, dark pleasure, watching members of his own class so relentlessly skewered. Aristocratic rakes in particular never fared well beneath Mrs. Delamere's pen.

Heat pulsed along Cam's veins. She wrote about men exactly like him.

He ought to be offended or disgusted by her temerity. He ought to shun her work. Yet it drew him, again and again. Until he never missed a single performance. He might carouse after the curtain fell, but before then, he was entranced. The stories filled him with possibility of what might be—especially where the heart was concerned. That fantasy realm held him captive with its promises of love.

But he couldn't focus on any of it with Childers and Hudson yammering on behind him.

"If you can't keep your mouths shut for the next hour," Cam warned his companions, "then take your gossip and your witlessness somewhere else. *Now.*"

Gaping like cod, Hudson and Childers lurched to their feet. They muttered to themselves as they slipped out the back of the box.

"Ladies, perhaps you'd like to go with your friends," Cam suggested politely to the courtesans.

The women, looking confused, rose gracefully and, after giving him a curtsey, exited the theater box, trailing the sounds of rustling silk and the fragrance of expensive perfume. Other men might consider him a damn fool for letting two beauties like those courtesans go—but there were always more women. Mrs. Delamere, however . . . *She* wasn't like any woman he knew.

Turning back to the stage, he sighed in relief. At least for now, he could enjoy the show. Eagerness sparked through him at what was to come. *The Sorrows of Cassandra* was one of his favorites. He never failed to cheer when Cassandra pushed her patrician seducer off a cliff and sent the bastard plunging into the Adriatic. The current burletta ended, and Cam and the audience applauded.

Intermezzo. Orange girls circulated around the pit. People moved about in the boxes, greeting one another, flirting, exchanging tales of scandal or else hoping to see something scandalous.

He wasn't much in the mood to plunge into the fray, so he amused himself by watching the proceedings.

The Imperial lacked the spectacle and stagecraft of Vauxhall, but that's not what drew him here. He checked his jeweled pocket watch. Just a few more minutes until the trials and bittersweet victories of Cassandra.

Voices sounded in the corridor behind him. He recognized them almost immediately. Lord and Lady Ashford.

"And a dreadful evening to you, Marwood," Ashford said, stepping into the box. His wife was right behind him. "May we join you?"

"Terrible night to you, Ashford," Cam answered at once. "Please, do join me." Though he wouldn't mind being alone to watch *Cassandra*, at least the Ashfords didn't talk through performances.

As the couple settled in, Cam turned his attention back to the stage.

The orchestra struck up a tune, and the audience murmured in excitement as they found their seats. Anticipation thrummed in Cam's chest.

Was Mrs. Delamere in the theater now? She had been the night before. He sincerely hoped so. Life had become a good deal more interesting once she'd entered his world. He would enjoy her seduction, as well.

She wouldn't be an easy conquest, and he didn't want one. He smiled wickedly to himself. Give him a challenge, and he couldn't resist. Whether it was horseraces, duels, or a midnight swimming competition in the Serpentine, he pushed himself whenever he could. He loved the thrill and danger of the hunt. She could tear him apart with her verbal claws. A strange eagerness clung to him at the notion. They were equally matched in wit and determination. She made all other women seem dull and colorless by comparison.

He wanted her. As neatly as that. He wanted every part of her.

Theirs would make for a fascinating story. And he did so love stories—the more complex, the better.

Chapter 6

Enter Alina.
Alina: Mother, it is a joyous day in the village,
  and yet you sigh.
Phoebe: I cannot explain this strange
  melancholy, my dearest daughter. I have a
  foreboding of doom.

The Shattered Heart

Why was she still here? Installed in the properties room, Maggie could hear the actors upstairs, performing the last act of *Cassandra*. The strains of the musical theme threaded through the piece as Cassandra bid her final farewells to the weeping villagers gathered around her deathbed. The audience had been sufficiently engaged in the performance, if their laughter, sobs, and applause throughout was any indicator. And yet, far from encouraging Maggie as she wrote, it made her pen all the more difficult to move.

She should have gone home to work. Or perhaps ventured to one of the taverns that didn't frown on female patrons, like the Foxhead. Yet the Imperial always felt like her most productive space, the most comfortable, and so she was here late, writing.

Attempting to write.

The brief inspiration she'd had when Marwood had visited her had faded quickly, like the sun in winter. Leaving her anxious and chagrined. He oughtn't be important to her creativity. She didn't want him to be. Firstly, because she wanted to be the source of her own artistic vision. And secondly, and most vital, she didn't want *him* to serve as any kind of muse.

Yet he hadn't been far from her thoughts these past days. The gleam in his eye glinted in the light of a candle upon a wineglass. The memory of his laughter played like a warm breeze along the nape of her neck. Worse . . . she'd dreamed of him. Her dreams had often been fertile ground for her work, and she kept a notebook at her bedside for jotting down ideas upon waking, so she wouldn't forget them. It was a dream of a young girl's broken weeping that had inspired *The Shattered Heart*.

But now, her dreams were of Marwood. Laughing. Teasing. Always out of reach. Always hidden in darkness. Sometimes he pursued, sometimes she sought him. It shifted and changed from moment to moment. But it was him in that darkness. The logic and instinct of dreams told her so.

She rubbed at her face as if to erase him from her mind. But she knew the tenacity of her imagination. Once it had hold of an idea, nothing could dislodge it.

Perhaps he could serve as the model for the villain of *The Hidden Daughter's Return*; there was always a villain. However, Alina needed a happy ending.

God, was Marwood to play the inspiration for Maggie's hero?

The thought was appalling. Viscounts weren't heroes. Rakes certainly weren't either.

Yet a *reformed* rake . . .

Maggie laughed aloud. No such thing existed. Not in real life, anyway. Eleanor's husband had been a rake, but not truly. His motivations to help his friend Lawford revealed his true heart.

Further, Maggie wasn't concerned with the real world. Hers was the realm of fantasy. So perhaps there could be a titled man, a wicked man, whom Alina rebuffs. But through epic displays of humility and self-sacrifice, this nobleman somehow becomes deserving of Alina's love.

That might work. Preposterous as the idea seemed.

The orchestra launched into the final crescendos. Perhaps Maggie ought to do the same and leave. Usually after performances, most of the actors wanted to celebrate surviving another night, and they often pulled Maggie into their festive wake. But this new piece had to be written, and getting into drinking contests with the repertory cast was not entirely productive.

Applause sounded, marking the end of *Cassandra*. Maggie allowed herself a small smile. Those were *her* words being performed. Though much of the audience's praise was for the actors, part of it was for her, too. *Her*. Who'd risen from such obscurity and dire circumstances to this. Having her writings enacted on a stage before hundreds of people every night.

In the crowded prop room, empty of everyone but Maggie and the Imperial's fat orange mouser, she stood and gave a slightly self-mocking bow.

The door suddenly swung open.

Why were people constantly interrupting her in here? She ought to find another place to hide.

Maggie spun around, her face reddening at being caught bowing to a cat.

Her embarrassment drained away when she saw that the person standing in the doorway was none other than Eleanor Balfour, Lady Ashford. Her old friend smiled at her with droll fondness.

"Soaking in the applause, Mags?" Eleanor asked, hands on her hips.

"Playing the part of countess, El?" Maggie answered. Her gaze roved over Eleanor's expensive gown and the fortune of gems she wore. How far Eleanor had come, and yet she was exactly the same person Maggie had known for so many years—wealth and privilege hadn't changed her at all.

Something else had, though. Something that shone like a light beneath Eleanor's face and made her smile and laugh with greater frequency than ever before.

Love. The kind of love Maggie only wrote about but never knew. She'd never had experience with it. In truth, if it hadn't been for Eleanor and her husband, Maggie might not believe it existed at all. But it did. Just not for her. Never for her.

Not with an aristo, in any case.

"Will you come up to the box?" Eleanor asked, coming into the prop room. "Daniel's asking to see you."

She reached out for Maggie's hand. Though Eleanor wore gloves, Maggie was dead certain that the kidskin covered ink-stained fingers. After all, Maggie's own fingers were permanently marked with ink. One of the hazards of the profession.

"Of course," Maggie answered, stepping forward. Though he was titled, Ashford was a decent enough man. Surprisingly, strongly principled and loyal. Handsome as hell. Utterly enslaved to his wife, which earned him Maggie's favor. Both with humble backgrounds, they had come by their successes through backbreaking work and countless sacrifices. If anyone deserved some joy, it was Eleanor.

Hand in hand, they left the prop room, winding their way through the maze of corridors and throngs of performers and workers. Everything smelled of sweat, face paint, starch, and sulfur. Peculiar scents that few would find pleasant. Maggie inhaled deeply. It was her home. The place that had taken her in when the rest of the world had turned its back on her. That could never be underestimated.

"Anyone else up in the box with you tonight?" Maggie asked, squeezing between a twist of acrobats.

"A friend," Eleanor answered.

Maggie stopped in her tracks. "That's hedging. Who is it?" she demanded.

A slightly shamefaced expression crossed her friend's face. "Marwood," she admitted.

Heat rushed through Maggie. As it had every time she'd thought about him.

"Absolutely not." Maggie tried to tug her hand free from Eleanor's grip, but her friend held her tight.

"Come on, Mags," Eleanor wheedled. She looked at her imploringly. "Daniel would really like to see you, and Marwood isn't as bad as all that."

"He's a plague," Maggie shot back, still tugging. "A gorgeous plague, I'll grant you, but there is absolutely nothing of worth to that man's existence other than his face." And his body. And the desire in his gaze when he looked at her. And his interest in her work. And the way he'd called her an artist, with actual respect. But she wasn't about to say any of that. He was an aristo, a rake, and to her, that's all he'd ever be.

Maggie continued, "You ought to know what kind of man he is, given that you write about him so much for *The Hawk's Eye*."

"Yes, he's something of a wastrel," Eleanor conceded. "But he's Daniel's friend, and so I must be friendly to him, too. It'll make Danny so pleased to see you," she pressed.

Maggie hesitated.

"Afraid?" Eleanor asked slyly.

Tipping up her chin, Maggie answered at once, "Of course not!"

"Then come up." Her friend tugged on her hand, urging her toward the door that led to the house.

Maggie clenched her teeth. Eleanor knew her weaknesses and how to bait her. "For the sake of our friendship."

"You're using our friendship as leverage."

They continued on, passing more stagehands, crew, and actors.

"What did you think of my performance tonight?" Mrs. Fortescue asked, stopping her.

"I suggest crying out as the duke leaves," Maggie answered. "That way you truly drive home the character's sorrow."

"I shall do precisely that!" the actress said, nodding eagerly.

Maggie and Eleanor hadn't gotten far before Mr. Dunn, another actor, stepped in front of them.

"I hear they are rethinking the casting for *The Hidden Daughter's Return*," he said pointedly.

"That's my understanding, yes," she said cautiously.

"I'm sure you have considerable influence in their decision," he pressed.

"I'm just the writer, Mr. Dunn."

"You are modest, Mrs. Delamere. You have far more sway in the workings of this theater than most."

"Perhaps," she said vaguely. "But I really cannot speak of it now. Excuse me."

Finally, they reached the point that led from the back-stage area into the house itself. A crowd of young men gathered at the door, offering bribes and trying to impress Darrow—the man watching the door—to let them back to see the actresses. When Darrow saw Maggie and Eleanor approach, he gave them a nod. He held the crowd back as she and Eleanor passed by, though one or two of the lads tried to slip past the door man. A few outraged yelps indicated their lack of success.

"Poor Darrow," Maggie said to Eleanor as they walked through the house. "Trying to maintain morality in a hotbed of wickedness."

"Some men thrive on challenge," her friend answered.

People milled and swirled in a proliferation of color and talk as they moved toward the theater's exit. Many chatted and flirted and gossiped—half the reason why they came to the theater in the first place. She didn't fool herself in thinking that they only came to watch the fruits of her labors. Yet more than a few audience members recognized her, stopping her to praise her work.

"You are too kind," she murmured to a knight and his wife, sinking into a curtsey.

"False humility," Eleanor chided with an amused smile as they moved on. "You know you're one of the best writers in London right now."

"Naturally," Maggie replied. "Yet I can't go around

saying that, or people will accuse me of arrogance. A quality admired in men, but not women."

Her friend sighed in understanding. "God forbid we females should take ownership of our skill and talent."

Maggie exchanged wry smiles with Eleanor. It was a true pleasure having such a good friend, and one who understood completely the unique struggles of being a woman making a living through one's pen. They never had to justify themselves to each other.

Of course, they hadn't seen each other nearly as much since Eleanor's marriage, but such was the way of the world. People moved in and out like tides. And while Maggie missed her friend, she was pleased a man as intelligent and doting as Ashford had been the one to win Eleanor's hand.

The earl was waiting for them as she and Eleanor entered the box. Sharply handsome and elegant as always, he stood at the entrance and bowed over her hand.

"Mrs. Delamere." Ashford straightened to his full, impressive height. "The pleasure of *The Sorrows of Cassandra* is eclipsed only by the pleasure of your company."

"And your ease with flattery is an art unto itself, my lord." Her answer came readily. They were not entirely friends, she and Eleanor's husband, but they were tentatively reaching toward a greater level of comfort. Admittedly, she had not been especially kind or welcoming to him when he and Eleanor had first begun their association with each other. But Maggie hadn't wanted Eleanor to fall prey to a nobleman. Experience had taught Maggie the bitter truth.

Awareness prickled along Maggie's skin, sinking even deeper to the nerves below.

Marwood stood at the railing, surveying the emptying theater. Tonight, he was dressed for going out, in a snug ink-blue coat, rose gold waistcoat, and white breeches. Yet his cheeks were shaded with a shocking amount of stubble, and his long black hair flowed loosely to his shoulders. It was as if a pirate had decided to dress up for a night at the theater.

His dark eyes raked her as he turned around. Stepping forward—she had to resist the impulse to move away from him—he took her hand for the requisite gesture of polite greeting. But while he wore gloves, she did not, and the heat of his large hand spread into her much smaller one. His fingers tightened slightly, almost instinctively. Did she pull out of his grasp or hold him closer?

She gave herself a mental shake. *Flee*, her instincts demanded. *Stay*, they also insisted.

"Why, Mrs. Delamere," he said, his voice low and lush as velvet. "How very condescending of you to join us aristos."

"I am always friendly with Lord and Lady Ashford." She managed to tug her hand free, and tucked it in the folds of her skirt. The contrast between her plain woolen gown and their evening attire suddenly seemed jarring. "And I cannot blame Lord Ashford for the fault of his noble birth. He's doing his best to correct that unfortunate condition."

The earl laughed—to her relief. She still wasn't certain how self-deprecating he could be, though he obviously had to be a man of good humor to be married to Eleanor.

"Come now, Mrs. Delamere," Marwood said with a sly grin. "I have been studying the culture of the Egyptians, and you judge us gentry folk more harshly than Osiris, the god of the dead, judges the souls of the departed."

"I had not expected you to read anything more than the latest scandal rag for references to yourself," she answered sweetly. Maggie glanced at Eleanor. "Not to give offense."

"None inferred," Eleanor replied.

"I might surprise you in many ways, madam," he said with that sinful smile. "I observe more than the turn of an opera dancer's ankle. For example, it hasn't escaped my notice that us toffs, as you might say, are always the villains in your work."

She folded her arms across her chest. He would not draw her out. He wouldn't affect her. "My writing comes from life experience."

Marwood went still, his gaze perceptive as he looked at her with dark eyes.

"Not all people of noble birth are wicked." He nodded toward Lord Ashford, who shook his head at his friend in exasperation. "There's proof."

"Are *you* wicked, Lord Marwood?" Maggie countered.

He bowed, a gesture that was both graceful and sensual. "Most assuredly."

That same rush of sensual awareness filled her, heated and drugging. She must fight against it. Fight him. She spread her hands. "My point is proven. Maybe some are good, but they are infrequent specimens."

"If you truly want to know the ways of the nobility," he said, winking, "you could accompany me on my evening revels, the way Lady Ashford did with Lord Ashford."

"That was for her newspaper," Maggie answered, placing her hands on her hips. "And it's impossible to overstate how little I care about the lives of the gentry, except the roles they play in my work." She knew she was being outright rude now, but the man seemed to enjoy needling her. He seemed as uncertain of her as she was of him, making them both fall into roles they were not entirely comfortable with.

What the hell should she do with him?

"I think you're doing a reasonable job of it." Damn him, he continued to smile at her. "Yet I don't believe you're being entirely fair in your depiction of aristocrats. Do you want to be accused of being unjust?"

"So long as people come to the theater, my lord," she returned, stepping forward, "I'm not especially concerned what I'm accused of. I've been called much worse than 'unjust.'"

There had been such cruel names, so painful, so injurious, that she'd once believed she'd never heal from their wounds. Yet she had. Not without echoes of old pain, however.

She didn't know why she'd revealed that to him, anyway. His brow lifted, and a fleeting look of anger crossed his face.

Before he could speak, she gave him the barest of curtseys. "It's late, and I've still much work to accomplish tonight."

"Am I being dismissed?" He laughed with incredulity.

"Not at all, my lord. I'm leaving." She gave Ashford a deeper curtsey. "Lord Ashford. A genuine pleasure."

"Likewise," he answered.

"I'll walk you back," Eleanor said, taking her arm.

"That isn't necessary," replied Maggie.

"I think it is." Ah, her friend was just as stubborn as she. The trouble of cleaving to like-minded individuals.

As the two women left the box, Maggie felt Marwood's gaze on her back. Perhaps it was for the best that she wasn't alone for the next while. Just a few minutes in Marwood's company had made her pulse hammer and her temper roil like a witch's cauldron. Left to her own devices, she might do something rash—like set fire to his theater box.

Or pull him close for a kiss.

Where had that thought come from?

She felt an unmistakable pull toward him, a heat and magnetism that pulsed down to her very bones. Yet he stood for everything she despised. How could she want him when the thought of him filled her with hot anger? The ground seemed to shake beneath her feet, throwing her off balance.

The Lord preserve her from wealthy, aristocratic rakes. Especially with sinfully handsome faces and pointed wits. They were the most dangerous.

Chapter 7

Enter Harriet, a maid.
Harriet: My lady, the wedding celebration will
*   begin soon. Shall you join the festivities?*
Phoebe: I shall, but I cannot help but feel a chill
*   in my bones. Something ill comes this way.*

The Shattered Heart

"You're in a damned odd humor," Ashford remarked to Cam once the women had left the box.

Cam settled back on the edge of the box's ledge, continuing to watch the rows of seats as they emptied. The Imperial, like every other theater, replicated the strata between classes, with the most expensive seats being located in the private boxes, and others divided between the pit and the benches, each separated by cost. Funny how the English couldn't resist clinging to their hierarchies, even when seeking entertainment.

He hadn't cared about pecking order when he'd been a boy of ten or so. He'd spent the summer at one of the family's country estates, and a troupe of strolling players had come through the nearby village. Reluctant, he'd been dragged to see a production of *Henry V.* A spell had come over him from the moment the young king had stepped upon the rickety wooden stage. It hadn't mattered that Henry's velvet robes had been patched and were shiny with wear. Or that the swords were painted wood. He'd been entranced, and spent the rest of the summer begging his parents to take him back to every performance.

That fever had never burned away, even twenty years later.

"I'm always odd," he countered, observing one of the stage hands beginning to sweep between the rows of benches. Sweet wrappers, orange peels, and sundry papers collected by the man's broom. The detritus of a night's entertainment, now merely garbage.

The memory of Mrs. Delamere's work, however, lingered with a thrilling glow. Even more exciting was the heated exchange he'd just had with her.

"You baited Mrs. Delamere," Ashford pointed out, coming to stand beside Cam. "I've never heard you provoke anyone so mercilessly."

Cam shrugged. "She intrigues me." He didn't mention that a need had been kindled in him, a new hunger that burned with an unusual intensity. It was unprecedented for his interest in someone to flare this fast, this bright.

"Clearly, you don't offer the same significance to her."

A corner of Cam's mouth rose as he considered the sizeable challenge ahead of him. "I am an optimist." He clasped his fingers together. "If she held me in such contempt, she wouldn't even bother talking to me."

"Perhaps she's only being polite," Ashford offered.

He gripped the rail, and lamplight glinted on the unfashionable wedding band he insisted on wearing.

Cam gave a snort. " 'Polite' is not a word I would associate with that woman. Witty—yes. Radical—indeed. Never been one for hiding her feelings, the bold wench."

"Don't call her that," Ashford said, voice hardening.

Cam stared back at his friend, the two men engaging in a quiet show of dominance, each waiting to see who'd blink first.

Neither yielded. They would have gone on silently battling each other, had not a youthful lad down in the pit called out to Cam in greeting, breaking the wordless duel.

After Cam returned the greeting, the tension between him and Ashford had broken.

Somewhat. "She doesn't want you, old man," Ashford said gently.

Not yet, she didn't. But Cam's campaign hadn't even begun. He was formulating his strategy, which was in itself a pleasure. She would not come to him easily. Mrs. Delamere was a prize worth winning.

"The thorniest plants offer the sweetest fruit," Cam countered.

Ashford shook his head. There was once a time when the two of them were the most unstoppable rakes in London, careening through the night as though packs of demons pursued them. But all that had changed. The light in Ashford's smile dimmed when his wife wasn't nearby.

What might that be like?

"In this case, that fruit is kept in a walled, locked garden that you'll never access," Ashford said.

Cam smiled and straightened. "I can jump a wall or pick a lock." He scratched at his jaw. Really, he ought to shave more, but it was such a bother, and, in truth, women seemed to particularly favor him when he resembled a highwayman. "Haven't had a challenge in a long while."

That's all that it was, wasn't it? The excitement of the hunt. To reach the hotly passionate woman beneath the veneer of cool wit. She'd shown her temper, simmering just under the surface.

God, what ecstasy they could create together.

Ashford pointed warningly at Cam. "Careful, blighter. Mrs. Delamere is Eleanor's best friend. She's not to be trifled with."

"Who spoke of trifling?" Cam lifted his hands.

Ashford's look was wry. "Have you forgotten? No one knows you as I do. Not even your father. You're even more wicked that I was—before Eleanor."

"Not everyone can find an Eleanor," Cam muttered.

Could he ever find a love like that? It seemed an impossibility. He'd rather be alone than risk disappointment and heartbreak. In the meantime, he had a pretty playwright to seduce.

Maggie couldn't think. As she and Eleanor walked backstage, her mind was too clouded with thoughts of Lord Marwood. Why did he bother her so much? It wasn't as though she was unused to being needled or baited. Yet that man in particular set her temper, and other parts of her, alight.

She cursed herself. She ought to know better. At the least, she should have developed some kind of immunity to men like him and their practiced seduction. A charming rogue like Lord Marwood could wreak havoc on her heart—and, apparently, her inspiration. She couldn't afford to risk either.

Maggie and Eleanor continued through the wings of the theater, then lower, down the stairs to where the dressing rooms were located. Eleanor chatted about hiring new female writers for *The Hawk's Eye*, but Maggie only half paid attention, barely making sounds of assent or engagement during pauses in her friend's story.

"You're troubled," Eleanor noted shrewdly, peering at Maggie.

"I'm perfectly well," she answered at once.

Eleanor shook her head. "It's not an illness. There's something else at work."

"As I said, I'm fine."

A young actress in the makeup and costume of an ingénue fortunately stopped her, giving her a welcome distraction.

"Was tonight better, ma'am?" she asked, her hands twisting together with anxious anticipation.

"Much better this evening, Miss Brown," Maggie answered. "Though I would pause right before the line, 'Your plans are ruined, your grace.' It will give more impact."

The girl nodded eagerly. "Thank you, ma'am." She hurried off, practicing her lines.

"I need to speak to the wardrobe mistress," Maggie said aloud. "There was a tear in Miss Brown's costume."

"Don't change the subject," Eleanor said insistently. "You're fluttering around like a butterfly on fire. Something's got you upset. What is it?"

Damn it. Eleanor knew her all too well. Maggie glanced around in the crowded backstage hallway, making certain no one overheard them. She pulled her friend into a small storage closet that smelled of dust, dried paint and vinegar.

"It's bad, isn't it?" Eleanor asked in the darkness.

Maggie exhaled unsteadily. "Terrible." Embarrassment heated her face, even in the darkness. How could she confess this secret to Eleanor? Yes, she was her dearest friend, but she was also a writer with a booming career. Professional shame flooded her.

At last, she said, "I'm . . . I can't write anymore."

"What?" Eleanor cried. "Impossible! You've always been able to write."

"Apparently, not always," Maggie said wryly.

Eleanor pressed, "Even when your lodging house flooded and then the Imperial burned down, and you had to write on a piece of wood, sitting on the curb, you still managed to do it."

Maggie rubbed at her eyes. "It's different this time. The words aren't coming anymore, El."

"I know that feeling," her friend said darkly. She added, sincerely, "I'm so sorry. It's a terrible feeling."

"Thank you," Maggie answered, warmed by Eleanor's honesty.

"What are you working on now?"

The Hidden Daughter's Return." She leaned against some shelves, feeling them poke her in the back like her reluctant Muse.

"Ah," Eleanor answered with understanding. "Alina's story. Damned sequels."

"Yes, damned sequels," Maggie agreed. Helpless fury and fear gnawed in her stomach. She groaned.

"How am I supposed to equal or better something that people loved? The board of directors for the theater is threatening me, demanding I hand over *The Hidden Daughter's Return* as soon as possible."

"And all of that is holding you back."

"Yes. No. I don't know." In her angry despair, she wanted to pace, but the closet was far too small, so she plucked an object off the wall—which turned out to be a pasteboard crown, and ran her fingers over the faux jewels adorning it. "It's got to have a *happy* ending. Anything else will have the audience riot."

"How difficult are happy endings? Besides, in all of London, no one has a better imagination than you," Eleanor added warmly.

Though Maggie smiled at her friend's belief in her, it couldn't quite erase the sinking sensation in the pit of her belly, or the heaviness that clouded in her chest.

"With the exception of you and Lord Ashford," Maggie replied darkly, "I haven't seen much to give me faith in happy endings."

"They're out there," Eleanor said. "Perhaps they don't seem very spectacular, but happiness can be found in the most humble of corners."

Maggie whistled. "That's very good. You should put it in your next article."

"I will." She could hear the smile in Eleanor's voice. There was a pause, then Eleanor asked more gently, "What are you going to do?"

Unhappiness surged at the well-intentioned question. After letting out a long sigh, Maggie said, "I simply don't know. This work *has* to be written but the burletta won't come to me, no matter how I try." She groaned again. "Perhaps there's too much riding on it.

I feel pressure on every side, yet I know its momentum can make or break me."

"We'll figure something out." Eleanor gripped Maggie's hand tightly. "We ink-stained scribblers stick together."

"Sisters of the quill," Maggie answered, her own voice thick.

Something had to break. But Maggie didn't know what. She had a terrible fear that it might be her own strength, and with Lord Marwood so close, she needed all the strength she could muster.

Chapter 8

Friar Ned: My child, you came to us ten years ago, a stranger with a babe in arms. Now you are beloved in the village. Yet I sense a heaviness in your heart. A secret within.
Phoebe: Oh, Father, I wish I might unburden myself, but the danger is too great.

The Shattered Heart

The words trickled out of her, drop by drop, like blood from an almost dry vein. Maggie sat at her table in the property room, her fingers digging into her hair as she stared at the paper in front of her. A handful of sentences littered the foolscap.

Each day since she'd spoken with Lord Marwood in the theater box, she'd been in an agony of waiting, wondering. Would he come back? And why should she care? He didn't matter to her. Not a bit. Her life had gone along just fine before he'd sauntered into it, and it would continue to do so long after he'd moved on to some other amusement.

Still, when a knock sounded on the door to the prop room, Maggie jumped in her seat.

"Yes?" she called.

Mr. Kingston poked his head in. "Two gentlemen are here to see you," he said in his musical Caribbean accent. "They're from the board."

Her throat closed as though someone were gripping it. Guesses about what they were doing there caromed through her mind. None of those guesses were particularly pleasant ones. Still, she could try for some optimism, thin as it might be. She took a deep breath, stood up, and straightened her shoulders.

Two expensively-dressed men entered the chamber. One was middle aged, tall and stout—Lord Abernathy—the other younger, shorter and lean—Mr. Edmunds.

She'd met them a few times before, under happier circumstances. Now, they both smiled at her, though she detected some strain at the edges of those smiles. Neither man looked particularly pleased to be there.

Well, she wasn't glad to see them, either. Their presence at the theater was not a welcome one.

"Good afternoon, my lord, Mr. Edmunds," she said with a false attempt at brightness.

Both men greeted her by name, with Mr. Edmunds bowing and Lord Abernathy offering her a small nod.

"I trust you are having a pleasant and productive day," Mr. Edmunds began.

"Pleasant enough," Maggie answered. "And yourselves?"

"Very pleasant," Lord Abernathy said.

It seemed that the only word anyone knew how to use was *pleasant*. Which was ironic, given that the tense, strained atmosphere in the room was anything but.

With the exhaustion of their vocabulary, taut silence fell. Maggie twisted her fingers together, then, realizing what she was doing, clasped her hands behind her back. Mr. Edmunds coughed into his fist. Lord Abernathy looked everywhere but at her.

She couldn't stand it.

"Is there something I can assist you with?" she finally asked.

"Ah, yes, well . . ." Mr. Edmunds looked at Lord Abernathy, who made an obvious *Go on* face. Yet when Mr. Edmunds continued to hedge, with more "Um, yes, ahem," Lord Abernathy could no longer wait.

"We've sent you three letters," he said, cutting through Mr. Edmunds's evasions. "And you haven't responded to any of them. May we inquire why?"

Maggie resisted the urge to pick up a chair and start swinging it. A fine sheen of sweat coated her body. Instead of striking out, though, she held herself still and faced them. "I've been busy."

"Writing the sequel to *The Shattered Heart*?" Mr. Edmunds asked.

"I'm working on it," she answered. Which was something like the truth.

"How soon do you think you will be finished with it?" Mr. Edmunds continued.

Oh, God. How to answer? "Difficult to say," she managed.

The two men exchanged uneasy glances. Clearly, she'd given them the wrong answer. Her mouth went dry.

"I'm very sorry to hear that," Lord Abernathy said.

"Why?" she couldn't help but ask.

"Because, Mrs. Delamere, we've come to tell you that you have two weeks to deliver the burletta."

"What?" she cried. She couldn't possibly have heard them properly.

Lord Abernathy explained, "We need the income from the sequel in order to keep the theater running. It cannot exist without capital."

"What if . . ." She swallowed hard, but the dryness in her throat made it almost impossible. " . . . I cannot give you the burletta within two weeks?" The question tore from her.

"Then," Mr. Edmunds said apologetically, "we will abandon production on the sequel, and find ourselves a new playwright to take your place. We already have several prospective writers lined up. Any one of them could pen something in a similar vein."

Only through force of will did Maggie keep from staggering backward. She planted her feet firmly as the ground listed beneath her. "You cannot be serious."

"We are serious, unfortunately," said Mr. Edmunds. "Our profit margin is dwindling, and we're soon going to lose money on the operations of this theater. The only way to secure its continued success is through staging the sequel. Your other works have been successful, but it's not enough to satisfy the board of directors."

"I thought we were turning a profit," Maggie said.

"We were," Mr. Edmunds said. "But operating costs have soared in the past few months. Nothing is coming cheaply, and we find our coffers dwindling faster than they can be replenished."

Lord Abernathy continued, "If you cannot provide the work for us, we have no choice but to look elsewhere for content for the theater."

"Art cannot be rushed," Maggie exclaimed hotly.

"Yet we aren't talking about art," Mr. Edmunds said

ruefully. "What we're discussing is profits. Though we like to stage artistic works, this is a business, after all. None of us can afford to take a loss given the expense of running a theater."

"Writing doesn't *work* that way," she said fiercely. "You can't squeeze an author like a sponge, and words just dribble out."

"You have two weeks from today," Lord Abernathy said. He seemed less apologetic than Mr. Edmunds, much more businesslike.

"We're quite sorry." Mr. Edmunds gave her a sympathetic look.

"But this is how it has to be," the other man said brusquely. He checked his pocket watch. "We've several more appointments today. So, we shall leave you to get back to your work. Good afternoon, Mrs. Delamere."

"Good afternoon," she said numbly as the two men filed out. Mr. Edmunds threw her one final contrite glance before leaving the property room.

Then she was alone. Beyond frustrated. Utterly devastated. Even in her wildest imaginings, she couldn't conceive of a worse situation for a writer. The world spun out of her power, and nothing she could do would bring it back under her control.

Chapter 9

*Friar Ned: Come now, there is no judgment in
the eyes of God.*
*Phoebe: I fear even God would cast me aside if
He knew my truth.*

The Shattered Heart

London thrived on madness. From its assembly halls
to its stockyards, Wapping to Westminster, Cam had
experienced firsthand all the chaotic lunacy the city
had to offer. Yet as he walked through the crowded,
bustling wings of the Imperial, he understood that
there was no greater madness than that of the theater.

Men in workmen's clothes carried painted scenery
flats. A trio of dancers spun and twirled in a corner,
practicing a routine while a woman at a piano accompanied them, banging out a tune to be heard above the
actors onstage rehearsing. One tenor sang scales. Carpenters hammered nails into boards, adding to the din.
It was as though someone had decided to take all possible sounds and set them in a barrel full of rocks, then
pushed the barrel down a hillside.

He'd been feeling restless and edgy all morning.

Like there was something, someone, he was meant to see.

As he'd sat at his breakfast, brooding over his tea, a woman's face appeared in his mind. Mrs. Delamere would likely have nothing but insults and vitriol for him, yet he needed to see her with an uncommon desperation. She'd engaged his every waking thought for days.

Excitement pulsed through him at the idea of not only seeing and talking with Mrs. Delamere, but watching her engage in the mysterious process of writing. So he'd called for his carriage and made his way to the Imperial. Where he'd been met by mayhem.

It was a measure of how hectic the theater was that no one stopped him and asked him his business. Cam made his way from the wings, down the backstage stairs, then down through the corridors. Reaching the property room, he decided politeness might garner him some good favor, so he knocked on the door.

No answer. Perhaps she was deeply involved in her writing. He knocked again, saying through the door, "Mrs. Delamere?"

Still no response. Was she ignoring him? He chafed at the idea. At the least, have the good manners to tell him to bugger off.

"Come now," he said, opening the door, "remaining mute is childish."

But he spoke to an empty room. Empty of Mrs. Delamere, in any event. The chamber's sole occupant was an orange cat, grooming itself atop the table. The animal regarded Cam with a disinterested yellow stare before returning to its task.

Not unlike Mrs. Delamere's reaction when seeing him, in fact.

Turning away from the property room, he stepped back into the corridor. A man holding a kit of tools walked past.

Cam stopped him. "Where is Mrs. Delamere?"

The workman shrugged. "Don't know. Hang on." He shouted at another man at the end of the hallway. "Oi! Frank! Where'd Mrs. Delamere go?"

"Can't say," was the shouted reply. "I'll find out." This bloke opened a nearby door and yelled into it. "Any of you lot know what happened to the lady what writes?"

An unseen person hollered back. "Mr. Kingston told Will who told Edgar who told me that she went to do some thinking!"

"She's gone off to think," Frank bellowed back at Cam and the first workman.

"Lady's somewhere ruminating on something," the man told Cam.

"I gathered that," Cam answered drily. "But *where* did she go to do this ruminating?"

"Where'd she go?" the workman called to Frank, who asked the same question of the unseen gent.

Finally, in the world's most deafening relay, the answer came back with the disheartening news: "She didn't tell nobody."

Disappointment hit him, quick and sharp. The lightness he'd felt when he had thought of seeing her again dissipated.

He wouldn't give up so easily. After handing the workman a coin for his trouble, Cam distractedly climbed the stairs.

Where might Mrs. Delamere go to think? To ponder this issue, he let himself into one of the theater boxes—

empty during the day—and leaned against the railing to watch the stage. Actors there continued to proclaim their lines and pose, guided by the direction of Mr. Fontaine, who seemed to be playing the part of the male lead. Given the awkwardness of the prose, the work the troupe was performing wasn't likely from Mrs. Delamere's pen. Unless she had suddenly lost her talent.

Doubtful. Ability like hers didn't simply stop like the last drops of wine in the flagon. Yet the whole of the artistic process remained obscure to him. He had no idea what went on in any writer's mind—especially hers.

But where was she? When he needed to be alone with his thoughts he sometimes went to White's—a place she couldn't go.

The racket from the actors, orchestra, and construction pierced his concentration. How could anybody get any thinking done with this bedlam? What he needed was quiet. Somewhere removed from all distractions. A little bit of greenery might be nice, too . . .

He stood upright. A garden or park would fit the bill. Yes, she might seek someplace pretty and relatively serene, far from the chaos of the Imperial.

London was full of parks and gardens, however. Hyde Park he dismissed immediately. Too big, likely too crowded, and full of the fashionable elite she so disliked. Same with St. James's Park and Kensington Gardens. Where, then?

The garden maintained by the Apothecaries' Company might suit. It was serene and uncrowded, save for a few medical students and the occasional resident of Chelsea, looking for some pastoral sanctuary in the heart of the city. And it was full of poisonous plants—

the kind Mrs. Delamere might admire and use as inspiration in her work.

Resolved, he quickly left the box, and hurried from the theater. His carriage awaited him, and he called up to the driver his intended destination. In an instant, they were driving west, toward the Embankment.

As the carriage wended its way through the streets, Cam held tight to his walking stick, and kept his gaze leveled straight ahead. His heart maintained a fast, steady rhythm in his chest. He rehearsed a number of things he might say to her—little jests and jibes that seemed to both exasperate and amuse her. He wanted anything but indifference. There was no hope of seduction if her response was apathy.

The carriage finally reached its destination, and Cam gave the garden's gatekeeper a coin. The grizzled old man waved him forward, and Cam stepped into the boundaries of the garden itself. It had been a cold summer, and the grounds showed it, the numerous specimens in their beds not nearly as lush as they were at other times. Cam paced up and down between the beds, his gaze uninterested in all the exotic plants, nor their scientific properties. At another time, he might be intrigued by the specimens brought back by Sir Joseph Banks from the distant corners of the globe. Or he might pause to admire the statue of Sloane, the garden's former owner.

Not today. Today he had one goal. To find Mrs. Delamere and . . . what? He wasn't certain exactly what, only that his need to see her outweighed all other desires.

A gardener in a dirt-stained apron approached him. "May I be of assistance, my lord? I can ask one of the students to give you a tour, if that's your pleasure."

"Has a woman been here?" Cam asked instead. "About this tall." He held his hand just below his chin. "Dark hair. Lovely little gap between her teeth. Figure like a tiny Aphrodite."

The gardener reddened at the mention of Mrs. Delamere's shape, but Cam didn't care. He'd describe the woman to her last beauty mark if it meant finding her.

"Can't say as I've seen anyone fitting that description, my lord," the man said, rubbing his hands on the front of his apron. "Only been two ladies here today, and they were both fair."

Damn it. His heart pitched low to his boots. Cam's world had never included this kind of piercing, consuming disappointment.

"I'm sorry, my lord," the gardener seemed compelled to say.

Cam tried to clear his expression. "No, that's . . ." He handed the man a shilling.

"Thank'ee," said the gardener. "Is there anything else I can do for you, my lord?"

Cam shook his head. "Please, return to your work."

The gardener ambled off, leaving Cam alone. Instead of sinking down onto one of the stone benches, Cam slowly ambled along a path. He carefully pushed aside a spray of vines that drooped in a green canopy. A handful of the plants here looked downright carnivorous, though most were rather pretty, in their useful way. And the garden was blissfully quiet. He'd have to suggest it to Mrs. Delamere as a place to gather her thoughts—when he did see her again.

She'd likely be at the theater tonight. He didn't want to wait that long.

His gaze fell on a bright crimson flower, its petals

unfurled in the afternoon sun. A small sign warned visitors that the plant contained a toxin, perilous to the touch. Mrs. Delamere would look quite delectable in red with her complexion and dark hair. As lush as the flower, and likely just as dangerous.

She would probably enjoy the comparison. Especially given the dark and often gothic nature of her works.

The thought made him pause.

The final act of *The Shattered Heart* took place in a graveyard, an eerie and atmospheric setting that perfectly suited the tone of the piece.

Damn him, why hadn't he thought of it sooner?

Turning, he stalked from the garden as fast as he could go without breaking into an outright run.

"Putney Burial Ground," he said to his driver once he reached his carriage. It was across the river, and a considerable chance to go so far, but he'd take it.

Traffic lightened as they proceeded farther from the city. More wagons from the country were coming in than leaving, bearing their goods for market. Cam barely paid it any heed. This was a wild gambit, one that would likely result in more disappointment. He should just turn around and go to White's to while away the rest of the afternoon with a good brandy and the latest news. A perfectly pleasant activity for men of his station. And yet he was compelled to pursue his instinct.

At last, after crossing Fulham Bridge, the carriage headed over to Upper Richmond Road. It came to a stop outside a small enclosed bit of greenery. Cam alit from the vehicle before his footman could open the door for him.

He'd only taken a few steps inside the burial ground,

with its evocative moss-covered headstones and above-
ground tombs, when he spotted her. She drifted
across the lawn, head bent, as though she was indeed
lost in thought. Occasionally, she stopped to run her
ungloved fingertips across the age-rounded top of a
tombstone.

She hadn't yet spotted him.

Pleasure and awareness hit him like a shot of the
purest whiskey, warm and dizzying. But he noticed that
a frown creased between her brows, and her mouth was
tightly drawn. Something troubled her.

A feeling struck him in a quick, hard jab. He rubbed
at the spot between his ribs, confounded. What bothered her? How could he make it right?

Others' problems were best avoided, and he made
it a general policy to do so. As a man of property
and means, there were always people coming to him,
asking for help. Sometimes they wanted money. Others
wanted his influence. But he'd learned how to say no,
or to evade those demands altogether.

Yet Mrs. Delamere's distress hit him on a visceral
level. A surge of protectiveness pulsed through him.
Perhaps there was someone else here in the burial
ground who was pestering her. Or maybe she was es-
caping something, or somebody, at the theater.

He must have shifted or made some sound, because
she glanced back. Her gaze fell on him—he felt it in a
rush of heat—and for the briefest, barest moment an
expression crossed her face. A look of relief.

Could he dare hope?

But hope didn't last long. Her expression was gone
in an instant.

Wariness and irritation replaced the look.

But he never retreated. So he crossed the small expanse of the grounds, coming to stand several feet away from her, then bowing.

"You are not an easy woman to find, madam," he said with a smile.

"That is by design," she answered, taking a step back. More distance between them. "No one knows of this place."

"The occupants do." He waved toward the head-stones and tombs. "Though they are remarkably silent on the topic."

She tilted her head, puzzled. "Tell me truly, how did you find me?"

He'd been compelled to find her—but he couldn't say that. "It's a rather lengthy saga," he replied. "I might turn my own quill to the writing of it. An epic poem in the tradition of Spenser's *The Faerie Queene*, full of adventure and peril, with you as my own Belphoebe. The huntress who always runs away from blokes."

Her mouth curved in what looked like a reluctant smile. "I prefer Britomart, the lady knight, fighting as fierce as any man."

He chuckled. "A better fit."

"You haven't answered my question." She planted her hands on her hips. "In this enormous city, you managed to find me in a little corner of Putney?"

"Perhaps I know you better than you realize."

Her lips pursed. "A distressing thought." Yet she didn't take another step backward.

He took the little victory, treasuring it like a found gem.

"I should hope nothing I do distresses you," he continued. "I only wish to give you pleasure."

Red stained her cheeks, intriguing him. "It's been so long since I've had experience with it."

"With what? Pleasure?" At her small nod, he said, "That's a damned shame. You deserve as much as you desire."

"And if my desire is great?" she asked, breathless.

"Then I am the man for you," he replied thickly, his every nerve alight, his body tight. He brought up his hand, and traced one ungloved finger down the side of her cheek. Her skin felt softer than dreams, cool and velvety beneath his fingertip.

Heat shot up through that point of contact, all the way through his body. He felt her in every corner of himself. If she felt this soft on her cheek, imagine what she felt like elsewhere. Imagine how wondrous it would be to explore her every inch, learn her intimately.

He wanted that. Wanted her. Desire pooled hot and thick, centering in his groin. It was a simple touch, just a fingertip to a cheek, and yet it affected him as strongly as if their two naked bodies were twined together.

Stunned by his response, he watched her pupils widen, and caught the sound of her breath as she inhaled sharply. More pink crept into her face. Her full lips parted. She seemed shocked by her reaction. Yet she didn't pull away.

For a moment, they only stared at each other, gazes locked.

Then, changeable as a summer storm, the good weather of her desire passed quickly. Her frown returned. She pulled back.

She paced away, turning so quickly that a lock of her hair came loose from its pins and fluttered behind her. "I can't be your amusement," she threw over her shoulder.

He followed, his longer legs easily closing the distance between them. "Who says you're my amusement?"

She stopped and leaned against one of the above-ground tombs, her arms crossing over her chest. "Tell me what you're doing here, then."

Though her sudden decision to face him made his pulse race, he made certain to keep a respectful space between them. She'd only run away if he tried for anything more. "Perhaps I wanted to see you."

Her brows rose in disbelief. "You hunted me down across London to talk?"

"You intrigue me unlike anyone I've ever met." As soon as the words left him, he realized they were true.

She had a way of pulling candor from him. As though she would abide by nothing less than authenticity. And he had to obey that demand.

Cam couldn't examine that revelation now. His concern was her, here, in this moment.

"We could talk of your writing," he offered. It was important to her. Everyone liked speaking of what mattered to them. But he cared most of all what *she* wanted.

Her mouth turned down. "Brace yourself for disappointment. While it's being written, I don't discuss my work with anyone."

"Surely exceptions can be made."

She shook her head. "Not for anyone. Even you, *my lord*." She pushed away from the tomb and started down one of the small paths crisscrossing the burial ground.

"But I understand nothing of your creative process," he pressed, aware that he sounded, well, almost desperate. Yet . . . what was this? He truly did want to know more about how her mind worked. "All I know about creativity is in the bedroom."

That got a startled laugh from her. Her blush returned. "Doubtless your myriad lovers could attest to that."

"They're not of concern to me right now," he found himself saying. "You are."

She regarded him with a piercing gaze, one he couldn't look away from. She seemed to see everything all at once, and it was odd and uncomfortable, yet strangely refreshing, as though all artifice fell away to the truth beneath. The self that never saw the light of the sun.

"Why would you care?" she demanded.

There would be nothing from her without giving of himself. She was too guarded, too wary. It was the toll he'd have to pay to cross the bridge into her mind.

"I cannot understand how you write of love, when it's so absent in the real world," he admitted. He picked up a leaf that had fallen from one of the trees, and twirled it between his fingers as they continued to walk slowly through the burial ground. "You create a fantastical realm of true love. The works you create . . . they make me . . ." He struggled to form the proper words, when he himself did not fully understand what he was trying to say. " . . . Feel things."

"You say that like it's not a good thing," she answered.

"For viscounts, feelings are not quite fashionable. Or useful. We are supposed to be dedicated either to the pursuit of entertainment, or else devoted to duty. Feelings have no place in any of that."

"Will they make you weaker?" she pressed.

"Perhaps." He couldn't believe he was having this conversation—with her of all people. She was his intended target for seduction, and yet he was opening up to her in ways he'd never experienced with anyone. "Yet I crave those sensations feelings give me. I cannot understand it."

"You don't need to understand it," she answered. "Only experience it."

"Where do you find them," he asked, "these stories you create?"

After a moment, she said, "Stories abound everywhere. In the faces of people, in the fall of light across water." Her shoulders lifted and fell. "I cannot help it. All it takes is a single image, a sound—a woman shaking out her laundry, a man's laugh as he leans from a window—and the thoughts come to me. I want to know more of them. Who they are. What brought them to this place in their lives. If they have any hidden joys or sorrows. And then . . ." She glanced down at her spread fingers, as though they held the answer. "My quill takes over."

The dreamy passion in her voice enthralled him. "Are you a mystic?"

If her voice was alluring, her low, husky laugh shot heat through him. "There's no god that speaks through me, and I'd never claim to be one myself. If anything, my inspiration comes from an empty belly. I don't write, I don't eat."

"False modesty," he scoffed. "There's more within your writing than the desire for steak and kidney pie." They reached the gate of the burial ground and, to his surprise, she didn't leave, but instead turned around to make another circuit around the enclosure. He stayed alongside her.

"I warrant," he continued, "that you made up stories

even as a child, before you thought of the commerce of writing."

A small, enchanting smile curved her mouth, and her gaze turned far away. "When I was small, we sometimes took the mail coach to visit my mother's family in Guildford, and I'd stare out the window. Just . . . imagining." She laughed again, lost in a private world. "I'd be so quiet, especially compared to my brothers, my parents used to jest that I'd fallen out of the coach. But I was only lost in my own thoughts."

This was the first she'd ever spoken of her kin. He gathered each piece of information about her, more precious than any moment at the theater.

"They must be bursting with pride now, your family," he said.

Whatever warmth or openness that had been in her expression immediately disappeared behind a wall of ice. One moment, she was soft and fond, and the next, she was distant and cold as the Arctic.

"That's none of your damn concern," she said through tight lips. She spun on her heel, heading for the gate.

"Mrs. Delamere—"

"Leave me alone," she tossed over her shoulder. She pulled open the gate and it groaned like a ghost.

He stretched out a hand toward her. "At the least, let me give you a ride in my carriage."

Her laugh was scornful. "Alone? With you?"

"I can wait. Or walk back."

She faced him, the bars of the iron fence between them, like a prison. "I want nothing from you or any of your kind." With that, she spun around and hurried down the street.

Should he go after her? That would only push her further away.

In a moment, he stood alone amongst the gravestones and tombs, wondering what had just happened. Her moods were unpredictable, suggesting an inner life he couldn't quite understand. Slowly, he made his way toward one of the above-ground tombs, and braced his hands on the carvings. Some rich man's final resting place.

The whole of the day had been one exercise in confusion after another. Capped now with her abrupt departure. They had flirted a small amount, but what they had really discussed went far beyond becoming lovers. What he suddenly wanted—and what he'd partially achieved—was knowing her more. This was a first for him with his paramours.

He didn't understand her. And now he didn't understand himself.

Chapter 10

Enter Lord Diabold and Fishhook, his servant.
Lord Diabold: How charming and fresh this
*   place is.*
Fishhook: But not for long, I hope, my lord.

The Shattered Heart

He couldn't know of what had happened with her family, and yet mention of them had soured any sense of intimacy she and the viscount had shared. When she and Lord Marwood had been talking in the burial ground, it was almost as if he'd truly cared about her process, about her work. As though she was more than another conquest.

His company had been more than pleasant. Like an urchin drawn toward a brightly-lit mansion, she'd been drawn in by him. He'd made her feel worthwhile, important.

He'd revealed things about himself she wondered if he'd ever told anyone. Lord Marwood had seemed just as surprised by the revelations as she had been.

But she'd been a fool to think of him as anything other than another aristo. Talk of her family had only reminded her of everything that she'd lost because of his sort. He might find her an engaging plaything now, but she always had more to lose.

She *was* going to lose everything. The board of directors would no longer wait for her to deliver. Yet what could she do? The board paid for the theater, its productions, and all of the expenses the Imperial incurred. She couldn't gainsay them.

There was no help for it. She would have to leave the Imperial. But she might not find another theater willing to take on the dead weight of a blocked playwright. So she would have to start over somewhere else—if such a thing was possible.

Her steps were heavy as she made her way back to the theater. It was drafty and noisy inside, smelling of fresh paint. Onstage, a handful of actors and actresses continued to go over their lines, reading from manuscript pages. Clowns practiced handstands. Fiddlers and a piper trilled out a popular song. And always came the pound of hammers and *hee-haw* of saws, building the latest set.

Returning to the familiar, controlled anarchy was a knife in her chest. The actors, the stagehands and workmen—she knew them all. In the absence of her blood kin, the cast and crew of the Imperial had become her family. Yet she had no choice.

The stage manager rushed past her, busy as always. "Mr. Kingston," she said to him. "A moment?"

"For you," he said with a smile, "always."

She choked past the hard lump in her throat. "Can we assemble everyone quickly? I promise it won't take long."

Mr. Kingston frowned. But he nodded. "Ten minutes."

"Take your time." She had no desire to speak, but better to get it over with as quickly as possible, like snapping a dislocated bone into place. There would be pain, but ultimately, it had to be done.

She waited upstage left as Mr. Kingston went about gathering the whole of the Imperial's collection of performers and crew. It took closer to thirty minutes, rather than ten, the process akin to snatching drifting feathers from the air. Music came to an abrupt halt, and a peculiar, unnatural silence fell as everyone in the building gathered around the stage and in the pit.

"I believe that's everyone," the stage manager finally said, appearing beside her.

Taking hold of his wrist, she said sincerely, "Thank you, Mr. Kingston. For all that you've done. This theater couldn't function without you as its beating heart."

He frowned at her again. "That has an ominous sound to it, madam."

All she could offer him was a strained smile. With feet like lead, she walked to center stage. The weight of dozens of gazes pressed down on her. Here they all were. Waiting. Someone coughed. An unnatural silence fell.

She swallowed. *Do it*, she thought. *Now, while you have the strength.*

"With the exception of my friend Lady Ashford," she began, pitching her voice so she could be heard, "everyone I care about most in the world is collected here right now. Which makes what I have to say all the more difficult."

"What ails you, Mrs. D?" one of the stage hands called out.

"Tell us," a costume assistant cried. "Whatever it is, we'll help."

Tears damped her hot eyes. God, how could she do

this? "I'm afraid there's nothing anyone can do. I . . ." Her throat burned, but she pushed past the pain. "I have to leave the Imperial."

Cries of shock and disbelief rang to the chandeliers. An actor yelled above the din, "Did Drury Lane finally lure you away?"

"My career in this theater is over, Mr. Hems," she answered. This was greeted with even more alarmed chatter. "Perhaps I may never write again. I apologize if this is short notice, but—"

Mr. Kingston stepped forward to stand beside her. "I won't accept it," he said defiantly.

She gave him a sad smile. "That's not for you to decide. I find myself in a very difficult position, and there's no choice for me but to leave."

"It's the board, isn't it?" the stage manager pressed quietly. "They told me and Mr. Fortescue what happened."

"What's he talking about?" shouted a violinist.

"Our board of directors insists that Mrs. Delamere present her next burletta within two weeks," Mr. Kingston said to the crowd.

This announcement was greeted with confused murmurings.

"And it's not written yet?" Mr. Hems asked.

"It's in process," she answered, unwilling, even now, to confess to the troupe the true state of her distress. "But it won't be ready by the time they want it."

"And if you don't deliver in time, Mrs. D?" Mr. Fontaine asked.

"Then I'm out," she answered flatly.

"Why do you have to go on account of them?" the violinist pressed.

Her hands clenched into fists. It was bloody unfair,

but she didn't have a choice. "They control the purse strings. Including whose burlettas are performed here." She pressed her trembling lips together. Damn it, she never cried, and yet here she was, on the verge of weeping brokenly in front of the entire cast and crew. "Once I'm gone, they'll find new writers to take my place." She shook her head. "I'm so sorry. I wish it could be different. I wish everything could be different."

With an almighty effort, she forced her back to stay straight, her spine unbended. The board could take everything from her, but she wouldn't give it the last shred of her dignity.

Mutterings and murmurings sounded among the gathered crowd. She couldn't make out what they were saying, but it sounded as though dissent brewed. At last, Miss Brown, one of the actresses, stepped forward from the people assembled in the wings.

"We won't take another cent of those toffs' money," the young woman said, tipping up her chin. "We'll work for nothing."

A chorus of agreement followed her announcement.

Maggie's heart broke. These dear, dear people. So generous, and yet so imprudent.

"That leaves the Imperial with no funding," Maggie gently reminded the girl.

"What if we went to someone else so you could stay?" Madame Hortense, the costumer, offered. "There are rich men all over London. Surely some of them will help."

Many voices joined in, saying, *Aye*, and *Let's talk to those blokes*. And, most touchingly, *To hell with the board*.

"We'll find a way, Mrs. Delamere," Mr. Kingston said softly, patting her hand. "Never you fear."

A tear finally escaped and rolled down her cheek. Bless these mad people. They believed in her, even when her faith in herself had been shaken to the core.

After the conversation with the troupe, Maggie quietly excused herself and left the theater. She needed to walk in order to think. There had to be someone who could take over for the board, but who?

She made her solitary way through London. She didn't know where she was going, only that she needed to keep moving, as if she could literally outpace her troubles. The neighborhoods around her transformed from the elegant buildings of Mayfair to the more business-oriented structures of the City.

She didn't pay much heed to where she was heading, too distracted by the churning in her belly and the knot of confusion in her chest. Yet when she looked up, she discovered herself in front of the offices of *The Hawk's Eye*. As soon as she saw the sign, including the notice "E. HAWKE, EDITOR AND PROPRIETOR," she realized that her feet had taken her to the one person who could truly understand the agonizing nature of her dilemma.

Stepping inside the offices, Maggie found herself in a large room filled with people hunched over desks. The scratch of a dozen quills charged the air, and the chamber smelled of paper, damp ink, and that peculiar scent of writers laboring under a deadline. A mixture of ambition, fear, and sweat.

At one end of the chamber stood a heavy door. Behind it, Maggie knew, were the printing presses where *The Hawk's Eye* was transformed from the scribblings of a band of writers into one of London's most popular scandal rags. It never failed to impress

Maggie that Eleanor had built this tiny kingdom, and, despite her own anguish, a bubble of pride rose in her to think that her friend had accomplished so much from so humble a beginning. In that, they were very much alike.

But Eleanor didn't have a board of directors threatening everything she'd worked for.

One of the writers, a young woman, glanced up from her work and spotted Maggie. "Mrs. Delamere!" She rose from her chair and walked toward Maggie. "Miss Hawke—I mean, Lady Ashford—is in a meeting, but I know she would be most eager to see you."

"I don't want to disturb—"

But at that moment, the door to Eleanor's office opened, and several people filed out, murmuring amongst themselves. Eleanor stood at the door, calling after them, "And make certain your sources are accurate. We don't want to be accused of slander."

"Isn't that our business?" a slightly older man asked with a cheeky grin.

"Scandal," Eleanor reminded him, one finger upraised, "not slander. An important distinction." She caught sight of Maggie, and smiled. "If it isn't my favorite histrionic hack."

"And my most beloved rumor-mongering harpy," Maggie answered, though the banter between them rang hollow in her chest.

Eleanor seemed to sense Maggie's distress, because she immediately came forward to take her hand. "What is it?" She glanced around when Maggie didn't answer. "Come, let's go into my office."

Maggie let herself be led, glad to have someone else in control for even the smallest moment. The fate of so many rested upon her shoulders. While she always felt the pressure to perform, now that weighed even more heavily upon her. The Imperial was so much more than a theater. It was, for many of the cast and crew, their home, their family. How could she cost them all that?

She needed to find other investors, but she didn't know who to go to. Financing a theater was a costly endeavor.

One name whispered in her mind. But she didn't want to consider him. It would be . . . too humbling. Not after the rude way she'd behaved toward him. He'd reject her in an instant, overwhelming her with humiliation. Could she stand that kind of mortification?

"Tea?" Eleanor asked, once she'd sat Maggie down in front of her desk and closed the door.

Maggie shook her head. Nothing tasted right ever since the two board members had appeared the other day. She couldn't remember the last time she'd eaten, and her head throbbed.

Sitting on the edge of her desk, Eleanor wouldn't relinquish hold of Maggie's hand. "What's happened? You look as though you've been bled."

"In a way, I have." Maggie exhaled. Then explained tersely what had happened with the board of directors. As she talked, the color also drained from Eleanor's face, and her friend gripped her hand harder, almost to the point of pain.

Maggie shook her head. "What am I to do, El? If I cannot come up with someone to fund the Imperial, I'm going to have to leave the theater so they can bring someone else in. And who will hire me again, if I cannot write? I may have to leave England. Start over somewhere else." She let out a strained laugh. "There's always America. I hear it's a country full of barbarians. They'd love someone like me."

"Bunch of ruffians in America." Eleanor smiled sadly. "You're too good for their sort."

"There's nothing else I can do." Maggie pulled her hand from Eleanor's grip. Too agitated to sit, she rose and paced back and forth in the confines of her friend's small office. She was a bird trapped inside a room, beating itself against the walls. Perhaps she'd knock herself unconscious, or brain herself.

"What about Daniel?" her friend offered. She pulled her legs out of Maggie's way. "He'd be more than willing to help with capital."

"Under no circumstances," Maggie exclaimed. Her heart shriveled at the thought. "I cannot go to my dearest friend's husband and whine for money."

"It's not whining," Eleanor corrected. "And I know that he couldn't refuse you. Not if I have anything to say about it," she added sternly.

Maggie stopped in her pacing and faced her friend. "That's exactly it, El. What if the theater flounders? What if *The Hidden Daughter's Return* fails, and Lord Ashford loses thousands of pounds?"

"The loss wouldn't bother him." Eleanor offered a wry smile. "I quail to say it, but my husband's a wealthy man."

"He might not be bothered by the financial shortfall," Maggie answered. "But *I* would."

"But—"

"Have you seen the garret in which I live? The plain dresses I wear? My decided lack of jewels and luxury?"

Frowning slightly, Eleanor said, "You live frugally, perhaps, but I wouldn't say you live like a Spartan."

"You know as well as I do that the life of a writer isn't precisely one of abundance," Maggie pointed out, "especially not where finances are concerned."

"Then take the money, Mags," Eleanor insisted.

Maggie placed her hands on her friend's shoulders. "The point I'm trying to make is that I don't have much in my life, but one of my greatest treasures is this." She gripped Eleanor's shoulders tighter. "Us. Taking his money would drive a wedge between us. Especially if the burletta fails. I'd never be able to look you in the eye."

A sheen appeared in Eleanor's eyes. "Mags—"

"And if anything were to happen to this . . ." Maggie glanced down at the space between them, a narrow span of air that contained the whole of their friendship, more meaningful than anything Maggie could ever bring to life with her pen. "I have you, I have the Imperial. The sum of my life, my heart. I cannot lose either. And that means I can't take your husband's money."

Eleanor's lips pressed together in a displeased line. "There's nothing I can do to convince you otherwise." Her friend shook her head. "Stubbornness, thy name is Margaret Delamere," she paraphrased.

"Alas, 'tis true," Maggie answered. She gave her friend a quick, hard embrace. "But never think I don't appreciate your generosity."

"I think I may have an answer," Eleanor noted, tapping her chin with one finger. "You're refusing to consider the obvious solution. There's one man who's always at the Imperial. Who seldom misses a performance, especially of one of your works. He's in his theater box without fail."

Turning back to face her friend, Maggie demanded, "No—"

Eleanor smiled wryly. "Lord Marwood."

Chapter 11

Enter Alina.
Alina: Good day, my lord.
*Lord Diabold: Good day, child. Strange—you
look familiar to me.*

The Shattered Heart

Cam considered himself to be a fairly unshockable man. He'd seen—and done—nearly everything. And that included watching a nude female aerialist at a rather risqué underground circus. As well as learning more of that same aerialist's acrobatic skill later in bed. He'd seen good women sin and bad men repent. It took a considerable amount to surprise or astonish him.

As he sat at his desk in his study, reviewing more reports from his steward, his butler appeared at the door.

"Yes, Robson?" Cam asked without looking up.

"A Mrs. Delamere to see you, my lord," the butler said.

Cam dropped the sheet of paper he'd been reviewing. He shot to his feet. "Here? Now?" He cleared his throat, and smoothed his hands down his waistcoat, calming himself and his thundering heart. "I mean, where is she?"

"I put her in the Blue Drawing Room."

After shrugging on his jacket, Cam strode quickly from his study and headed down the hallway. Why the hell did he feel in such disarray? He couldn't string two thoughts together. But the notion that she was here, in his home, waiting for him, careened through him like lightning. What brought her here?

Pausing outside the door to the drawing room, he straightened his coat and waistcoat. He checked the folds of his neckcloth in a nearby mirror, and raked his fingers through his long hair. It had a tendency to get knotted and wild whenever he sequestered himself in his study. It wouldn't do looking like some kind of brigand.

Finally, he was satisfied with his appearance. He rubbed his hands on his thighs, ensuring his palms were dry. Only then did he draw a breath and open the drawing room door.

She formed a dark curved outline against the window as she stared out at the street. At his entrance, she turned, facing him. The expanse of the drawing room stood between them, but he felt the burn of her gaze as if they were only inches apart. Heat shot through him. He felt alive, yet drugged, profoundly present, but also a hundred miles above the ground.

Emotion flickered in her gaze. Caution.

The last time they'd seen one other—had it been only yesterday?—she'd been angry. They'd quarreled over something. The mention of her family had sent her to blazing, and she'd stormed off, refusing his offer of a carriage ride. He'd been convinced then that nothing in God's magnificent creation could get her to amble calmly along a path with him again, let alone willingly seek him out. Yet here she was.

He needed his composure. So he strolled to the bell pull.

"The hour's late," he said casually, "but I have an excellent cook who would like nothing more than to prepare tea for us."

"I must disappoint your cook," she answered, her voice slightly hoarse, "as I find myself short of appetite."

He pressed his hand to his chest. "Surely, it isn't the present company."

"It is not." Her fingers twisted in the ribbons of the bonnet she held. Agitation vibrated from her in nearly palpable waves. Yet she looked far from fragile. Instead, she was as thorny as a rosebush.

She was still as upset as she'd been the previous day. And just as before, he wanted to pull her close and tell her that everything would be well. Everything would be taken care of. And if someone had hurt her . . . he'd hurt them back.

He'd also get an elbow in the gut or a knee in the groin should he attempt to embrace her. That much he knew for certain.

She shook her head when he waved toward a settee. So he remained standing, his hands clasped behind his back, as she seemed to struggle with the proper words.

"I came to . . ." Her voice sounded strangled. "You must allow me to . . . That is . . ." Her words trailed off, and she looked as though she wanted to be anywhere but here.

"Given your profession," he said dryly, "I should think you'd be more adept at forming sentences."

She glared at him, which was a sight better than the misery he'd seen on her face moments before.

"Let me apologize, damn it!" she growled.

He walked quickly to an inlaid cabinet against a wall. Opening one of its doors, he pulled out a crystal decanter and a glass. Women usually kept cordials or other such concoctions, but he was a bachelor, and so he filled his glass with a strong shot of whiskey. He threw the drink back.

Once the alcohol had burned its trail down his throat and into his belly, he said, "Please repeat that."

She marched over to him and held out her hand. It took him a moment to realize that she demanded her own drink. Taking a clean glass from the cabinet, he splashed a little whiskey into it.

"Not enough," she said.

He poured her a generous serving of the drink, then handed it to her. Their gloveless fingers brushed as he passed her the glass, and they both inhaled sharply at the contact.

As she lifted the glass to her lips, he noticed her hand shook, causing the whiskey inside to spill a little over the rim. A droplet rolled down the side and onto the floor. She didn't seem to pay any heed.

Instead, she drank the whiskey in one gulp.

Well.

"Just take my apology."

"Of course."

Her exhale was soaked in the pleasant scent of whiskey. "I am sorry, my lord, for how I behaved yesterday. It's only . . ." She glanced away. "I'd had something of a shock the other day and I'm afraid I took it out on you."

He said nothing, watching her—angry and, yes, contrite. What had made her apologize? It wouldn't happen unprompted, would it?

"What?" she pressed, looking back at him with her wide hazel eyes. "No demands for groveling?"

"There are many things I'd like from you," he said at last, "but I never want to see you grovel."

She set down her glass on a nearby table, breaking away from their shared look. "I . . . Thank you. I don't merit your civility. Not the way I've been speaking to you."

"It's good for me," he said with a wry smile. "Always it's, 'Yes, my lord,' and 'Whatever pleases you, Lord Marwood.' I need to be put in my place every now and then. Who better to see to my humility than a sharp-tongued playwright? And a famed one, at that."

Her laugh came soft and self-deprecating. "Hardly famed. Notorious, perhaps."

"Notoriety is far better than holy obscurity."

She fought to contain what looked like a smile. "Perhaps you've got a bit of the scribe in you as well."

Now it was his turn to laugh. "I can appreciate fine writing far better than I can create it. If I stumble across any bit of wit, it's pure happenstance."

"Well," she said, a glint in her eyes, "you've kept up with me at times, so I would say you have some measure of cleverness."

He tilted his head. "Was this part of your apology?"

Mrs. Delamere walked away from him, positioning herself again to look out the front window. "It seems the worst in me comes out whenever I'm around you."

"Not the worst, surely." He decided he didn't want to dull his senses with another drink, so he left the cabinet and its comforting spirits, and crossed to stand behind her. He had an excellent view of the back of her neck rising above the collar of her spencer. The urge rose to run his fingers over that curve, and the soft whorls of dark hair that curled at her nape, but he fought it. "I can be far more terrible."

"So the scandal sheets say," she threw over her shoulder, though she smiled as she said it.

Outside, gleaming carriages and finely-dressed pedestrians passed, and he wondered how they appeared to her. The theater provided her the opportunity to see men and women of every stripe, every class. Yet here she was, in the thick of London's elite. Did she feel uneasy? Contemptuous? Given how little love she had for high society, the latter was the far more likely option.

Again, he had to wonder what had happened to her to cause such animosity to grow within her. Her accent wasn't precisely low, but it didn't resonate with the higher echelons of the city. Writing for money—especially for the stage—wasn't considered a very polite way for a woman to earn her coin. Whatever she had achieved, she'd done so by force of her own will.

"I'm sure that you'll find a way to immortalize my bad behavior in one of your characters." He was careful to keep his hands at his side, rather than test the texture of that curling hair at her nape. "The unconscionable rake Lord Blarwood."

Her quick laugh was more rich and potent than drink. "And the virtuous, beleaguered widow, Mrs. Blelamere."

"I believe we have a success on our hands," he decided.

She pressed her hand to the glass, and a small corona of heat radiated out onto the smooth surface.

Turning to face him, her shoulders straightened, as though she was bracing herself for an ordeal or a blow.

"I have . . . a proposition for you, my lord." Each word seemed to be pulled from her, slowly, painfully.

His every nerve shot to attention. "Yes?"

"Might you consider . . . becoming the patron of the Imperial?"

He straightened. "Are you jesting?"

"I jest about many things," she said at once, "but never something so important."

"Then I agree to your proposition," he said without a moment's hesitation.

She started. "Truly?"

"Yes, truly." His heart took up a hard pace.

She narrowed her eyes. "Would you be willing to fund the entire theater for the run of a single play?"

"It needn't be limited to one play. I can bankroll the entire season." He spread his hands, indicating the elegant furnishings of the drawing room, its imported china lined up on shelves, the cut crystal of the chandelier hanging from a rosette carved into the coved ceiling. "What else am I going to spend my money on? Gilded phaetons? Portraits of my magnificent self?"

She shrugged. "Those courtesans in your theater box don't come cheaply."

"You don't have to concern yourself with the cost of my female company." He frowned, remembering her sudden apology. "Much as I enjoy the thought of being a patron of the arts, this seems a rapid turnaround. Did the owner of the building raise the rent?"

"The rent is the same," she answered.

"Something is different, though. There's a board of directors that foots the bills. What happened to them?"

Her expression turned hard, mask-like. "They want me out if I don't deliver by an impossible deadline."

Fury on her behalf coursed through him hotly. "Bunch of philistines, to think that art can be rushed to production. I'm to take the board's place," he deduced.

She crossed her arms over her chest. "For the run of *The Hidden Daughter's Return*."

"But no longer."

Mrs. Delamere shook her head. "If the play is successful, I'll buy out your share and find another patron."

"I'm truly that repellent to you?" he said softly.

"Repellent, no." She clasped herself tighter, and looked away. "You . . . unnerve me."

A shiver of electricity shot through him at her words. But "unnerve" could mean many things. Not all of them good.

"You think my patronage will come at a price."

"Won't it?"

Anger rose up. He felt unjustly accused, and though he deserved his reputation, he was never the kind of man she painted him to be. "For all that you think you know about me, I'm not a leering villain, hell-bent on forcing Mrs. Blelamere into my bed." He took a step toward her. Seduction had never been further from his mind, especially as a condition to the proposed arrangement. "If a woman becomes my lover, it's because she wants to. No blackmail required."

She said nothing, so he stalked to the door and held it open. "If that's what you truly believe, then you're welcome to find your way back to the Imperial. I'd offer you the use of my carriage, but we both know you'd refuse it. As you refuse everything from me."

Her exhale was long and ragged. She unclasped her arms from around herself, and looked embarrassed. "Again, I find myself needing to apologize. That was . . .

uncalled for." Her brow furrowed in contrition. "Though I haven't given much cause in my life to think well of toffs—I mean, aristocratic men—there's little to excuse my behavior."

He moved away from the door. "Your apologies are getting better."

Her lips curled in a slight smile. "It must be all the practice." She looked at him with her shrewd writer's eyes, then walked toward one of the vitrines displaying the blue and white china that gave the drawing room its name. "These pieces of porcelain are nearly transparent, the quality's so fine. Like painted eggshells."

"Beautiful, but utterly useless," he said, coming to stand beside her. "Too breakable. That's why they're kept in a cabinet."

"Durable things are apt to be rougher," she murmured.

"But they last," he noted, "and get the job done."

"Sometimes." She sighed. "Will you fund the theater, my lord?"

He felt her presence beside him. She was small, but it was as though she was a much bigger person, more will and self, that had been concentrated into a red-hot coal of a woman. If he tried to clasp her close in his hands, he would surely be scorched. But he wanted that heat, that fire and burn. Everything else seemed cold in comparison.

Yet he meant what he said. If they were to experience pleasure, it would be because they *both* wanted it. Shared and desired.

"I will," he said at last.

He thought he heard her let out a held breath.

"Thank you, my lord." No mistaking the relief in her voice, though it contained a hint of trepidation.

"As for you buying me out at the end of *The Hidden Daughter's Return*," he continued, "we'll take things on a play-by-play basis."

She looked as though she wanted to dispute that point, but checked herself, and only nodded.

Cam held out his hand. "A handshake is in order. It's how us *gentlemen* close a deal, and shows that we take our commitments seriously."

"So you *can* be serious." She took his hand, and the press of palm to palm was like a lit fuse, soon to explode.

"Please don't let anyone know," he said in a confiding tone.

She vowed, "The secret shall perish with me."

They shook, yet their hands continued to hold for a moment longer than was truly required. But it was necessary, because he knew her even better now. He'd wanted her before, yet with just this small taste, he hungered for more.

Chapter 12

Lord Diabold: Have we met before, little girl?
Alina: I do not believe so, my lord.
Lord Diabold: [to Fishhook] Does she not
*   resemble someone we know?*
Fishhook: Perhaps so, my lord. Perhaps all
*   children resemble one another.*
Lord Diabold: No, she is unique.

The Shattered Heart

The actors were restless. From her seat in the pit, Maggie watched them rehearse Act One of *The Hidden Daughter's Return*—again. None of them needed the manuscript pages anymore. They had already memorized what brief words she'd written. As they went through their paces, several of them shot her questioning glances fraught with unspoken meaning. They were actors, after all, and experts at communicating without words. The whole cast seemed to want to know: when was she going to give them more?

"I have no bloody idea," she wanted to shout, though in truth she kept her silence. She had thought that once the issue of financing the theater had been resolved, the words would come like a tapped spring. But no, her mind was dry as ever, her quill unmoving in her hand. What did she need to get her writing again?

Inspiration felt a very far way off—a gleam of a promise of a possibility, hidden behind very tall mountains. Something had to change, or she really would have to leave the theater altogether and learn a new way of earning her bread. A terrifying thought. She'd been writing for over a decade now, and was hardly a fresh girl eager to take on a new world. What could anyone her age and with her limited skills do? There was always returning to the stage as a performer—but she had never truly enjoyed nor excelled at that art.

Then what? The only answer was to keep hammering away at *The Hidden Daughter's Return*, but without inspiration, she was adrift.

Knowing the cast and crew watched her, she kept from burying her head in her hands. Instead, she continued to watch the rehearsal with a pretend smile on her face. All the while, her stomach knotted and an impotent rage built within her. Something had to give. She needed that spark, that kindling to life of her art. Where to find it?

Awareness danced down the back of her neck. As if . . . she was being watched.

Turning in her seat, she beheld the long, lean form of Marwood standing at the very back of the theater. But he wasn't observing the performers onstage. Arms crossed over his chest, leaning against the doorway, he looked at her.

Only a day had passed since they'd made their bargain—followed by a restless night—and yet her stomach turned into a beehive.

How was it that he could look like a gentleman and a pirate at the same time? It was as though she could feel his dark gaze burning into her from a span of thirty feet. As though no distance at all separated them. It didn't help that when she had slept, her dreams had been of him, offering promises of more than money, if only she said *yes*.

His mouth tilted at the corner, as if he could read her thoughts. Pushing away from the doorway, he strolled down the aisle toward her. Damn, but he did move beautifully—fluid and masculine and aware of his own magnetism.

Briefly, she considered fleeing. Retreating backstage to one of the dressing rooms then locking the door behind her. He unsettled her too much, and she was already too rattled by her inability to write.

But no. She wouldn't run.

So she remained seated on the bench and watched him walk to her. A few of the actresses stuttered their lines. A quick glance over revealed that Marwood's unexpected appearance had caught the attention of the performers, as well. God knew he distracted her. Especially after yesterday, when he'd revealed a side of himself—more mature, more thoughtful—than she would have liked. If only he'd remained the shallow rake, how much easier her life would be. Yet he defied easy classification.

At the moment, he was pure charisma, ambling toward her with effortless virile appeal. He looked aw-fully proprietary, too, as though he owned the place. Which, in a way, he did.

Instead of sitting next to her, he flung out the tails of his long coat and sat in the row behind Maggie. He set his hat, gloves, and walking stick on the bench. A man making himself at home.

"Good morning, Mrs. Delamere," he said. A perfectly commonplace greeting, and yet the sound of her name on his lips felt like a stroke along her bare skin.

"Lord Marwood," she answered evenly. Turning back to the stage, she continued to sense his presence behind her. Strange. She had the feeling that if he'd taken a seat beside her, she could have adjusted and acclimated to him more. But he'd deliberately put himself out of her view by sitting behind her, forcing her to be even more aware of him. Wondering where he was looking. Hearing the sounds of him simply existing.

"It's awfully early for you to be awake," she said, keeping her gaze on the stage, where the rehearsals had resumed.

"Investments need tending," he replied smoothly.

"This one may prove the exception," she answered, forcing herself to keep looking forward. "Your attendance at the theater isn't one of the conditions of your investment. None of the board members ever made their presence known."

He chuckled. "They did a poor job of it, then. Witness the fact that they were so ready to abandon their resident scribe."

"True," she acknowledged, "and yet, until that point, they were exemplary in their responsibilities by giving the Imperial complete artistic freedom."

He shifted, and then suddenly, he stepped over the bench and sat himself next to her. Only a few inches separated their thighs, and he wasn't exactly a big man, but he had what actors often called *presence*.

Awareness of him prickled through her, pinpoints of light that brightened her most darkened recesses.

"An unimaginative lot," he said with a wave of his hand. "This is a rare and splendid opportunity to be a patron of the arts. I, for one, am not going to waste it."

"Don't most benefactors simply write out cheques and wait for the finished product?" she pressed. Part of her wanted to lean closer to him, absorbing his heat, while the other, self-protective part still demanded she run. She recognized those feelings. They led straight to ruination.

"The dull patrons, perhaps. But that's not me. No," he continued magnanimously, "throwing money at the Imperial is so . . . boring. Here I've been watching plays for most of my life, just a member of the audience, but now I've got a chance to be so much more."

She couldn't be churlish about his generosity. Still, the thought of him hanging about, close by . . . well, the idea was simply alarming. How could she get anything done if he was always around, distracting her?

Warming to his topic, he went on, "Lorenzo de Medici wasn't merely tossing handfuls of lire at Botticelli. He helped guide and shape the painter's art."

She raised her brows. "And you propose to do the same for me."

He pressed a hand to the center of his chest. "I am your servant, madam." But he ruined the humility of his words and the gesture by grinning wickedly.

"Here I thought you were a man of modernity," she answered. "And would treat the theater as a business prospect. Like a mine or a canal."

Marwood made a gruff sound of disinterest. "I don't know anything about mining or digging canals. My brain is stuffed, however, with nearly a lifetime of plays. I know theater backwards and forwards and every other direction. There's not much else I'm good at—well, beyond one skill in particular," he added as an afterthought.

As though she'd forgotten. As though Maggie hadn't overheard one of the dancers weeks ago speak wistfully of her time as Marwood's lover.

"The way he touched me," the dancer had sighed, stepping into her rehearsal clothes. "Like he was . . . I don't know . . . *discovering* me."

"Blimey," another dancer had giggled. "What does that mean?"

"It means he was good, idiot," a third young woman had growled. Then the three dancers caught sight of Maggie and scampered away, leaving behind a cloud of laughter and perfume.

That conversation now played through her head, and she couldn't stop herself from glancing down at Marwood's long, elegant hands. They hadn't known any rough labor, but bore slight calluses from a horse's reins. What would they feel like on the softer parts of her own body?

She didn't want to know.

Yes, she did.

Oh, damn everything.

"May as well get used to it, Mrs. Delamere," he said now, breaking her reverie. "I'm here to stay."

"How delightful," she answered through her teeth. Rising, she said, "Stay or go, my lord. It's your right, your decision. But your investment won't be good for anything unless I get time to write. Alone."

No written words were forthcoming, but he didn't need to know that.

"I'll check in on you," he said, nodding. "Give you encouragement."

"Encouragement isn't necessary."

"You say that now, but you may need it in the future."

"I have my methods, my lord," she pointed out. "I've developed them over many years. Doubtful they would change now."

"Stagnation is the enemy to artistic development," he proclaimed.

She raised a brow. "I thought you didn't know how the creative process worked."

His grin showed him to be undeterred. "I am a quick study."

Maggie sighed. "Very well. You can stay."

"I didn't know you had that power to control the comings and goings of this theater," he said drily.

She didn't, of course. But she wasn't about to tell him that. "If you'll excuse me, Lord Marwood. I have work to do."

He gave her another smile, this one full of wickedness. "By all means, let your artistic inspiration fly."

Without sparing him another glance, she turned and walked up the aisle. How in the name of all nine Muses was she to get anything accomplished with that man around? He made her life a tangle. And yet, imagining her world without him seemed strangely bereft. And that was a thought she did not want to pursue. Better to try to immerse herself in the realm of the fantastic rather than reality. It was so much more safe in the land of make-believe.

Chapter 13

Lord Diabold: 'Tis passing strange. Fishhook,
  make some inquiries.
Fishhook: I will, my lord. [aside] After I partake
  of my morning ale.

The Shattered Heart

Cam took a sip of tea, staring out at his table, empty of everyone but himself. It was a serene, quiet morning, with the wrens singing in the garden and pale sunlight gilding the breakfast room. He preferred to dine without the presence of footmen, so he was alone with his breakfast, his newspaper, and his thoughts. A perfect recipe for peace.

And yet he was restless. Edgy. After Mrs. Delamere had left him in the theater two days ago, he'd done his level best not to return to the Imperial—for his own sense of stability. He'd never panted after a woman for long. Either they became lovers, or he moved on. No one woman distracted him for more than a fortnight.

Yet he couldn't stop himself from thinking of Mrs. Delamere. Dreaming of her. His waking thoughts circled back to her again and again.

He needed to prove he was his own man. Yesterday, he'd gone to his fencing academy. For hours, he'd worked out his restlessness by going up against opponent after opponent. A few had even commented that he'd seemed in a rare driven humor. And despite leaving the academy hours later, coated with sweat, he'd been no calmer than when he'd arrived.

Now, Cam set his teacup down. Edginess danced along his nerves. He needed another outlet for his energy. Something hard and fast and physical.

He rose and tugged on the bell pull. In a moment, his butler appeared.

"Have my horse saddled," Cam said to the servant. "I'll take Whiskey." The high-spirited gelding was always ready for a good run.

Moments later, Cam mounted up, the horse prancing sideways beneath him. He seemed just as eager as Cam to feel the distance disappear beneath racing hooves. Hyde Park would prove too sedate for his liking.

It was always a frustrating ride to Hampstead Heath. Traffic never relented in the city, a tangle of carriages, carts, horses, people and the whole of the world's commerce all crammed streets that were always too narrow to contain everything. Yet within half an hour, he and his horse were tearing across the green, with the watercolor sky above and the rolling grass below.

There was a peace in this. The communion between horse and rider. It emptied his mind, made him an animal of muscle and drive. Somewhere, he lost his hat, but it didn't matter. All that counted was speed.

Yet while the horse gave him everything it could, he had to protect the beast. After an hour, he finally gave the horse a rest, and they slowly walked back into town.

As he entered his neighborhood, he saw Ashford riding in the opposite direction. They lived near one another, so it wasn't much of a surprise to see his friend. Ashford hailed him.

They pulled up alongside each other, guiding their horses off to the edge of the road so they wouldn't block traffic.

"You look like you've ridden to Edinburgh and back," Ashford remarked dryly, eyeing Cam's disheveled state and the sweaty condition of his horse.

"The Hebrides, actually," Cam answered.

"Trying to run away?"

"Came back, though."

Beneath the brim of his hat, Ashford's eyes narrowed. Cam had the uncomfortable notion that his friend saw far beyond the surface he presented. "Out with it," Ashford said.

"With what?" Cam feigned innocence.

Ashford pointed his riding crop at him. "None of your playacting. What's in your craw?"

"Mrs. Delamere suggested I become the new patron of the Imperial," Cam said, "and I agreed."

His friend looked stunned. "That's unexpected." For a long moment, Ashford sat silent and contemplative in the saddle. Then, he said, "A party."

Cam frowned at him. "Come again?"

"Eleanor and I will host a dinner party. You and Mrs. Delamere will be among the guests," Ashford explained. "We'll introduce Maggie to influential people. Gain more support for her and her work. Who knows? We might even drum up business for the theater."

The idea made sense, although Cam did have some concerns. "Who else will make up the party?"

"Believe it or not," Ashford said wryly, "the *ton* didn't completely abandon me when I married Eleanor. We've retained a substantial number of friends—good people who also possess rank and influence. They'll come. In fact," he added, seemingly warming to the idea, "with Eleanor's assistance, we'll make it into one of the most highly sought-after invitations of the Season."

"She doesn't mind you volunteering her or her home?"

A flush spread over Ashford's cheeks. "There may be a bit of manly groveling involved."

"It's rather a shame I won't get to see that." Cam laughed.

"No one but my wife will ever witness such a thing," his friend said darkly.

"Will your lady wife agree to the scheme?" Cam asked.

"I can be . . . persuasive."

"Please, don't speak of that."

Ashford touched the end of his riding crop to the brim of his hat. "I'll send word around when I know more."

They exchanged farewells, each riding in separate directions.

A dinner. With Maggie. It was an entirely new environment for them to interact with each other. She'd hidden from him at the Ashfords' wedding, but things were very different between them now. So different, in fact, that he had no idea what to expect.

Unsettling. And thrilling.

The makeup brush felt strange in Maggie's hand. A quill suited her better. But the brush glided far more easily over the skin on the back of her hand. A quill's nib would scratch, and she didn't want to hurt herself, just provide a means of distraction.

She sat alone in the makeup room at the theater, using liquid kohl and one of the head cosmetic artist's brushes to draw on her hand and arm. Her skill as a visual artist wasn't precisely deft, but she kept the design basic. Only curlicues and simple flowers. It was mindless work. Her thoughts were distracted, and her brush followed the loops and whirls of her own mind.

They piled on her, those thoughts, one atop another, like a stone cairn anchoring her to the ground. The board's decision. Marwood's rescue. Marwood himself. Her inability to write. So many worries. She needed a solitary diversion, which had brought her here, to the snug confines of the empty makeup room.

Her hand rather resembled those illustrations she'd seen of women in Arabia and India, with their elaborate designs painted upon their bodies and faces. Though she didn't flatter herself to think she possessed half those women's skill in adorning herself. For them, the patterns held meaning and beauty. For Maggie, they merely illustrated the cloudy, chaotic state of her mind.

Footsteps creaked on the floorboards behind her. Glancing up to gaze in the mirror, she beheld Eleanor's reflection. Her friend watched her with a measure of interest and concern. It likely looked as though Maggie had taken leave of her senses—drawing on herself like a piece of paper or a canvas.

"I'd no idea you were a painter, too," Eleanor murmured, her gaze on the design.

"As you can see," Maggie said, holding up her hand for a closer inspection, "I'm not."

Her friend made a dismissive sound. "I would wager that if you were seen wearing that on Bond Street, you'd start a new fashion."

Maggie snorted in disbelief. "Playwrights are hardly the arbiters of taste. And a *failed* playwright is more likely to be a pariah."

Eleanor drew up a chair. "You aren't *failed*," she insisted.

With a rough exhale, Maggie set down the makeup brush. "What else would you call a writer who cannot write?"

"Temporarily blocked," Eleanor said gently.

"Doesn't feel temporary," Maggie muttered. Though that wasn't entirely true.

She couldn't admit it. Yet she couldn't deny it, either.

"It is," her friend insisted. "And I think I may have something to help with that. Give you a change of scenery, perhaps generate some new ideas." She reached into her reticule and produced a letter, which she handed to Maggie.

"What's this?" Maggie asked.

Eleanor's lips quirked. "Funny thing about letters. You don't actually learn what's in them until they're opened."

Maggie called her friend a very colorful, descriptive name, which made Eleanor chuckle. Examining the letter, she noted that it bore the seal of the Earl of Ashford. Made sense, as her friend was the Countess of Ashford.

Breaking the wafer, Maggie opened the letter and read. "An invitation," she said aloud.

"To a dinner," Eleanor confirmed. "Daniel thought it would be a good idea to introduce you to some of the most influential members of society. And," her friend added, eyeing the drawings on Maggie's skin, "it could be a pleasant diversion from your current situation."

Panic immediately clutched Maggie. "A formal dinner?"

"Since I married Daniel, I've hosted several for influential members of Parliament. They're far less intimidating that you might think."

"But . . ." Maggie fought to swallow, and she felt cold all over. "I've never attended a dinner party. Certainly not like this kind." She waved the invitation in the air. "It's all been casual. Just a group of friends gathered together for a meal and some wine."

"And that's exactly what this will be," Eleanor said at once. "Except you have to wear gloves at the table, and don't eat off your neighbor's plate."

Despite her friend's assurances, Maggie couldn't stop the pounding of her heart at the idea of sitting down to a ritualized dinner with the elite of England. She was a secondhand shop-owner's daughter, not a society flower trained in the ways of the aristocracy.

Eleanor took her unpainted hand and gave it a squeeze. "It will be so easy, my dear. I'll tell you everything you need to know. And if an ink-stained scribbler like me can learn how to take a meal with toffs, surely you can, too."

Still, Maggie twisted with uncertainty. "I'll make a fool of myself."

"Impossible," Eleanor swore.

"I won't know anyone there," Maggie objected.

"You'll know me and Daniel, of course," her friend declared. "And Lord Marwood."

Maggie sat up even straighter. "He'll be there?"

"Naturally," Eleanor said. "He's one of Daniel's closest friends. And, as the new benefactor of the Imperial, he can help acquaint you with society's elite. Speaking of which, you never told me Cam had taken over as the patron," she scolded gently. "You understand you can tell me anything."

"There wasn't time," Maggie mumbled, guilt tingeing her voice. She should have spoken of it sooner to Eleanor, but she had been too preoccupied.

"It doesn't signify," Eleanor said with a wave of her hand. "All that matters now is that you agree to come. Do say you will. I promise that everyone we're inviting will welcome you. They stood by me and Daniel after our wedding. They'll do the same for you. No judgments. Just good friends and good conversation."

Maggie rubbed at her face, mulling over the prospect. On the one hand, the idea of a formal dinner party sent terror through her like a hundred stinging wasps. On the other hand, her attendance could help bring in new, wealthy theatergoers. She could mingle with the influential ranks without being shunned.

And Marwood would be there. She could picture his twinkling dark eyes across the table from her, see his wry smile. He'd already proven himself her ally. Just knowing that he'd be nearby sent a thrill of anticipation through her.

And wasn't *that* a distressing notion?

"All right," she finally said. "I'll go."

Eleanor beamed. "Excellent! I'll be sure to have the cook prepare jelly tarts."

One of Maggie's favorite dishes.

"But I can't promise I won't do something ridiculous or outrageous," Maggie added. "Like challenge everyone to a belching contest."

"Where belching's concerned," Eleanor replied, "no one can top Daniel. He *was* a rake of the first water."

"What a remarkable thing for a wife to brag about."

"You'll need something to wear to the dinner," Eleanor noted. "Your costumer, Madame Hortense, provided me with the right clothing for my schemes. We could make use of her now."

"Let's pay Madame a call," Maggie said.

They both stood. Looping her arm through Maggie's, Eleanor said, "I've been dying to have you over for ages."

"You never asked." They proceeded from the makeup room toward wardrobe, down the hall.

"Because I knew you'd always say no." Eleanor grinned. "Now you cannot refuse me."

Shaking her head over her friend's impertinence, Maggie laughed. But she felt a prickle of remorse. She would have turned down the invitations, believing Eleanor was only trying to be polite, but not because her friend truly desired her company at one of her elegant soirees. Yet she should have known that Eleanor genuinely wanted her there. Her pride formed a high, stone wall sometimes.

She and Eleanor had always been close, ever since Eleanor had been reviewing plays and burlettas for sundry newspapers, and had introduced herself to Maggie one night. Both had been stunned and secretly pleased that they were two women forging their paths in the field of writing. A friendship had soon blossomed.

They reached wardrobe, and found Madame Hortense scolding one of the seamstresses over a crooked hem. When the costumer caught sight of Maggie and Eleanor, she cried out loudly in "French" accented exclamations of dismay.

"These girls," Madame Hortense lamented. "They know nothing of quality workmanship. Go, child," she snapped at the seamstress, who hurried off, clutching a faux ermine cape.

"*Alors*," the costumer said once the poor girl had gone, "how might I assist you today, ladies?"

Eleanor pushed Maggie forward. "She needs a dress for a dinner party."

"One of *your* dinner *soirées*?" Madame Hortense asked. At Eleanor's nod, the costumer clapped her hands together. "But this is *magnifique*! For so long, I have wanted to dress this one. Always, she wears the plain gowns. Now I can finally adorn her the way she was meant to be beautified."

Maggie suddenly felt like a prized cow. She held up her hands. "I insist on something simple. And modest," she added, seeing the way Madame Hortense eyed her bosom. Maggie had an ample chest, and she had no desire to display it for all of high society to see. She was already part of a slightly scandalous line of work. No sense in making it worse by having her bosoms spilling out over the damask tablecloth, as though she were some kind of tart advertising her wares.

A glowing spark already existed between her and Marwood. If she were to literally reveal more of herself to him, she wasn't certain if that spark wouldn't burst into flame.

Now, Madame Hortense heaved a sigh. "Very well. Though I have a peacock-blue gown cut to here," she motioned to halfway down Maggie's chest, just above her nipples, "that would make you shine."

"No, thank you," Maggie said, picturing herself losing an olive down the front of her gown.

"I believe I have just the thing." The costumer disappeared into another room that held the majority of the wardrobe.

Madame Hortense returned after a few moments, a gray silk gown draped over her arm. As per Maggie's directions, the bodice was modestly cut, though pretty seed pearls adorned the neckline, so it wasn't dowdy. "This will be *très jolie* with your coloring. With the right jewelry and," she added, looking at the painting on Maggie's hand, "some gloves, you will be exquisite."

"I don't want to be exquisite," Maggie objected. "Just respectable."

"A little scandal adds zest to a dinner party," Eleanor noted.

"So long as *I'm* not the source of that scandal."

As Madame Hortense began taking her measurements, Maggie couldn't repress another flare of anxiety. She would be entering into a whole new world, one she'd scrupulously avoided. She believed that the nobility were born deceivers—she knew from firsthand experience. Yet now she could no longer hold herself apart. For the sake of the Imperial, and her own reputation, she had to throw herself into the deep end of the bathing pond.

What would the night with Lord Marwood bring? She would be entering into his world. Eleanor would be there but despite the presence of her friend and the other guests, Maggie couldn't help but wonder.

How safe would she be with *him*?

Chapter 14

*Fishhook: A cup of ale and a pretty wench.
There's nothing better to fit a man's hand!*

The Shattered Heart

Laughter and the chiming sounds of crystal and silver rang out over the expanse of white damask.

Seated at the Ashfords' dining room table, Cam looked down its length, toward where Mrs. Delamere was seated. Candlelight cast a warm gleam over all the company, though it seemed to caress her skin, turning her even more luminous. While her gray silk gown boasted a high neckline, he'd never seen her in something so elegant. With her dark hair trailing tendrils down her neck, she fairly glowed like a pearl, fresh from a tropic sea.

It might have been considered rude, or too bold, but he couldn't tear his gaze from her. He'd made conversation with this dining partners, but his eyes had been for Mrs. Delamere alone. She drew him in without even trying.

She had been placed toward the middle of the table as a matter of her lower status in the social hierarchy.

Cam, being the highest ranked male after Ashford, sat at Lady Ashford's side. The company, consisting of Cam, Mrs. Delamere, Lord and Lady Ashford, and two other aristocratic couples, was small enough that everyone's conversation could be heard easily and comfortably.

Also as a matter of her being the lowest ranked woman, Mrs. Delamere had been required to enter the dining room on the arm of Baron Fordyce, the man with the lowermost title. Yet none of the other guests seemed concerned with this. Only Mrs. Delamere had seemed a little uncertain at first. She'd gazed cautiously at the company, and had eyed the spread of elaborate dishes and silver as though they'd contained hidden secrets she needed to solve.

Ashford had said, waving toward the table, "You are most cordially welcome to my home. It seems like a lot of fuss, but we just like good people and good food."

Mrs. Delamere had rallied herself then, and replied, "I hope you don't like good people *as* good food, my lord."

"Only if they're dull conversationalists," had been his answer.

"Then, I'd think their meat would be tough and bland," Maggie had said.

"Good point." This had been from Lady Ashford. "We must all endeavor to strike the perfect balance between being *too* scintillating and *too* tiresome, lest we wind up as dessert."

The tension had been broken as the guests all chuckled. And from that point on, Mrs. Delamere had settled down.

Now she seemed to be genuinely enjoying herself, chatting amiably with Lady Fordyce and the Viscount Scarborough. Her face seemed lit from within, and her laughter was low and rich as it tumbled out, her head tipped back to reveal the smooth column of her throat.

Nothing was more provocative than the line of her neck. Cam wanted to run his tongue up that flesh, tasting her skin—far more delicious, he suspected, than any sweetmeat laid before him at this table. He was a man who loved the sight of women in bright colors and low necklines, yet the demure cut of Mrs. Delamere's gown combined with the subtle but lustrous hue stirred him. Made him want more. Whetted his appetite.

She caught his gaze on her, and a pink stain crept into her cheeks. But she didn't look away. She actually lifted her glass of wine, and he returned the gesture. Together, they drank. The room seemed to shrink to contain only them.

The others remained present, though, and Baron Fordyce said, "You must have many fascinating tales to tell of life in the theater, Mrs. Delamere."

"The theater is nothing if not replete with stories," she answered with a laugh. "Most of them not suitable for polite company."

"Do tell us one," Lady Scarborough pressed. "I promise we won't be too scandalized."

Mrs. Delamere cast a quick, questioning glance toward Cam, looking for guidance. He gave her a subtle nod. If anyone would appreciate the outrageous nature of theatrical life, these guests would. Lady Ashford had selected her guests with care.

"The tale I'm thinking of involves a degree of intemperance," Mrs. Delamere said.

"That is something with which none of us have had experience," Ashford replied drily.

Her shoulders relaxed, and, after taking another sip of wine, began. "There was an actor at the Imperial whose name I shall not mention. He was known for his fiery, compelling performances, and, alas, his love of strong spirits."

"The two often go together," Cam murmured.

She smiled at him with acknowledgment of that fact. "Yes, the two often walk hand-in-hand with one another. The pressures of artistic genius, I suppose."

"Or the fortification of Dutch courage," Lord Scarborough said, and chuckled.

"The two might be inseparable," Mrs. Delamere acknowledged. "A performer is driven to be on stage, to interpret the role, to feel deeply. It's their job, in truth. But that sensitivity leads them to need the support—or, perhaps, even the numbing effects—of alcohol. After a while, one cannot be without the other." She shook her head, then offered a bright smile. "But I won't ruin the story with melancholy reflections."

"Do go on, my dear," Lady Ashford urged.

Mrs. Delamere said, "We were doing a musical performance of *Romeo and Juliet,* which I had adapted into an operetta. The nameless actor, whom I'll call Mr. Gin, was to play the part of Romeo, though he was a little advanced in years for so youthful a role. In truth, he would've made a better Friar Lawrence, but Mr. Gin insisted he would take the lead. And, for the most part, he performed the role admirably."

She warmed to her subject, and went on. "One night, the curtain was set to rise in five minutes, but Mr. Gin was nowhere to be found. We scoured the entire theater, and even a few nearby pubs. All to no avail. We could only assume he was ill, for he'd never missed a performance."

"Couldn't you have sent someone to his home?" Lady Scarborough asked.

"There wasn't time," Mrs. Delamere answered with a shake of her head. "There was no choice but to send Mr. Singh up as his understudy. So the play went on without Mr. Gin."

"How did you find the performance?" Cam wondered.

"Excellent," she replied. "Mr. Singh is extremely talented, and now takes the romantic lead roles at the Imperial. Women sigh over him like schoolgirls. And no wonder. He's exceedingly handsome."

"I've seen him," Lady Fordyce said, and she did sigh. Her husband shot her a slightly annoyed look, though at her reassuring smile, he seemed to ease.

A thought threaded traitorously through Cam's mind. Had Mrs. Delamere and this Mr. Singh ever taken their relationship beyond the professional? Theatrical life was known for its rather fluid morals. Performers often became lovers. And while Mrs. Delamere wasn't an actress, she was intimately involved with the Imperial—including the crew and cast. But how intimate was this association?

It oughtn't matter to him. Yet heat and tension crept along his bones, and only a sip of wine helped release some of that tightness.

Mrs. Delamere was here, with him. That's all that concerned Cam now.

"We were midway through Act Three, Scene Five," she said.

"When the lovers must part after their night together," Cam noted.

A gleam of appreciation shone in her eyes. "You know your Shakespeare, my lord."

He resisted the impulse to preen under her admiring gaze. Instead, he affected a careless shrug. "Seen a bit, here and there."

She gave him a wry look that showed she didn't quite believe his nonchalance. Yet she went on. "It's an affecting scene. Hardly an eye without tears in the house. But just as Mr. Singh says, 'Let me be ta'en, let me be put to death,' suddenly Mr. Gin rushes onto the stage."

"Oh, no!" cried Baron Fordyce.

"Oh, yes." Mrs. Delamere closed her eyes in remembrance. "He'd found a duplicate of Romeo's costume and had thrown it on, but with considerable disarray. It looked as though Romeo had just gotten into a street brawl with some angry Capulets." She opened her eyes, and they shone with horrified amusement. "The alcohol fumes wafting off of Mr. Gin were nearly visible from the balcony. Mr. Singh and Juliet staggered from the smell. Then, Mr. Gin launches into the next line from the play."

" 'I am content, so thou wilt have it so,' " Cam said.

"Ah, your modesty is false," Lady Scarborough chided playfully.

"Perhaps a little," Cam admitted with a grin. "But, what happened next?"

"Mr. Gin knew that line, but he forgot the next, so Mr. Singh had to fill in for him. 'I'll say yon grey is not the morning's eye/ 'Tis but the pale reflex of Cynthia's brow.' Then Mr. Gin remembered the following line. Poor Juliet, she didn't know which lover was her doomed soul mate. And so it went, each trading lines as Romeo until 'Dry sorrow drinks our blood. Adieu, adieu!' Finally Mr. Gin tottered off the stage and fell asleep in the crypt. The rest of the performance went on as normal, but no one ever forgot the time we had two Romeos."

There was loud laughter, and some tittering.

"Is that true?" asked Lady Fordyce, sitting at Cam's elbow.

"Every word," he confirmed. "I was there to witness it."

Once more, Cam caught Mrs. Delamere's eye. She seemed to radiate with brilliance, wit, and beauty. He felt a pulse of heat that had nothing to do with the candles or the wine. It was all her. She had been wary at first, but now she'd risen in self-assurance, confident and clever.

If only the other guests could simply disappear.

He wanted her all to himself.

Maggie had forgotten that men and women separated after dinner. She and the other female guests were escorted from the dining room by Eleanor. Yet Maggie couldn't help but cast a look over her shoulder. Sure enough, Marwood watched her, heat in his eyes. A blush spread through her body, settling low in her belly.

Had any man looked at her the way he did? Not just with desire, but with admiration? She couldn't remember anyone else who'd done so. Only him.

She'd been aware of him all through the meal, and yet, for all her heightened perception of him, he'd actually focused her with his easy smile and ready intelligence. Whenever she'd grown nervous that she wasn't behaving properly around Eleanor's elegant friends, she had only to look at Marwood, and she felt more confident. He knew her. He wouldn't let anything happen to her.

More than a writer's curiosity had made her study him throughout the meal. He'd been relaxed, sure of himself. As he'd bantered with Ashford, she watched the easy camaraderie between the two men. It appealed to her, observing this give and take of repartee, showing the years of familiarity and comfort they shared.

She'd also watched him as he'd dined. He had excellent table manners, but managed to imbue the mundane act of eating with a sensuous quality. As though he relished every mouthful. Every swallow of wine. He proved himself a lover of pleasure, and she couldn't help but think how that might translate from the dining room to the bedroom.

As she and the women settled back in the drawing room, a servant came around with a tray of lemonade and sherry. Maggie took the sherry.

"I wish it was something stronger," she murmured to Eleanor.

"Me, too," her friend confirmed.

"Mr. Kingston keeps good whiskey in the bottom drawer of his desk," Maggie said lowly. "Maybe another time, you and I could grab a nip."

"Would he mind?"

"After a rehearsal, he's the first to pour a glass. I doubt he'd begrudge me a drink."

Eleanor drifted away, and Lady Fordyce came to sit beside Maggie on the settee.

"I should have loved to be an actress," Lady Fordyce confided. "Save for the fact that it would have thrown the family into dreadful scandal."

"Surely you did some amateur theatricals," Maggie offered.

The baroness reddened. "At school, I was the best Lady Macbeth. But don't tell my husband. He'll think I'm trying to manipulate him into politics."

"Just steer clear of any witches," Maggie advised.

"I'll do my best."

They chuckled together, and another band of tension eased from Maggie. Eleanor's friends were truly gracious and welcoming people. They didn't look down their noses at her, and seemed genuinely interested in her life in the theater.

An uncomfortable realization struck her. In her work, and in life, she'd painted all aristocrats with the same brush. But they weren't all like she'd imagined. Some were cruel and snobbish, it was true, but mostly, they were people of all stripes. Just like commoners. These noblemen and noblewomen were kind to Eleanor, as well.

A small thread of embarrassment crept through Maggie. She'd been so very uncivil to Lord Marwood, when he'd shown her considerable generosity and kindness. In his way, he'd been honorable, and she'd been . . . a shrew. Her face reddened to think of it.

How narrow-minded she'd been when thinking of the gentry. Yes, one of their ranks had been base and cruel to her. But they weren't all like that long-ago villain. Now, she'd never be able to write about them in the same way again.

If she could ever write again. Right now, that seemed unlikely. But should her Muse ever return, she would have to do some serious reevaluation of her perspective.

It was an unsettling thought.

Shaking off her unease, she chatted amiably with the other ladies over their sherries. Eleanor talked of the recent influx of scandal at *The Hawk's Eye*. Lady Fordyce discussed her children, and the charity project she managed for widows and children of fallen soldiers.

"If you don't think me too impertinent," Lady Scarborough said, blushing a little, "I brought some of my butterfly collection. I'm something of an amateur entomologist."

"But that's wonderful!" Eleanor exclaimed. "Let's wait for the men to join us, and we can all have a look."

Maggie gazed at the door in anticipation. She caught herself mid-glance.

Marwood had been so incredibly handsome in his evening finery, just this side of civilized. This was his world, and he fit into it perfectly, like onyx in a jeweled setting. She looked forward to seeing Cam again, yet he'd been an aggravation not that long ago.

Her perceptions were shifting, altering. She barely recognized herself anymore.

After a few more minutes, the door finally opened. A slight whiff of tobacco proceeded the men as they entered the drawing room. Last to come in was Marwood. His gaze went straight to her. Her stomach leapt.

Her world was off its axis.

He didn't go to her, though. Instead, he stood before the hearth, outlined in firelight.

Eleanor explained that Lady Scarborough had brought her collection of butterflies for the amusement and edification of the other guests. A footman was dispatched to retrieve the case, and, in moments, the servant reentered, carefully holding a wooden frame. He handed it to Lady Scarborough, who set it on a table that had been positioned in the middle of the room. The company gathered around it, admiring.

Maggie had never seen such brilliant colors. Blues and reds and elaborate patterns of white and brown. Everyone exclaimed over their beauty.

"These are from South America," Lady Scarborough explained. "This is a Callicore hydaspes, from Brazil."

"A tropic and fantastical place," Maggie noted.

"I believe it must be," Lady Scarborough answered. "This is Morpho anaxibia," she continued, her finger hovering over a brilliant cerulean and black butterfly. "And this," she went on, indicating the third and final specimen, "is Siproeta epaphus, first seen by Western eyes only three years ago."

"They're lovely," Eleanor said.

One had spots, like eyes, as though it was looking at the others. The bright blue one was smaller than the others, yet it still radiated with brilliance. Maggie heard herself murmur, "They look like characters on a stage, ready to speak their lines."

"So they do," agreed Lord Ashford.

"And if they *were* characters onstage," Marwood said, "what would their story be?"

Lady Fordyce clapped her hands together. "Oh, yes, Mrs. Delamere. What's their tale?"

A frisson of panic gnawed coldly at the base of Maggie's neck. Could she spin a story here, now? She'd been blocked for so long, she doubted she had the ability to create anything anymore.

She glanced at Eleanor, who looked worried, knowing Maggie's dilemma.

Then she gazed at Marwood, standing on the opposite side of the table. His smile was small, intimate and encouraging. "Go on, Mrs. Delamere. You can do it."

An idea blossomed.

Eleanor spoke. "I think perhaps we should—"

"The blue one is the lady," Maggie said without thinking. "The other two are her suitors. One is a nobleman, the other is just a humble worker. Though she herself is not a butterfly of consequence, she is courted by these two handsome males."

"Which will she choose?" Lord Scarborough asked.

"Herein lies her dilemma," Maggie answered. "At first, her heart tells her to pick the humble worker. But the nobleman shows unexpected depth." She couldn't stop herself from looking at Cam, but she was overcome with a rare bout of shyness, and glanced away.

"She must pick one," Baron Fordyce said.

"Indeed, she must," Maggie replied. "So she sends them on dangerous quests, all the way to the ends of the earth. To bring her back hidden prizes. To face monstrous beasts. And they both show incredible courage and tenacity, returning again and again from each task."

"But if they both return, how can she choose?" asked Eleanor.

Maggie gave the company a wicked grin. "She doesn't. She takes them both to be her husbands, and the three of them live in wedded bliss for the remainder of their days."

Shocked but titillated laughter rose up from the others. Followed by applause.

"You are a free-thinker, Mrs. Delamere," Lady Scarborough said with a wide smile.

"I know what audiences respond to," Maggie said. "They like to be shocked." Once more, she looked at Marwood. His eyes gleamed warmly as he gazed back.

Something within her loosened, grew light. At the same time, her pulse sped just to look at him, sharing an intimacy even in the midst of the other guests.

The company broke apart into smaller groups then, and, sensing an opportunity, Maggie slipped from the drawing room to find the retiring chamber. Once she had finished and washed, she started to return to the drawing room, making her way down a darkened corridor.

A form approached her from the other end of the hallway. She recognized him even in the shadows. There was no mistaking Marwood's broad shoulders, or the smooth grace with which he walked, as though merely walking was a prelude to seduction.

Her mouth dried as he neared.

They stopped, standing not two feet apart. Dimly, she heard laughter and conversation from the drawing room, but she and Marwood were alone in the corridor. She knew only his presence, felt the heat radiating from his body, and the intensity of his gaze upon her.

"Nicely done," he murmured, his voice like a caress upon her skin.

"They were just stories," she said quietly.

"You never create 'just stories,'" he answered lowly. "They're far more than that. And the guests recognized that. They see how special you are."

A bloom of warmth flooded her face. "And you?" she felt compelled to ask. "How do you see me?"

"I'm not much of a poet or a writer," he said softly. "Words are awkward things for me to manipulate."

She gave a breathless laugh. "You wouldn't be so adept at seduction if you couldn't speak persuasively."

"There are times when words are paltry substitutes for actions." His voice deepened, darker than the shadows linking them. "Now is one of those times."

He stepped closer, bringing his hand up to stroke along her jaw. She shivered at the contact. Yet she didn't move away. He'd been the embodiment of sensuality at dinner, in the way he'd consumed his food and drink, and how he looked at her. The need to experience that for herself blazed. All her reasons for staying away from him fluttered away like flakes of burnt paper.

She held herself still, waiting. She couldn't catch enough air. It seemed very scarce all of a sudden.

Though he wore gloves, she still felt the impact of his touch, resonating in rich, sonorous waves through her body. Time itself seemed to stutter to a halt as he drew the back of his fingers along her cheek, down to her chin. She felt his gaze upon her face, then drop lower, to her mouth.

Was he . . . ? Would he . . . ? Nothing seemed more vital than to feel his lips against hers—despite every warning in her mind shouting that this was a very bad idea. She couldn't bring herself to care. All she wanted was his kiss. She *needed* it.

And then . . . Tipping her face up, he kissed her. Just a brush of his lips at first, a velvet slide back and forth across her mouth. Gentle. Almost tentative.

But that caution didn't last. They both deepened the kiss at the same time, their mouths opening to savor. Oh, did he taste wonderful. Tobacco and port and heat and desire, all combined into one heady flavor she couldn't get enough of.

She braced her hands against his chest, feeling the
rapid rise and fall of his breathing, the pound of his
heart. He might be an inveterate libertine, but she understood this kiss affected him as much as it did her.
They had flung themselves off a high precipice, falling
through the warm blue sky into boundless sensation.

His tongue brushed against hers, sampling, learning. Wanting more, reckless and heedless of what it
might cost her, she opened for him. He groaned low
in his chest, an animal sound of need, and drew her
closer, his hand cupping around the base of her neck.
Lost in his taste, his caress, she spun deeper. Her hands
stroked up his chest, until she gripped his shoulders,
feeling them firm and tight.

This was more than a kiss. This was an invitation to
sin. And she craved that sin.

One of his hands clasped her waist, pulling her closer
still. His touch burned through the silk of her gown to
the flesh beneath. He held her tightly, possessively. As
though he never wanted to let her go. His other hand
moved higher up, skimming her ribs. Until . . . his palm
rested just beneath the curve of her sensitive, heavy
breast. A sweet ache filled her, demanding more.

She pressed into him. He was hard and unyielding everywhere, taut with muscle and desire. Even
through the fabric of her dress, she felt the evidence
of his desire—firm, insistent. A small mewl escaped
her. This couldn't be real, could it? Yes. Need rioted
through her.

He moved, urging them backwards. Her back met
the wall, and his body surged against hers, engulfing
her. Though he wasn't a tall man, she felt surrounded
by him, deliciously imprisoned between his body and

the wall. And his hands . . . were everywhere. On the curve of her hips. Her breasts. Learning. Searching.

One of his thumbs grazed her tight nipple. Sensation careened through her, as bright as the sunrise. She moaned into his mouth.

Her own hands weren't idle. Maggie wanted to feel all of him. She cupped the hard arcs of his shoulders, and traced down his arms, rigid with strained sinew. Her palm skimmed up his solid chest, and beneath her touch, his heart throbbed, fast as a drum. With the richness of her imagination, she pictured him without his clothing, and, oh, what a sight that would be. Not a trace of softness anywhere on him.

Dizziness enveloped her as she became drunk on him. On the sensations they created together. She wanted more. And more.

A nearby sound made her break the kiss. She tore her lips from his and glanced anxiously toward the noise.

A servant carrying a decanter crossed at the far end of the hallway, not even glancing in their direction.

Marwood reached for her again. She stepped away. Trembling wracked her body.

What had she been thinking? He was her *patron*, for heaven's sake. An aristocrat. She'd been down this path before and knew the consequences. A gulf as wide as the Atlantic separated them, as it should. They couldn't cross that ocean.

"That . . ." She exhaled. "Cannot happen again."

"The devil it shouldn't," he rumbled. "It was good. Damned good."

"Precisely why we can't do it anymore." She took another step away, ensuring that she wasn't within touching distance. "You're my benefactor. Technically, I work for you."

"To hell with technicalities." He held out a hand. "We both want more."

She shook her head. "We can't have it. It makes everything too complicated, too confusing. I've been led astray by an aristocrat before, and I cannot do it again."

"Who?" he demanded.

"I've no wish to speak of the past now. But just know that this mustn't continue." When he seemed ready to object, she said quickly. "Please. Respect my wishes."

He cursed softly. His lips compressed into a tight line. But finally, he nodded. "As my lady desires."

"I'm no one's lady," she answered.

"That's debatable," he said.

A burst of laughter from the drawing room made her snap to attention. "We've been gone from the company for a long time."

"I'll go first," Marwood volunteered, though he sounded reluctant.

"Thank you."

His look was wry. "Don't thank me. There's much more I'd like to do with you. But I'm a sodding gentleman."

At that, he turned and walked back down the corridor, then disappeared into the drawing room.

Pressing a hand to her chest, Maggie exhaled again. *Good God.* Had she really done that? The heat lingering in her body proved that she had, in fact, kissed Marwood. What could it mean? He was handsome, yes, and sensual, and seductive and dangerous as the devil. But more than that, she'd seen admiration in his gaze. An appreciation of more than her physical self.

He seemed to want *her*, not just her body. Even more risky.

She'd done the right thing. There were lines that simply shouldn't be crossed. Class and money were two of them.

Yet he'd given her more than physical sensation. Earlier, he'd urged her to create a story, and she'd done so. He'd helped shape that ability when she'd thought she'd lost it. She wanted more—but couldn't have it. There had to be another way to break her creative barrier.

Things would be different between her and Marwood now. They couldn't pretend that the kiss hadn't happened. Smoothing her hand down the front of her borrowed dress, she vowed that she would carry on anyway. He provided financial support for the theater. Nothing more. And if she craved anything beyond that, she would just have to learn to live with those unfulfilled desires.

Chapter 15

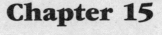

Phoebe: Too well I remember the blush of desire.

The Shattered Heart

Cam couldn't contain his restlessness. He paced back and forth in his study, needing his body in motion as his mind churned.

Less than twelve hours had passed since he and Maggie had kissed. He couldn't think of her as "Mrs. Delamere" any more. She was Maggie to him now.

Twelve hours wasn't very long, when considered in perspective of existence. And yet it felt as though each hour contained a lifetime. He'd been unable to sleep, too roused to do much more than stare at the canopy of his bed, counting the minutes until sunrise. His thoughts had kept flashing to Maggie. What she'd been doing at that very moment—blamelessly sleeping, or awake, like him.

He picked up a small, cricket ball-sized globe from his desk and tossed it from hand to hand.

Cam had kissed too many women to remember. Starting at the age of nine, when he'd pressed his lips to the cheek of a pretty dairymaid, who'd laughingly told him he'd be a regular Casanova once he'd reached maturity. Since then, he'd done much more than kiss a girl's cheek. He'd kissed every part of a woman's body. He enjoyed kissing, especially as a prelude to more.

But kissing Maggie . . . had been a sensuous experience unto itself. And while his body had wanted to take the kiss further, he'd also been oddly satisfied with just the feel of her mouth against his. The kiss had been as gratifying, as enjoyable, as lovemaking itself. She had been responsive, knowledgeable, eager. He could have kissed her for hours.

Staring down at the small globe in his hand, it was as though he was a titan holding the world. Such a small thing, the Earth. In the vastness of space, it wasn't more than a speck. Less than forty years ago, William Herschel had discovered another planet. The universe expanded as human knowledge strove to comprehend its vastness.

Was this how Herschel felt, seeing that glowing dot and realizing that it wasn't just a glimmer of a star, but possibly a whole world? In the span of a few days, Cam's knowledge of himself had expanded a thousand-fold. Including the fact that he and Margaret Delamere fit together perfectly.

She'd been heat and sweetness, strong and silken. And so bloody responsive. He hadn't known how she was going to react to his kiss, but she'd far surpassed any expectations. She wanted him, as much as he wanted her.

But she'd been adamant that they couldn't take their relationship any further. It would complicate things, she'd said. As if everything wasn't already as complex as one of those wrought iron tavern puzzles, nearly impossible to figure out.

And she'd alluded to her past, with another titled man. Someone who clearly had hurt her. The thought filled him with blinding fury. *No one* caused her pain.

The rest of the evening had been strained, with her staying on the opposite side of the drawing room. As if she didn't trust him. As if . . . she didn't trust herself.

But he didn't have to completely exile himself from her presence. After all, he was technically her patron. He could check on the progress of her work.

Cam called for his horse to be saddled, and in moments, he was on his way to the Imperial. Though traffic was thick as always, he eventually reached the theater.

After giving a boy a coin to watch his horse, he went in through the side entrance. A comedy troupe rehearsed their tumbling and patter onstage, frenetic as young foxes. He peered out into the house. No sign of Maggie. Well, there was no reason for her to watch the jesters go through their paces.

The Hidden Daughter's Return demanded her attention. Likely, he'd find her in that property room downstairs. She did say she'd want her privacy, but he'd poke his head in, just for a moment. Perhaps she was hungry. Or wanted something to drink. Writers could be a forgetful lot, especially when attending to their quill rather than their own needs.

There were other needs that would demand attending—sensual needs. But she'd insisted that wasn't an option. He had to abide by that, even though a quiet theater's property room could be a delicious place to make love, full of possibility.

Pushing that fruitless thought from his mind, he ventured down into the bowels of the theater. He passed more workers and assorted performers, all of them wishing him a respectful good day. He sensed their gazes on him with renewed interest after the other day's scene. He merely returned their greetings with polite nods.

The door to the property room stood open. Stepping inside, he found the cat once again, though it showed him far less deference than the other inhabitants of the theater. A glut of objects crowded the room, an abundance of stories in painted paperboard and wood. But at the long, heavy table where Maggie usually sat, there were only sheets of paper. No playwright.

He ought to turn around and leave—he shouldn't read her work while it was in process, but he stepped forward anyway. His hand shot out and took hold of one of the pieces of paper. Cam already had proof that her handwriting was appalling, but perhaps he could apply his intellect to deciphering the scrawl. His heart beat fast. Finally, he had his chance to read her latest work before anyone else.

Yet, as he held the paper up, he frowned. Not only were the words nigh illegible, they were all scratched out. She'd taken her quill and scrawled across them, drawing what looked like angry, dark hash lines through her words. As if . . . she'd hated what she'd written.

An examination of the other papers showed the same thing. Even a man with his resources knew that paper was not inexpensive. Yet sheet after sheet revealed that she had attempted many times to write, only to undo her work with furious scratches. What the devil could it mean?

He pocketed one of the papers, then strode from the property room. Though he feared a repeat of the information relay from the other day, he stopped a woman carrying an armful of faux-ermine.

"Where is Mrs. Delamere?" he asked.

"Think I saw her in the offices upstairs with Mr. Kingston," the woman answered, "my lord."

"My thanks, madam."

The woman reddened and ducked her head. "Of course, my lord." She hurried away, most likely to share the story of her brief run-in with the Imperial's patron. Gossip was always a valuable commodity, and no doubt it had tremendous worth in a theater. Thank God no one knew about the kiss. That would flood the gossip market.

After asking a stagehand for directions, Cam climbed several sets of stairs and walked down numerous hallways to discover the stage manager's office. It was a cramped little room, stuffed with papers and a few commedia dell'arte masks. Standing in the middle of this chaos was the Jamaican man, deep in conversation with Maggie.

His gut tightened at seeing her again.

She'd replaced her gray silk gown with a more mundane russet wool, but that didn't diminish her beauty. If anything, it revealed how she had a natural radiance that wasn't dependent on a sophisticated dress or ornate hairstyling.

"It won't make sense to have the dog act come on at the beginning," she said, seemingly unaware that Cam hovered in the doorway. "Those always get the audience riled, and if we place it first, no one will settle down for a melodrama."

"We'll have the same problem if we put it as the intermezzo," Mr. Kingston noted.

"Then it'll have to go at the end," she answered. "Better to finish with a dog rescuing a baby from a river than have the audience leave after the first act."

"True," the stage manager agreed.

Cam knocked on the doorjamb. Both Maggie and Mr. Kingston glanced in his direction. While the stage manager looked openly happy to see him, Maggie at first looked startled—alarmed—almost. Then caution crept into her face.

"If you're continuing to conduct business," Cam said, leaning against the door, "I can wait."

"We're finished, my lord," Mr. Kingston said. He glanced down at a sheaf of documents in his hand. "These are the bills from our lumber suppliers, and they want attending to."

"I ought to get back to writing," Maggie said, and it was only then that Cam noticed she said the words with the same enthusiasm one might utter, *I ought to eat this handful of grubs.* She reluctantly moved toward the door.

"Might I speak with you?" he asked lowly as she approached.

"There's nothing to talk about," she said hastily, glancing at Mr. Kingston.

"It's about this." From his pocket, he produced the piece of paper with her scratch marks.

Her eyes widened, and she snatched the paper from his hand, then crumpled it into a ball. Gripping it tightly in her fist, she hissed, "Not here."

"Everything all right, Mrs. D?" the stage manager asked.

"Perfectly well," she answered, too brightly, too fast. She glared at Cam. "Come on."

In an instant, she had sped ahead of him. Puzzled, he trailed after her, watching with curiosity as she wove through the maze of the theater. She was like a doe being chased by hunters. Several minutes later, she led him into his private box.

She whirled on him. "You're not here to talk about . . . last night?"

Heat roared through him, recalling the feel of her mouth, her willingness and strength. "Would you like to discuss it?"

"No," she said flatly.

"Then we won't."

She looked briefly relieved, then she shook the fist holding the discarded paper. "What are you doing with this?"

"More to the point," he said, sitting himself down, "what does it mean?"

"It means nothing," she snapped.

He raised his brows. "Does it? Because it appears to my untutored, mildly-literate eye that whoever was writing that seems rather stymied. As if"—and here it finally dawned on him the significance of all that used but useless paper—"the author couldn't get past an obstacle or block."

She spun away from him, and her hand opened as if what she held burned her. The paper dropped to the ground noiselessly. Yet it seemed as though it weighed ten stone. He was surprised the whole building didn't shake with the impact.

"Don't tell anyone," she croaked.

He was beside her in an instant. For one of the few times in his life, he found himself at a loss in how to act toward a woman. He ached to put his arm around her, offer her his solace, his strength. But she'd made it clear they were to keep distant from each other. He had to do something, however, so he placed his hand upon her shoulder. At the least, she didn't shrug him off. Yet he discovered anew the shock of how slight she was, rather than made of steel.

Her expression was bleak as winter, and that alone sent a bolt of fear through him. She always had such fortitude, especially last night, yet now it seemed to have deserted her.

"How long now?" he asked gently.

For a moment, he thought she wouldn't answer. Then, "Months."

A writer without the ability to write? Dear God. What unimaginable suffering, especially for a woman of her talent. That pain seemed to flow from her into him, and he realized now what a bloody fool he'd been not to have noticed until now. The actors had been rehearsing the same scenes over and over again. She'd seemed especially quick-tempered whenever he'd caught her working, and there had been that momentary panic on her face when he'd asked her to create a story around the butterflies. And the fact that the board of directors had been pressuring her to produce. Now he understood her fear. Because she was blocked. He should have seen the signs sooner.

"I'm sorry," was all he could say.

She rubbed impatiently at her face. "Always thought it was a myth. There were too many ideas, too many stories out there. I never thought it would befall me."

"How did it happen?" He didn't want to make a bad situation worse, but it seemed incomprehensible that she should suffer such a devastating loss.

She threw up her hands. "It's this sodding sequel. Everyone wants it. Everything's resting on it. And it has to have a damned *happy ending*," she added with disgust. "What do I know of happily ever after?"

He'd never experienced a hurdle quite like this one

before. It seemed bigger and more insurmountable than anything he'd encountered. What could he do? How could he help? His own powerlessness angered him. But anger would solve nothing. She had enough rage for both of them. Another tactic, then.

He turned her gently to face him. She looked furious with herself.

"Seems to me that you made one for yourself." He searched for the right words. "None of this would be possible without the hard work you put in," he went on. His thoughts churned as he struggled to say the proper thing. "Happy endings . . . simply don't occur. They need . . ." Pieces began to fall into place as he spoke, understanding coming with them. "They need to be made."

His own words seemed to shake them both.

"Onstage, all that needs to happen is the curtain falls, and the couple is united and happy forever." She glanced disgustedly toward the stage in question, as though it was the source of her misery. "Real life doesn't operate so neatly. The curtain doesn't fall. Life goes on. And whatever happy ending I might have earned has evaporated, like my ruddy writing ability."

"Listen to me, Maggie." He gripped her shoulders tightly. "It's not gone. It's still there."

If she minded him using her Christian name, she did not say. Instead, she only shook her head. "You don't know that."

He gave her a tiny, tiny shake. "I *do* know that." He needed it to be true. For her, and himself. He needed the words from her pen to sustain him.

She gazed up at him with wide, suffering eyes. "I cannot write a word, Marwood. All these people"—she glanced toward the performers and members of the stage crew—"depend on me. They *need* me to write, just as you do. And the more I think on that, the less the words come. They're dammed up. And I'm damned." She clenched her jaw, as if to keep back tears or a scream of fury.

A workman onstage dropped his hammer, and Maggie jumped at the sound. Cam could see the pulse beating at her throat, and the wild, trapped look in her gaze. As if she truly was a deer that had been herded indoors, and now sought escape, only to find herself imprisoned by all these walls.

"You need to leave this place," he said suddenly, an idea striking him with the same force as the hammer hitting the ground.

"I can't," she growled. "I've committed myself to this theater and all the people who call it their home."

"Not *leave* leave. Nor desert it entirely," he explained. "Just . . . get out of London. Go somewhere quiet. A change of scenery."

She looked at him as though he'd put a turnip on his head and declared himself pope. "I'm not exactly brimming with funds to send myself off to the country."

It all made sense, and he couldn't help a small flare of pleasure at his own cleverness. "There's a perfectly enormous manor just thirty miles from the city." He smiled. "Empty of all occupants, but fully staffed. Lovely place," he continued. "Got its own forest, a lake. Nice, picturesque village just a half an hour away on foot, should you desire company. Say the word, and it's yours for as long as you want."

"And what is this Utopia?" she asked suspiciously.

He beamed at her. "My country estate."

Chapter 16

Harriet: Will you not dance, my lady?
Phoebe: I cannot this day. A dark presence
  hovers close.

The Shattered Heart

Maggie stared at him for a moment. Then she closed the distance between them, leaned in close, her face very near his, and took a deep inhale. He looked vaguely appalled.

"No brandy or wine fumes on your breath," she said, taking a step back. "So I know you aren't drunk. But then there's no explanation for your outrageous offer."

"It's my bloody property," he said with a scowl. "I can do with it what I like. Including offer it to you. Temporarily, of course."

Throwing up her hands, she exclaimed, "But it makes no sense."

"It makes perfect sense," he replied. "Aside from the staff, there's no one at Marwood Park. Someone ought to get some use out of it."

She eyed him cautiously. "What about you?"

"Sundry interests keep me in town. You may find

this incredible, but yes, I do have responsibilities. I meet with my man of business twice weekly, and that cannot be done by written correspondence. Further," he continued, "the Robertsons are giving a ball in three days' time, and I told them I'd be there. You'd have the place completely to yourself."

Trees, fields. A property empty of everyone but the staff. All hers. The idea was appealing. With a name like Marwood Park, it sounded rather vast and bucolic. Certainly a far cry from anything she'd ever known here in London. She was a city creature, born and bred. Yet here he offered her the opportunity to experience not only the country, but a country estate, with servants and parkland, and who knew what else. Her writer's curiosity brimmed with excitement—and, she had to admit, getting away from London with all its pressures was definitely an incentive.

Yet, despite Marwood's gallantry toward her, she still kept a part of herself in reserve. After what had happened at the Ashfords'—that blistering kiss—she wasn't certain what might follow between her and Marwood. They'd crossed a line, and it might not be possible to go back.

"I haven't any means of paying you back," she finally said.

He frowned deeply. "Why do you insult me thus?"

"Forgive me," she said quickly. "I'm . . ." She glanced away, then back. "Trust is a commodity that I don't have in abundance. Life taught me to hold it very dear."

"If I may ask . . . what . . . ?"

She knew this moment was coming, and yet it didn't frighten her to talk of it now. Not with him. It was her deepest secret, and yet it seemed right to tell him of it. She wanted no secrets anymore.

"My parents owned a used goods shop, and I worked there. A young nobleman came in one day—I was barely past my fifteenth birthday. He wanted to sell some silver. He spotted me at the shop and . . . well . . ." She gave a small shrug. "I was smitten. I thought he was enamored, too. At least, he led me to believe he was."

Cam held up his hand. "I know where this tale is going. He seduced and abandoned you."

"Not a very unique story, I'm afraid." She smiled sadly. "I was another pregnant girl on the street after that."

"A baby?" His eyes went wide.

Her smile faded. Maggie shook her head. "She . . ."

"I'm sorry," he said simply, the words holding far more sympathy and understanding than any florid declaration.

She nodded, feeling the sudden prick of tears behind her eyes. Grief was an odd thing. It came up out of the shadows, like a thief stealing happiness. But she'd had a long time to come to terms with her sorrow, and the memory of her stillborn daughter was tucked away into the velvet-lined cabinet of Maggie's heart.

"Not much for trusting aristos after that," she said flatly.

"Why would you?"

"I'm learning," she said, her gaze meeting his, "that they aren't all alike."

"Tell me his name so I can find and castrate him," Cam growled, his expression thunderous.

Her mouth twisted. "Last I heard, he'd disappeared on a trip to Argentina."

"Too bad," Cam said bitterly. "I'd like nothing better than to cut his bollocks off."

"What a sweet thing to say," she exclaimed.

His expression gentled, and he took a step closer. "There's nothing I want from you in exchange for having you stay at my home in the country. Nothing that has to be given. Consider it my responsibility as your patron," he added with a gentle smile.

"It's not precisely proper," she felt compelled to note, "having me stay at your home."

His smile widened, and, oh, was he a wickedly beautiful man. "My dear, you work at a *theater*. For some, that's one step up from a brothel."

"Our rate of disease is slightly less," she answered. But he did have a point. She'd never meet the King, and there were certainly households into which she'd never be received. Yet decorum and respectability had little value to her now.

"It's settled then." He rubbed his hands together briskly. "I'll dispatch a letter this very day to have my staff prepare a room for you. Tomorrow morning, I'll send my carriage either to your home or the theater, as you prefer, and thence to transport you to Marwood Park."

"Your *carriage*?" She shook her head. "That, I cannot accept."

He raked his hand through his hair in frustration. "It's a small matter—"

"Not to me," she countered, but gently. "Call me foolish if you wish—"

"Obstinate," he corrected.

"That, too," she said with a smile. "But there are limits to how much I can take from another person.

The mail coach is suitable, and I'll pay for my own fare."

He looked as though he wanted to argue, but seemed to think better of it. She could indeed be obstinate. It was a part of herself that she actually prized. For if she didn't have that stubbornness, she would have collapsed in on herself long ago, and likely disappeared from the face of this earth.

"Sometimes," she said with a self-deprecating little curve to her mouth, "obstinacy is all that keeps us moving forward."

He folded his arms across his chest and nodded. "Sage words, Mrs. Delamere."

"No going back," she reminded him. Something tugged at her, a need that wanted fulfilling. "Might you . . . call me Maggie again?"

Though his expression remained neutral, she could sense the gratification in him that she'd made this request. As though it was something that only the two of them could share.

"I'd like you to call me Cam," he said softly.

She felt the look of surprise on her face. Not *Lord Marwood* or even simply *Marwood*, but his own first name—a privilege he likely didn't bestow easily. Even Lord Ashford, his closest friend, called him by his title. Yet here was even more intimacy, like an invisible, silken cord binding them closer together.

"As you wish," she said just as softly. "Cam."

A hush fell over the two of them as they stared at each other. The theater box felt as small as two cupped hands, holding them in a warm, protected space. Beyond which lay a world of uncertainty. But here, they were sheltered, alone with each other. She had taken lovers in the past, but this felt far more intimate, this display of humanity and vulnerability.

"I look forward to having you in my home," he said quietly.

Simple words, yet they made her blood speed. What would it be like, to be so far from the city? To be in a place that was entirely his? It would be still another intimacy, another piece of him gently, slowly assembling to form a complete picture of a man. Not the rake, or the rogue, but his truer self. And that would be the greatest understanding of all.

The gig jostled and swayed as it drove down the tree-lined lane. Perched beside the driver, Maggie held tight to the seat, though there was little chance of being thrown to the road. Her one small valise sat at her feet. It contained a few changes of clothing, but most importantly, it held a dozen sharpened quills and a whole sheaf of fresh paper. All she would need for this unexpected trip to the country.

"You going to be a maid at the Park?" the driver asked as they crossed a stone bridge.

"I'm a guest."

The man raised a dubious brow. "Right."

She didn't feel the need to defend herself to this man. His opinion didn't matter. Yet she had worn her best traveling coat and bonnet for this excursion, and it stung a little how even this country driver didn't think she measured up.

A thrill of anxiety shot through her, despite—or because of—the pastoral setting. Would she be even more uncomfortable in Marwood's . . . *Cam's* estate than she was in London? Already, she felt the shift from the city to the country. The air smelled of soil and grass instead of coal and animal refuse. Wind ran its fingers through the trees, a far cry from the sounds of bellowing coster-mongers and rattling wagon wheels. Though the sky was gray, it held the purity of a dove's wing, rather than the stain of smoke. On all sides of her, rolling farmland stretched out, marked with low stone fences, hedges, and trees she couldn't name.

It was all a little unnerving.

It became even more unnerving when the gig crested a hill, revealing an enclosed vale below. Deer grazing on the lawns lifted their heads like sentinels at the cart's approach. Dominating the valley was a massive baroque-style three story building of sand-colored stone. Tall windows lined the front, and an old tower rose even higher above the roofline. It was a stately place, and imposing, yet it seemed perfectly comfortable nestled at the bottom of the dale, as though it had always been there and would continue to exist in perpetuity.

Maggie let out a long, slow exhalation. Dear God, this was Cam's *home*? Perhaps he might only reside here part of the year, but it was a testament of his wealth and position that he could claim such a place for himself. Marwood Park could hold two Imperial Theaters inside of it.

It seemed incongruous with what she knew of Cam. He was anything but formal and daunting. In truth, he seemed to enjoy flouting decorum. But this house had likely been built long before he'd been born. It was simply part of his birthright. Yet even *that* intimidated her. The Cam that owned this house seemed so much farther above her than the one who had kissed her in a dark corridor.

The gig rolled down a long curving drive, finally coming to stop in front of a set of tall black doors. Almost the moment the cart stopped, the doors opened and several servants came bustling out—two liveried footman, an older woman in a lace cap, and a middle aged man with a starched white shirtfront.

"Mrs. Delamere?" the woman asked.

"Yes."

The older woman nodded toward the footmen, who stepped forward. The strapping young men seemed confounded by Maggie's small valise, likely expecting something much more substantial. One of the footmen gingerly took the valise and carried it inside.

"We're so glad you've arrived," the older woman said kindly once this operation had been carried out. "I am Mrs. Dyrham, the housekeeper. This is Mr. George, the butler. Welcome to Marwood Park."

The remaining footman held out a gloved hand to help her down from the gig. Maggie couldn't help but send the driver a quick, slightly defiant look. He reddened.

She took the footman's proffered hand and stepped down from the carriage, her traveling boots crunching on the gravel driveway. Closer now to the front of the house, it looked even bigger and more daunting, a symbol of everything she wasn't.

As if sensing her discomfort, Mrs. Dyrham said sincerely, "Lord Marwood was most insistent that we give you a warm welcome. Everything is in readiness for you."

"Thank you, Mrs. Dyrham," Maggie answered.

Mr. George bowed, and said, "Just this way, if you please." He gestured toward the open front door.

With her small entourage—the first time she'd ever *had* an entourage besides people at the theater—Maggie entered Cam's country estate. Inside, it was just as formidable as the exterior. After crossing through a small entryway, Maggie found herself in the middle of an enormous wooden-floored hall with vaulted ceilings. Ancestral portraits hung on damask wallpaper, and crystal chandeliers sparkled in the late afternoon light. The air smelled of wax and lemons. Beyond the hall, Maggie caught sight of another long room, this one lined with mirrors. Perhaps wealthy folk liked looking at themselves. One of their many eccentricities.

"Are you hungry?" Mrs. Dyrham asked, her hands clasped at her waist. "I have tea and cakes, whenever you desire."

"Perhaps later, thank you," Maggie answered. It was disconcerting to have people attending to her needs after having taken care of herself for so long. She wasn't entirely certain she liked it.

"Let me show you to your room, then."

"If you'll excuse me," Mr. George said, bowing again. He disappeared with the silence of a trained professional.

Once the butler was gone, Mrs. Dyrham led Maggie into another hallway, this one containing an enormous walnut staircase that wound upward to the next floor. Maggie tried very hard not to gape like a buffoon at the richness of the house surrounding her. She'd never been inside a nobleman's home before—her aristocratic seducer had always met her at various inns—and this one seemed especially fine. More mirrors and fine paintings of likely Italian origin hung upon the dark wood-paneled walls. Everywhere her gaze fell, she found objects of incomparable cost—vases, tables, china. The house seemed imbued with the kind of wealth and privilege that seemed both hard won and effortless.

This isn't your world, everything seemed to whisper.

She'd half a mind to turn around and walk back to London. But no, she ought to stay for a day or two, or else risk seeming churlish and ungrateful.

"Forgive the state of the house," Mrs. Dyrham said unnecessarily. Everything gleamed and glowed from the labor of many. "We don't expect anyone until the Spring."

"This is far beyond anything I could have expected," Maggie answered. She would not put on airs, and had to be truthful.

"The master wanted you to have the Tapestry Bedroom." The housekeeper opened a door lining the hallway and waved Maggie inside. Together, they entered the bedchamber.

Almost at once, Maggie knew. "I can't sleep here."

Mrs. Dyrham frowned worriedly. "Is something wrong? Is it not large enough?"

"Madam, my entire living quarters could fit inside this bedroom." Maggie spread her arms open to take in the expanse of the chamber. As the Tapestry Bedroom's name suggested, the walls were hung with what had to be Flemish works depicting castles and forests. In the center of the room stood a galleon of a four-poster bed. It was a singularly impressive room, and entirely unsuitable for her.

"The tapestries keep the drafts out, so you needn't worry about being cold," Mrs. Dyrham explained.

"It's not the cold that concerns me," Maggie said sadly. "I know I wouldn't sleep a wink in a place this grand. Isn't there something smaller? A nursemaid's room or its equivalent."

"I don't know if the master would like it," the house-keeper said dubiously.

"But *I* would like it," Maggie replied, "and you seem like the sort of woman who wants her guests to be comfortable above all else."

Mrs. Dyrham clicked her tongue. "Ah, you know my weakness, Mrs. Delamere."

"If Lord Marwood has anything to say about it," Maggie added, "the blame will rest solely with me."

The housekeeper tapped her chin thoughtfully, then said, "There's a governess's room that's just off the nursery on the next floor. It's very . . . snug."

"Sounds perfect."

The housekeeper tugged on the bellpull. In a few short minutes, two housemaids appeared. "Prepare the governess's room for Mrs. Delamere." Once the house-maids had bobbed their assent and disappeared, Mrs. Dyrham turned back to Maggie. "If I cannot interest you in something to eat or drink, perhaps you'd like to see the other room the master had readied for you."

"Yes, please." Maggie had no idea what this other room might be, and her writer's curiosity was piqued at the thought.

She followed the housekeeper back down the stairs, then through a series of extraordinary chambers, each lavishly furnished. They finally reached a doorway set at the very corner of a hallway, which Mrs. Dyrham opened. She gestured for Maggie to go in.

It was a bright, cheerful room, with yellow flocked

paper on the walls and numerous bookshelves stocked with leather-covered volumes. Windows lining one wall looked out onto a lush garden. A blue and white china vase held yellow roses that scented the air delicately. But, as lovely as the room was, nothing entranced Maggie half as much as the substantial desk that stood at one end of the chamber. It faced the windows, so that whomever sat in it simply had to look up to see the garden. A stack of fresh paper waited atop a blotter, and several sharpened quills lay beside a silver inkpot.

It was the perfect room for writing.

Maggie took a hesitant step forward. "Is this . . . mine?" she breathed.

The housekeeper chuckled. "Indeed, so it is. The master was very specific in selecting the Yellow Chamber for you. He was particular about everything that has been placed here."

Approaching the bookshelves, Maggie saw that they contained Dr. Johnson's dictionary, as well as a complete set of the *Encyclopaedia Britannica*. Everything a writer might need whilst penning her latest work.

She pressed a hand to her chest. No one had ever given her a gift quite like this one.

"It's extraordinary," she said, half to herself, half to Mrs. Dyrham.

"Aye, well, I cannot say that I've seen the master ever make such a fuss over one guest before." The housekeeper clucked. " 'Make certain she has this,' 'Be sure she has that.' As though I don't know how to make someone feel welcome at Marwood Park!"

Maggie turned to face Mrs. Dyrham. "I suppose now you'll regale me with tales of how wonderful he was as a child, too. Visiting the poor with food taken from his own plate. Never causing a lick of trouble as he studied diligently in the nursery."

The housekeeper snorted. "A hellion, more like. And a considerable pain in my backside."

"Not much has changed."

The bright room was filled with laughter as Maggie and Mrs. Dyrham commiserated about the ongoing trial that was Cameron Chalton, Lord Marwood.

"I must be getting back to my duties," the housekeeper said after wiping her eyes. "If there's anything at all you might need . . ."

"I'll be certain to ask."

Mrs. Dyrham curtsied, then exited the room, leaving Maggie alone. A soft silence filled the chamber, interrupted only by a bird singing in a nearby tree. There was a profundity to the quiet, as though everything in the world had fallen away, leaving Maggie fully alone with herself, perhaps more so than she had ever been.

Yet she wasn't entirely alone. Cam's presence was all around her, in the small touches that surrounded her in this room, in the care he'd shown when making arrangements for her stay here in his home.

She drifted around the yellow room for a while, her fingers lightly touching the spines of the books, her palm resting on the stack of paper that awaited her pen. She even smelled the roses. This all felt like a dream, like someone else's life. But, for a time, it was hers. And Cam had made it so.

She sat herself at the desk and picked up a quill. But what if the words couldn't come to her here, either?

Setting the quill down, restlessness pulsed through her. Perhaps a stretch of her legs was in order.

She wandered out of the writing room and ambled slowly down the hallway, feeling a touch as though she was sneaking around. She peered into other chambers, all of varying size and magnificence. Some were small parlors or drawing rooms, furnished for family, and others were larger and stately, meant for public gatherings. After winding her way through the labyrinthine corridors, she discovered one closed door tucked away in a corner.

It might be someone's private room, but she had a limitless—and shameless—curiosity, and so she tried the door. It was unlocked, which, for a writer, was as good as an invitation. So she went inside.

Honey-colored wood paneled the walls instead of the darker, heavier material used throughout the rest of the house. The chamber was only around ten feet by ten feet, containing a writing desk, numerous bookshelves, and glass-fronted cabinets. In a previous century, it would have been called a closet, a room in which a gentleman might repair to be alone with his thoughts and his most prized possessions. Not much, it seemed, had changed in these years—except perhaps for the gentleman who would occupy the chamber.

Voices sounded outside. She didn't want to be accused of creeping around where she wasn't welcome, but she couldn't leave without drawing attention to herself. So she quickly shut the door.

She was alone in the chamber. Perhaps a small exploration might be acceptable.

The best way to know someone was to look at their library. So Maggie immediately went to the bookshelves and examined the spines. They were almost entirely bound editions of plays, beginning with medieval mystery plays, through Shakespeare and Jonson, all the way up to Mrs. Inchbald.

So, this must have been Cam's private chamber.

Though she stopped short of going through the drawers of the writing desk, Maggie gave herself free rein to look around the room. There were framed and unframed drawings, sketches of landscapes and fantastical scenes.

In the glass-fronted cabinets were shards of Greek and Roman pottery illustrating scenes from the theater. A few fossilized bones and shells also lined the shelves, as well as objects that Maggie could make no sense of: a thimble, a tortoiseshell comb, a square of paper that had once been wrapped around a boiled sweet. Whatever these things were, they obviously held personal worth to Cam, and she could only guess at what that might be.

She sensed him, as though he stood just behind her, warmth exuding from his body. Here, she peered into the most inner reaches of Cam, past all the polished veneer to find the truth of him beneath. The way she had felt his real self in his kiss.

Heat pulsed along her at the remembrance of his lips against hers, the need and urgency absent of artifice. He hadn't been a rake with a reputation, but a man, with desires and demands of his own.

He was over thirty miles away, still in urban, urbane London. They were farther apart than they'd been in a goodly while. And yet, standing in his chamber, in his home, she'd never felt closer to him.

Chapter 17

*Phoebe: How I long for home! But it will be
    forever denied me.
Harriet: This is your home now, my lady.
Phoebe: Is it, truly?*

The Shattered Heart

The evening stretched out before Cam in a long, seamless void. As he dressed for the night, he contemplated his options. Restlessness and dissatisfaction gnawed at him like rats.

There was an assembly given by Lord Frances, which would be filled with all the usual characters gathered from High Society, including mamas eager to match their daughters up with a viscount. That option he rejected almost immediately.

It was too early to visit a gaming hell, but even if it was midnight, Cam thought of the card tables and the men crowded around them, shouting, wild, desperate. No appeal there, either. Not since he'd become involved with Maggie.

The theater? Tonight at the Imperial was a rare bill without any of Maggie's works. Drury Lane or Covent

Garden could suit his needs. He wasn't so beholden to the Imperial that he had to be there every night. Yes, he'd try Drury Lane, and see what sort of entertainments and diversions he might find there. Macready was performing this evening, so at the least, it would prove moderately engaging.

He dined alone at his favorite chophouse. All the while that same, strange restlessness continued to shift beneath his skin. He felt as though he meant to do something . . . but what? What was missing?

After a pint of good ale and a bellyful of beefsteak, his head remained no clearer. A walk might do him good. Outside the chophouse, he dismissed his carriage for the night and walked to Drury Lane, his legs taking the pavement with long, impatient strides. People scurried out of his way.

The theater was far more grand than the Imperial—much larger, and calculated to show off its patrons in a rarified atmosphere. After paying for his ticket, Cam went into the lobby, looked at the elegant display and felt . . . underwhelmed. But why?

Maggie likely would have something to say about the painted friezes and crystal chandeliers of Drury Lane. Using spectacle to cover up the lack of substance, she'd likely mutter. He smiled at the thought.

A woman with an ivory fan must have thought he smiled at her, because she made eyes at him over the top of her fan. She was attractive, blond and slender, dressed in the height of fashion to show off her figure. At best, all he could summon was a connoisseur's appreciation for something pretty, yet she moved him—and the rest of his body—not at all. He gave her a slight bow before moving on through the crowd.

Where would he sit? He kept no private box here. As he debated this, someone called his name.

He turned, and there was Mr. Frederick Vesey, an amiable young gentleman and heir to a substantial estate and iron fortune. They had met several times at social functions, and Cam had found him pleasant, and generally game for the more unconventional amusements of high society.

"Didn't expect to find you here, my lord," Vesey said, shaking Cam's hand. "Aren't you usually at the Imperial?"

"A man can expand his horizons," Cam answered. "It keeps him from the decay of old age."

Vesey nodded. "Quite sage. Come and join me and my companions in our box."

"Excellent." Cam followed Vesey through the corridors of the theater. Odd how out of sorts Cam felt in this place. He'd been at the Imperial so much in the last few weeks, Drury Lane was a peculiar echo—similar, but not entirely the same. As though a stranger was wearing the clothes and performing in the habits of an old friend.

Vesey led him up several flights of stairs, then down a hallway, until he pulled back a curtain to reveal one of the theater boxes. Inside, a handful of gentlemen and ladies chatted and flirted in the manner of young people eager to experience the pleasures of sophisticated life.

Introductions quickly followed. Cam bowed at the women and shook hands with the men. Some of them he knew, others he was less acquainted with. But the world of the *ton* remained a small one, and in one way or another, he had familiarity with everyone.

All except one young woman. She sat unobtrusively

in the corner, hands neatly folded in her lap. Unlike the other ladies, her dress was cut a little more modestly. If one was being generous, one might call her hair color dark amber, or a more prosaic light brown. She did have bright blue eyes, which brought forth a quiet attractiveness in her somewhat understated features. The girl looked every inch a respectable young woman of means, completely proper, honorably demure. Dull as broth.

"Lady Sarah Frampton," Vesey said brightly, "may I present Lord Marwood. Lord Marwood, Lady Sarah."

Cam took her slim hand and bowed over it. He recalled her now. The only daughter of the Duke of Wakefield, she had been out for several years now. Her maid sat quietly in the corner.

"My sincerest pleasure," he said as he bowed.

"Likewise," she murmured, with a surprisingly husky, sensuous voice. The kind of voice that belonged to a much more worldly woman. It was like drinking from a plain ceramic cup, only to discover it held a rich French wine.

Despite her seductress's voice, he and Lady Sarah would likely have nothing in common. She was a virgin, untutored in the ways of the world.

Maggie's voice sounded in his head. "Judging a play before the curtain goes up," she said disapprovingly. Or he imagined she would say.

Likely, she wouldn't be much interested in the people in the theater box, and more engaged by the theater itself. Observing how it was constructed, and the way in which the stage was lit, or the quality of the orchestra as it played a preshow air.

Suddenly, the thought of sitting through a play written by a contemporary author other than Maggie felt like a ridiculous exercise. He didn't care what other new playwrights had to say—he only cared about her work, and whether or not she found Marwood Park to her liking.

Turning to Mr. Vesey and his friends, Cam said, "The play hasn't begun. We should all leave now and go to my home for our own gathering. There's billiards, cards, and music, if that appeals."

The ladies clapped their hands and the gentlemen murmured their approval.

"Capital idea," Vesey declared.

"We're in agreement, then," Cam said.

"Not everyone is in agreement," Lady Sarah said.

"Can you not join us?" Cam asked.

"It wouldn't be very seemly of me to do so," she answered.

"Of course," he replied smoothly. He bowed as she rose and drifted out of the box, her maid following.

Cam's thoughts returned to Maggie. Had she seen the writing room he'd had prepared? What did she think of it? Damn, but he hoped it pleased her. He hoped everything at Marwood Park pleased her, and that she'd find her absent muse while in residence.

Thinking of her, his mind and body flashed back to the kiss they'd shared. God almighty, he'd enjoyed kissing before, but nothing could match what it was like to kiss Maggie. She'd been fire and steel, alive. Strong and passionate. A woman who knew herself and what she wanted. And Lord help him if he didn't find that unbearably arousing.

He wanted more. But would he ever have it?

"Shall we go?" Vesey asked, interrupting Cam's thoughts.

"Yes, let's," he answered.

Soon, transportation was arranged for everyone, and in less than a half an hour, a party assembled in Cam's drawing room. Footmen rolled back the carpets and moved furniture to the side of the chamber, while one of the ladies seated herself at the pianoforte. Wine already poured in abundance, and laughter filled the room. Some of the gentlemen ambled off in search of billiards, but most remained.

A card table was set up in one corner of the room, and two couples played piquet. The stakes were as high as everyone's spirits, and Cam again wondered what Maggie would make of this—four people wagering in an evening what ordinary folk made in a year. Before he'd known her, he wouldn't have thought twice about how much was being bet, but now . . . there seemed no turning back to his old way of thinking.

"I heard about your masquerade a few months ago," Vesey said. "Got a little wild, didn't it?"

"We should have one now!" one of the women cried.

"Masks would defeat the purpose," Cam pointed out. "We already know the identities of everyone here."

The woman deflated a little. "Well," she said brightly, "we'll have dancing, of course."

"Not just dancing, I hope," Vesey said eagerly.

The woman winked. "We'll see where the evening leads."

A lady at the piano didn't bother with country dances. She skipped the preliminaries and went right into a waltz.

Cam's limbs felt heavy and weary. He had no taste tonight for dancing. But he was the host, and had, for some reason, proposed this evening's entertainment, so he approached Lady Wigan, an attractive, dark-haired widow. The type of sophisticated woman he favored, with few illusions about the world, but an appetite for pleasure.

Would she kiss as passionately or with such openness as Maggie?

"We ought to begin the festivities," she murmured. "Don't you think, my lord?"

"By all means, let's start the fashion." He bowed, then held out his hands.

She slid her palm against his, and placed her other hand upon his shoulder. He lightly held her slim waist. She seemed to be wearing a minimum of undergarments.

No mistaking her intent as she stepped nearer, closing the respectable distance between them. She stood so close that the front of her bodice brushed against his chest, and he was enveloped in the rich floral curlicues of her perfume. She smelled of roses and worldly temptation.

Did Maggie like the roses he'd requested for her writing room? Some women didn't care for the scent. He should have thought of that. But he'd assumed that, after the acrid smells of London, the spicy sweet fragrance would come as a welcome relief. He'd also been specific about the color of the roses. Yellow would suit the chamber's décor, but they also signified friendship and good cheer. She had need of both.

"My lord?" Lady Wigan asked, breaking his train of thoughts.

Oh, yes. Dancing.

As the music started in its familiar rhythm, Cam's body instinctively moved in time with the tempo. Other couples joined in. Lady Wigan was skilled at dancing and she made a good partner. And yet, as Cam spun her around the room and her body swayed with his, he imagined another woman in his arms.

Maggie ought to know how to waltz, though he had no idea how often she danced. Theater folk were known for their love of merrymaking. But she kept herself slightly separate from the others at the Imperial, the weight of responsibility always heavy on her shoulders. She needed joy in her life, too. Perhaps when she returned from the country, he could arrange a small gathering for her and some of her friends. Just a moment's respite from her constant pressure.

She would fit well in his arms as they waltzed. She wasn't a very big woman, but then, he wasn't the tallest bloke, and they would partner nicely. Perhaps they could also ignore society's dictates and dance close, so he could feel her body move in time with the music. Dancing was an excellent metaphor, one that had, many times in the past, led to other rhythmic activities. Yet, much as he needed to know every aspect of her, he simply wanted the pleasure of the dance, and to see her smile up at him as they turned and spun, caught up in a private world that belonged to them alone.

"I'm enjoying our dance, too, my lord," Lady Wigan murmured.

He blinked, belatedly realizing that he'd been smiling down at the pretty widow as if he was looking at Maggie. Rudeness wasn't in his vocabulary, not where women were concerned, so he kept smiling.

"It's a pleasant evening," he said lightly.

"Indeed," Lady Wigan agreed, "there's nothing quite so agreeable as excellent company. I do so take pleasure in making new friends."

"As do I," he said automatically. Flirtation felt rote, a script he'd memorized long ago. Yet the words continued just the same, no matter how little he meant them.

Remorse crept through him. Lady Wigan deserved better. A hazy veil had been drawn over the night. She couldn't help it if everything and everyone suddenly seemed pallid and dull. It wasn't her fault that the one person he wanted with him currently resided at Marwood Park.

"I believe that Mr. Vesey might be in need of a partner." Cam was careful to keep his tone gentle, but the meaning beneath the words was clear.

The young gentleman indeed stood by himself with a glass of wine, watching the dancers with a cheerful, expectant look on his face.

Lady Wigan's own sophisticated expression didn't shift. But she seemed to know what Cam meant. "Of course. We cannot have anyone left out of the fun."

She slipped from Cam's grasp, and they bowed and curtseyed to one another. Then she crossed the chamber to stand beside Vesey. Immediately, the young gentleman asked her to dance, and she readily agreed.

Cam positioned himself at the edge of the room, watching as Lady Wigan and Vesey whirled their way around his drawing room. She appeared to have recovered quickly from switching partners, and now she and Vesey laughed together as they danced.

He considered joining the card players, but the idea of sitting through hand after hand, even with high stakes, seemed flat. How could he wager so much money, when it could easily go to fixing some of the Imperial's more shabby sets, or repairing or replacing a few threadbare costumes? The same went for billiards. The men playing would expect him to bet, and he had no interest in throwing money away on a game. Not when he knew that money could be used to better purpose, like new costumes for the performers. Come to think about it, some of the props had been looking a little careworn lately, too.

Ribald comments flowed as freely as the wine. Couples were already making eyes at each other, preparing to pair off for the night.

He'd invited all these people over to his home for an evening's entertainment. Now, he wondered how soon everyone would leave so he could go to bed—alone. He could revisit the kiss with Maggie. A kiss that continued to reverberate through him with heat and need.

But he was obligated to play host, and so for the duration of a very long night, he did just that. All the while, his thoughts were far away. She would sleep tonight in the quiet of the countryside. He used to hate the silence whenever he'd travel from the city to the country. In the past few years, however, it had become more and more restorative. He hoped she would be able to get some rest.

He hoped she found whatever it was she needed. At least one of them should be satisfied. God knew, he wasn't.

Chapter 18

Phoebe enters. Sees Lord Diabold, who does not observe her.
Phoebe: The day I dreaded has finally arrived!

The Shattered Heart

Setting down her quill, Maggie stretched her back, working out the knots that had gathered after hours of writing.

She'd written ten completed manuscript pages today. Though the words seemed to flow from her unhindered now, she could ill-afford to court another bout of writer's block. Part of her wanted to push on, knowing how much was at stake with this work. But a Muse was an erratic being. Whatever Maggie was doing at this point to keep that creature happy, she had to keep it up.

Better not to test her luck. Ten pages was a marked improvement over no pages at all.

She still couldn't believe how vast a sea change had occurred. She'd had a bare hint of it in London, when she'd spent time with Cam, but this was even greater. Now, everything flowed. From a barren desert to a flood of words. Fear had given way to amazement.

She felt reborn, yet more herself than ever before. She didn't know why the change had happened, only that it had. Something about this place—being surrounded by Cam's presence—seemed to unlock something within her.

She fell asleep dreaming of her work, and woke with it fresh in her mind. It was as though a dull, dry husk covering her had fallen away. Her wings were fresh, still wet. Delicate. She worried still that those wings might tear. But she had to press forward, and not let doubt tug her down.

After sanding her paper and making certain the ink was dry, she put the sheets in the top drawer of her desk. Rising, she gave her back another bend, feeling her spine make a satisfying *pop*. Before, her back would lock up with frustration and terror. Now, it was with the tension born from hours of work. She'd never been so glad to feel the familiar pain.

The cup of tea beside her had gone cold, but she didn't call for another. It already felt peculiar to have people waiting on her. In the days that she'd been at Marwood Park, she still hadn't acclimated to life with servants. She kept saying *please* and *thank you*, a habit she doubted she would ever drop. They might be paid for their work, but that didn't mean that Maggie would take the servants' work for granted. In that, she supposed she would never make a good aristocrat. Not that the chance was forthcoming.

Nor would she take it, if it was offered.

Still, she mused, there were considerable advantages to having wealth and power. That was never in doubt. And now that she had been staying at Marwood Park, she'd begun to dream of a country retreat of her own.

Obviously, it would have to be on a smaller scale than this vast estate. However, the idea of having a place to escape to from the din and burdens of the city seemed a delightful, albeit distant, fantasy.

If having a country place meant this same outpouring of creativity, how could she *not* afford to have it? She couldn't crawl back into that dark cavern of creative barrenness again. That way lay misery. Now, everything was open and bright. Better, even, than it had ever been before. Her opinion of the gentry had altered so much—perhaps that helped open the doors to her creativity. She could write aristocratic characters as *people* now, not villainous archetypes.

It frightened her just a little, how much she felt inspired. She clenched with anxiety, anticipating the retreat of her muse. Yet that fickle creature seemed to have taken up residence—for the moment. Maggie would have to take advantage while she could, and if her muse fled again . . . she'd think of it later. This was all about *The Hidden Daughter's Return*. Future calamity had to remain in the future.

Though she'd done a good day's work, restlessness continued to push at her. Several hours remained until dinner. How to fill the remaining time?

Reading held little interest—she was too unsettled, and it was always difficult to read someone else's work when she was thick in her own. She never had time or interest in the usual feminine pursuits such as embroidery or painting.

A thought whispered: *explore*. She hadn't seen every part of the house. It was overly massive to take in all of it in one round of exploring, and she'd been too busy working to do much investigation beyond her first days here. Should she ask Mrs. Dyrham to show her around? No, the housekeeper was always busy with some aspect of running the domestic arrangements at the estate.

Stepping from her writing room, Maggie ventured out into the corridor. She could just picture gentlemen in plumed hats and lace-draped ladies strolling up and down the hallways, engaged in witty, calculated banter. Someone would be plotting the theft of a necklace to fund the purchase of a prized racehorse, and that, in turn would serve as the basis for future prosperity. The family fortunes would at last be restored.

For now, Maggie had only herself to keep her company. Indeed, there had been several days where the silence had unnerved her, with its absence of human voices. Thank goodness for the voices of her characters in her head, or else she might have been driven to distraction by the quiet.

Yet, her time at Marwood Park was improved by the constant courtesy the staff showed her. Every day, too, little things appeared on her desk. An ebony quill sharpener. A small rhyming dictionary. Sweetmeats in a gilded box.

She knew precisely who was behind these small gifts. She hadn't returned to his private closet since the first day she'd arrived, but she felt Cam around her at all times. When she woke up in the morning and fell asleep at night. Especially when she sat in her writing room, chosen and outfitted especially for her by his own directives.

She passed a chamber and drifted into it. This was some lady's drawing room, judging by the soft colors and china painted with large roses. Did it once belong to Cam's mother?

Maggie picked up a miniature portrait on a small writing desk. A dark-haired, dark-eyed child grinned impishly back. Her mouth curved in a smile. She would recognize that grin anywhere.

She set the portrait down and moved out of the drawing room.

None of her lovers in the past had shown her the same courtesy, the same attention. Were these calculated manipulations on his part? Some form of courtship? Thank God he wasn't here, because he would have seen how much these gifts were working. She caught herself pressing the little book of rhymes to her lips, running the leather binding over her mouth, as if it served as a substitute for the man who'd given it. She pictured him, with his long, dexterous hands, using the pen sharpener, and felt heat building low and unrelenting. He did possess wonderful hands, and it was all too easy for her now to picture those hands on her, caressing her, learning her. He'd be an apt student, who'd come to know her as well as she knew herself. Cam was gifted in that way. She'd no doubt he'd be talented in bed. His kiss had revealed that. And much more.

Maggie entered a room filled from floor to ceiling with weapons. Pistols, axes, swords. A little boy's dream of a chamber. Doubtless young Cam came here often to arm himself for pretend battles.

It was strangely easier to hold him at a distance when they were in London together. There she had well-constructed defenses. But here, with him far away, she could at last indulge in the fantasies that grew more and more abundant. Her imagination didn't fail her.

While she'd been here in the country, she often took walks to clear her thoughts. But it left her mind free to wander and picture scenes she had no right to picture. Cam pressing her against the trunk of a tree, his body's length and his lips against hers. Hitching up her skirts, slowly, slowly, revealing her flesh to his touch and the sunlight. They could bring a blanket, and lay down upon the grass, their kisses and touches growing deeper, hotter. He'd bare her breasts to the sky, caressing and suckling them to aching points. Meanwhile, his clever hands would be busy beneath her skirts, teasing her to readiness. And then . . . and then . . .

Oh, she could imagine the *and then* all too well.

Another portrait of him hung in the East Hall, and all at once she found herself standing in front of it. He was a much younger man in the painting, just returned from his Grand Tour, if the Italian landscape behind him was any indicator. Yet the wicked, knowing gleam was already in his eye, that tormenting smile on his lips. Lips that had caressed hers with wicked sensuality . . .

She shook her head, trying to bring her attention back to the portrait in front of her. It depicted a man with the whole world before him, who was eager to taste life's pleasures.

She went into his bedchamber. It was a substantial room, dominated by a large canopied bed. Maggie couldn't help but imagine them together in his expansive bed, doing all sorts of wicked things to each other.

What was he doing right now? Was he just waking up? Perhaps he took a meal as he read the reviews for the previous night's theatrical performances. Or maybe he was too busy recovering from last evening's debauchery to have much head for reading.

A frisson of something hot worked its way up her

spine as she contemplated him carousing with one of the Imperial's dancers, or an urbane widow.

He can do as he pleases, just as I can. It was just a kiss. But that didn't stop an ember of jealousy from smoldering inside her.

She shook her head at herself. He was her patron, while she was the writer supported by his generosity. A business arrangement. That was all. No matter what his gifts did to woo her. Regardless of what her imagination painted in her mind and upon the canvas of her body. Kiss or no kiss.

For several minutes, she watched the rain from the window in Cam's bedroom. There should be a storm in *The Hidden Daughter's Return.* Perhaps it could trap Alina and her suitor, the disguised Prince Frederick, together in a cave or cottage, forcing them to confront their feelings for each other. The whole scene could be beautifully lit in cool blue, acting as counterpoint to the hot emotions her characters would be feeling.

Damn him, but Cam was right. Her mind felt expansive in this place, no longer hemmed in by cramped walls or responsibility. His presence drifted closely around her, providing shelter in its way, as if keeping the howling winds of doubt at bay.

She'd seen much of the house. Where else could she go? The East Wing had been largely unexplored. She remembered that Mrs. Dyrham had mentioned that it contained the schoolroom, where Cam had spent his formative years.

Before she could question her own footsteps, Maggie headed that way. He remained a mystery to solve. What could she learn about him in the security of his absence?

Servants curtsied and bowed as she passed. After turning down several dead-ends, she finally had to ask a maid directions. The girl helpfully led her up a flight of stairs to the very top floor of the house.

"Here it is, madam," the maid said, waving her toward a fairly plain wooden door. "The schoolroom. Though it hasn't been cleaned in an age. Let me get some other girls up to tidy before you go in."

Maggie smiled. "In a theater, dust is as common as, well, dirt. Nothing I haven't seen before, and nothing I'm afraid of."

The maid looked dubious, but stepped aside, allowing Maggie entrance. Opening the door, Maggie found herself in a medium-sized room with tall windows lining one wall—rain sheeting down them now—and plain wooden floors. Three child-sized schoolroom desks were arranged before a chalkboard. A drawing of a man with outsized genitals scrawled across its surface. So, Cam had been the last one in here.

The maid stammered at the picture, and hurried forward to erase it with her apron.

"No, leave it," Maggie said, holding up a hand. "I think the artist might enjoy seeing his handiwork someday." She gave the maid kind look. "You don't need to mind me in here. If you have other responsibilities, feel free to attend to them."

The girl bobbed her thanks, then hurried away.

Alone in the schoolroom, Maggie allowed her curiosity free rein. The bookshelves held the usual primers and hornbooks, many of them with a boy's handwriting scratched in the margins. A few of the marginalia contained such zesty commentary as, "Bollocks," and "arse," along with more crude drawings. Diligent scholar, that Cam.

Arranged in one corner of the room was proof that there were some tasks to which Cam applied himself. Toy soldiers stood in formation, awaiting orders to march to glory. Nearby was a set of ninepins.

The real Cam drew even closer to her now. He was a man who'd once been a mischievous boy who loved to play, and test boundaries. No wonder he liked coming to the Imperial and thumbing his nose at convention.

He probably drove his tutors to madness. But then, like any boy child of means, he would have been sent to public school. Eton or Winchester or some other bastion of rich male privilege. She opened the top of one of the desks and inside lay a toy soldier. Maybe he'd deserted his unit to follow a comely young village maiden. Or, more likely, he'd had enough of bad rations and not enough rum, and had run off to seek his fortune away from the front lines.

Her parents had always wondered why Maggie couldn't play with her poppets like a normal girl. Instead of having a Papa and a Mama and a baby, she'd enacted bloodthirsty revenge tragedies, with the Mama doll choosing plunging to her death from the dresser rather than be forced into marriage with the Papa doll.

How was her mother? Did she ever think of her lost daughter? Mother was too cowed by the authority of Maggie's father to ever defy him. But maybe, just maybe, there was a day when Mother was cleaning and found Maggie's dolls, and remembered, if only for a little while, her strange girl who couldn't play "ordinary."

Moving on to the second desk, she found it contained a notebook. For half a moment, she considered whether or not she ought to open it. Perhaps it was someone's private journal. But then her boundless, shameless curiosity took over, and she sat down. She opened the notebook and read.

The Pirate Prince
By Cameron Chalton
1801
Enter JACK BELLINGHAM. *A dashing young man with dark hair and dark eyes.*

A play. Written by Cam. Calculating the year, she realized he'd written it when he was in his teens. Perhaps when he was home for a holiday. Bored by being kept indoors, and seeking diversion.

There was no choice in the matter. Maggie had to read it.

Secret identities, setbacks, betrayals, love. A full-scale pirate battle onstage, complete with cannon fire and swordfights. Exactly the sort of story a young man might create.

She read until the sun set, and had to light a candle. When she finished, she read it again, then set it pensively aside. The world shifted slightly, realigning itself.

Why did he tell no one? Not even her? Why had he kept this a secret, inhabiting the role of rake and reprobate, when, in truth, there was another part of him, a hidden self full of dreams and adventure, and, yes, prose that wasn't appalling. His writing was, in fact, good. Had he stuck with it, there might have been a career in it for him.

If viscounts had careers.

It wasn't unheard of for noblemen to write. Though they seldom did so for profit. Art for coin was beneath them.

It stunned her to realize that he was more than a theater-goer, but was, in fact, an aspiring playwright. It was a shame for him to deny this part of himself. Yet society had created a role for him, too, and he had no choice but to play the part of the dissolute nobleman. He possessed a degree of freedom, but he dwelt within a prescribed persona.

Could she ask him about this? He hadn't told her about this very private aspect of himself. If she did say anything, not only would she have to admit to reading his personal writing, it meant bringing them into unexplored territory, far away from patron and artist. That seemed too charged, too dangerous.

It would be a secret they both kept.

A soft tap sounded at the door. Maggie quickly replaced the notebook in the desk and turned around. Mrs. Dyrham stood in the doorway. She gave a knowing smile when she glanced at the chalkboard.

"What did I tell you?" she said wryly. "A hellion."

"Nothing I've seen contradicts that," Maggie answered.

The housekeeper laughed. "Would you be wanting dinner? I can have it ready in a trice."

It surprised Maggie to discover she was, in fact, hungry. "In a moment. Might I ask you something? I hope the question isn't too impertinent."

"That's to be decided, isn't it?" Mrs. Dyrham asked pertly, though she smiled as she said it.

"What are they like, the marquess and marchioness?"

The housekeeper tilted her head to the side as she considered this. "Very respectable. Always treated us servants with courtesy."

Naturally, Mrs. Dyrham would say this. "What are they like as a married couple? I assume it's one of those typical aristocratic marriages—full of responsibility and politeness."

"Well, it may have started that way," the housekeeper admitted. "It didn't begin as a love match, but it evolved into one. A very happy pair."

Maggie felt her brows rise. "Truly?"

"Indeed. Surprising that they only had two children, if you get my meaning."

Maggie wasn't entirely certain she wanted to picture Cam's faceless parents as being carnal.

"A very blessed union."

With this model, it made sense that Cam would not wish to marry. How could he hope to achieve the same kind of happiness, seeing such a paradigm? Instead of making it achievable, a good marriage might seem all the more distant and impossible. No wonder he seemed dedicated to the life of a rake.

A day of discoveries, this. She would need far more than a day to make sense of everything.

A clattering sounded in the hallway behind the housekeeper. His face shining with sweat and excitement, a footman appeared.

"Mrs. Dyrham," the servant panted. "You're wanted . . . downstairs."

"Goodness, Jacob," Mrs. Dyrham exclaimed. "What is it?"

"The master." Jacob looked at the housekeeper, then at Maggie. "The master has arrived."

Chapter 19

Phoebe: Harriet, come quickly!
Enter Harriet.
Harriet: My lady?
Phoebe: You must make certain Alina does not
leave the cottage. Else everything is ruined.

The Shattered Heart

As Cam strode into the entry hall, shaking rainwater off his caped greatcoat, he was met by a host of servants, including Mrs. Dyrham and Mr. George.

"My lord," the butler intoned. "Your communication announcing your intention to reside here must have gone missing in the post."

"It's missing because it was never sent." Cam handed his wet coat and hat to a nearby footman. Outside, a groom was seeing to his tired horse. His carriage, with his belongings and valet, followed at a more sedate pace, given the conditions of the roads. "A spur of the moment decision, George."

"Of course, my lord," the butler agreed with his usual imperturbable demeanor. He drifted off to do whatever butlers did.

"I'll put you in the drawing room with some tea while your rooms are being prepared," the housekeeper said with her usual good humor. She knew him well—almost too well.

She strode off, discreetly snapping orders to footmen and maids.

Cam turned. In a nearby doorway, Maggie lounged, her arms folded across her chest, a faintly amused expression on her face.

How many days had it been since he'd last seen her face, heard her voice? It seemed, now, to have been a fathomless stretch of time, marked only by perpetual gloom. For all that it was raining like the devil outside, something bright and shining opened up inside him to look upon her now.

How had his imagination painted her with so muted a palate? She was dark and light and vivid with life. A torch in a room full of candles. This place was as familiar as his own heartbeat, and yet now it, like his pulse, was made new again. Because of her.

He'd tried, without success, not to think of her constantly en route from London. But she'd drawn him ever forward, even when the rain had poured down and a sensible man would have stopped at an inn for the night. He couldn't have waited. It urged him on, like a whip.

His pulse thundered in his ears now, and echoed low in his groin. Despite the damp, heat throbbed through him just to see her again. His gaze wandered to her mouth, full and ripe.

"London must be experiencing a new low in entertainment," she murmured. "To bring you all the way out here in search of diversion."

He dragged his eyes back to hers. "No diversion needed," he said with a calmness he didn't feel. His body was all readiness. Hours in the saddle hadn't dimmed his reaction. If anything, the horse's pace continued to resonate, mirroring his own heartbeat. He wanted to pull her into his arms, feel her mouth against his, taste her once more. "The tenants' cottages are due for inspection."

She lifted a brow. "I would have thought a man of your stature would leave that to his estate manager."

"Some things I prefer to do myself." She looked delicious, with the firelight lining her curves. Though her dress was modest, it couldn't hide the lusciousness of her figure. His mouth actually watered. He needed to savor her again. "Why, madam, do you accuse me of some ulterior motive?"

Pressing a hand to her chest, she said with wide eyes, "Never say such a thing."

He crossed to her, and she straightened. She smelled of spice. He forced himself to keep his hands at his sides instead of pulling her even closer.

His fantasies in London had been rich, detailed. He'd dreamt of her nightly. That kiss had been only the beginning his imagination. In his dreams, she'd whispered, murmured. Urged him on. Teased him. He'd half-convinced himself that it was only a byproduct of one kiss. But having her so close now, he understood. It was far more than simply a body's hunger. He craved *her*.

Instead of kissing her again, as he longed to do, he offered her a smile. She returned it, though, he had to admit, her smile was somewhat more restrained. Almost . . . wary.

"Does the house not suit you?" he asked, concerned.

"It suits me very well," she said at once. "The writing room . . ." Her eyes turned misty, faraway. "Never would I have dreamed of such a place for myself."

"Every writer deserves it," he answered. He'd give her far more. She had but to express any desire, and he'd fulfill it.

"Here I thought we were all assigned hovels and garrets when we chose the life of the pen." A corner of her mouth turned up, then she sobered. "But, truly, it's beyond my imagination, and I've got a substantial imagination. Thank you."

He waved his hand in dismissal of her praise, though inside, he felt that torchlight burn even hotter, flare brighter. Generosity had always been simple, trifling. He had means. He could give anyone anything. It hardly signified. But with her, he wanted to give and give until she had everything she ever wanted. And even then, he wouldn't be satisfied.

"Simple enough to arrange," he said. "I did none of the heavy lifting."

"I see you're determined to be modest, which doesn't suit you at all." She set her hands on her hips. "How am I to recognize you if not by your swagger and braggadocio?"

"My roguish good looks," he answered.

"But London is full of wicked-looking men. At any given moment, there are fifteen gents all swanning about, looking like Byron."

"Firstly," he corrected, "I do not *swan*. I stride about with masculine, virile purpose. And secondly, Byron imitated *me*, not the other way around." Could she tell that every word she spoke set him higher and higher aflame? His true self, the one that longed for love and did, in fact, dream, had been buried by his role as the reprobate heir. But with her compassion and clear-sightedness she wore away at his veneer. The polished surface gave way to the rough rock beneath.

"Everything you say is debatable," she noted.

"Perhaps so," he conceded, "but I'd like to get out of this damned drafty hallway and have myself a re-vivifying cup of tea. Or better yet, whiskey. In case you hadn't noticed, it's raining fit to bring the second Great Flood, and I was just out in that biblical mess."

She stepped to one side and waved him toward the drawing room, where, he could just see through the open doorway, tea was being laid out. He noted with satisfaction that the whiskey decanter was also present on the sideboard.

"Playing hostess in my house?" he asked her. "The height of impertinence."

"I only imitate my betters," she said with a teasing glint in her eyes.

Though his legs ached from riding, energy continued to move through him. Riding often invigorated rather than tired him, no matter the length of the journey. But despite this, he couldn't remain standing, not when Maggie sat down on a divan next to the tea accouter-ments. So he took a chair opposite her, stretching his legs out as much as he could to keep the blood flowing.

Here she was, in his home. After all the fantasizing, all the long nights with his own hand taking the place of her body in his imagination. He'd been in this room hundreds, perhaps thousands of times. Yet she changed the feel of his home. They were here together, sitting down to tea as if it were a natural and routine thing. Yet nothing about it felt ordinary. Not with her.

She glanced at the arrangement of teapot and cups and sugar bowl, a slight frown creasing her brow.

"I . . ." She cleared her throat. "This is a custom with which I'm not familiar. Not anymore."

"Surely you drink tea," he drawled. She did look fine on that divan. Fine and right, as though she was meant to be there all along in this drawing room, in this house, and this corner of the countryside. She'd lost none of her resiliency, yet there was a kind of welcoming softness to her now that hadn't been present in London. As if a brittle shield had broken away, revealing a woman who looked the same, yet glowed with fresh life.

"Either alone or with people at the Imperial," she answered. "We're not the sort to stand on ceremony. I used to pour tea for my family . . ." Her voice trailed off, and a shadow crossed her face. "I have brothers, you know. Two of them. I haven't seen or spoken to them, since . . ."

"Were your parents cruel? Did they spurn you?" Fury ate at him to think of it.

"I used to rail against them," she replied instead. "Especially my father. He was the one who cast me out when they discovered I'd been ruined. Strangely, for a while, I blamed him more than the nobleman who'd seduced me." Her expression softened. "But I stopped hating my father a long time ago. Now I just miss him."

Guilt throbbed through Cam. He'd been so eager to get away from the marquess's influence, never realizing what a privilege it was to have a father who cared.

She seemed to forcibly throw off her melancholy. "That was a long time ago, and now I've become barbaric in my habits."

"Nothing in my home appears to be broken, you're

wearing shoes, and the house isn't a smoldering ruin," he noted. "So you aren't quite that barbaric. Earthy, perhaps."

A corner of her mouth tilted up. "A politic choice of words, my lord."

He held up a finger. "That title doesn't exist when we're together. It's just Cam and Maggie."

Red spread delicately across her cheeks. A fascinating color, and one he could spend several hours contemplating. "So it is," she murmured. "Meanwhile, as we debate this, Cam and Maggie have no tea."

"Ceremony is an empty thing." Courtesy would have to wait, so he stood and ambled over to the table containing the tea. "It exists only to fill the lives of hollow people." He poured them each a cup, and handed her one. She murmured her thanks and took a sip. Again, that sense of rightness surged through him at so small a moment. It meant nothing, but it felt as though it meant everything—this little domestic scene. She wasn't interested in his title. She cared about him as a man. She engaged him on every level—more than anyone ever had.

He swallowed a mouthful of tea as he watched Maggie do the same. Warmth followed, chasing off the chill. He still wouldn't mind a nice dram of whiskey, but for now, tea would do. Several moments passed as he and Maggie sat in companionable silence. The fire was lit, and it crackled with shared confidences. Rain pattered against the windows, while inside, all was snug and comfortable. Yet he didn't feel quite comfortable. His sprawled pose was only a façade. Alert and edged, he was attuned to her every small gesture, every rise and fall of her chest as she simply existed—yet that existence fascinated him.

"You're enjoying your stay here, then," he said after a while.

"Dare I flatter you by saying yes?"

"In all things, you are daring." Brightness resounded in his chest to hear her response. He'd given her something, something she valued. "And your time here has been . . ." How could he phrase this carefully? It had caused her such pain before. "Fruitful?"

A wicked little smile curled her lips. "Forbidden fruit, perhaps?"

"Nothing is forbidden," he answered.

"So says a man who gives free rein to his appetites."

"If everyone followed my example," he said, "think of what a happier place this world would be."

After what felt like an eternity, she said, "It's been very fruitful."

He wanted to jump up from his chair and pull her into a tight embrace. Something inside him unmoored and soared up, up, higher than the ceiling and clouds, to drift among the stars. It was everything he wanted. Yet . . .

"Why do you sound doleful?" he pressed.

She set her cup down. "It's this place," she admitted after a pause. "I don't want to like it here." She reddened again. "That sounds ungrateful, and I don't mean to be."

"No, I see." He also put down his cup, then leaned back in his chair, folding his hands across his abdomen. He fought against the leaden ball that threatened to sink in his chest. "The city girl doesn't care to admit how she enjoys the country."

"It's more than that." She looked around the room, as if her words were hidden behind the furniture, or crouching behind the curtains. "This place . . . isn't real."

"Don't tell that to my family and ancestors," he said dryly. Easier to hide behind humor than reveal how his emotions were tied to her every word. "They'd be inordinately displeased to learn that the source of their wealth was just an illusion, and we're actually sitting in the middle of a blasted heath."

She sent him a stern look. "It's not real *to me*. What I know . . ." She searched the room again. "The smoke of London. Cramped little rooms and yesterday's meat pies. It isn't having an army of servants waiting on me. It isn't rooms so vast, I could stage a full-scale opera inside them. It's not this profound quiet, the kind of quiet that only privilege can provide."

Understanding hit him, and the lead lifted. "You're worried you might get too used to it."

"This"—she waved her hand at the warm, elegant drawing room—"is only temporary. Eventually, I'll have to return to what I know."

"Marwood Park is always available for you, whenever you want." *He* wanted it. Having her here, being waited on, cared for. But he had to tread lightly. She was a woman who looked upon generosity with a chary eye—and he couldn't fault her caution.

"We both know that isn't true," she said ruefully. "What if . . . what if I can't write when I go back, because I'm too used to this?" Her admission seemed to dismay her, and she stared out the dark, rain-coated windows, which reflected the room.

This was delicate territory. A writer admitting her fear of not being able to write anymore. It was like stealing someone's ability to breathe. He'd have to tread gently, because she was an artist, and because she was her. He'd already walked that narrow line with her before, and had to continue with his subtle handling of the subject.

Yet coddling her wouldn't do. She never seemed to take kindly to being cosseted. It wasn't her way. She was steel and fire, and responded best to a challenge.

"What rubbish," he finally said. "You think that because you've had a few fresh-baked scones and took a walk down some garden paths, that you've suddenly lost the thing that makes you who you are?" He snorted. "That's not the woman I know who told the gentry to kiss her arse."

"When did I say that?" she demanded, looking cross. Good. That was better than the self-doubting melancholy that had enveloped her a moment before.

"Everything you write is a great, big *Bugger off* to aristocrats like me," he countered. "Those characters— Count Le Cyr hunting down Drucilla, and the robber duke, and all the others. With your history, it's no wonder. You don't have to shake your head at me. It's true. Denials are beneath you."

"You know me so well?" she fired back hotly.

"I've seen all of your work," he rejoined. "Multiple times." He leaned forward. "*I know you*, Margaret Delamere. Not everything, but enough. I've seen you on the battlefield. You're a warrior carrying a blazing pennant. Nothing changes that. Not that arse who seduced you. Not me. And certainly not this damn pile of bricks," he added, glancing up at the ceiling. "So if you're concerned that you won't be able to take up your quill again once you go back to London, stop it now. Your determination doesn't simply go away. Nor does your talent. It's always a part of you, and sod off if you ever forget that."

For a long while, silence reigned. All that could be heard was the rain and the fire. Maggie stared at him, her eyes bright, her breathing shallow.

Had he gone too far? Did he push too much? He did think he understood a part of her—on paper, at least. But a writer wasn't entirely her work. Conflating the two was a tricky, dangerous business. He had seen her defiant spirit in action—against him, and against the world. But one's sense of self was insubstantial, and hers, he discovered just then, hers was vital. Even the hardiest of trees could be uprooted in a storm, and maybe he'd blown a little too hard.

Damn it, this was too important to ruin with his clumsy attempts at encouragement.

An apology formed on his lips.

Then, she smiled. A true smile, broad and brilliant. And, damn, did it make her even more beautiful. Desire roared back to life.

"Ah, hell," she said after a moment. "How can I resist such sweet words?"

"You can't." His voice was calm, but he let out a long mental exhale, while his body was tight and aching. "And while you're here, I'll stay out of your way."

She tipped her head. "This temperamental writer thanks you. Only . . ."

"Yes?" he prompted.

Leaning forward, she pressed her hands together. "It might be a bit . . . scandalous. Us here. Together. Alone."

"Thirty servants, not including the gardeners and stablehands—that's not alone," he pointed out.

She lifted a brow. "Servants don't count in the eyes of society."

"Why are you concerned about scandal?" He spread his hands. "You don't run a boarding house for young ladies. And the Imperial isn't precisely rich with virtue."

"My reputation helps or harms my work," she noted. "Especially in the court of public opinion. A man may do as he pleases. He can father scores of children out of wedlock and no one would think the lesser of him. I daresay other men might consider him a champion stud. But if even the slightest spot of rumor attaches itself to a woman . . ."

"She's a pariah," he finished.

"Audiences might stay away from my performances on principle," she confirmed.

He rubbed at his chin. "I'll hire a companion for you. Someone from London, or the village. That should keep the gossipmongers silent." He hated the idea of bringing someone here, interrupting his time alone with Maggie, but he'd hire dozens of chaperones, if that's what she wanted.

Her fingers tapped together as she frowned in thought. Finally, she said, "For all my protestations, I don't want more people running about. It's a careful balance I've struck here, and any new factors could upset it."

"And the chinwaggers?" he pressed.

She pursed her lips. "They can go hang. Especially if *The Hidden Daughter's Return* is a success."

"Forgive me for this breach of decorum," he said, standing, "but this calls for a celebratory drink." He walked toward the sideboard and poured two healthy glasses of whiskey.

"Isn't a celebration a little premature?"

"There's always a reason to celebrate." He turned and held up the glasses. "It's raining. It's not raining. I fell asleep. I woke up. All perfectly acceptable rationales for celebration." He walked to her and handed her the glass of amber liquid. "Here's to telling the blatherers to go rot." He held up his drink.

"To country houses and fresh-baked scones." She clinked the rim of her glass against his, and together, they drank. After a sip, she said, "My god, this is good stuff. But then, I'd expect no less for a rake of your caliber."

"For the next few days," he said with a wry smile, "I'm a gentleman farmer, not a citified profligate."

She laughed. "A farmer. That would be a sight—you out in the fields, behind a plow."

"I do other kinds of plowing."

"That, I believe." She glanced at him through her lashes. Heat rushed through him. And when her fingers brushed his, the heat became a conflagration.

She murmured, "Now, quiet, I have excellent whiskey to enjoy."

They each continued to sip at their glasses, and more warmth coursed through him. The whiskey. The woman. Each potent and fiery.

He didn't often congratulate himself on his deeds. He seldom judged his actions, preferring to *do* rather than wallow in contemplation. But at that moment, he silently applauded his decision to come to Marwood Park. It had been, in its way, inevitable, and now seemed one of the best choices he'd made in a long, long time.

Chapter 20

Alina: Mother—
Phoebe: Hush, child. Run! Run and play inside.
Do not come out until I call you.

The Shattered Heart

Her quill was just a nub. More sharpened pens lay at the ready—they greeted her every morning, so Cam must have directed his staff to prepare them for her.

With each small gesture, pieces of her carefully forged armor had fallen aside. He seemed determined to prove he was more than a title, more than privilege. It was a physical sensation, this bending toward him. She felt it like a caress, urging her to softness. Part of her wanted to cling to what she'd known, foreseeing danger and pain ahead if she let herself be unguarded. But another part of her wanted to relent. She'd been on her own for so long, and here he was, gentling her like a wild mare. Yet he didn't tame her. It was more like he accepted her wildness.

She would miss pre-sharpened quills when her time at Marwood Park came to an end. But she'd been cutting her own pens for years. She'd done it before, she could do it again. Now was only a temporary luxury.

Maggie stood and took several paces around the room, stretching her tight legs. Despite Cam's words yesterday, it was difficult not to worry about what would follow when she returned to London. This place—this house—inspired her. After breakfast this morning she'd rushed to her writing room and scribbled out half a dozen pages. Things between Alina and her disguised nobleman were heating up—lingering glances, accidental touches. An unspoken affinity that grew even when they were apart.

Though she wasn't entirely certain about some of their scenes together. Did they work? She had only herself to judge the merits of her work.

Maggie could imagine several handsome young actors in the role of the aristocratic lover, yet every time she thought of the character, it was Cam she pictured. Cam's voice saying the nobleman's lines. Cam's leanly muscled frame cutting a fine figure upon the stage. She'd never written with anyone in mind before. Not a specific actor, nor even a person she knew as an acquaintance or friend. She might be stirred by a face, but that was as far as it went.

This new inspiration unnerved her, yet felt strangely fitting. She could try to push it away, but what would that serve? She might lose her creative direction, and she couldn't risk that. Besides, it was almost comforting, having Cam inside her mind. A strange alloy of uneasiness and solace.

Earlier, when she had gone to breakfast and had found Cam already at the table, she'd started in surprise, half expecting to see him dressed in the disguise of a hunter. She'd half a mind to call him "Frederick," though the character and the man were separate. She was no Pygmalion, enamored by her own creation.

Cam had been his usual elegant self, smiling at her from one end of the breakfast table, a stack of correspondence beside him, and one long hand curled around a cup of coffee.

He *wasn't* Prince Frederick. She'd had to remind herself of that. And she most certainly wasn't Alina. Though they shared some commonalities, Maggie refused to identify herself with her heroine. There was a difference between the make-believe world of the theater and real life, and woe betide any author who mistook one for the other. Frustration inevitably followed the blurring of those lines. She'd had enough disillusionment in her life.

They had chatted amiably over breakfast, as pleasant as two birds sitting upon the same branch. Nothing of consequence had been spoken, yet it had been a pleasant way to start the day, seeing him across the expanse of mahogany, the sunlight glinting in the curls of his dark hair.

Alina and her prince ought to share a meal together, too. It nurtured intimacy. Drew people together. An old ceremony of binding, the breaking of bread.

"Another roll?" Cam had asked her, as she'd stared off in thought.

"Yes, please," she'd said distractedly. But she'd only taken a few bites before the urge to write again had compelled her to leave the table and return to her office.

"Storm the battlements," Cam had called behind her, laughing.

She'd barely had enough presence of mind to mumble some farewell before she'd been back at her desk, penning the newest act in the saga of Alina and Frederick. A servant had brought her a tray for tea, but Maggie had barely touched it, too engrossed in her work.

True to Cam's word, he hadn't interrupted her all day. In fact, the few times she'd gotten up to stretch her legs and back, he'd been absent from the house. Mrs. Dyrham had told her that he'd been out inspecting cottages, just as he'd claimed the day before. It wasn't a ruse.

For all that she appreciated him staying out of her way, it felt strangely empty in the house without him there. Odd, given that she'd been doing perfectly well without him before. Most likely it was because she was used to having people around at the Imperial, and she'd reverted to her old ways. That had to be it. But would it have hurt him to send Maggie a note, letting her know his whereabouts?

At last, with the sun slanting lower towards the treetops, she was finished for the day. Or, at least, she thought she was. Uncertainty gnawed at her. Was she on the right track with this story? So hard to tell when she was in the middle of it.

Perhaps a walk in the gardens would assist in settling her thoughts, give her some perspective. The rain had cleared out overnight, leaving the day brilliant and golden. Yes, some fresh air would truly help.

She pulled on her shawl, then left her office. Hardly had she gone a dozen steps, when Cam rounded the corner of the hallway, and they both pulled up short. He was in the process of unbuttoning his greatcoat, with a footman trailing behind him, ready to relieve him of the garment. His hair stood up in windblown waves, taking years off of him. Remarkably, he'd shaved, as if wanting to give his tenants a good impression.

He also looked perfectly edible. Strapping and dark, glowing with robust health and masculine purpose. His skin would be cool to the touch at first, but with that underlying heat beneath. Divested of their clothing, wrapped together beneath the sheets, they'd both warm up quickly.

"The scribe emerges," he said with a smile.

"The country gentleman appears," she countered, though she couldn't help returning the smile. Could he read her thoughts? She hoped not.

He eyed her shawl. "Going for a stroll?"

She hesitated. "You could join me," she heard herself offer.

His fingers stayed on the buttons of his coat. "Excellent suggestion."

A bubble of excitement rose within her. She tried to smother it with self-deprecation. "Every now and again, I have a good idea, but it happens seldom."

Cam looked stern, almost angry. "Don't say such things, even in jest."

That was unexpected. "The gardens?" she prompted.

His severe expression fell away, and he offered her his arm. "To the gardens."

Together, they left the house and went onto the wide back terrace, then down into the garden. As they walked sedately along the path, her hand on his arm, he felt solid and warm beneath her touch. Even through the layers of clothing she sensed the leashed strength of him. Though Cam was a known libertine, she didn't doubt he could fight, too, and fight well. But then, he might put that taut body of his to other, more sensual uses . . .

"What a shock," she said, pushing those thoughts

away. "To hear that you were actually tending to your responsibilities."

"I'm not all gallivanting and debauchery," he agreed. "Though my schedule is rife with them," he added cheerfully.

Was that what he did in London while she was here in the country? Did he take some willing woman to his bed and lavish her with the fullness of his erotic knowledge? A man like him, as he'd just acknowledged, wouldn't go very long without female company.

A hot, angry knot formed in her stomach. She tried to force it away. Retreat behind the wall of ice she'd diligently built. Yet those blocks of ice kept melting from the heat of her unwanted possessiveness. *She* wanted his hands on her, his mouth pressed to hers.

They might have kissed, but it made no sense for her to feel this way. They had no claim to each other—certainly not in that way. No obligations. No commitments. The kiss didn't factor into anything.

Even so, this feeling was alien. After her ruin, she rigorously ensured that she wouldn't allow herself to feel anything akin to jealousy toward her lovers. Though they had kissed, Cam and she hadn't even gone to bed. This was irrational, ridiculous. He could sleep with a dozen elegant, worldly widows and it shouldn't matter to her in the slightest. It didn't. No, it didn't bother her at all.

They passed beneath a topiary arch, and he glanced up at it. "I really ought to come to the country more," he mused. "But it was always a little dull." They walked on toward a dry fountain, a statue of the goddess Diana atop it, cool and chaste. But there was nothing chaste about Maggie's thoughts. It was far too easy to imagine herself as Cam's lover.

"And now?" she asked.

He looked down at her, a slight curve to his lips. "I find new interests here."

Their gazes locked. His eyes, she saw now, were not a uniform dark brown, but contained small flecks of green and gold, like autumnal leaves. They were far richer, more complex, than she'd believed. His gaze was a palpable thing, stroking her with warmth, all the way through her body to linger low in her belly and between her thighs.

"Will you . . ." She cleared her throat, and licked her lips. His gaze followed the quick swipe of her tongue, and his eyes darkened. "Will you help me?"

His voice was a low rumble. "Anything."

"I don't know if I can do this," she admitted. "It goes against everything I've believed for over a decade. But somehow . . ." Heat crept into her cheeks. "It feels right."

"Whatever you desire," he said lowly.

"I need you . . ."

His nostrils flared. His jaw tightened. "Yes."

"To read my play," she said.

"I think you did that on purpose," he said wryly.

"I truly do need your help," she said, though in fact, she ought to have expected the look of initial disappointment on his face. "And I never have let anyone read my work until the act is complete. Consider yourself lucky."

His expression cleared, changing from one of frustration to excitement. He looked like a man who'd been given a new phaeton with a nude, willing woman waiting inside it. As though every dream had been fulfilled at once.

It floored her, how much her work meant to him.

"Do you mean it?" he exclaimed. "I can read the next acts of *The Hidden Daughter's Return* before anyone else?"

"Not the whole burletta," she amended. "There's a scene I'm not certain is working, and I think it might assist me if we read it aloud."

"We?"

"I'll read for Alina, and you can be Frederick, the prince in disguise."

"Ah." He smiled. "A disguised prince. I like it already."

They started walking back toward the house. "A premature judgment. You haven't seen it yet."

"But if it has disguises and princes and the daughter of a wronged woman, it's already in my favor."

Inside, they both went into her writing room. Maggie grabbed the sheets of manuscript pages and brought them forward. She held them, and Cam stood very close beside her, his body radiating heat and the fragrance of his cologne. A tantalizing combination.

Glancing down at the dialogue, she realized too late that perhaps reading aloud with him wasn't as brilliant an idea as she'd initially believed. Yes, she wasn't certain about the quality of the work, but there were elements of the scene that could be . . . dangerous. But he was already scanning the page before him, and he'd been so eager, so excited, she hadn't the heart to change her mind now.

"Something isn't quite working in this scene," she explained. "But I'm not certain what. If I hear it aloud, it might help me pinpoint what bothers me about it."

"I begin here?" he asked, pointing with one long finger to the first line.

"Yes," she answered. "Normally, the lines are sung, but as I sound like an angry boar with laryngitis when I sing, I'll spare us both that indignity."

"Come now, I'm sure you don't sing as badly as that," he chided.

She cleared her throat, then sang a measure of "Over The Hills and Far Away."

Grimacing, he pulled back slightly. "Not an exaggeration, then. I've heard finer sounds from drunken toothless sailors."

Scowling, she said, "You needn't agree so enthusiastically." But she couldn't blame him for his response. "Back when I was acting, my singing voice was a detriment. I could never land the lead because I couldn't trill, 'Barbara Allen.'"

His brows rose. "A scribe *and* an actor?"

"I didn't start in the theater as a playwright," she explained. "After . . . what happened with my seducer, I wasn't . . ." She cleared her throat again, surprised that the pain could come again so suddenly and without warning. A buried thorn. Pushing through it, she tried to make her voice as brisk and businesslike as possible. She had told him some of her history, but not all of it, and she needed him to know. She wanted no pretenses between them. "I hadn't anywhere to go. Pregnant as a sow and not a place to lay my head."

A thunderous look darkened Cam's face. He looked fit to kill. "I still cannot believe he got you with child and abandoned you. That bloody bastard. I'll travel to Argentina, hunt him down, and gut him." He paced away, ready to take action.

Oddly, his anger on her part soothed her, muting the pain. "Much as I appreciate your thirst for his blood, I'd rather you not hang for his murder."

"Someone should kill him," Cam muttered.

"I'll settle for maiming," she said, perfectly serious. "Though I doubt that chance will ever be made available to us. We can only hope that providence stepped in, and he was eaten by piranhas."

Cam shook his head, as if dispelling his rage. Yet it still seemed to cling to him, a dark haze of anger. Fury—on her behalf.

Not even her own family had given her as much. Her father had literally tossed her from the front step, cursing her and calling her all variety of names that still burned like brands upon her skin. Her mother and brothers had been forbidden to speak with her—on pain of excommunication from their father. If only one of them had been strong enough to stand up to him. Once, she'd tried to talk to her mother in the Smithfield market, but her mother had just turned and hurried away, saying nothing.

The pain still cut her to this day.

"I managed," she said, though she didn't know why she felt the need to appease him. "Found myself a boarding house run by a kindly woman. She saw me through the bad days, when I . . . Well, you know I have no child now."

He stepped to her, taking her hands in his. Giving her solace. More than desire poured through her, though she felt that as well. There was a profound relief, as if, at last, she had someone with whom to share her burdens. A man strong enough to bear their weight.

"I'm so damned sorry," he said earnestly. "Sorry that you were alone through that."

Maggie nodded slightly. "Those were dark times,

but they weren't without respite. The room next to mine was let by Joseph Delamere, an actor at the Haymarket. A good man, Joseph. Kind. So witty."

He'd been older than her by decades, and pre-ferred the amorous company of men. Of course, she'd been shocked to learn such a thing, but she gradually learned it was far more common than she'd ever been taught. Such desire was illegal, and Joseph suggested that he and Maggie should wed, with her receiving the protection of his name. In turn, he would have the respectability of a wife. A disguise. It had saddened her then and continued to distress her now that he had to keep such an integral part of himself hidden. There had been one man, a Mr. Douglas, who had been Joseph's particular companion. It was a strange arrangement, to be sure, but she'd agreed to Joseph's proposition, and together, they'd made a life, sharing it with Mr. Douglas.

"He helped me get my first parts," she went on. "First at the Haymarket. Later at what was a new the-ater called the Imperial. Mostly I played maids and other secondary roles, because of my demonstrated horrendous singing ability. Every now and then, I got breeches roles. Those were fun." She smiled at the memory of the freedom that came with wearing pan-taloons rather than skirts. She'd even had the chance to wield a prop sword in a few stage duels. One of the most exhilarating feelings she'd ever had.

"I should have liked to have seen you in breeches," Cam mused, clearly delighted by the idea.

"Perhaps you did," she answered pertly.

His gaze misted over at the thought. "I would have remembered."

"Entirely possible," she agreed. "Though at the time, the Imperial's stage was ruled by Miss Eloise Lucchetti, and I doubt you would have noticed me behind her, ah, magnificence." Especially given Eloise's preference for wearing gauzy gowns that revealed quite a lot beneath the lights.

He pressed a hand to his chest. "The divine Lucchetti. How could I forget?"

She swatted him. "Never you mind about her. She's married now with half a dozen children."

"And I have no interest in her now," he answered.

She flushed. "Ah. Well . . . Mr. Delamere saw me scribbling little scenes and skits, and he encouraged me to try my hand at actually writing a burletta. It seemed so ludicrous at first—who was I, to presume that my odd mind could produce something anyone would want to watch."

"Mr. Delamere knew, though, even when you didn't," Cam pointed out. "The seeds of talent were in you."

"Took some time for them to come into flower. When I think about those works from my early years . . ." She shuddered. "It's best that those early endeavors went unperformed. But, with practice, I did get better. And eventually, they did stage my work at the Imperial."

"Your husband must have been very proud," Cam noted.

"Alas, he died of fever only a month before the first performance," she said sadly. Poor Joseph. Still with many years left in him, yet the sickness had come on quickly and without mercy. At the least, he'd died with her and Mr. Douglas beside him. Maggie and Mr. Douglas still corresponded, and, five years later, he'd finally found himself a new companion.

"There's the whole of it," she concluded. "*The Tale of Mrs. Delamere, or, A Fallen Woman's Ascent.*"

"I do love a story with a happy ending," he said, smiling faintly.

"My story isn't finished," she pointed out, and held up the sheets of her manuscript. "This could be my second fall."

"Or your greatest triumph." He glanced at the papers, then back at her. "Nothing keeps you down. I've learned that much."

"That's uncertain. As of late, I think my greatest obstacle is myself."

"Time to get out of your own way," he declared. "Now," he continued, taking a few strides so he stood beside her once more, "let's see what kind of trouble you and I can get into."

He hadn't even read the scene yet, but he'd no idea how much she feared his words would prove true.

Chapter 21

Lord Diabold: After ten years, I have found you!
Phoebe: I wish I had run farther.

The Shattered Heart

Cam's words might have been light, but inside, all was chaos.

Logically, he'd known that Maggie had endured considerable trials. She wore her experience like a mantle, shrouding her in strength and wisdom. Yet he'd never truly understood until that moment how much she'd faced on her own. Seduction, pregnancy, the loss of the child, marriage, the death of her husband. All of it on her own.

It was a wonder she hadn't been bloodied and defeated by everything life had thrown at her. Yet she continued to stand, shoulders back, head up. Her strength and tenacity were marvels he couldn't fully comprehend, but damn if he didn't appreciate them. There was nothing fragile about her—unlike so many people he knew, women and men alike. What had he suffered that could match her experience? Nothing.

He was small and unworthy in comparison. But he

wanted to rise to that challenge. Become a better man. For her.

With those large, fathomless eyes of hers, she watched him now. Waiting. Yes. He could never forget. Not only had she shared a wounded part of herself with him, but she wanted to share her work. Both were precious.

He glanced down at the sheets of paper. Calmed himself. He'd wanted to read her work for so long, but now . . . Now he only wanted to know her. To learn all of her.

He couldn't let her know how much her revelations shook him. She'd retreat, and that was something he couldn't endure.

"I'm shocked to read this," he said.

Her brows lifted. "Too scandalous?"

"No—your handwriting is legible."

"I took pains to transcribe this into a slightly more readable form," she said primly. "But I thank you for reminding me that my penmanship is wanting."

"*My* handwriting is wanting," he corrected. "Yours is as indecipherable as madness."

She made a face. "The purpose of this exercise is to ensure that I'm on the right path, not a critique of my penmanship."

"I shall oblige you, madam. I'm Frederick, I assume," he drawled. "Unless," he raised his voice an octave, "I'm to play the heroine, Alina."

Maggie grimaced. "Vow to me now that you'll never use that voice again."

"I swear," he said, returning his tone to its usual lower register.

She fidgeted with the papers, with them rustling beneath her fingers like restive leaves. "Let's get this over with."

There were times to badger her. Other times it wouldn't be appreciated. Her obvious nervousness touched him deeply.

He cleared his throat, and read. " 'Why do you tremble so?' "

She looked down at the script pages. With his gaze, he traced the intricate curl of her ear, the soft tendrils of hair swept up in a loose knot, and the delicate curve of skin of her nape.

" 'What you see is anger, not fear,' " she read, a slight tremor in her voice. Yet when she spoke again, there was more strength, as if she discovered herself. " 'You have played me false.' "

" 'It is only the sin of omission,' " was his response.

" ''Tis more than that,' " she returned, glancing between him and the written lines. " 'For so long, I believed you to be a simple man, a good man. But 'twas a mask, and nothing more.' "

" 'All masks have truths beneath them,' " he answered.

" 'More of your practiced seductions,' " she rejoined. The woodenness had left her now as she warmed to the role. In truth, she'd stopped reading, and seemed to be reciting the lines from memory. Her gaze locked with his.

" 'With others, perhaps, I have played the part of libertine,' " he said, glancing between her and the paper. He didn't want to look away from her, but he had no choice, needing the written words for reference. " 'Never with you.' "

" 'Ha!' " she cried. " 'Further deceit. You forget, sirrah,

the fate that befell my poor mother. She was unwise with a man of genteel birth, and fell victim to his enticements. I shan't be so imprudent.' "

" 'Is there nothing that can convince you of my sincerity?' "

" 'Nothing,' " she returned at once, eyes flashing.

" 'Then shall I ever be your slave, if only to prove the authenticity of my affections. For, madam, you hold my soul in your palms, and if you are its captor, then I welcome my imprisonment.' " Each line seemed to resonate within him.

Without thinking, he'd lowered his voice, his gaze straying to her lips. She looked ripe, ready for tasting. Her breathing came quickly.

" 'I do not want the keeping of your soul,' " she murmured, glancing, too, at his lips.

" 'It seems neither of us have a choice in this matter. I am yours, madam. Soul and body.' " The words resounded like bells, tolling low and deep and true.

He could not stop himself. He lifted his hand, bringing it up to cradle the firm line of her jaw. She was all softness and strength beneath his touch. The sensation of her skin burned through him, a wildfire of feeling. He tipped her face upward. Her gaze fastened to his.

Time itself drew to a stop, the world ceasing in its rotation, the sun affixed in the sky. Slowly, he brought his face lower, lower, until he felt the soft warmth of her breath against his mouth. He was drawn down, down, into an intoxicating inevitability. Need burned him, unrelenting. He hungered. He wanted.

She raised herself up, meeting him.

Their lips brushed against each other. Once. Twice. And then they sank deeper, opening into the kiss. She was softness and warmth and delicious spice. They tasted each other, tongues slick and seeking, velvet rich. She was open to him, and he was drunk, dizzy with her. Each gave, each took, and together, they were a force unstoppable.

They had kissed once before, yet this was more than sudden desire. He explored her now with the full sense of recognition.

It was hot and needy, but also tender. *I know you, too*, she seemed to communicate with each stroke of her lips and tongue. *We cannot hide from each other.*

The script fell from her hands, drifting to the floor with a rustle, but he barely noticed. He drew her closer, along the full length of his body, as his hand cupped the back of her head. She felt both fragile and ferocious.

Heat roared through him, into every corner of his mind, his body. He was harder than he'd ever been, his cock an insistent force as it strained against the front of his breeches. And, damn and bless everything, she pressed even closer, cradling his length against the soft curve of her belly. She gasped into his mouth at the contact. He groaned.

He filled his hand with the lush abundance of her breast. The point of her nipple grazed his palm. She sighed at the touch. And her clever, bold hands gripped his backside, urging him even closer.

Cam growled.

Yes.

But the sound seemed to break her from their shared reverie. One moment, she was hot and eager against his lips and in his arms, and then—nothing. He was left holding empty air.

His eyes blinked open, as if waking. She stood in front of him, over a foot separating them. Her arms were at her sides, her fingers spread, as if holding something back. Herself, perhaps. She looked dazed, but wary. Almost . . . afraid. Wild.

Only through sheer will was he able to keep from reaching for her again.

"They'd never allow a kiss onstage," she said on a shaky exhale. "Certainly not one like . . . like that. They'd close us down for indecency."

"No audience here," he said, taking a careful step toward her.

She didn't back up, but wrapped her arms around herself, self-protective. "But *I* can see. This wasn't supposed to happen again. We agreed."

"Maggie—"

Taking several paces away from him, she shook her head. She scooped up the sheets of paper and busied herself with straightening them. Then she walked quickly around the desk, placing it between them. She refused to meet his gaze. "This session wasn't as productive as I'd hoped."

"On the contrary," he said gently. "The work is strong. And so are we."

"I need to—" She collected herself, and, as if gathering her courage, looked him full in the face. It was still there, the desire that blazed between them. He saw it in her gaze, in the softness of her lips and the rapidity of her breathing. Yet he also saw her will of iron, and how she refused herself the pull and hunger they shared. "This scene isn't right. I need to rework it."

"I think it went beautifully," he said softly.

"Maybe. Maybe not. I don't know." She turned her back to him, staring out the window. "It needs time."

"Some things cannot be rushed," he agreed. A long pause. Then, "See you at dinner."

Her only response was a nod.

He was more than animal need. With stiff, awkward steps, he took himself out of her writing room. He paused at the door to glance at her one final time. She'd gripped her arms again, as if anchoring herself.

He turned and strode away. Energy pulsed along his veins. He craved her with a ferocious desperation. Cam called for one of his horses to be saddled. In a matter of minutes, he was riding away from the house, needing to quench the fire that blasted him. Fortunately, the animal was young and full of spirit. It let him push them both to their limits, tearing across the countryside. Hills and fields and sky rolled by as he lost himself in movement and being. Yet he couldn't outrun his thoughts.

Between their first kiss and this last one, he knew her now, more fully than he'd known her ever before. The embers of his desire had only grown as a result. The strength of her, the gentleness and ferocity of her heart. This was no mere physical demand. It had strengthened into something more, something more intricate and rich.

In the past, he'd fled such complexity. He lived for pleasure. But now . . . now every part of him ached for her. Including his own heart.

A small stream appeared ahead, and, at his urging, the horse leapt over it. A brief moment of soaring and flight. As if he could loose himself from the bonds of the earth. But he wanted to remain tethered to the ground if it meant more of her.

Did he even have a heart? He'd longed for love, but believed it to be impossible. No woman ever came close to touching him as deeply as Maggie touched him now. He'd originally thought of her as something he could enjoy, take simple pleasure from and move on.

She'd changed all that. With her bravery, her intelligence. Her passion. Through her eyes, he saw he could be so much more than the dissolute aristocrat. She'd made him into more than he ever believed he could be.

He saw her as a person. He was enriched.

But fear still encircled and trapped her. If anything more were to happen, it would be because she wanted it. He would accept nothing less.

He rode on, but no amount of speed could help him leave behind this insistent need. Cam had a feeling that there wasn't enough countryside in England and places beyond that could help him outpace his hunger for Maggie.

The morning dawned soft and gray, a low-lying mist clinging to the ground as if too sleepy to dissipate. Maggie sat at her window, watching the world brightening by degrees. Sleep had eluded her for most of the night, but she'd stayed in her room, too concerned about running into Cam to venture forth and seek some diversion in the library or work out her concerns by writing.

She pulled her wrapper close around her, shifting in her seat. Curse her for being a coward. Yet she was afraid—mostly of herself.

Hearing her words on his lips last night had shaken her deeply, like hearing sheet music finally performed.

It had become alive at that moment. Real. As he'd become even more real to her, if such a thing was possible. Now he filled her mind and resonated through her body.

A long, restless night hadn't dimmed her desire for him. If anything, it grew with each hour, until she ached with it. But could she trust herself with him? It seemed like her old habits were returning. Another nobleman. Another foolish fall loomed.

But Cam wasn't that man. She wasn't so muddled that she couldn't make the distinction between the two. She'd learned far too much of Cam. He wasn't heartless, wasn't cruel. He was generous, kind, thoughtful. Courageous. And that's what worried her. It would be so much simpler if he'd stuck to the role she'd created for him. But he refused to be shoved into that part, and therein lay the danger. How could she protect herself?

Hiding wasn't in her nature. It chafed against her like manacles. She would not allow herself to retreat. If she'd followed that strategy in her life, she would never have made a name for herself in the theater. She would have been unremarkable as a ghost. Flight never gained her anything. She had to face what she feared.

Though it was still early, she put up her hair and dressed for breakfast. It was unlikely that Cam would be awake at this hour, anyway, but if he was, she would face him. And tell him . . . what? That they should never kiss again? She wanted more. To what end? Was everything inevitable? Or did she have power in this?

The only way to know what would happen was to confront the man who was her solace and temptation.

Glancing in the mirror, she noticed the shadows

beneath her eyes from a night without sleep. She was pale, too, and her features looked brittle. A wry smile touched her lips. If she attracted him in this state, then surely his interest was based on more than the physical.

Silently, she left her little room. He hadn't remarked on the fact that she'd chosen the governess's room instead of the sumptuous bedchamber that had been originally prepared, though surely he knew she'd done so. At the least, he didn't try to cajole her into something with which she wasn't comfortable.

She made her way downstairs, passing servants on their morning duties. Strange how much work one house with two residents could cause for the staff. But Maggie had to reconcile herself to the fact that she was there to be served. Still, she wouldn't mind returning to her more solitary, self-sufficient ways, once her time at Marwood Park was over.

And it would come to an end. All of it. She needed to remind herself of that.

Reaching the breakfast room, she started. Cam was already seated at his meal. He didn't notice her at first, so she had a moment to look at him. Unlike her, he didn't appear haggard at all. He was polished and shaven, gleaming with health and vitality. Pale sunlight outlined the dark corona of his hair, which fell in waves nearly to his shoulders. A bandit prince.

Despite her exhaustion, hunger flared to life. Not for the meal arrayed on the sideboard. Hunger for him. The feel of his mouth continued to haunt her. The taste of him teased her senses. He was a man who knew how to kiss. As though kissing was itself actual lovemaking. He'd shown her once before, but now she understood completely. The man was dangerous to her sense of stability.

She still barely believed that she'd possessed enough sense to stop their kiss yesterday from going further, when every inch of her had craved more. She *still* wanted more.

Maggie must have made a sound, for he looked up, and their gazes held across the length of the breakfast room. Another flash of heat resounded through her, centering between her thighs. He stood. Two impulses warred within her: running to him, and running away.

Instead, she walked into the chamber with a confidence she didn't feel. "Good morning." Internally, she winced. What a mundane thing to say.

"Morning," he answered.

She was almost gratified to hear the slight rasp in his voice, as if there was a possibility that he, too, didn't find complete rest the night before.

"I trust you slept well," he said neutrally.

"Yes, thank you," she answered. No sense in telling him how he'd tormented her all night with memories of his kiss, and the need to take that kiss into hotter territory. "You?"

"Dreamless as a cat," he replied.

"You must not have had a cat," she said, sedately filling her plate from the sideboard. "When they sleep, they twitch, dreaming of chasing birds."

"Perhaps I dreamt of chasing other things," he rumbled.

She turned to face him. "Cam—"

He held up his hands, a wry look on his handsome face. "No need to worry about your feathers, Maggie.

This tomcat has no intention of hunting you in the breakfast room." His expression heated. "I want you willing."

More warmth rushed through her, but she cooled it. "And if I'm never willing?"

He seemed to keep his face carefully dispassionate. "Then it goes no further."

She didn't feel assured by this. The greatest danger was herself . . . and her desire.

Strange to have this conversation while she held a plate of eggs and toast. She moved toward the table, but sat at the far end. If she took her place beside him, there was too great a risk that she'd abandon her food altogether and feast on something—someone—else.

Once she took her seat, he, too, sat. A cautious silence enveloped the room as they both ate.

Finally, she said, "I'm surprised to see you awake at this hour."

"It's Sunday," he said, as though that explained everything. At her blank look, he explained, "Church."

"Aren't you afraid lightning will strike you once you cross the threshold?"

He gave her a sardonic look. "Skeptic. Whenever I'm in residence, I attend church. Part of my responsibilities as the lord of the manor." He paused, considering. "Will you come with me?"

It would be a momentous thing, to be seen with her at the parish church. Almost a declaration.

"Much as your invitation is appreciated," she said at last, "I'm afraid if I went, I'd be the greater hypocrite."

"Surely you haven't sinned that much," he chided. "Less than me, certainly."

"That may be true. But I think I'll forgo the pleasure."

"As you wish," he said with a nod. "But you'll be missed. The villagers have never met a genuine playwright before."

"Another time, perhaps." Though she doubted such an occasion would ever exist. For all their desire for each other, she and Cam could never truly dwell in the same world. Too much divided them. Now, and always.

Chapter 22

Lord Diabold: You could not hide from me
   forever.
Phoebe: Though I wish it were so. Base
   deceiver!

   The Shattered Heart

Something wasn't right. Cam didn't have to be an expert in human nature to read the signs. Maggie had appeared that morning at breakfast, moody and uncommunicative. She'd picked at her food, then left with barely a mumbled farewell. Mrs. Dyrham reported to him later that Maggie had been spotted pacing the Long Gallery, back and forth, like a caged cat.

   She wasn't writing. That worried him. She'd been aglow with the fires of creativity. Had it been the last kiss? Was that what had thrown her off? From a distance, Cam could only guess at the mysteries of the writer's mind. True, he'd taken a stab at the process himself during his youth, but he'd known that it was a path he wouldn't have been allowed to follow, and so the practice remained opaque.

   When she'd emerged from her cloud for luncheon,

she continued to move her food around her plate, barely forming sentences. Writers. Who understood them?

"All right." He abruptly stood from his chair and walked around the dining table to stand beside her. "Go upstairs and change. Something comfortable. Something you can move around in easily. Then meet me on the East Lawn."

She glared up at him. "I'm in no humor for picnics or dalliances."

"Neither a picnic nor a dalliance are being offered." He tugged on the back of her chair, pulling her away from the table and the meal she tortured. "Go on."

"Cam . . ." she said warningly, coming to her feet.

"Trust me," he answered.

Irritation fell away from her face, yet she didn't look happy. Still, with a curt nod, she left the dining room, heading in the direction of upstairs.

Cam had his own preparations to make.

Fifteen minutes later, he stood on the wide expanse of the East Lawn, which was bound on three sides by low hedges. As a child, he'd played at blind man's bluff here, chased after hoops with sticks, and been a rough and tumble boy, horsing around with whomever would tolerate his rambunctiousness. Now, he was a man, and had a man's purpose for being out here—the pursuit of a woman.

Maggie appeared at the edge of the lawn. True to the directive, she wore an old, loose gown, which played nicely about her legs and ankles as the breeze blew, outlining her form through the soft cotton. He followed her gaze to his chest.

He wore a padded vest.

She looked over to a blanket, spread upon the grass.

But instead of picnic accouterments, two practice foils lay side by side, along with a smaller padded vest and two fencing masks.

"Where did those come from?" she asked, approaching.

"Never a shortage of things in a huge pile of rocks like Marwood Park," he answered, picking up the second vest. "I used to practice my fencing with my brother over holiday breaks."

"Did he ever best you?"

"Once, and only once." He handed her the vest. "Put this on."

Her brows lifted.

"You told me you've played breeches parts," he explained. "Surely you know how to use a sword."

She tied on the vest, and while it did cover up her womanly assets, it still hugged her body nicely. "I was principal boy in a number of pantomimes. Cherubino, in a spoken version of *Figaro*. Viola, in *Twelfth Night*."

"The duel with Sir Andrew," Cam confirmed. "So you have picked up a sword or two in your time."

"In my time," she agreed. She eyed the two blunted weapons. "Though it was very long ago."

"Surely it will come back to you in a trice." He reached down, plucked up one of the practice foils, and presented it to her. "The body remembers."

She did not take the weapon from him. "*My* body might suffer from amnesia."

"Only if it was a character in one of your plays. Come now." He offered her the sword again. "Fear can't be the thing holding you back."

"I'm not afraid," she snapped, though there was a trace of nervousness in her voice. "This exercise seems pointless."

He brandished the tip of the sword. "Indeed, the points have been carefully filed down."

"You are a wit, sirrah."

"I'm a better swordsman than wordsmith," he admitted, "but I promise I'll let you win a bout or two, just to assuage your pride."

"My thanks," she said sardonically. "Yet I still fail to see the purpose of all this."

Seeing as how she didn't take the blade, and seeing as how he wasn't above a bit of showing off, he gripped the weapon and took a few practice moves, careful to keep the sword well away from her. He went into dueling stance and made a handful of feints, speaking as he did so.

"You've been prowling around the house like an irate bear," he said between cuts and parries.

"A bear!" she growled.

"A she-bear, to be certain, and a lovely one at that, but a bear nonetheless." He lunged, knowing full well it showed off his physique to its full advantage. Shameless, that's what he was. And he didn't bloody care. "Whenever I find myself with a case of the angry bears, I've discovered the best way to shake them off is a bit of exercise. Riding, or fencing."

"I cannot ride," she said.

"But you can fence."

"A little."

"A little is more than enough." He stopped in his exertions and was gratified to see the gleam of interest in her eye. Though she was an exceptional person, she was a woman, and most women seemed to be aroused by the sight of a man practicing a deadly art. "I can teach you as we go."

He offered her the sword once more.

This time, she took it.

"Ah, gloves first," he said, an anticipatory thrill already glinting in him.

They both pulled on pairs of leather gloves with gauntlets. Hers had belonged to his brother when Michael had been a boy. "Masks next," he directed.

The fencing masks went on, covering their faces. He was sorry to lose sight of her behind the rather cumbersome thing, but better that than have either of them face an injury.

She held her sword. "And now?"

"Now, we begin."

He raised his sword in a salute, and she mirrored the gesture. Then they both took fighting stances. Hers was hampered somewhat by her skirts, but her form was admirable. At least, he enjoyed looking at her, alive and ready to act and move. She didn't appear to quail as she readied herself for what was to come.

He decided to go easy on her. He would only prove himself a bully if he made a show of besting her, and it wouldn't reflect well on either of them. So he started slowly, with one gentle pass, only to establish the lines of combat. She avoided the strike, parrying nimbly. The reverberation of steel against steel thrummed up his arm and into his body. Almost erotic.

He tried a simple combination, just a cut to her left hip, which she blocked. Yet she wasn't content to simply defend herself. He deflected her cut toward his head. A neat move, quickly executed. So he countered with a right cut, and again, she parried.

Cam held himself back. For all her adept skill, he was still a trained swordsman, and she knew how to fight onstage, but not truly duel. Yet their blades crossed again and again, and they circled one another. What he thought might be an indulgent exercise quickly turned into a more serious interplay of weapon against weapon. As she advanced and retreated, struck and defended, she revealed the sharpness of her mind, thinking several moves ahead like a chess player.

It was no hardship to see her in motion, too. Lithe and agile, she moved with strength and purpose. There was a time or two when she lost her balance, and once her sword fell from her hand. She wasn't an expert. But she was good, far better than he'd expected, and as their blades met, vibrating with intent, it resounded in his mind, his body. He felt it everywhere. Especially in his cock.

Easy to translate this activity to another, the push and pull, struggling delightfully for the advantage. Oh, she'd be a passionate one in bed, clever and willful. They could wrestle for control—yielding, taking. It was as though they generated invisible arcs of lightning between them, shaped by the energy of their bodies and unspoken sensual purpose.

This was the first time he'd ever fenced while aroused. He'd never fenced with a woman before. But he was hard and wanting, even as he concentrated on their bout. Which made the anticipation and dance all the more delicious, because neither seemed willing to relinquish control.

She must have grown equally hot, because her strikes and defenses came faster, stronger. Until, at last, their swords crossed, held.

Reaching up, Maggie tore off her mask. Hair pins came with it, for her hair came cascading down in a dark, silken tumble. Some strands clung to her damp, rosy face. She panted, full lips parted. The sight was unbearably stirring, his body almost in pain with wanting.

He tugged off his own mask. Cool air touched his skin and along the nape of his neck. He, too, breathed hard. Not from exertion.

They each pushed forward, swords still crossed. Closer and closer they drew to each other, until only inches and steel separated them.

She rose up onto the tips of her toes and kissed him. Cam felt himself fall, losing himself. Lost to everything but her.

Their swords dropped to the ground. They broke apart just long enough to pull off their gloves, as if by mutual agreement they needed the sensation of skin against skin.

He wrapped his arms around Maggie, one hand splayed low on her back, the other tangled in her hair, drawing her as close as possible. She clutched at his taut forearms, feeling the strain of muscle beneath her hands. He trembled faintly, and she was dimly aware that she did the same, shaken with desire like a blade of grass in a storm.

His arousal was hot and insistent against her, and she reveled in this evidence of his hunger. She wasn't alone in this—they would be devoured together by their need. She would gladly meet oblivion if this was the means of her destruction.

Cam kissed her like his fate depended on it. As though he wanted only to touch and taste and know and bestow pleasure. She savored the taste and feel of his lips against hers, hot and demanding.

Vaguely, she was aware of being lowered to the grass. It didn't matter that it was broad daylight on the East Lawn.

"More," she breathed against his lips.

"Anything," he growled. His hand touched her ankle, and she nearly jumped with the exquisite sensation of these two points coming into contact. Just an ankle and a hand, but they held everything in the world. Everything she would ever want.

All her previous objections drifted away, like leaves on a breeze. *This* was what she wanted, needed. She'd been so foolish to deny it for as long as she had.

His mouth never left hers as his hand skimmed higher, under her skirts, tracing along her stocking-clad calf with gentle, rough fingers. She moved her hands restlessly over him, frustrated by the padded vests between them. Feeling him everywhere became imperative.

He'd almost reached the top of her stocking. Soon, he'd touch the softness of her thigh, and go higher, higher. And then . . . he touched her. Intimately.

She bowed up beneath his caress. Mindless pleasure raced through her. A delicious ache built as he stroked her with his long, clever fingers. Heat and need roared through her. She couldn't control the movement of her hips, pushing against him, searching for more.

"That's it," he murmured against her mouth. "Take everything."

"I . . ." And then she couldn't speak as the climax shattered her. She cried out with release, exquisite sensation flooding her as he brought her over the edge.

When the last waves throbbed away, she lay spent and sated, sprawled in his arms.

"God, Cam . . ." She couldn't find other words.

"Yes, Maggie," he answered thickly. "Yes."

But she wasn't finished with him. Not by a long mile. She reached for him, her hand lingering over the placket of his breeches. His jaw was taut, and his wicked, wicked gaze held hers as she began to unbutton him.

Applause and whistles pierced the air.

She immediately pulled her hand back. He tugged down her skirts, and covered her body with his as he snarled at their sudden audience. Glancing up through the shelter of his arms, she saw half a dozen men and women standing at the very edge of the East Lawn, all of them in traveling clothes.

"Oh, God," she said, closing her eyes and letting her head fall back to the ground. "They're here."

"You know them?" Cam demanded as the applause continued.

"I didn't think they'd come here, not with the season in full swing." It was a kind of apology, though her own culpability was questionable.

"Who, damn it?"

Cries of "Brava!" and "Author!" drifted across the grass.

"They're from the Imperial," she muttered. "And they're here to make nuisances of themselves."

So much for solitude. The unfinished passion between her and Cam would continue to burn, and could run rampant if it wasn't soon satisfied. She'd be left with nothing but ashes.

Chapter 23

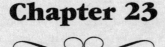

Phoebe: What a foolish child I was to ever think you charming.

The Shattered Heart

Cam often enjoyed playing host. What was the point of having as much as he did if he couldn't share it with others? He hosted guests at his home in London, and he'd thrown house parties here in the country. It pleased him to hear the hallways ringing with laughter, to empty his cellars, to dance and talk and play with others around him doing the same.

At any other time, he'd relish having theatricals at Marwood Park. They'd make for amusing company, full of grand gestures, wild humor, and performance.

It would also drive his father mad, which was itself an inducement.

But with half a dozen men and women from the Imperial now under his roof, it meant his time alone with Maggie had come to an abrupt end. Yes, he would have liked to have taken the encounter with Maggie further toward its natural conclusion. He needed her in his bed, but he could wait. The greater disappointment came from not having her to himself—that was something precious to him.

Cam now walked down a hallway, bearing a bottle of whiskey—mostly for himself. Music and singing emanated from the Blue Parlor. The theatricals disported themselves as the staff readied their rooms. Thank God Marwood Park was a great sprawling heap of a place, with plenty of room for everyone. The actors and actresses of the Imperial had taken control of his house with charming, cheerful audacity. Cam hadn't seen Maggie since they'd arrived, and for that, he could only smile through his teeth. The whiskey would be most welcome.

He could have turned them out, but he wasn't such a churl. No, he'd let them stay for . . . well, his patience had a finite limit, but he'd wait to see what that limit might be.

Entering the Blue Parlor, he found a young actor, Mr. Hems, at the pianoforte. Hems accompanied Miss Brown, who sang an Irish air, while two other actresses, Mrs. Cavendish and Mrs. Llewellyn, gossiped on the sofa. Mr. Fontaine stood beside the fireplace, cradling a snifter of Cam's French brandy, talking with Mr. Singh and—hallelujah—Maggie.

She'd changed from her fencing practice dress into a modest green gown, but he remembered with visceral clarity the feel of her against and beneath him. Her taste. Her fire. Even now, with this house full of guests, the flame had been lit and could not be extinguished.

Looking happy and comfortable, she chatted with her friends. Unseen for now, Cam caught the edges of their conversation.

" . . . only a little fire," Mr. Singh explained, "but enough to shut the doors for a week."

"Was anyone hurt?" Cam demanded.

"No," Mr. Singh said. "It happened just before we went home for the night. The damned cat knocked over a candle."

"Please tell me you didn't get rid of the cat," Maggie pressed.

"He's fine," Miss Brown said with a laugh, "but he lives with Mr. Kingston now."

"Who told us you were away in the country," Mr. Fontaine went on. "And we thought, 'Let's go visit Maggie. She's been awfully wretched and downcast, wouldn't it be a treat to go and cheer her up?'"

"But," Mrs. Cavendish exclaimed from the sofa, "no one told us that Lord Marwood's 'little country house' you were staying at was such a rambling citadel. An impressive and wonderful citadel," she added, catching sight of Cam in the doorway. She lifted her glass of sherry in salute as he came further into the chamber. She was a handsome woman of middle years, perfectly suited to play the Tragic Mother. She also winked at Cam, reminding him that she and the others had caught him very nearly *in flagrante* on his lawn.

"We've lost guests in the hallways and corridors," Cam said. He poured himself a whiskey and carefully set the bottle aside. It would probably be drained by dinner, but there was always more. "Sometimes, at night, you can hear them sobbing."

Mrs. Llewellyn, an ash blond perhaps a few years older than Cam, gave a theatrical shiver. "Oh, don't say such things. They turn my blood to ice. To ice, I tell you!"

"Never fear, madam," declared Mr. Fontaine. "I shall lay down my very life if necessary to protect you."

"Unless a starring role was at stake," Mr. Singh said dryly. He appeared to be around forty, good-looking and lively enough to enact Mercutio. "Then you'd throw your own grandmother into the millpond with a boulder tied to her feet."

"Only if the parts were Hamlet or *the Scottish play*," intoned Mr. Fontaine. He was an older gentleman, white at the temples, but still hale enough to attempt these roles. "Though for Lear, I'd lock grandmamma in a room with only bread and water."

Meanwhile, the singing continued.

Cam sought Maggie's gaze, and found it. She gave him a sardonic look, long-suffering but full of affection for these ridiculous people. They were both appalling and amusing. He'd spent time with theatricals before, of course. A number of his past lovers had been actresses, and he wasn't averse to buying a round of drinks for the entire cast of a work he'd enjoyed. They had a madcap vitality that demanded attention. Some other time, he'd be more than happy to give them that attention. But, damn it, he just wanted to be alone with Maggie.

"How long do you plan on staying?" Maggie asked, reading his mind.

"As long as Mr. Kingston can spare us," Mrs. Cavendish answered. "He's got workmen fixing things as fast as they can, but you know how they lollygag and goldbrick. Don't they understand that *art* is at stake?"

Cam would write a letter to Mr. Kingston, promising double wages to the workhands if they could finish the repairs within the week.

"Art, and box office," Mr. Singh said.

Cam decided he liked Mr. Singh.

The singing stopped, at last, though it was very prettily done. Miss Brown stepped forward. "Do tell us, Mrs. D. How fares *The Hidden Daughter's Return*?"

"Yes—we're all clamoring for it!" added Mrs. Llewellyn.

Cam stiffened. He'd been very careful not to address the topic directly out of deference for Maggie. And, after the last day, when she'd snarled and prowled the house, he wasn't certain how she'd take being questioned bluntly about her latest work.

But, to his surprise, she smiled. "I find my inspiration has been abundant as of late."

"Oh ho!" cawed Mr. Fontaine. "Wondrous news!"

"I'd hardly call it 'wondrous,'" Maggie demurred.

"No, no, no, my dearest lady." Mr. Fontaine strode into the middle of the room and struck a heroic pose. "This is indeed marvelous, and I declare before all the company that it calls for a celebration."

Cries of approval and excitement followed this announcement.

"It's hardly worth a party," Maggie said, interrupting the demands for a fête. "I'm not yet finished with Act Four out of five."

"Nevertheless," pressed Mrs. Cavendish, "in a barren world, your words feed our starving souls—"

"And pocketbooks," Mr. Singh added.

"Thus we *must* grab at whatever joy we can," Mrs. Cavendish continued. "Tonight, we must feast, and have wine, and song."

"Dancing, too!" Miss Brown threw in. "Do let us have dancing."

Everyone turned to stare at Cam. He was, after all, the man whose house would provide for this revelry. All the actors looked at him with imploring eyes. Maggie, meanwhile, looked apologetic. Clearly, this had gotten away from her.

In response, Cam tugged on the bell pull. The butler appeared in less than a minute. "We're having a party tonight, Mr. George. Make all the necessary preparations. Oysters, champagne, cakes. And there will be dancing afterward."

"Of course, my lord," the butler murmured, then disappeared.

Shouts of "Huzzah!" and "Bravo!" filled the parlor. As the actors celebrated the upcoming celebration, Maggie slipped across the room to stand beside him.

"I've spoken to them about," she murmured, "about . . . what they saw on the East Lawn." She blushed.

"And what did you tell them?" he asked quietly. Heat surged through him at the memory.

"That if they were to tell anyone in London about it, they could jeopardize not just my reputation, but the fate of the play and the theater. They agreed to keep silent."

"Good. Do I need to buy their silence, too?"

She shook her head. "They'll do as I ask. They're my friends, and they also know that damage that befalls us could affect their own coffers."

"Sentimental and venal."

"Like all actors." She paused. Then, softly, she said, "Thank you."

"I see no reason to thank me," he said sincerely.

"For putting up with them," she replied. "I admit, they can be rather . . . boisterous."

"They're your friends," he answered simply. "If you care about them, so do I."

For a moment, she merely looked at him. Then she reached down and took his hand. That simple contact rocked through him. Far more than heat, far more than hunger, it reached into him and bound them together with gossamer threads that could not be broken.

"Lord, how you fidget!" Mrs. Llewellyn complained as she dressed Maggie's hair.

"I'm not an actress anymore," Maggie offered by way of apology. She perched on a small, low bench in her room, studiously avoiding looking at herself in the mirror on her washstand. "It's been an age since anyone fussed over me."

"They ought to do it more, my dear." Mrs. Llewellyn spoke around a mouthful of hairpins, each of which she seemed determined to shove into Maggie's unruly curls. "You're as fresh and bright as a rose."

"This bloom has faded."

"Pfft! You know very well that you could give me a run for my ducats if you decided to go back on the stage."

Maggie wasn't certain about that. She much preferred writing to acting, shaping the words and the world rather than being a passive player in it. Still, it was somewhat gratifying to receive the compliment from an acknowledged beauty.

She tugged on the bodice of her dress borrowed from Miss Brown. When Maggie had initially packed for her stay here at Marwood Park, she'd made no preparations for parties. All her clothing was day dresses and simple gowns, nothing suitable for a formal dinner, let alone a small gala. Fortunately, for all her innocent looks, Miss

Brown was far more experienced than her appearance would have one believe. The young actress had packed several evening gowns, and, as they were close in size, it had taken only a few alterations to make this dress fit.

Alas, Miss Brown had a much smaller bosom than Maggie, and that was something that couldn't be adjusted. Maggie's breasts were abundant in this gown, offering far more expanse of bare flesh than she was truly comfortable with. At least Mrs. Cavendish had a spare necklace of paste stones—but Maggie wasn't certain if the necklace hid or highlighted the swells of her breasts.

What would Cam think of her in this borrowed glamorous gown? Nerves danced along her skin in anticipation.

What would Eleanor say if Maggie told her what had transpired? She tried to imagine her friend's reaction. Maybe Eleanor would scold her. Or perhaps she would applaud. Maggie herself didn't know how to feel.

"There," Mrs. Llewellyn said, affixing the last of the pins. "Stop playing the shy duck, stand up, and have a look at yourself. If this doesn't knock that viscount of yours on his arse, nothing will."

"He's not my viscount," Maggie said automatically, but that wasn't true. After their kisses, she'd begun to think of him as hers, in a deep, primal way. It was dangerous, reckless. And yet she couldn't stop herself. Not after this time alone with him. And those kisses . . .

"You don't need rouge on your cheeks, that's for certain," laughed Mrs. Llewellyn. "Not when I mention that delicious man." She held up her hands. "No need to glower at me, my dear. I know he's forbidden."

Maggie hadn't even been aware that she'd been glaring at her friend. She tried to make her expression as placid as possible. But she knew any protestations she made about Cam's availability would only ring hollow. There was no way in hell she'd sit idly by and let any of these well-intentioned flirts have a go at her viscount.

"You haven't looked at yourself," Mrs. Llewellyn chided. "I want you to admire my handiwork."

Drawing a deep breath, Maggie finally beheld herself in the mirror. It wasn't a full-length mirror, so she had to take several steps back in order to get a better view. She wasn't by nature modest or shy, but somehow tonight it seemed much more important that she send him reeling.

She needn't have worried.

The borrowed gown was deep ruby silk, lustrous in the candlelight, and setting off the slightly olive hue of her skin. It boasted short, puffed sleeves, and a gleam of glittering stones nestled at the band just beneath the pleated bodice. It bore no other ornamentation, yet none was necessary. Its simplicity revealed far more than excessive flourishes and flounces.

Maggie's usually untidy mane of curls had been tamed into a high chignon, but a few tendrils had been left loose to curl enticingly beside her face and down her nape. She looked as though she was moments away from being ravished, or invited ravishment.

"How you shine," Mrs. Llewellyn sighed.

Maggie resisted turning and preening. But yes, she did look quite well in the gown. As pretty as she'd ever seen herself. Even more so than at the Ashfords' dinner. And while she'd observed Cam in his evening finery before—a mouthwatering sight—he'd never seen her in such a revealing gown. Her pulse raced in expectancy of watching him look at her.

"Thank you for your labors," Maggie said.

"A pleasure. Now, let's not keep your viscount waiting," Mrs. Llewellyn said, looping her arm through Maggie's.

"You're looking very well tonight, too," Maggie said, noting the other woman's peacock blue gown.

"I am," Mrs. Llewellyn agreed, "but I've a feeling that no one else will notice." She said this without malice.

They proceeded from Maggie's small room down the hall. After threading through the corridors, they reached the main staircase. Talk and laughter already floated up from the ground floor, where the rest of the guests must have assembled. Cam was down there somewhere.

"I'll let you make your entrance solo," Mrs. Llewellyn said, stopping on the landing. "Go on. I'll follow presently."

Swallowing hard, Maggie gripped the bannister and slowly, carefully made her way down the stairs. Down one flight, then another, until she paused at the final landing. Cam stood at the foot of the stairway, resplendent in a dark blue coat that hugged his wide shoulders, and white breeches that reminded her of his deft skill as a swordsman. He truly did have a remarkable form, lean and muscled, with a barely restrained potency. With his dark hair brushed back from his angular face, he looked every bit the pirate lord.

Her pulse set off at a sprint, speeding faster than ever.

She made a small noise, just enough to let him know that she'd arrived. And when he glanced up at the top of the stairs, he froze, like a tiger sighting its prey.

Maggie wasn't above exploiting the theatricality of

the moment. She *was* from the theater, after all. So she took the steps at a leisurely pace, letting him look his fill. If she'd feared his response to her in this gown, she needn't have worried. Raw hunger flared in his gaze as he watched her descend. He looked moments away from dragging her off to some darkened corner and taking her the way a beast claimed its mate. And, God, how she wanted that. Heat washed through her in liquid pulses. Every part of her felt sensitive. She didn't know that one could make love with just a look—but that's precisely what she and Cam did as she made her way to him.

Before she even reached the bottom step, he met her on the stairway. As if he couldn't stop the pull between them.

He stood on one step lower than her, but she still had to look up at him. His eyes darkened even further.

"The hell with the guests," he growled for her ears alone. "I'm going to take you upstairs and have you for dinner. And dessert. And breakfast."

Her stomach clenched with need. "We can't be rude," she murmured.

"It's my damn house," he rumbled. "I'll do what I bloody well please."

"Let's have our party," she said softly. The anticipation would make whatever happened all the sweeter.

He didn't look pleased by this notion, but tipped his head in acknowledgment. "As my lady wordsmith desires."

There were many other things she desired, and a party was very low on that list. But for tonight, she'd live the dream that she'd never known. Tonight, she'd be the heroine of her own tale.

Chapter 24

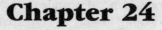

Phoebe: I was ruled by my passions, run wild with desire.

The Shattered Heart

During dinner, the parlor had been readied for dancing. The pianoforte waited with sheet music. As everyone drifted in after dinner—ignoring the custom of separating the sexes—the air was rich with the happiness that good food, good wine, and good conversation could provide.

The actors had entertained Maggie and Cam through dinner with all the latest London gossip. There was never a pause in the dialogue. Everyone had something to say.

Except Cam. Maggie had noticed how quiet he'd been through the meal. Not rude or sullen just . . . preoccupied. But, judging by the fiery looks he'd been sending her across the dining table, she could well imagine what consumed his thoughts. Maggie blushed her way through the meal, too overheated to do much more other than pick at her food and sip at her wine.

Now that the repast was over, the entertainments were to begin.

Cam seemed determined to keep apart from her, as though he didn't quite trust himself to be within touching distance. In this, he was wiser than her. After his declaration about his need for her, she wanted nothing more than to peel that coat from him and perform many explorations with her mouth.

Chairs were drawn into a half circle, and the actors challenged each other to perform monologues from different plays. Maggie sat opposite Cam in the arc, and forced herself to pay attention as Miss Brown recited from *The Way of the World*, and Mr. Singh performed as Pisaro from Aphra Behn's *The Forc'd Marriage*. Spirits were high, and the performances were excellent—but neither Maggie nor Cam seemed to pay them much mind. She felt a little poorly for being such an inattentive audience, but Cam distracted her too much to give her full concentration to the wit of the playwright Congreve. He kept looking at her with sinful promise in his dark gaze. Her stomach gave an answering leap in response.

"Song!" Mrs. Llewellyn cheerfully demanded. Mr. Hems manned the pianoforte, and soon everyone— with the exception of Maggie—took turns singing.

"Our host, too," chided Mr. Fontaine.

With a small, wry smile, Cam stood beside the pianoforte. He murmured something to Mr. Hems, and the first bars to "Let Us Drink and Be Merry" started. Cam sang in a fine baritone:

> *Let us drink and be merry, dance, joke and rejoice*
> *With claret and sherry, the oboe and voice.*
> *The changeable world to our joy is unjust,*

All treasures uncertain, then down with your
    dust.
In frolics dispose your pounds, shillings, and
    pence,
For we shall be nothing a hundred years hence.

Applause sounded after he finished, leaving Maggie to puzzle out the meaning of his selection. It seemed a *carpe diem*, to take what was offered for as long as it was possible, for the future was uncertain. Of that, she knew. Her own fortunes were obscured in shadow, but she had dwelled in the dark for too long.

"Now dancing!" Mr. Hems insisted after the last song was sung.

Yes, dancing. That would get her into motion rather than sit and simmer in her need.

Mr. Fontaine took on the role of musician, and sat down at the pianoforte. Country dances were first, and as they were evenly numbered in terms of men and women, everyone had a partner as they lined up. Maggie was paired first with Mr. Hems, then Mr. Singh. And while she enjoyed the dancing, the speed of her heart didn't have to do with the lively steps.

Finally, it was her turn to partner with Cam. The tune began, and they bowed and curtsied in preparation for the dance itself. Then they moved. His hands grasped hers as they came together and turned. Neither she nor Cam wore gloves, so the heat of his skin burned hers. As did the fire of his gaze as they went through the figures. Country dancing had never felt especially arousing to Maggie before, not like the intimate waltz, but as she and Cam teased each other with their touches, coming together, then breaking apart, then uniting once more, she felt on the verge of combustion.

The dance ended, yet she felt the hot echoes of his touch after they parted. She went for a drink of punch to cool herself down, but it didn't help her thirst.

It was too late for her. She had tried everything she could to protect herself, but the damage had been done. The walls around her had fallen. She was as undefended as a country meadow, and she couldn't find it in herself to regret it. Yet she was not the same girl who'd tripped unknowingly into pain. Maggie knew what she wanted now, felt alive and strong with purpose. Nothing could turn her from her desired path.

The fire burned low in the grate, throwing shadows and gold across the small bedchamber. The house had at last fallen silent after hours of revelry, with everyone finally adjourning to their rooms. Though, given the way Miss Brown and Mr. Singh had been eyeing each other throughout the evening, Maggie rather assumed that not everyone was going to bed alone tonight.

Yet here she was, curled up in a chair in front of her fire, clad in her chemise and night rail. Entirely on her own. Cam had been sending her heated looks all night, but he'd only bent over her hand and given it a kiss of parting before retiring to his room. The lingering impression of his lips on her flesh continued to radiate in sultry echoes. But he'd made no other move to take their dance any farther.

In confusion, she'd gone up to her little bedchamber and readied for bed. Yet sleep refused to come. She was abuzz with awakened sensation. She'd half a mind to see to her own needs, as she'd done on long lonely nights before. But the idea was dismissed. She had no hunger for anyone else's touch—only Cam's.

Should she have been more bold? Whispered an invitation to come to her room after everyone else had gone to sleep?

Or—and here was a thought—why did she wait here, when she knew from her rambles where his room was, and how to get there? Nothing ever came to her just sitting idly by, hoping something would happen. She'd never taken that approach to life, and she wouldn't begin to now.

Resolved, she stood and searched for her slippers. As she did, something sounded at her door. A soft tapping.

Heart lodged firmly in her throat, she walked to her door. Opened it.

Cam stood in the hallway.

He'd lost his cravat and coat, and had rolled up his shirtsleeves, revealing sinewed forearms. He carried no lamp or candle, but his eyes gleamed in the darkness. His jaw was tight, his body alert, primed, as he balanced on the balls of his feet—ready to pounce.

They both seemed to know why he was there.

Wordlessly, she stepped aside to let him enter. He brushed past her, and that small contact made her shiver with awareness. Once he was inside, she closed and locked the door, the sound like a decision being made.

Just the same, a question burned in his eyes as he turned to face her.

"Stay," she whispered.

"And your regret?" he asked, his voice a low rasp.

"There will be none." And she meant it. For whatever the future brought, this night belonged to them. She would hoard it like treasure and never rue her choice.

He was in front of her in an instant, no hesitation, no indecision. His strong arms wrapped around her, and she felt through the thin fabric of her rail and chemise that he was already primed. He blazed, he burned. She wanted to be scorched.

"Glad you picked this room," he rumbled. "It's far from the others, and we're going to be very noisy."

Arousal built like a flood, overwhelming her. "I'm usually very quiet." Much as she enjoyed the act of lovemaking, it had never inspired her to delirious vocalization.

"Not tonight you won't be."

Her head spun.

They came together in a scorching kiss, filled with unadulterated hunger. Mouths open, as if they could consume each other, as if they would subsist on this alone and be happy. She sank into a maelstrom of sensation. His hands roved her body, cupping her arse, stroking up her ribs to rest beneath the rise of her breasts. When he finally took her breasts in his hands, his thumbs raising the tips to hard points, she moaned.

"The first of many," he promised, and licked her bottom lip. "Damn it, I want to go slow. Don't think that I can. I've wanted you for so long."

There was a comfort in knowing she wasn't alone in this colossal need. "Then don't go slow," she urged.

He took her mouth again, shaping pleasure with his hands as he caressed her. Everywhere he touched she felt alive and bright. Her own hands were not idle. Finally freed of his heavier clothing, she could feel his body, its strength, its solidity. He was primal and male, precisely right. She cradled his length between her thighs. They seemed determined to get as close to each other as possible, fusing themselves into one.

He tugged off her night rail. Cool air touched her skin, but she barely felt it, heated by desire and him. With slightly shaking fingers, he undid the ribbons at the top of her chemise. The neckline gaped open. He slid the fabric aside, baring her breasts.

"Goddamn it, you're beautiful," he growled.

At that moment, she felt beautiful. The most potent, powerful woman in the world. To have him look at her like this, as though she contained everything.

He dipped his head, and she gasped as his lips found her nipple. He spoke over her damp flesh, teasing her with warmth. "There's another."

She couldn't care that he was being proved right, not when he licked and sucked, drawing her sensitive flesh between his lips, rousing her to madness. His hand found her other nipple, and he rolled it between his fingers, gently pinching. A sharper cry escaped as sensation rocked through her.

Yet she had power, too. She brought one of her hands down the hard length of his torso, tracing contours of muscle, over the flat plane of his abdomen, lower still. Until she cupped his length. Then it was his turn to moan.

Oh, did he feel marvelous. Thick and eager. For her. She stroked him through the fabric of his breeches. He arched into her touch, reveling in the desire they sparked in each other. Unashamed of pleasure.

When she stroked him more firmly, he stayed her. "I'll make this last," he vowed, growling.

In an instant, they were at the bed. He shucked clothing as they went, first his waistcoat, then his shirt. Bare-chested, he stood before her in the firelight. There wasn't an ounce of spare flesh on him. He was carved with an artist's eye, hard and taut, with dark hair curling along the planes of his chest and trailing lower to vanish beneath the waistband of his breeches. He was desire and sensuality embodied. She wished at that moment for a painter's skill, that she might immortalize his image.

They both worked the buttons of his breeches, releasing him. When the fabric slid down, she wasn't entirely surprised to see that he wore no undergarments. His cock sprang free, and he groaned in relief and pleasure as she took him again in her hand. The living reality of him took her breath away.

He broke away long enough to strip away the last of his clothing. At last, he was nude, and perfect. Of course, she'd seen naked men before. But they weren't as beautiful as Cam. They weren't *him*.

"Keep looking at me like that," he rasped, "and this will be a very brief night."

"We'll make it last," she said, echoing his words.

"Damn right, we will." He eyed the narrow bed, meant for a solitary occupant. "Small."

"We can squeeze tight."

His look was wolfish. "Got plans before that." He gently pressed her back, until she sat on the edge of the bed. Putting her on level with his cock. She had a fair idea of what he wanted, but then he did surprise her when he knelt between her legs.

"Truly?" she asked breathlessly.

"This is my feast," he rumbled. His broad hands slid

her chemise up higher, revealing the tops of her thighs. Then her sex. "Look at you, shining for me."

She couldn't be embarrassed by how ready she was for him. They knew each other. No hiding, no half-truths or constructed identities. The moment was raw and real, the realest of her life.

Muscles in his back shifted as he bent down. His breath fanned over her soaking flesh. And then she clapped her hands over her mouth as his lips and tongue found her. With one hand, he gripped her thigh. With the other, he held her hip in place with enough force to bruise. But she didn't care. All that mattered was him as he made her his banquet. Long, hot glides of his tongue. At her entrance. Around her bud. No part of her went untasted, unexplored. He found her world and learned it through the most profound, intimate touch possible. And, God, did it feel exquisite.

He slid two fingers into her passage. She bucked at the sensation. With faultless instinct, he worked her, mouth and fingers, until she writhed, lost to all rational thought. Heat and sensation built in her, higher and higher. It was tight, rising. She couldn't bear it. It was too much. Too good.

Her climax ripped through her, unrelenting. Scorching and perfect. She bowed back, unable to keep herself upright.

But he didn't yield. He brought her over again. And again. Until she was nothing but pleasure. Formless. Endless. She was loosened from her body, but fully within it, as he worshipped her.

She could take no more. She fell back to the bed, limp and boneless, replete.

He lifted his head and licked his lips, looking like

a man well-satisfied. As well he should. Maggie had never before experienced such pleasure, and in the giving of it, he was an expert.

"Oh," he murmured, "but there's more. Much more. So many lovely things I want you to feel."

"I've got nothing left in me," she gasped.

"You misjudge yourself." He rose over her, lithe as an animal. Carefully, he sat her up, then he stretched out onto the bed. His cock angled sharply upward, pointing to his navel. He held out his arms. "Ride me, Maggie. Take us both there."

At his words, need surged anew. She pulled off her chemise, then knelt on the bed, straddling him. He swallowed hard, body gleaming, desire personified. His shoulders were broad, his rippled torso shiny with sweat. Firelight carved him into sculptural perfection, all hard planes and knitted muscle.

One hand she braced on his shoulder. The other she used to guide his cock toward her entrance. Then she sank down onto him.

They moaned together as he slid deeply into her. He felt . . . he felt like everything. She was alive with him, filled completely.

"Cam," she gasped. "Yes."

"Maggie," he rumbled. "Goddamn it, Maggie. You're . . . perfect."

"I—" But she couldn't speak, not when he shifted his hips, moving within her. She became instinct and need. She moved slowly at first, then with growing speed as sensation gathered. Beneath her, he was taut and hard, throwing himself fully into the creation of shared pleasure. His head was thrown back, the tendons in his neck straining as he too was submerged in sensation.

Release overtook her and she had no means of quieting herself. Her cry of pleasure was one of liberation, freed from the confines of her body. The climax took her all the harder this time because he was within her, because it was theirs to share.

He pulled up on her hips, lifting her. Just in time for him to spend. He was not silent, either, his groan of ecstasy full-throated and unabashed.

She collapsed on top of him. His arms came around her to hold her close, their bodies panting and slick. He pressed a kiss to the top of her head, burrowing close amongst her curls.

"Maggie," he said on a satisfied sigh. "Lovely, lovely Maggie."

His words caressed her. If she was a fool, she could not blame herself. She had done everything she could to protect herself, but in the end, it had been for naught. Despite it all, the many ways she'd shielded herself and the fortifications she had built, nothing had been able to save her from the demands of her own heart.

Chapter 25

Lord Diabold: 'Twas said that a woman heavy
with child was seen in these parts, but I never
imagined that woman would be you. If that is
so—
Phoebe: No!
Lord Diabold: There is a child. My child.

The Shattered Heart

Much to his dismay, Cam awoke in his own bed. Alone.

It wasn't the first time he'd done so after a night of pleasure. Normally, he didn't mind. But this morning, he wanted Maggie beside him, soft and warm and sleepy. Lush and lithe as she lay between the crisp sheets. Would she stretch and smile? Would she crossly cover her head with a pillow, cursing the morning? Either would be delightful.

Last night had been . . . revelatory. He and Maggie had made love twice more, their positions creative in order to accommodate her narrow bed. His body stirred at the memory. Yet it had been more than that. More than shared pleasure. As though . . . there'd been an intimacy beyond the physical. They'd been drawn together by something vast and secret, a bond shared only by them.

He stretched now and rose, nude, from his bed. After taking care of his needs, he washed and threw on a robe to attend to his toilette. He hated to shave—what an irritating chore—but when he saw Maggie again, he was going to have to kiss her. And it wouldn't do to scrape her soft skin with his stubble. So he whisked soap into a lather, and began the tedious process of shaving.

It would have been impossible to stay in her room last night. The bed was too small for two people. But a little bit of discomfort would have been nothing for the wonder of having her in his arms all night. His main motivation for returning to his own chamber had been those damned theatrical friends of hers. Maggie had said they wouldn't go telling tales about Cam and her. Yet he didn't want to take chances and give them more fodder.

He didn't give a camel's arse about gossip about himself. But Maggie had to be protected.

Rinsing the soap from his cheeks, his thoughts drifted back to last night. He hadn't words to describe it. His body felt well-used, yet energized. For all his experience in bed, his time with Maggie surpassed everything. The lovemaking itself continued to resonate through him, as though it recognized what it was to truly know and care about the woman with whom he was making love. Hunger gripped him. He wanted her again. And again. As long as she would have him, he wanted her.

If only his sodding guests would leave so he could be alone with her.

Shaving completed, he bathed quickly, then rang for his valet and dressed. He found himself lingering over his appearance, ensuring everything was just right. Would she prefer the green coat or the russet one? Should he wear the clothes of a rustic gentleman, or a town aristocrat? In the end, he settled on a dark brown coat with matching breeches, and an evergreen waistcoat. White cravat, of course. He wasn't a barbarian.

Thus attired, he took a steadying breath and headed downstairs. He'd never been nervous seeing a paramour. But now his heart took up a steady, hard beat beneath his ribs and his palms dampened.

Lively chatter trilled from the breakfast room. So, the theatricals were awake and availing themselves of his larder and pantry. He didn't know six people could eat so much. Like locusts, they were. Locusts with a penchant for reciting Shakespeare.

He didn't hear Maggie's voice amongst the others, though she had a tendency to be rather quiet when the others were around. Difficult to compete for attention in the midst of that cacophony. He sighed. He wasn't certain he had the temperament today for keeping up with his guests. They were entertaining, but exhausting.

Stopping a footman en route to the breakfast room, he asked, "Is Mrs. Delamere inside?"

The servant shook his head. "Took her breakfast early, my lord. Before anyone else had risen. She's in her study now."

Cam dismissed the footman and debated. Normally, he wouldn't dream of disturbing Maggie at her work, but he needed to see her this morning. Even if only to look at her from the doorway, then slip silently away.

Decision made, he strode to her writing room. He tapped softly at the door.

It opened right away, revealing Maggie on the other

side. "Are you alone?" she asked, looking up and down the hallway.

"Yes."

Relief filled her face, and she tugged him inside, then shut the door quickly behind them.

Before he could speak, she was in his arms, kissing him. He didn't question it, merely kissed her back with the need that seemed constant. His chest felt tight, full. It had been only hours since they'd last seen each other, but it seemed so much longer. Lifetimes.

Yet it was almost worth the wait. She was sweetness and heat, unashamed of her passion. He went hard in an instant. There wasn't an abundance of furniture in the room, but there was a sturdy desk . . .

She pulled back just enough to hold his gaze. "This is real, then," she murmured. "Not a product of my imagination."

"Real as the ground beneath our feet and the air we breathe." She felt so damn good in his arms, as though they'd been fashioned to fit together.

Letting out a shaky breath, she said, "It's a little . . . daunting." She searched for the words. "All this. You and I. I didn't expect . . . I'd no idea . . ." She shook her head, speech seeming to evade her.

"Neither of us did," he said, adding to her confession. "Scared witless as an owl."

She lifted her brows. "Didn't think anything frightened you."

"Unknown territory," he admitted. "I know the world, but not what it's like to have a lover like you."

Gazing at him from beneath her lashes, she said, "You know me."

"I want more," he growled. He kissed her again, greedily. Yes, that desk might do just fine . . .

Fear dissolved, excitement taking its place. *Yes. This. Her.*

A knock sounded on the door. Cam tore his mouth from Maggie's, and forced himself to take a step back. He'd given instructions earlier that this room was sacrosanct, and no one was ever to be disturbed while within. Unless very important circumstances dictated otherwise. Perhaps one of the actors had burned down the South Wing in an attempt to reenact the Sack of Carthage.

"What?" he demanded after he made certain that Maggie had righted her hair and clothes.

The door opened a crack. George poked his face in, just enough to speak.

"Forgive me, my lord," he said apologetically, "but you have a visitor. Mr. Jeremy Cleland."

Damn it. "Show him into my study."

"Yes, my lord." The butler receded.

Alone with Maggie, Cam exhaled roughly, dragging his hands through his hair. "Christ—literally."

"Who's Jeremy Cleland?" she asked.

He tugged on his waistcoat. The news of Jeremy's arrival had been a bucket of icy water, and all of Cam's burning desire cooled. "My cousin. And a vicar."

Cam hated leaving Maggie, but family was family, and he had no choice.

He found Jeremy waiting in his study, as he'd instructed. His cousin stood near the bookcase, examining the volumes there.

"Jeremy," Cam said, coming into the room with his hand extended.

"Marwood," his cousin answered, shaking his hand

and smiling. He was dressed in simple clerical black, his blond curls pushed back. He had a long, angular face, handsome enough to ensure good attendance in church—at least from the female parishioners. A good speaking voice, too, deep and cultured, which had to make sermons moderately endurable.

"Do you normally entertain such, ah, colorful guests?" Jeremy asked, reddening. His cousin was a bit of a naif, but well-suited for the clergy, which was fortuitous, as he was a third son of an earl, leaving his options for inheritance somewhat limited. A good living had been purchased for Jeremy, and he'd been fulfilling his duties as vicar for the past three years admirably. "One of them insisted I serve as Friar Tuck in a pantomime Robin Hood."

So, he'd met the theatricals. "You get used to them. Somewhat. You're a long way from your vicarage," Cam noted.

"I was visiting my father in London," Jeremy explained.

Their fathers were brothers, and Cam had grown up with the younger Jeremy trailing after him. He was a gentle sort, more fitted to reading than roughhousing.

Good thing Jeremy went into the church. Cam could well imagine the young girls of Jeremy's church sighing after him, and claiming need of spiritual guidance in order to secure some time alone with him.

Cam saw Jeremy seldom, as they didn't precisely move in the same circles. "How fares your parish?"

"Very well," Jeremy said. "Christened three babies in the past month. We have a new grange hall, made possible by local donations. But my congregation does seem to have a consuming desire to see me married. They invite me to dinner after dinner, and seating me next to single women. Soon I'll be fat as a bishop from all those meals."

"Yes, I didn't want to be rude and remark on your bilious cast and heavy paunch," Cam said dryly. "Good to hear that everything is well out in the realm of the holy."

Jeremy laughed. "I'm no saint, as you well know."

"But a bit of a prig," Cam teased.

His cousin chuckled again. "Better a prig than an inveterate sinner, like some."

"It'll be much more fun in hell than heaven. At least the amusing people will be in hell."

"Remind me of that when the devils are prodding you with pitchforks."

"Perhaps you aren't as virtuous as I'd thought," Cam mused. "Much as I enjoy seeing you at Marwood Park, you have a flock that needs tending."

Jeremy looked caught. He sighed. "I'll be blunt. Your father asked me to come."

Understanding hit Cam. "He thought I was in need of divine assistance."

Jeremy smiled ruefully. "After you'd become the patron of a theater, the notion may have crossed his mind."

"And what of your mind?" It was too early to drink, but the whiskey did look tremendously appealing as it sat nearby on a shelf.

His cousin shrugged. "You're a grown man, and know your own will. I can offer a listening ear, and counsel when it's welcome. But I don't preach to the unconverted. It's about as welcome as a fly in an iced cake. Nevertheless . . ." He heaved another breath, clearly reluctant. "Word's been going around that you've been keeping low company."

Cam's hackles immediately rose. There was nothing

low about Maggie. She elevated *him*. "You know better than to believe slanderous rumors."

"I'd been inclined to agree," Jeremy said ruefully. "Except . . ." He glanced toward the door and the hallway beyond, toward where the theatrical troupe had ensconced themselves.

"They might be outrageous," Cam answered coldly, "but they're good people."

"Creatures of God?" Jeremy asked with a raised brow.

"Aren't we all?" Cam fired back.

After a moment, Jeremy nodded. "Far be it for me or anyone to cast stones. However," he pressed, "though you are an investor in a theater, it seems like it's getting on time for you to move on from actresses. Even the most incorrigible rake can reform. Think of your friend Ashford. Never seen him happier since he married."

While that might be true, Cam had no desire to have the marriage agenda pushed on him by anyone, especially his young cousin. "Remind me to invite you to dinner," he said. "I know several eligible women who'd adore being wed to a vicar."

Jeremy's mouth curved into a wry smile. "Point taken. However, there's one thing I feel I ought to give you." From his pocket, he pulled out a small, black book and handed it to Cam.

It was a Bible.

"I've marked a few sections that might be informational," Jeremy said, still smiling. "The usual favorites. Prodigal son, and so forth."

"Thank you," Cam said, slipping the Bible into his own pocket. He thought for a moment. "May I suggest some reading of my own?" He walked to the bookshelf and, after perusing the titles, pulled out one slim, red-covered volume, which he presented to Jeremy.

"*The Highwayman's Seduction* by A Lady of Dubious Quality." His cousin read aloud, and frowned. "I generally don't read fiction. Just theosophical treatises."

"You might find God in those pages," Cam said dryly. Only Jeremy would be unaware that the Lady of Dubious Quality was one of the most popular writers of pornography currently active. Her identity had been the object of much speculation, many insisting that a woman couldn't possibly write such superb filth, but to Cam's mind, it was entirely feasible. Who better to know what a woman wanted in bed?

"My thanks, cousin." Jeremy slowly put the book into his own pocket. He sighed. "I shall tell your father we had a very productive discussion of *religious* texts," he said dryly.

"It wouldn't be an untruth," Cam said.

Conflicted, that's what Jeremy was. He had the wild impulses of a man, but the conscience of a saint. Cam had to wonder if Jeremy was still a virgin. Wouldn't surprise him.

"If I may say, coz," Jeremy added, peering at Cam, "you do seem . . . different. Calmer. More at peace."

Cam's thoughts immediately flew to Maggie, and, as they did, he felt a softness come over him. A soothing, warm cascade—even as his heart sped just to conjure her image.

"Perhaps I have undergone my own kind of spiritual awakening," he admitted.

A corner of Jeremy's mouth tilted up. "A *female* spiritual awakening?"

"As though you know anything about it."

Jeremy reddened. "I'm not entirely untutored in the ways of the world."

"When it comes to women," Cam answered, "you're

an utter novice. I'd be happy to teach you a few things."

"Let's save that lesson for another day," his cousin quickly answered. "Well, I've given you my words on keeping company with the fast set, so my duty has been discharged, and I'm expected back in London. I hope to see you again under less pious circumstances." Jeremy offered his hand once more.

Cam shook his hand. "My den of iniquity is your den of iniquity." He meant it. For all that he was of a man of the cloth, Cam always enjoyed his cousin's company and dry humor.

"I'll just see myself out." Jeremy picked up a flat-brimmed hat, bowed, and strode from the room. He left the door open, and after he'd gone, Mrs. Llewellyn appeared.

"Coo," she said, fanning herself. "Who's that delicious morsel of holiness?"

"My cousin," Cam answered.

The actress laughed. "A bit of irony. The rake and the rector."

"Technically, he's a vicar."

Mrs. Llewellyn shrugged. "Must be something they feed your family, to produce such handsome men. Reckon we could bottle it and make millions."

Cam shrugged. He had no need of more money. All he wanted was time with Maggie. And it seemed in very short supply.

That night, the group assembled at dinner. As usual, the conversation flowed easily, and was full of merriment and wordplay, along with several impromptu speeches.

But even such pleasantness had to reach an end.

"My darlings," Maggie said to the gathering. "You know I care deeply about each and every one of you."

"And we adore you, Mrs. D." Mr. Fontaine raised his glass, and the rest of the table followed suit, even Cam.

She continued, "But you have to leave."

"Throwing us out?" Mrs. Cavendish cried.

Maggie only smiled. "Please understand that this comes from a place of deepest affection and esteem. But, much as I value your company, I simply cannot write with your dear, dear faces around me. I find myself too distracted by your presence, and it jeopardizes the progress of my work."

"Of course!" the company exclaimed in unison.

Cam wanted to stand and applaud. "I'll make arrangements for your departure in the morning," he murmured.

"You are all kindness, my lord," Mr. Singh said.

"A toast to our generous host," Mr. Hems added, lifting his wine. Cheers resounded across the table, and another of Cam's bottles of wine met an honorable end.

Across the table, Maggie met Cam's gaze. She winked.

God bless clever women. Perhaps Cam would get his wish for more time with her after all. But for how much longer?

Chapter 26

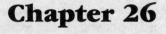

Lord Diabold: Fishhook, search every cottage
until you find that girl.
Fishhook: With pleasure, my lord. I do love a bit
of viciousness.

The Shattered Heart

Maggie stood beside Cam the next day, kissing and hugging the actors as they piled into two carriages. She made promises to correspond when she could, though she had little intention of actually doing so. What she needed, wanted, was peace. Space and time to write. And solitude with Cam.

She was keenly conscious of him as they waved farewell to the troupe. The world had shifted, changed profoundly, since they'd made love. It felt larger, somehow, expansive. Fear and excitement and arousal all warred within her as she watched the vehicles drive away. Soon, she and Cam would be alone together. But as much as she wanted that, she didn't know what it all meant.

At last, the carriages disappeared around the drive.

Cam breathed a sigh of relief. "What a delightful bunch of histrionic parasites," he said brightly.

She chuckled as she and Cam turned to go back inside. "A hard life, being an actor. Meals are scarce and unreliable."

"Explains the devastation they wrought on my pantry and cellar."

"They're shameless, too." They reached the entry hall of the house. The servants busied themselves cleaning up after the guests had finally left.

"And you?" he asked lowly, his gaze burning. "Are you shameless as well?" He took her hands in his, then pressed kisses to her fingers, one after the other.

Need washed through her. It took only this to bring it to life again. He could set her ablaze with the simplest words, the most basic touch.

"Only for some," she murmured.

"Some?" He lifted a brow.

"A very select some," she conceded. She couldn't help it—a thrill went through her to hear his jealousy. She would not have believed he could feel possessiveness for his lovers. And while she valued her independence, it excited her on a primal level to know he wanted her for himself.

As she wanted him. The thought of him taking any other woman to his bed shot twin bolts of despair and fury through her. Whenever she looked at him, touched him, the idea pulsed in every corner of herself: *mine.*

But he wasn't hers—was he?

He must have sensed her drawing back, because he said, "Now that the house is cleared, you can retreat into your writing grotto without fear of being disturbed."

She shook her head. "My mind's still cacophonous. Can't seem to string two coherent thoughts together."

"Another fencing bout?" he offered.

"I've no head for foils and fighting right now. A walk, perhaps."

He brightened. "There's something I can show you. A folly you might not have seen. It's a fair distance from the house, but you'll like it."

"Why is that?"

"It will appeal to your sense of the dramatic. A faux hermitage built fifty years ago."

"A hermit's cottage? What an odd thing to construct on your land."

He looked wry. "Used to be having a hired hermit on your property was the height of fashion."

"So theatricality runs in your blood," she noted.

He considered it. "Entirely possible. We Chaltons do have a flair for the dramatic." Cam continued, sounding like an excited boy, "The place is long abandoned. I heard the hermit went off to become a mercer in Sheffield. Nice and remote. Got a gloomy Gothic feel that might suit you."

"I'm not *gloomy*," she replied. "I'm *profound*."

"Then this place is good and profound, being mostly ruined."

"Must've been a wonderful place to go to as a boy."

He grinned. "Oh, it was. Made for a good knight's castle, or a pirate's fortress."

She could just imagine him there, playing amongst fallen stones and raising all manner of hell. Oh, there went her heart again, softening like melting wax. She was in grave danger, and couldn't seem to do anything about it.

"I'll take you there," he continued. "That is," he added, almost shyly, "if you so desire."

She softened further at his tone. He wanted to please

her, this aristocrat used to having his every whim fulfilled. Now, he wanted to serve her. He would be her ruination.

"I can think of nothing more inspiring," she answered.

He brightened. "You'll want to change your shoes into something sturdier. It's near a half mile from the house, and we'll have to tramp through the woods."

Reluctantly, she disentangled their hands, then hastened up to her room to grab a spencer and don walking boots. Fortunately, she was used to traipsing up and down the rough cobblestone streets of London, so she was prepared for a country ramble. She decided to leave off her bonnet. Annoying things, those ridiculous hats, and since the estate was private, she didn't have to worry about scandalizing anyone with her appearance.

She met him downstairs. Her heart gave that funny little jump it always did whenever she saw him. He'd put on a long coat, but also forwent a hat. Good. She'd be able to see his dark hair gleaming in the pale sunlight, and see it ruffle in the breeze, like the pirate he was.

Instead of offering her his arm, he took her hand. Such a small thing, yet the tenderness of the gesture made her throat tighten. He kept undoing her at every turn.

Together, they went out the back of the house. He guided her through the formal gardens, until they reached a break in the hedges, then he led her across a sweep of lawn toward the edge of a forest. It seemed there was no end to the estate.

They neared the edge of the forest, thick with trees that she couldn't identify. She'd always wanted to know the names of trees and plants, but there were few opportunities in London for botanical pursuits. She'd always been too busy. But now, she had more time. Yet she couldn't concern herself with plant nomenclature when Cam walked beside her.

Finally, they breached the woods, the sunlight growing speckled and the air cool and clean.

"So you ran wild through here," she noted as they picked their way through the trees.

"They'd only see me at mealtimes," he agreed, "and only then if I'd forgotten to nick something from the larder."

She could just picture a dark-haired rascal tearing through the forest, grime-smeared and grinning as he made mischief wherever he went.

"How different our lives were," she murmured. "My earliest memories were behind the counter of my family's used-goods shop, sorting the piles of things that came through every day. It hadn't been a carefree childhood," she mused, "but it had been all I'd known, and so it was precious to me."

Precious and lost.

She shook off that melancholy thought, and concentrated on the pleasure of walking through a sun-dappled forest with an exceptionally handsome man holding her hand. Perhaps Alina and Frederick could steal away to some woods, and there come to learn more of each other, away from expectation and prescribed roles.

As they walked, Cam pointed out certain trees, shrubs, and late-blooming flowers. He possessed a considerable knowledge of the forest, far more than she would have expected from a nobleman who spent most of his time in the city. But then, he spent his youth here. He regaled her with a few folk tales of the area, including the ghost of an abandoned bride that was said to lurk in the woods, and the legend that an entrance to the fairy kingdom existed beneath a massive oak.

"Tried for years to get that damn thing to open for me," he muttered.

"So you could seduce a few fairy maidens?" she asked slyly.

"You impugn my honor!" he exclaimed.

"Have you any?"

"Precious little." He sighed. "Much to my father's consternation."

"And what would he think of you keeping company with a notorious female playwright?" She asked the question lightly, but the need to know scoured her.

"He'd give me another of his bloody lectures," Cam said darkly. "Or send my cousin the vicar back to counsel me. But," he added quickly, glancing at her face, "I've never heeded his advice. Always a sore spot between him and me. Man means well, but he can take his opinions and go rot."

He tried to soothe her, she could tell, but she wasn't able to stop the lowering sensation in her chest and stomach. She and Cam were so far apart, so distant, the chasm of class and position wide and unbridgeable. It was no use pretending—this thing between her and Cam could never last.

It might not survive for long. Life back in London held no room for an affair. She had her work. He had his life as a dissolute nobleman. The two could not be compatible. She had to take what she had now. It was hers to revel in while she could. So she made herself smile and shrug, and focus on the canopy of leaves overhead, the man beside her, the feel of his hand in hers. All of it, she would secret away inside herself to cherish in the cold future.

After fording a small stream, they walked up a rise, and there it was: the hermitage.

"Told you it was a picturesque ruin," Cam said cheerfully, gesturing toward the crumbling structure.

"It is, indeed," she murmured as they neared. It was a small cottage built in a neo-Gothic style, though the glass in the trefoil windows had long since gone. One of the sides had also tumbled down long ago, leaving a half-wall, and ivy ran riot along the masonry. As she and Cam stepped across the threshold, she looked up to see that most of the roof remained intact, though holes here and there seemed to let in patches of sunlight. A handful of birds, startled by the appearance of the newcomers, took flight, chirping their surprise.

The structure itself had once been a neat rectangle, though the loss of one of the walls made it slightly crooked. An old, rotted table and a chair were shoved to one side, but if there had been other furnishings, they were long gone.

She and Cam picked through the ruin, hand-in-hand, accompanied by the sound of their boots on the floor and the wind tousling the leaves of nearby trees. More birds continued to trill, calling to each other.

"Feels like one of those cottages from a fairy story," she said softly, "fallen under enchantment. Doubtless, we'll find a sleeping prince here."

"Let him keep sleeping," Cam said. He turned to face Maggie, his gaze darkening, his features growing sharp with hunger rising to the surface. "This place belongs to us alone."

He bent and kissed her. Thoroughly, deeply. Always, it seemed, they had this need between them, that burned scorching and fast, taking them over in less than a heartbeat. He grasped her other hand, and they stood, fingers interlocked, palms pressed together. The front of her pelisse brushed against his chest. She leaned into him, feeling how unyielding he was, how solid and hot. He licked into her mouth and she moaned. She didn't know herself when she was with him. Or perhaps this was who she truly was, feverish and famished for his touch, his taste. A woman ruled by desire for this man.

She felt herself slowly backed up, until the half wall bumped against her bottom. Then his hands were at her waist, lifting her. She sat upon the remainder of the wall, her hips perfectly fitted with his as he stood between her legs.

"You intended this," she breathed between kisses, glancing down at how well this position aligned them.

His grin was full and unabashed. "A good chess player always plans several moves ahead."

"Is this a game?" she asked.

His expression sobered. "Not to me." He kissed her again, even more deeply, with the taste of urgency and desperation.

"Or me," she whispered, though she wasn't certain he heard her. She gripped his shoulders, holding him tightly to her.

Cool air touched her legs. He gathered up her skirts with hands that faintly shook. They were alone. He desired her. She craved him, growing slick and needy with wanting. How had she lasted a whole night without him?

How had she lasted at all, when *this* was what she craved so fiercely? This devil, this rake, this gentle soul who loved beauty and dreams. He was more, so much more, than she had ever believed.

His hands paused at the tops of her thighs, just below the hem of her drawers.

"Maggie, my lovely girl." His voice was unsteady and hoarse. "I need you so much."

"Take what I give you," she answered.

"And what do you give me?" he pressed, lips against hers.

"Everything."

He groaned. Then slipped his fingers through the opening in her drawers. She jolted at the touch. Another animal sound escaped him to find her damp and ready. She felt shameless, to be doing this in the out of doors, where anyone might find them, but she didn't care. She only wanted him and this moment.

He caressed her, drawing her moisture up and through her folds. Circling her bud, he drew rings of fire that echoed throughout her body. Tenderly, relentlessly, he stroked her, shaping pleasure and more pleasure, a bright wall of fire. It crashed down on her in a cascade of sparks and flame, and she threw back her head, crying out her release. A full-throated cry, away from listening ears. Luxuriating in sensation.

He fumbled for the fastenings on his breeches. And then he was pressed against her—the rigid, thick length of his cock, velvet soft but hard as steel. He guided himself up and down her folds, coating himself in her wetness. The frenzy had her again, as if her climax had never arrived, and she craved him with a furious madness.

Cam slid into her thickly. She gasped, and he gave another feral sound. Positioned as she was, she could see him disappear into her as he thrust, and the sight pushed her over again. She came almost at once.

"That's my love," he crooned to her, his hips moving, his hands tight on her waist. His speed increased. Bands of red stained his cheeks and across the bridge of his nose, and sweat gleamed on his brow and neck. Her climax unleashed something within him, for he pounded into her ruthlessly. She adored it. Seeing him without control, driven to his own madness because of her. They were animal together, making fierce sounds, losing themselves in this carnal fury.

He managed—just barely—to pull out before his own release hit. She watched his seed spill, loving the rawness of it, how there was nothing pretty but everything real about this moment.

They held one another, panting, sweat-slick yet fully dressed. Feeling the beat of their hearts pounding together. Gradually, mote by mote, her thoughts gathered.

How long would all this last? How could it sustain itself once they had returned to London? She had the Imperial, a thousand responsibilities, and nearly fifty people depending on her. He was a nobleman, born to a life of ease and privilege. Despite Cam's insistence, she knew that his father was a man of rank and power. He'd never approve of Cam keeping any kind of lasting company with her.

Two worlds, existing simultaneously, yet always apart.

Their time together seemed as fleeting as warmth in the autumn. Yet she clung to it, to him, as tightly as she could. Maggie had done everything she could to protect herself from heartbreak, but to no avail. Already, an ache spread through her. There was no backing out now, no shielding herself. But she knew, in the deepest corners of her mind, it would end at some point—it was just a matter of when.

Chapter 27

Enter Fishhook, dragging Alina.
Alina: Mother! Help!
Fishhook: It is so much better when they
*   struggle.*

The Shattered Heart

Cam woke, knowing that Maggie wasn't beside him. She'd slipped from bed before sunrise, telling him that she needed to write. He'd fallen back asleep with a smile on his face.

Once they'd returned from the folly, they had raced to his rooms, and there spent the remainder of the day and night in bed. Such a wondrous luxury to make love with her in a true bed, to see her bare flesh wrapped in his sheets, watch her head thrash on his pillows. They'd bathed together—though bathing was hardly the word for what they'd wound up doing in the tub—taken a light supper in his rooms, and made love some more. Drunk on each other, they couldn't seem to get enough. God knew Cam's appetite was hardly sated. He wanted more and more. He would never get his fill of her.

And so, as the first rays of daylight peeked through

the curtains, Cam shifted and stretched, wishing for the warm, soft body of Maggie next to him. He rose from the bed, then washed and dressed quickly. With long, purposeful strides, he made his way downstairs. Until he came to her writing room, where again he knocked.

A muttered answer was his reply.

He opened the door, and found Maggie bent over her desk. Her quill moved speedily across the page, the nib scratches over the pages sounding like an eager bird. She didn't even look up when he came inside. Just kept writing, writing.

Cam crept out of the room, backing up noiselessly. He shut the door with equal care. If she was writing again, like hell would he disturb her. He grinned to himself, warmed at the sight of her hard at work. If the small snippet he'd read had been any example, this was going to be a damned fine play. And it was being written under *his* roof by *his* lover.

He paused as he walked down the hallway. She was his lover. And he was hers. A surge of possessiveness gripped him. Apart or together, they belonged to each other now. As it was meant to be. Since the first time he'd seen one of her works performed, they belonged to each other.

After giving instructions for the staff to take Maggie a breakfast tray, Cam ate his own morning meal. Though he would have preferred to have her beside him at the table, it was enough to know she was nearby. Besides, he would never take away that valuable independence of hers. It was one of the things he respected about her. She might be his lover, but she was her own woman, and he admired the hell out of her for it.

He spent the day out, making arrangements for repairs to a few of his tenants' homes. Overall, everyone's houses and farms were in good condition—but winter loomed on the horizon and a leaky roof made for a long season.

When he returned for a small midday meal, Maggie waited for him at the table. She greeted him with an eager kiss.

"No distracted mumbling," he said, wrapping his arms around her. "That's an improvement over this morning."

She shrugged. "I can't be expected to make decent conversation when I'm working. Consider yourself lucky I made any sounds."

"You're writing, then?" he asked slowly.

A small, wry smile curved her mouth. "I feel . . . motivated."

He lifted a brow. "And what stimulated you?"

Lovely, rosy color filled her cheeks. "As if you weren't there, filling me with inspiration."

"That's a new word for it." He grinned.

She swatted him, but smiled, too. "Let's eat. Much as your company . . . inspires me, I've got more words to write today. And," she added, her eyes heavy-lidded, "I'd like to keep my nights free."

Desire dug its claws into him. But he had to respect her wishes, and so he reluctantly let her go so they could take their meal. She sat next to him, and they talked of the proposed repairs to the tenants' homes. The simple nature of their conversation should have bored him. Yet he found, as they chatted about roofing materials, that it didn't matter what they discussed. He was warm and easy in her presence, yet gleaming with awareness and life. They didn't need to exchange witticisms or barbs.

Just this unpretentious conversation about a mundane topic delighted him.

All too soon, luncheon was over. She kissed his cheek and distractedly slipped away, already in her imaginary world. He watched her go, both reluctant to part with her and exhilarated that she was hard at work.

Maybe he did inspire her. Was it possible? She seemed to think so.

He was a rake with a title. Very little was ever expected of him. He hardly pushed himself beyond those narrow margins. There was no reason to demand more of himself.

But Maggie seemed to believe him a kind of muse. If that was true . . . Light filled him, buoyed him up past the grayness of the world. After thirty years on this earth, years spent in idle dissolution, he'd finally found his true purpose. He meant something to her. And nothing could have fulfilled him more.

Though Cam had several possessions in his study at Marwood Park, he didn't consider himself a particularly sentimental man, given to bouts of nostalgia for times long past. He kept a few favored things that reminded him of a fond moment—the playbill from the first time he went to the Imperial, a rose-colored stone taken from an Italian ruin during his Grand Tour, a wrapper from a boiled sweet he'd had on a trip to Brighton—but overall, he preferred to dwell within the realm of what was rather than what had been.

Yet he knew he would always remember this time with Maggie as the best of his life. He'd grow white-haired, and think back with painful longing to the week they spent alone together at Marwood Park, wishing he could reclaim it, relive it all over again.

Strange to feel yearning for something currently in his possession. But he was aware of a precise, sharp finiteness to every moment he spent in her company. And the more he grabbed at it, held it tight, the more it seemed to slip from his fingers.

They had fallen into a routine once the theatricals had decamped. He normally eschewed routine. The word itself sent prickles of unease and discomfort along his skin. Yet in this instance, he reveled in the habit he and Maggie created. It both eased and excited him, knowing how the day and night would fall into place, anticipating each hour.

After waking, he and Maggie bathed together, which often delayed breakfast by at least an hour. It also completely ruined the floorboards, over which bathwater inevitably spilled. He didn't care about the expense. He'd have the floors replaced a dozen times over if it meant caressing Maggie's water-slick flesh.

Sated, dressed, they would break their fast and discuss plans for the day. Cam always had estate business to attend, and Maggie would outline the scenes she intended to write, her face alight with the excitement of creativity. He loved to watch her as she described her work, and see the play of emotions in her expression—joy, enthusiasm, determination. She couldn't know the pleasure he gleaned from these conversations, knowing he was the first to hear of her work. He felt as though he knew her better than perhaps anyone else, and that was a rare gift.

Maggie was more potent and driven than any steam engine, and that passion was contagious in Cam's own work.

He never thought he'd care for much beyond the pursuit of pleasure, but she inspired him to work, and make something of himself in some capacity besides gallivanting around. He had done the same for her, but it seemed it went both ways. They would part after breakfast, her retreating to her writing room. He would either discuss estate management with his steward or else ride to his tenants' cottages and farms to check in on them. Disappointment at not seeing her during the day weighed on him. Yet he couldn't begrudge the fact that her creativity flowed, and that she was deeply involved in something she loved to do.

Every now and again, he espied her walking alone in the garden, her head down. The breeze would catch bits of muttered dialogue, which made him smile. He knew better than to interrupt her or demand her attention. There was a particular pleasure in waiting for her, anticipation rising like a tide, unstoppable, knowing that they would come together once the sun had set.

Neither bothered dressing for dinner. They had no pretense. Instead, they spoke of everything that had happened during the day. She teased him a little about being a gentleman farmer, but listened and asked questions with genuine interest when he talked about helping refurbish the church, or inspecting a late season lamb. He let her dictate the course of the conversation about her work—it proved to be a delicate subject, depending on how the day's progress went. She could be sunny as a meadow some days, sullen as a waterman on others.

Life with a moody artist had its share of tightrope walking. Yet even that gratified him deeply. He felt rich, inhabiting himself fully, aware of the world surrounding him with a newfound clarity. Instead of chasing meaningless pleasure, he had a purpose, a goal: to strengthen his role as the head of his estate, and to make Maggie happy.

After dinner, they retired to the study to read or play chess or simply sit by the fire, letting the day fall away. She would be golden with firelight. He came to adore that little gap between her teeth, because it meant she smiled, and each smile was a jeweled gift.

Cam would draw his chair close to hers, and as they talked, they would touch—small, playful grazes or longer, meaningful caresses. Sometimes they made it to the bedroom. Other times, he'd lock the door and they'd make love right there in the study. On his desk. Spread before the fire, or interlocked in a chair.

He loved the urgency and heat of those times. But he also loved when they lingered in his bed, taking their time, exploring, learning. She had a spot on the back of her neck that, when bitten, made her shiver with pleasure. He relished when she straddled him and held his hands down, a woman in control. But more than that, more than making love, he prized the languorous hours afterward, intertwined, dozing, murmuring nonsense and truths as the fire burned low. Then they would sleep, replete.

Thus followed the pattern of days and nights. Glimmering and astonishing. Part of him mistrusted this sense of fulfillment. He'd never known anything like it before. It could not last. Yet another part of him gulped the time down greedily, like wine, until he was drunk with it and demanded more. And more.

"I think . . ." she murmured one night, while they were still glistening and gasping for breath. " . . . I think I might be . . . happy."

"Don't sound very sure of yourself," he answered.

"I don't have much experience with the emotion," she confessed.

He realized that he didn't, either. He knew enjoyment, and physical satisfaction. But true happiness . . . That had been a foreign language he couldn't speak. Now he possessed fluency.

"You should," he said hotly. "Every day. Every hour."

"Life doesn't work that way," she said with a sad smile.

"Then I'll do my damnedest to change that." He took her in his arms and covered her lips with his, and they didn't speak again for a very long time.

They never talked of the return to London. As if keeping silent meant it wouldn't come to pass. Where once he eagerly awaited the completion of *The Hidden Daughter's Return*, now he feared it, knowing that once it was done, he and Maggie would have to go back to the city. And then? Would she agree to remain his lover? Or would the pressures of London life tear them apart? He dreaded the answer.

Lying in Cam's bed one night, Maggie watched the flames in the fireplace die. They had exhausted their fuel and couldn't burn any longer. A chill crept slowly into the room.

She and Cam were wrapped in nothing but each other. To Maggie, the silence felt unusually strained, and she fought a shiver.

"How are the plans for the refurbished grange hall coming along?" she asked, fishing for something to talk about.

"Very well," Cam answered. "Funny thing someone mentioned the other day—the space is big enough for assemblies or even, if you can imagine, play performances."

She smiled. "That would be marvelous. Strolling players always need a new venue. Or even," she added, her smile widening, "some amateur theatricals."

"With the villagers as the actors?" he asked quizzically.

"Why not? I'm sure with a deft hand"—she gazed at him meaningfully—"they could be coaxed into some fine performances."

He chuckled, and she felt the depth of his laughter vibrating in her own body. God, these moments felt so precious, so fleeting. She already ached with their loss, even with his arms wrapped around her.

"Perhaps they might perform a work of yours," he teased.

That made her laugh a little. "Perhaps."

"And how fares the tale of Alina and Frederick?" he asked softly.

The incipient chill in the room crept into her veins. Damn. She'd been hoping not to speak of this. Not for some time yet.

Should she tell him? Dissembling to him was an impossibility. Yet once she revealed the truth, everything would change.

But she couldn't lie. He had to know everything, even if it cost them their utopia.

"I've finished," Maggie said.

He blinked at her, but it was willful ignorance. The

world felt as though it had dropped out of its gravitational arc, and now spun wildly out of control. His stomach sank with the motion. Something leaden settled in his chest.

"The Hidden Daughter's Return," she explained, though it didn't need further explication. "It's done."

Cam sat up, propping himself against the headboard. "Congratulations," he said hollowly. "You completed it today?"

She glanced away. "Two days ago."

"You didn't say anything until now."

"No." Her gaze slid to his, shadowed and unusually hesitant.

An entire unspoken conversation flowed between them. But there was no recrimination from him. If he'd had his way, it would've taken her months, years to write one simple five-act work. But as they stared at each other, they recognized that what they'd both wished for couldn't come to pass.

"And now?" she asked.

"What do you want?" he replied softly.

"I want . . ." She wrapped her arms around herself. " . . . To stay here. I want to go home. I want everything."

"Then I'll give you everything." He drew her close. "This doesn't have to end."

"You know it does." She gazed up at him, but resolve shone in her gaze. "I never saw myself as a nobleman's mistress."

"You're a damn sight more than that." He swallowed, his heart beating furiously. He spoke words he'd never thought he would say. Something he never believed possible. "Maggie, I love you."

She inhaled sharply. Her eyes glittered. She brought up her hand to cup the side of his face. "I love you, Cam," she whispered.

His heart broke free from its chains, soaring upward. He felt himself grow to encompass the universe. Simple words, but they changed everything.

"But . . ." she continued, "it isn't enough."

He wouldn't let doubt swamp them now. "Anything you want is yours."

Her mouth quirked. "Even you can't change the English class system. Eleanor and Ashford were the exception. I'm known publicly as a playwright. But she was an unknown. The rules cannot be changed to suit the whims of you and I."

"Maggie—"

She waved her hand. "I ask for the impossible. I ought to be happy with what we have."

"Yet you aren't," he said flatly.

"I'm greedy, Cam. I want everything. I want you."

"You have me." He'd never felt more strongly about anything in his life. "Always."

"That's a promise you cannot make. What if you meet a nice duke's daughter—?"

"I won't."

"But you *might*," she insisted.

"To hell with nice duke's daughters. I don't want them. I want you."

"Yet it can never be permanent," she said quietly. She shook her head. "It cannot work, Cam. If I become your mistress . . . it will ruin me. Ruin my career."

"I'll give you everything," he said at once.

"I don't need things," she answered. "I don't want a cottage in St. John's Wood, or jewels or gowns, or any of the things I know men give their lovers. I'd be happy with just having *you*. But we both realize that the world isn't just you and I. There's society."

"No one else matters." His jaw hardened with determination.

"If I do become your mistress," she pressed, "what do you think will happen to my profession?"

He was silent, knowing and despising the answer.

"Exactly," she said softly. "Word will get out that I've become your lover. It might draw in audiences for a little while, lured by the scandal. Then the public's interest will either turn against me, or die out. I could even lose what audience I've already got."

"I'll keep the Imperial filled to the rafters," he vowed.

She shook her head. "You cannot guarantee that." Her voice clogged with emotion, and her eyes gleamed. "I've worked so damn hard, Cam. Built myself up. I earned my place with my work, not with scandal. Losing it all . . . would kill me."

Fury rose up in him. Not at her, but at the truth of her words, and the ugliness they represented. Bloody social hierarchy. A stone wall built upon a thousand years of tradition. Impossible to scale, indestructible. He never hated anything more than he did at that moment.

"There's got to be another way," he insisted.

"I've thought of all the possibilities," she said sorrowfully. "The only way to avoid that kind of scandal is marriage, and we both know it's impossible. You're a viscount. I'm a lowborn playwright."

"I don't want this to end," he insisted. He scrabbled for a handhold as the ground crumbled beneath him.

"It has to. You've said it to me yourself—you're

not going to wed, and if you did, it couldn't be to a commoner who makes her living from her pen." She pressed her fingertips to his mouth when he began to object. "Please. We only have tonight."

The bitter truth of her words was like ice and steel in his gut. Logically, he'd known that what they shared at Marwood Park couldn't last, but he'd held out a foolish hope. That time would stop. That the world was different. But neither of those things had come to pass. The planet spun. Viscounts and playwrights did not form lasting romantic relationships. Not without destructive scandal. There were facts that even he couldn't ignore.

"One night." He brought his mouth down onto hers, and wrapped their bodies together. If this was all they had, he wouldn't waste a moment. He would imprint himself onto her, as she'd been branded onto him. Whatever the future brought—those long, cold, empty years—he'd be damned if he would ever let them forget each other.

She was part of him now, and always would be.

Chapter 28

Phoebe: My dearest child!
Lord Diabold: She belongs to me, now.

The Shattered Heart

Maggie left Cam while he still slept. Other times, she had done so in order to write, but not today. She couldn't let herself linger another moment in his arms. Her resolve would waver, and she could not allow that to happen. She'd spoken the brutal truth last night: continuing with their affair in London was impossible. For so many reasons, not the least of which was protecting herself.

She let herself look at him a moment while he slumbered. The sheets had bunched around his waist. He slept on his back, allowing her view of his hard chest, the dark hair sprinkled over the planes of his pectorals and trailing lower. A body made for pleasure, that had given her so much of it. But it was his face she held most dear, still angular, even in sleep, with stubble tracing the lines of his jaw, his brows forming dark slashes as he dreamt. Of her?

How she longed to press one final kiss to his lips.

But if she did, she risked waking him, and he might try to convince her to stay. Or at least continue their liaison in the city. Neither were possible. He hadn't offered her a future, leaving her only her work and writing—which would suffer if she became his mistress.

Quietly, in the predawn hours, she crept back down to her room and packed up her few belongings, including the completed script for *The Hidden Daughter's Return*. As she bound it with twine and slipped it into her valise, she realized with a sad pride that it was her best work to date. Happiness was a tapped spring, inspiring her. Would she ever reach the same heights again? Unlikely. Not when the sun had winked out of the sky, leaving her in cold darkness.

Before the sun rose, she took her leave of Marwood Park. A laborer drove her to the village inn, where she planned on taking the mail coach back to the city. She'd no doubt that Cam would offer her the use of his carriage, but no, she would leave as she came, on her own.

As the wagon rolled down the lane toward the village, she fought with every fiber not to turn around and take one final look at the house. That would be too much, too painful. She could only look forward, to the ribbon of road leading her away from him and back to the rest of her life. A solitary, lonely life.

I'm not alone, she reminded herself as she headed to the inn. *I've got the theater. My work. My friends.*

It wouldn't be the same. Not when she left a happiness she'd never thought possible.

The journey to London seemed much longer than her trip out. She shared the coach with a family and a parson, and while the conversation flowed easily between the other passengers, she had nothing to offer.

Instead, she stared out the window the entire journey, not caring if she drew curious stares from the others. Let them wonder.

Her heart sank as they left the countryside, and the landscape grew more and more urban. She'd always loved London, its excitement and variety. Now, it felt grimier and grayer than ever.

The coach deposited her at a bustling inn at the center of town. But rather than heading home to sleep, exhausted as she was, she went straight to the Imperial. People were there at all hours, and she couldn't bear the thought of being alone.

"Mrs. Delamere! She's back!" Cries of enthusiasm and joy met her as she entered the theater. She noticed the newly-repaired section of the wings as performers and stage hands swarmed around her, offering handshakes and even embraces. She met them all with a painted-on smile.

"Is it finished?" Mr. Kingston asked eagerly.

Did the stage manager know that he spoke of more than *The Hidden Daughter's Return*?

"It's finished," Maggie answered.

Celebration and cheers followed, but Maggie didn't join in. She was back where she belonged. Yet she was more alone than ever.

She slept in one of the property rooms at the theater. Going home to her solitary bed would have been too difficult. It was easier to stretch out on a threadbare couch and doze fitfully. She could pretend that everything was normal, that nothing had changed. Lies, of course, but she was a storyteller, even to herself.

Yet as the cast and crew gathered in the morning for

the first reading of *The Hidden Daughter's Return*, she met with an unwelcome surprise.

Cam.

He was in the pit, dressed for town, looking achingly handsome and more than a little angry.

She hurried down to him, her whole body desperate for his touch, yet she managed by sheer determination not to throw herself at him.

"What are you doing here?" she hissed.

He glowered at her. "I'm the benefactor for this production. That hasn't changed." He was ice cold. "I intend to follow this work all the way through its production." Then his eyes blazed behind his frigid mask. As he bent closer, he spoke low and quick. "Like a goddamn thief, you left. Not even a bloody note. Badly done."

"I didn't know what else to do," she said, hating how bleak her voice sounded. "Had I lingered, spoken with you . . . I don't think I could've left."

He inhaled sharply, his jaw tightening. "Searched the whole goddamn house," he growled. "I didn't want to believe you could go without a word."

"I'm sorry," she said, dull with misery. "They say that when you've been wounded by an arrow, the best thing to do is pull it out, sharp and fast."

He only shook his head. "I just wish . . . it could've been different."

"As do I."

Agonizing as it was, she had to turn and walk away. A second desertion. But one in which she had no choice.

A long table was set up in the middle of the stage. Overnight, Maggie's transcriber had made several copies of *The Hidden Daughter's Return*, and now those copies were distributed to the performers, Maggie, Mr. Kingston, and Mr. Sitwell, the composer. There weren't enough for all the people in the theater, but everyone gathered around the table to listen to the first ever full-cast reading.

Cam remained in the pit. Attentive, but removed.

She tried not to keep glancing over to him, but her gaze found its way to Cam without any effort on her part. Or rather, it took too much strain to *not* look at him. Strange to see him here again, where they'd first come to know each other. But Marwood Park was where they'd truly learned who they were, and to have him back in this environment felt odd, unnatural. They were meant to be together in the fields surrounding his country estate, or wrapped together in his bed.

Now they were strangers in the city again. And it felt profoundly wrong.

Roles were assigned and reassigned, and finally, after copious amounts of tea and coffee were consumed, everyone settled down to the reading. The score would come later, but Mr. Sitwell would be present in order to assess the work's musical needs.

Absolute silence reigned as the cast spoke their lines aloud. There were a few chuckles here and there when a bit of comic business came up. And—even better—sniffs and quiet weeping during the emotional, sentimental scenes. Maggie was on edge the entire time. She tried to keep her attention on the document in front of her, rather than anxiously scanning everyone's faces. This work was a departure for her. Not the least of which was the fact that it had a happy ending. She didn't know how that might be received, after delivering tragedy upon tragedy.

Finally, the last line was uttered by the actress playing Alina.

"'A limitless future is ours,'" she read.

More silence. Maggie knotted her hands in her lap. Not only was this the first time that anyone had ever heard this work, it was also Cam's initial listening to the entirety of the burletta. His opinion, more than anyone else's, carried the most weight.

And then . . .

Clapping. But it didn't come from any of the cast or crew. Where, then?

It originated in the pit.

Cam. He'd stood. Applauded. His eyes shone, but his expression was opaque.

In an instant, everyone else followed suit. They, too, had gotten to their feet. And to a one, they clapped. That had never happened during a reading before.

An edged joy overwhelmed her in a bittersweet tide.

Rehearsals began in earnest the following day. The performers stood on stage, holding copies of their scripts, learning their lines as they did rudimentary blocking—as decided by the actors, led by Mr. Fontaine, and Maggie. Mr. Sitwell was in the back, working on the music,

For Maggie, it was a blessing to throw herself back into the process of work, surrounded by so many people. She was all over the stage, advising on how a line should be read, suggesting a particular pose or action, and guiding the whole process.

Yet all the while, she felt conscious of Cam, sitting in the pit. Whenever she glanced over at him, he watched her, not the actors. Heat and cold washed over her each time, and a harrowing sense of loss that felt like a cavern in her chest, empty and echoing. She'd slept at the theater again—if one could call it sleep. Anything to keep herself from feeling his absence. But that was a futile pursuit. She couldn't envision a time when she would not want him, miss him.

Strange that she'd written so much of heartbreak, and had experienced it so bitterly with the death of her daughter, yet this was a new pain. What she had felt for her seducer had been a juvenile infatuation, crumbled to dust with the cold realization that she'd been just a diversion to him. But loving Cam, knowing that he loved her, and that it wasn't enough . . .

She couldn't eat. Barely slept. More torment came in the form of thoughts that the fate of the Imperial rested on the success of this work. If she survived the next few weeks without winking out like an extinguished candle, it would be nothing short of miraculous.

She ran herself ragged. That was the only succor in this sea of misery. Work had to be her solace, for that was all she had left.

And yet, hours into the rehearsal, a voice cried out at the entrance to the theater.

"Stop this play at once!"

Everyone stilled as an irate, prosperous-looking middle aged man strode down the aisle.

Cam intercepted him. "I'm Lord Marwood," he said with supreme aristocratic coldness. "What's the meaning of this?"

"This play can't go on," the stranger said.

Exclamations of shock rose up from the crew and performers.

Mr. Kingston shouldered his way to the front of the stage. "According to whom?" he queried, an edge in his voice.

From inside his coat, the man brandished a sheet of paper. "I'm Mr. Scanlon, from the Lord Chamberlain's office. This play is unlicensed. Only the Theater Royal and Covent Garden have patents to perform spoken word plays."

"But this work is a burletta," Maggie objected.

"I hear no musical accompaniment," Mr. Scanlon sniffed. He cupped a hand to his ear and made a show of listening to the silence.

"It's to be provided in the next few days," Cam growled. "We can summon the composer at once. Go and fetch Mr. Sitwell," he ordered one of the stage hands. The man hurried off.

"All activities in this theater associated with this work must cease immediately." Mr. Scanlon looked haughty as he made his pronouncement. "Or else the theater itself will be closed permanently." With that he turned and stalked out.

Mr. Sitwell finally appeared onstage, panting. "I have the first measures of the score here." He held up a lined sheet of paper.

"Too late," Mr. Kingston groaned.

Panic spread within moments. Everyone was in an uproar.

"Quiet!" Cam shouted, his arms spread wide. As one, the crowd silenced, turning to him. Maggie fixed all her attention on Cam.

"I'll find a way to fix this," he continued in a more

sedate voice. Though this seemed to pacify most of the group, restiveness continued to rustle among them.

"We've already announced the opening performance," Maggie felt obliged to point out. Fear tore at the edges of her composure, making her tattered and threadbare. Lead lined her stomach. Disaster seemed moments away. "It's in just two weeks' time. We've presold tickets for the first three nights. Any delay, even a few days, is a costly one. There could literally be a riot if we don't meet the audience's demands for a timely performance." Theater-goers in London were notorious for breaking into violent unrest at the slightest provocation.

"Scanlon said that activities in the theater weren't permitted," Cam noted. "But he didn't say that the rehearsals couldn't continue."

Mr. Kingston frowned. "If we don't rehearse here, there's nowhere else we can go."

"Untrue." He turned to Maggie and offered her a wry smile. "My London home has a ballroom that's currently out of use. It can more than easily accommodate the performers."

"And we'll be expecting you to work double-time, Mr. Sitwell," Maggie added, looking at the composer.

"Of course," he answered.

"Then it's settled," said Cam. "Rehearsals will continue at my home."

At this announcement, cheers went up amongst the cast and crew. Meanwhile, Maggie could only stare at Cam. His smile continued for her, but it was small and poignant.

Tears burned her eyes. Damn him. The burletta would go on. Her career was safe. She was getting most everything she wanted, but it cost her all she had.

Chapter 29

Phoebe pulls Alina free.
Phoebe: Run, my love! Never look back.
Alina: But, Mother—
Phoebe: Doubt not my love for you. Now go!
Alina runs away.

The Shattered Heart

Early the next morning, Cam made a visit to the Lord Chamberlain's office. Aside from his Parliamentary duties, he was unused to visiting places of such import. He tried not to feel too out of place as he made his way down gleaming corridors and past soberly-dressed men, finally finding himself in an antechamber where another bloke ushered him into the Lord Chamberlain's office proper.

The meeting went quickly, to Cam's surprise. The current Lord Chamberlain was the Marquess of Hertford, an old friend of Cam's father. In moments, he'd extracted a promise that the Imperial would reopen within three days. He provided a few sheets from Mr. Sitwell's score as further evidence that this was to be a burletta, rather than a play.

He strode from the offices with renewed confidence, and went straight home.

"We're back in three days," he announced to the gathered cast and crew.

The news was greeted with the usual boisterous celebration. Maggie, too, seemed pleased.

"Thank you," she said quietly amidst the merriment.

"Wasn't much," he answered with a shrug, meanwhile he soaked up her soft words of gratitude.

She drifted away. Mrs. Llewellyn sought him out, drawing him aside to one corner.

"She's been sleeping at the theater," the actress confided. "Isn't eating, either."

Alarm shot through Cam. "She's ill?"

"Not with any ailment of the body, my lord."

God damn it. He had to do something. But what? And how?

"Make sure someone escorts her home every night," he said, low and quick. "And get her favorite foods. Anything. The most expensive. It doesn't matter. Charge everything to me. Then stand over her to ensure she eats them."

Mrs. Llewellyn raised an eyebrow. "She won't like a minder."

"I don't care. She needs one."

"As do you, my lord." The actress gave him a sympathetic smile and drifted away.

Given Cam's extraordinary predilections, his household staff accommodated a crew of actors quite readily. All the furniture in the ballroom was quickly and efficiently cleared out, spirited away to chambers unknown. He'd hosted numerous private assemblies at his home in London before, but usually when the large chamber was emptied, it was so that the rich and powerful could dance and debauch. These actors were an entirely different sort. They worked for a living. Extra food—and a considerable amount of it—was prepared in the kitchen, available at all hours for a hungry performer. And they were frequently hungry.

He wished that the room had been cleared in order to give a ball in Maggie's honor. Though she didn't like too much fuss for herself, he knew she'd appreciate a bit of theatricality where an assembly was concerned. An orchestra would be set up at one end of the ballroom, playing daring waltzes. He'd dance with her in front of everyone, staking his claim, letting all in attendance see that he and Maggie belonged to each other.

But such a thing couldn't be, and instead, the ballroom was the setting for all her work.

Some chairs remained in the chamber, arranged in rows to simulate the pit. Cam installed himself there to watch.

Cam observed the process of a performance taking shape. How the actors learned their lines, the way in which their physical actions were coordinated and agreed upon, their discovery of the characters and motivations. He'd rather naively believed that plays and burlettas simply sprang into being, but it was a collaborative and fluid development. There was a pleasure in watching this unique progression, seeing how a community was built through the mutual desire to create art. He'd never seen anything like it.

Less enjoyable—agonizing, in truth—was seeing Maggie, yet being unable to touch her or talk privately with her. They were polite strangers, separated by a wall of glass. He felt a constant chill, as though he could never get warm again. When he wasn't watching the rehearsals, nothing gave him pleasure. Hints of mild gratification, perhaps, but that was it. His food tasted of dust, his wine could've been water from the Thames.

The house fell silent every evening when the theatricals left. It echoed with their absence—especially Maggie's—and he couldn't stand the quiet.

So he'd take himself out after work had ended for the day. Tried to go back to his old ways of ballrooms and gaming hells. Fetes and pleasure gardens. Conversations that held no meaning. Empty flirtations acted out of rote, but not desire. He always went home alone. The idea of touching another woman actually made him feel ill, as if poisoned.

He observed himself at a great distance, like a puppetmaster pulling strings, mouthing pleasantries, but far removed from truly feeling anything.

Having Maggie in his home—and then leaving every night—added to the chill. This was where she belonged, yet she could not be a part of it.

She seemed to understand this, too. Every now and again during rehearsals, their gazes would catch and hold, dark acknowledgment that their affair was at an end laying heavily between them.

At those times, he wanted to drag her upstairs, use every seductive trick at his disposal to make her change her mind. To make her his. But she had her resolve, and he had to honor it. It would be cheap and dirty to trap her into something she didn't want in her heart.

Three days passed in a crucible of speed and slowness. He and Maggie were unfailingly polite to each other, yet with a strain beneath. She appeared thin, pale as paper, and worn down. Worry gripped him.

"I have an excellent physician," he said to her one day as the actors were off taking yet another meal, leaving them alone in the ballroom.

She frowned at him. "I'm not sick."

"Don't work yourself so hard," he cautioned. He had hoped that Mrs. Llewellyn might have kept to his directive, but either the actress neglected her duties, or somehow Maggie managed to elude the older woman's care.

"I've got no choice," she answered flatly. "It's either work or . . ." She glanced away and shrugged.

Damn. She suffered, too. There was and there wasn't comfort in this. And the worst of it was that he could do nothing to alleviate her pain. Or his own.

It was too soon when the days elapsed. Lord Chamberlain made good on his promise that they could resume rehearsals at the Imperial. Rejoicing greeted this announcement, yet heaviness settled in Cam's chest at the news. As the actors celebrated, he looked at Maggie, sitting alone. Her expression was somber. Their gazes met. The bleakness in her eyes matched his own.

She would no longer haunt his home. He couldn't decide whether to rejoice or mourn all over again.

"You look like hell," Ashford said to him one night over steaks at their favorite chophouse. There was less than a week until opening night, and Cam had retreated from the Imperial as the sets were being constructed. The theater-going crowd circulated rumors that this next work by Margaret Delamere was going to take the scene by storm and tickets were already sold out for the first five nights' performances—an unheard of event.

"Thank you for your solace." Cam consulted the bottom of his tankard, and found it disappointingly empty. He waved the barmaid over for a refill, and hadn't the interest or energy to return her flirtatious smile.

Ashford studied him. "It happened. You fell in love with her."

"Of course I fell in love with her," Cam snapped. "I'm not an imbecile."

"That's debatable," his friend countered. "Only thing in your favor is that you had the good sense to give your heart to a woman as excellent as Mrs. Delamere."

"And yet here I sit, miserable as a tiger with a thorn in its paw." Why did his tankard hold so little? He kept draining it too quickly.

"Perhaps a dark-haired, lush-figured mouse can pull that thorn," Ashford suggested.

"She *is* the thorn." Cam tipped his head back. "She won't be my mistress, and I cannot give her anything more."

Ashford steepled his fingers together. "Have you considered a more . . . permanent arrangement?"

Instinctively, Cam shook his head. "I cannot do that. Marriage isn't for me."

"Such certainty."

"Always has been," Cam said at once. He loved Maggie, but couldn't marry her. So, he would have no wife at all.

Maggie had her reasons, too, for keeping them apart. She had her work, and he had . . . well . . . not much, now that he thought about it. A life of empty pleasure. But she needed to protect her career. He had to respect her choices.

He continued, remembering Maggie's objections, "Your wife's scandal sheet would make mincemeat of her reputation if we kept on as lovers."

"Eleanor would never do that to her friend," Ashford answered at once.

"But there are half a dozen more newspapers that would eagerly take on the responsibility of skewering her."

Ashford's silence confirmed what Maggie had suspected and Cam feared. She truly would become a pariah if their relationship became publicly known. Her livelihood would be in ruins.

With a detachment he didn't feel, he shrugged. "It's decided already that everything will pass on to Michael and his son when I shuffle off this mortal coil."

"And her low birth?" Ashford pressed. "That isn't a factor?"

"What the hell do I care who her parents are?" Cam snarled.

"Your father would be mightily concerned."

"That's not an issue. He'll have to abide by whatever I want."

"Then I don't see a problem," Ashford noted.

"It simply cannot be," Cam retorted angrily. "I'd marry her if I could, but I don't want to ruin her career."

Ashford leaned back in his settle, his gaze level on Cam's. "Why don't you stop listing all the things that cannot be, and listen to what your heart tells you *can* be?"

Rather than answer, Cam took another drink. But

his friend's words continued to reverberate through him for the rest of the night.

Maggie sat in the pit, listening to the very same scene she and Cam had read together.

Mr. Singh, in the role of Frederick, declared to Miss Brown, " 'With others, perhaps, I have played the part of voluptuary. Never with you.' "

Pain threaded through her as she watched the rehearsal. How had she not seen how closely her words had mirrored her own life? And how would she not recognize the agony her writing would cause her later?

Mr. Singh went on, unaware of her suffering, " 'Is there nothing that can convince you of my earnestness?' "

" 'Nothing,' " Miss Brown returned hotly.

" 'Then shall I ever be your slave, if only to prove the truth of my affections. For, madam, you hold my soul in your palms, and if you are its captor, then I welcome my imprisonment.' "

Maggie wanted to run from the theater and never return. She envisioned herself leaving the coal-smeared buildings of London behind, heading deeper and deeper into the green countryside.

But her only destination would be Marwood Park, and she could never return there again.

So she remained where she was. She had to contribute to the upcoming performance. Too much rested upon it for her to simply abandon everything.

Her hands twisted in her lap as she continued to observe the rehearsal. She barely glanced at Mr. Kingston as he seated himself beside her.

"Opening night's close at hand." Though he'd overseen countless other productions, an unusual excitement threaded through his voice. He, more than anyone, would understand the gravity and importance of this burletta for the health and prosperity of the Imperial.

"So it is," she answered. When silence followed this comment, she finally looked over at Mr. Kingston to find him watching her closely.

"Yet you greet the news as if it were the fishing report," the stage manager noted.

She forced a smile, the small action physically hurting her. "No one wants this work to succeed more than I."

"I don't doubt that. And yet, my dear," Mr. Kingston said with a quiet sympathy that broke her heart, "you're fading away before my eyes. We can all see it."

"See what?" she asked, though she knew the answer.

"That you're finally in love."

The word itself caused another spike of pain, as though someone had actually forced a stiletto between her ribs. "It doesn't matter."

"I think it does," he said softly. "A rare thing, love is. So rare that we cannot toss it aside when finally it comes into our grasp."

"It's a choice between success and happiness," she managed thickly.

"Do they have to be mutually exclusive?"

"For me, they do." She exhaled, bleakness creeping through her bones. "Happy endings only happen onstage, Mr. Kingston."

Empathy shone in his dark eyes. "Fate is a cruel author."

She'd no answer to this, and feared that if she tried to speak, she would actually weep for the first time in a decade. So she only nodded.

He patted her hand. "If you need anything, you've only to ask."

Despite her wishes, a few stray tears dropped down her cheeks. She rubbed at her face. "Thank you," was all she could utter.

Mr. Kingston left her then. She continued to watch the lovers onstage go through their travails, but the excitement she felt at watching her work gain life was gone. Yet it was all she had left.

As the financial backer to *The Hidden Daughter's Return*, Cam needed to present himself as wealthy, powerful, and supremely confident in the success of this venture.

He surveyed himself in the mirror as he dressed for opening night. He'd chosen his clothing with deliberate care—including a dark green coat, white breeches, and a jeweled pocket watch.

His hands shook so much that he actually had to summon his valet to help him with the buttons of his white satin waistcoat. He tried to hold himself still as the valet brushed down his coat, tidying him, making him appear flawless.

"Please don't fidget so, my lord," the servant said.

"Viscounts don't fidget," he answered, taking shelter behind his title.

"Of course not, my lord."

His conflicting thoughts slammed into each other. *The Hidden Daughter's Return* had to succeed. Not just for the theater's sake, but for Maggie's as well. Her reputation as a playwright could be made tonight. Or devastated. All he wanted was for her to have as much achievement as possible. He wanted her to soar to the moon on the wings of accolades. But if the burletta was a success, then the Imperial would no longer need his financial support, and Cam and Maggie would have no reason to associate with each other anymore.

Pain lanced through him, and he nearly doubled over, as if he'd been stabbed.

"Are you all right, my lord?" his valet asked, peering at him with concern.

"Small bit of opening night agitation," Cam answered, and forced a smile. "Nothing that a little whiskey can't repair."

"I'll fetch it, my lord." The servant bowed and left Cam's bedchamber.

Cam exhaled and tried to resist the impulse to run his hands through his hair. He'd only disorder himself, and he'd appear at the theater looking more wild than confident.

What was the point of anything anymore? Returning to his old ways of women and wickedness tasted of soot and sorrow. Nothing seemed worthwhile.

They could possibly go back to their previous patterns, with him in the theater box, and her behind the scenes. Physical agony pierced him at the thought, to be so near her yet apart. Might be better than nothing, though.

Someone tapped on his door. It opened, and Jeremy poked his curly head in.

"Sorry to stop by unannounced," his cousin said. "I told the footman I'd see myself up."

Cam wanted him gone. He had no humor for anyone's company right now, least of all the spiritual counsel of his vicar cousin. Yet he heard himself mutter, "'S all right."

Stepping into the room, Jeremy gave a small, apologetic smile. "I'm surprised to find you home at this hour."

"I'm due at the theater in a few minutes," Cam said brusquely.

"Then I'll speak quickly. This book—" He pulled from his dark coat a familiar slim volume. Cam recognized it as *The Highwayman's Seduction.* "What do you know of its author?"

"Little," Cam grunted. "No one knows much about her other than the fact that her pseudonym claims her to be a woman of the nobility."

Jeremy nodded, looking thoughtful. "You see I wanted to know more about her. The Lady of Dubious Quality . . ." He frowned. "Cousin, something seems to be troubling you."

"I'm as happy as a whore in a soldiers' camp," Cam growled.

Jeremy didn't seem put off by his deliberately crude language. "Yes, I can see that," he answered mildly. "Yet you're pacing fit to burn a hole in the carpet, and you always did that as a boy whenever you were upset."

Cam stopped, unaware until that moment that he'd been striding up and down the room like a caged animal.

Could he unburden himself to his cousin? Ever since he'd spoken with Ashford, fears and desires had been gnawing at him with jagged teeth, growing in intensity by the hour.

If Jeremy thought less of him, or went telling tales to Cam's father, what did it matter?

"There's something I want," he said at last. "Something I can't have."

"Why not?" Jeremy asked.

"Because I can't," he snarled. Anger and frustration welled.

"That's not much of a reason." His cousin stood by the fire, his expression mild and sympathetic. Surprisingly, Cam found it to be soothing, rather than irritating. "Will anyone be hurt if you go after what you want?"

"What's with these damned questions?" Cam fired back.

"Forgive me," Jeremy murmured. "But in my line of work, I often find that the answers someone seeks are usually in themselves."

"You want me to pray my way to a solution," Cam sneered, feeling mean and not caring.

Jeremy only smiled. "Prayer is just another way of communing with ourselves, and by so doing, we find the Divine."

"Just give me your damn counsel," Cam grumbled.

His cousin spread his hands. "I cannot tell you what to do, Marwood. Only you know the answers to your questions."

"I'm not supposed to seek God?"

"He's with you whether you want Him to be, or not. And, believe it or not, Cam, He wants you to be happy."

Sardonically, Cam said, "So this happiness is just handed to me on a silver plate."

Jeremy chuckled. "Of course not. Nothing is given to us. We have to work at being happy. It's not our right, but it is our choice."

Cam pondered this. "Are you happy?"

His cousin's smile faltered a little. "I am content, which is what I can hope for right now. But we're not speaking of me. It's you that concerns me." He took a step forward, and placed a hand on Cam's shoulder. "I cannot help but wonder, Marwood, what it is that keeps you from what you want?"

"Her objections."

"What are those objections founded on?"

"Fear," Cam answered.

"Hers—or yours?" Jeremy pressed.

"Ours," Cam realized. Until Jeremy had questioned him about it, Cam had not realized how much fear influenced him. He hadn't pressed his suit harder because he didn't want to face disappointment. Yet he'd always chased it—the dream of love. But it wasn't a dream any longer. It was real. And he could have it, if he could convince Maggie that their love was worth fighting for.

He could only hope that she would have him. An imperfect man who would always strive to make things perfect for her.

"You're a bloody fine vicar," Cam finally said to Jeremy. "That's not a jest. I mean it."

"Took some practice," his cousin answered with a wry smile. "Though I can't help feeling I'm going to soon incur the wrath of your father."

"Leave that to me," Cam said. He glanced at the clock on the mantel and swore. "I'm late."

"Not too late, I hope."

Cam strode toward the door. "What was it that you wanted to talk to me about?"

"Ah. It can wait."

Stopping at the door, Cam threw over his shoulder, "If you've got any prayers for me, say them now."

Chapter 30

Lord Diabold: After her!
*Phoebe: No—you have taken everything from
  me. I shall have my vengeance.*
*Phoebe pulls out a dagger. She stabs Lord
  Diabold.*
Lord Diabold: I am killed! [dies]
Phoebe: And now, I must meet my justice.
Phoebe is taken away by the magistrate.

The Shattered Heart

Maggie stood in the wings, her stomach and hands in knots. Opening night was never an easy prospect, but tonight—oh, tonight, she was nearly sick with anxiety, alternately hot as a furnace and cold as an icehouse. Clammy sweat clung to her back, and it was impossible to swallow even a sip of wine to calm her nerves.

Tonight's bill included two separate works: *The Hidden Daughter's Return*, and a comic operetta which would follow the intermission.

Backstage was in commotion as last minute preparations were made. A touch of paint on the flats, a ripped hem. Though the cast and crew of the Imperial were no strangers to premieres, a new tension clung to everyone, all of them aware of how much was at stake tonight. The theater's fate rested on the success of this evening's performance. The burden weighed like sandbags on Maggie's shoulders. She might not be onstage, speaking the lines, but *she* was the author of those words. Having her name on the playbill all but guaranteed that if the burletta was a failure, it would be attributed to her, not the performers.

Everything depended on this night.

And Cam was missing.

The curtain was set to rise in five minutes. Maggie had already peered through the heavy velvet drapes and blanched with fear and excitement to see an entirely full house. Heat and chatter pushed her back behind the curtain, but the sea of faces had left its impression on her. Lord, she'd never had a completely sold-out theater. Eleanor had already come backstage with Ashford to wish her the best of luck, but they had retreated to their box. Actors and crew also approached her to offer their best wishes. A superstitious lot, in order to trick the theatrical gods into giving them exactly the opposite, the crew said they hoped for an utter disaster, and that she might break a leg, as well.

Still no Cam.

Would he come tonight? Of course he would. How could he not? This represented a huge investment of his time and reputation—if such a thing mattered to him. He wasn't so petty that he'd avoid the performance. Yet his continued delay made her already twisted stomach flip. She needed him beside her. His steadying presence. His very being that made her believe she could do anything.

"We have to start," Mr. Kingston said, appearing beside her. "The crowd's restive and won't wait, not even for his lordship."

Maggie inhaled, then nodded. "Let's begin."

At Mr. Kingston's signal to the conductor, the orchestra played the overture. With the first notes, Maggie's heart flew up higher than the catwalk. This was it. *The Hidden Daughter's Return* was finally happening.

Applause sounded as the curtain rose. When Miss Brown, in the role of Alina, stepped onto the stage, the ovation grew, then silenced as she sang the first line.

" 'This world is brand new. Will I founder on the shores, or sail onward toward a golden future?' "

From that point onward, the crowd seemed to fall into an enchantment. They sniffled, they chuckled. They were with Alina through the whole of her arduous journey toward a happy ending. The villain was appropriately hissed. Sighs accompanied Prince Frederick's appearance, handsomely portrayed by Mr. Singh.

But Maggie had little time to stand and watch. While everything onstage might appear calm, backstage was pandemonium, and she remained at its center. She directed the stagehands as they moved the scenery into place, and guided the dancers into formation when it was time for the brief musical interlude. Though Mr. Kingston managed the stage ably, there were too many questions and variables for him to take care of everything himself. Maggie acted in support of him, as well as providing leadership for the thousands of questions and minor problems that arose during an opening night performance.

When she turned around to remind Mr. Fontaine of his entrance, she ran right into Cam. Her stomach unknotted, and the weight pressing down on her lifted.

He looked . . . animated was too mild a word. He seemed to vibrate with energy and purpose and appeared handsome as a devil in his evening clothes. But he was panting, and his hair was completely disheveled.

"Where have you been?" she hissed in her backstage voice.

"A last minute visit from Jeremy and then damned traffic," he gasped, also lowering his voice to accommodate the action onstage. "Had to. Run. Here now." He paused to collect his breath. "Maggie, I've got to tell you—"

"What's my lighting cue?" a crewman asked.

"When she says, 'You are playing me false,'" she replied.

When he left, Cam said urgently, "Maggie, I—"

A stagehand appeared. "Mrs. Delamere, do we bring the throne out with the blanket on it, or will Mr. Singh carry it in?"

"Put the blanket on now," she answered.

The crewman disappeared to ready the prop.

Maggie turned back to Cam, who was looking quite cross. "Please—I can't talk right now. The performance is happening."

He didn't look happy about it, but he nodded.

Now she just had to survive the next few acts.

Cam felt ready to explode.

His carriage had snarled in the worst traffic London had seen in recent memory, thickening considerably near the theater. He'd been forced to get out and literally run the remaining mile to the Imperial, all the time conscious of the fact that the burletta had already begun, and Maggie was facing opening night without him by her side.

At last, he'd finally reached the theater and dashed inside. There she'd been, beautiful and pale in the ambient light, looking harried but also in control as cast and crew buffeted Maggie. His heart had felt ready to burst at seeing her. This was truly going to happen. The moment was now.

Then the bloody interruptions. One after another. Cam couldn't fault anyone for needing Maggie's help, but it was so damn inconvenient. Especially when he was about to offer her his name and eternal devotion. He'd planned the speech in his head en route to the Imperial, but all that eloquence scattered like so much buckshot with the constant disruptions.

But he had to honor her request, and so kept silent as chaos ruled around him.

Soon, his heart whispered.

From her position in the wings, with Cam at her side, Maggie watched as *The Hidden Daughter's Return* unfolded onstage. She heard the audience's every laugh, every exclamation and sob. Each sound reverberated through her with the force of an explosion. God! Did they like it? Hate it? Periods of long silence came and went, where none of the spectators made a single noise.

She hadn't realized she had been twisting her hands together, until Cam gently disengaged her fingers and clasped one of her hands in his. Warmth spread up her arm, into her body. Calming her. Centering her. With him at her side, she felt capable of anything.

"Breathe," he whispered.

She let out a long, slow exhalation. Her heartbeat continued to flutter, but not as rapidly.

He gave her a smile of encouragement. She managed to return the smile, though hers was a little wobbly around the edges. Cam was here. He was beside her. He'd never wavered in his support of her, when she'd all but given up on herself. Yet he had stood fast, encouraging her to fight for what she loved, for what she believed in. It was a gift she would always cherish, long beyond this one moment, whether *The Hidden Daughter's Return* was a success or not.

Together, they watched the rest of the burletta's performance. A few more crewmen came up to her with questions, but it seemed as though they'd straightened out most of the problems on their own.

No one forgot a line. No cues were stepped on, and the music flowed.

And then . . . it was over. The actors and actresses bowed, and exited the stage.

More silence.

Maggie sent Cam a terrified glance. He held up a hand, bidding her patience.

All at once, it happened. Thunderous applause and cries of "Bravo!" resounded in the theater. Whistles and foot-stamping provided accompaniment.

Her heart shuddered to a halt, then it started back up again.

Cam turned to her. "A success." He grinned. "A goddamn bloody success!"

The performers around her also smiled and clapped, thrilled by their triumph. Everyone embraced and patted one another on the shoulders. Maggie found herself torn from Cam's grip as the troupe encircled her.

"We did it, Mrs. D!" Mr. Singh shouted above the din.

"Because of you," Mr. Fontaine added.

Maggie looked at the shining faces surrounding her. "We all made *The Hidden Daughter's Return* flourish." Her gaze found Cam, standing at the edge of the group, who added his applause to the others. Pure joy radiated from his expression. "*All* of us."

As the audience's ovation continued, Maggie urged the performers, "Now go out there and accept your adoration."

Holding hands, the cast wove their way back onto the stage. As one, they bowed. The clapping shook the rafters and floorboards.

Suddenly, Cam was beside her again, his hand gripping hers. Before she knew what he was doing, she discovered he pulled her toward the stage. The curtain hadn't yet fallen, and Cam gestured to one of the stagehands to keep it raised.

"What are you doing?" she cried.

"Making sure you get your due," he said, smiling broadly.

Panic assailed her. She hadn't been onstage before an audience in a long, long while. "Cam, I—"

But then the lights blinded her, and there she was, on the stage, in front of hundreds of men and women. She blinked, feeling like a bear emerging from its hibernation.

Cam held up one of his hands. "Ladies, gentlemen," he called over the din. "A moment of your time." He waited while the audience quieted, the noise subsiding to a murmur. "You've already met our esteemed cast, but I'd like everyone here to make the acquaintance of this woman. Mrs. Margaret Delamere, the author of tonight's work!"

The ovation started up again, louder than before. Maggie felt buffeted by it, nearly knocked over by a wave of sound. She'd listened to the clapping for her work before, but had never once accepted that ovation in person. Not once had she experienced the accolades so viscerally. So physically. It made it that much more genuine.

Tears threatened to spill.

"Take a bow," Cam whispered.

She did. The experience was both dreamlike and deeply, profoundly real.

Cam deserved his recognition, too. But before she could speak, he continued, addressing the crowd.

"Some of you already know me," he said, pitching his voice so that everyone could hear him. "I am Cameron Chalton, Viscount Marwood."

The crowd murmured amongst itself.

"And," Cam continued, looking at her, then back out at the audience, "I love Mrs. Delamere."

Gasps replaced the applause. Several women sighed, especially the female performers.

Stunned, Maggie could only watch as he turned to her. "I've said it before," he continued, ignoring everyone but her, "and I will go on saying it every day for the rest of my life."

"Cam—"

"Let me finish," he said gravely. "I rehearsed this speech a dozen times, and I won't let you deprive me of my moment."

Though inside, she was in complete disorder, stunned by his declaration, she managed a nod. "Pray, continue."

"Without you," he continued, "my life was like an empty stage. Hollow, silent. Devoid of meaning. But when you came onto the scene, everything changed. It became full of pageantry and light and life. I was enacting the role of the rake, but the most important part I could ever play is that of your lover and friend. And it wouldn't be an act, Maggie," he said with utter sincerity. "Every word from my lips would be true. As I would be true to you. Eternally."

Maggie's head spun. Her palms dampened. She barely knew herself. All she knew was him, at this moment, and the words he spoke.

"Eternity is a long time," she whispered.

"And that's what I want. Every morning and night. Especially the night," he couldn't seem to help himself from adding.

The audience tittered.

She dimly heard them, but her focus was on Cam. He was so achingly handsome, so dear to her. "How could I have imagined that a life without you would be worth living?" she asked softly. "I want whatever you can give me. To blazes with the scandal."

A tentative happiness lit his face. "You will have everything."

To her utter shock, he lowered himself down onto the footboards, until he was on one knee. He continued to hold her hand as the audience, performers, and crew looked on.

"Marry me," he said.

For several moments, she could only stare at him in astonishment. She couldn't believe what he was saying. Yet the truth in his eyes and the shaking in his hand revealed that he couldn't be more sincere.

"But . . ." she stammered. "I'm a commoner."

He grinned. "Nothing common about you."

"Don't be deliberately obtuse," she said. "Not now."

"I'm perfectly serious," he answered. "You'll always have your art. I can and will never take that away from you. As for wealth, title, and reputation. They mean nothing unless you're beside me. And I need you beside me, Maggie. Say yes."

Trembling seized her. This was a monumental decision. One that would change her life forever. She would no longer be simply Margaret Delamere, playwright, but Lady Marwood. A viscountess. While some women longed for a title, she desired only her independence. But Cam would give her that freedom. She trusted him to do that. She wouldn't have to change for him. If they were wed, the scandal wouldn't go away, but it would be lessened by marriage. Whatever trouble she and Cam would face, they would face together. She could endure any scandal with him beside her. Eternally.

And he was doing this in public, before a literal audience. His commitment to her was real. She could never doubt that.

"Say yes!" a man in the crowd shouted.

"Say yes!" echoed hundreds of voices.

"Do it!" exclaimed the actors.

She took a deep breath. And then, loud enough to be heard from the very back of the theater, she replied, "Yes."

"Huzzah!"

"Bravo!"

"Three cheers!"

The audience erupted into applause and celebration,

just as the cast and crew of the Imperial did. The orchestra launched into a celebratory tune.

Cam stood. His gaze never left hers. Gasps sounded when he wrapped her in his arms. He kissed her, in front of everyone. Maggie thought she saw a woman actually swoon in scandalized shock. But what did it matter, when she and Cam had each other?

The curtain fell.

Epilogue

*Friar Ned: Though we have seen sorrow here,
there is yet hope for a new beginning. All
things are possible in this wondrous world.*

The Shattered Heart

One month later

Ensconced at Marwood Park, Cam sat behind his desk, perusing an issue of *The Hawk's Eye*. He hadn't read the papers in a long while, but his man of affairs thought today's issue might interest him, so he read.

> "*Though it has been a month since the debut of* The Hidden Daughter's Return, *the burletta continues to have an unprecedented run lasting nigh four weeks. Tomorrow will mark the final performance of this work, though not for want of ticket sales. No, it's known that the management has decided to pull the burletta in order to increase demand, which seems limitless.*
>
> "*Word has it that another work of Mrs. Dela-*

mere's is in progress. Theater-goers are breathless with anticipation."

He'd show her the article later. For now, he had business in the village. But afterwards . . . they could celebrate her triumph in private. He never tired of rejoicing in her successes. And there were so many more to come. Of that, he was certain.

Though the carriage was always at her disposal, Maggie could not abandon her habit of walking everywhere, even the distance from Marwood Park to the village. She strolled there now, enjoying the countryside's shift into crisp, bright autumn. Everything seemed clear and sharp, from the sound of leaves crunching beneath her boots to the sting of cool air on her face.

Her cheeks heated now, thinking of how energetic she and Cam had been last night. She supposed one might attribute their enthusiastic lovemaking to the early stages of marriage, but Maggie suspected that it would always be thus. It burned hot between them, as it had from the very beginning. A fire like that couldn't be extinguished.

It felt good now to stretch out her well-used body. Wedded life far surpassed anything her capacious writer's imagination could have conjured.

Not everything had been sunshine, however. His father had been nearly apoplectic when they'd announced they would be wed by special license. He had gone several times to the marquess—sometimes returning home in a rage—yet Cam had been persistent and eventually, the proud Lord Allam came around.

Cam had noted to her later that his father had seen how much Maggie had transformed Cam. For the better. Lord Allam couldn't begrudge the love his son had finally found, and he was even present at the wedding itself. He was still cool to her, but Cam assured her that, in time, his father would thaw.

She couldn't help but feel a stab of unhappiness that her own family hadn't attended her wedding—her father, mother and brothers all absent—but the cast and crew of the Imperial had been there, and Mr. Kingston had been the one to escort her down the aisle. Naturally, the wedding breakfast had been decimated by the actors, to the amused astonishment of the other guests. Cam had only laughed and called for more champagne.

The village at last came into view. Before her stay at Marwood Park, she would have insisted London was the only place for her, but rural life agreed with her— and her Muse. The words came readily now, as if freed from a cage. They flew like birds, wheeling and sleek in the sky.

She bypassed the shops and instead headed to where builders were hard at work constructing a large structure. Though the grange hall had been refurbished, the village had agreed to a new building. It wouldn't be finished for at least another month, but already she could see it would be the pride of the village—a twostory edifice in the modern style, which would serve as a free lending library, meeting hall, and even space for theatrical performances. All of it was funded by Cam.

Today it was no surprise to find him overseeing the work. He came here most days when she was writing.

Even though she'd been with him only a few hours ago, her pulse hitched to observe him standing with a group of workers. He looked dark and dangerous in his long black coat, a panther amongst housecats. Later, she promised herself, she'd demand to see him in that coat—and nothing else.

For now, she approached sedately, playing the role of somewhat humble wife.

When Cam spotted her, he smiled and waved her over. The workmen dispersed after he gave them further direction. She linked her arm with Cam's and wandered a few paces away from the construction site.

He kissed the tip of her nose. "How fares *The Triumph of Alina*?"

"Like you," she said, "I'm building the framework before the decoration can be added. And what of your project?"

Cam became businesslike. "We should be finished before the first real frost. And to inaugurate the building, the villagers have decided to stage their own production of *The Hidden Daughter's Return*—with your permission, of course."

"They have it," she answered.

"Here's an odd thing," he noted. "They've asked us both to oversee the production."

"That's not odd," she said brightly. "That's wonderful."

His smile returned, and widened. "I rather thought so, too." He drew her close, heedless of who might be watching. "Would you have written an ending such as this for us?"

"I doubt it," she said with a laugh. "I'm known for my tragedies."

"The Hidden Daughter's Return changed all that," he pointed out.

"It changed a considerable amount," she noted.

He kissed her, in full view of everyone. But then, that was Cam. He didn't care what others thought. When at last he lifted his head, he said earnestly, "My life, for one. And my heart."

The sincerity in his words made her shiver with pleasure.

"And what of the action that transpires once the curtain has fallen?" Maggie asked when she regained some composure. He could still kiss her senseless.

He looked serious and beautiful, this wicked man who held her soul. "That, my love, is for *us* to write."

Don't miss the next smart and sexy novel in
Eva Leigh's
Wicked Quills of London series!

Temptations
of a Wallflower

Coming Spring 2016!

Have you had a chance to read
Eleanor and Daniel's story?
If not, don't miss

Forever Your Earl

Available now!

Read on for a sneak peek . . .

*Though London presents itself to the world
as the apotheosis of all that is moral and
upstanding, it might shock our readers to learn
that the appearance of virtue can be a very
clever disguise. It is the opinion of this humble
periodical that wickedness and deception are far
more common than our readers may apprehend.
Thus the necessity of this most respectful scrap
of writing—that we may, through the revelation
of the scandalous activities of our Town, provide
necessary guidance. But leading a life of probity
may be difficult, especially when presented with
temptation . . .*

The Hawk's Eye, May 2, 1816

London, 1816

A man rich in wealth and scandal walked into Eleanor
Hawke's office.

Eleanor was no stranger to scandal. Anything immoral, disreputable, shocking, or titillating made its
way into the pages of her newspaper—particularly if

it involved the wealthy and elite of London Society. She detailed all of it for her thrice-weekly publication, *The Hawk's Eye*. Nobody wanted to read about ordinary shopkeeper Mr. Jones who might or might not be spending time with the humdrum widow Mrs. Smith.

No, *The Hawk's Eye* sold strictly on the basis of its publishing the latest scandalous doings of Lord This and Lady That. All, of course, under the pretense of decrying the lack of morals in this fair city, and that publishing these lurid activities served as object lessons to the young and impressionable.

And it was Eleanor's job as owner and publisher to see to the moral education of London.

Which was utter rubbish, naturally.

But scandal put bread on her table and kept the rain off her head, and she readily immersed herself in it— the spirit of free enterprise, and all that.

Still, when Daniel Balfour, the Earl of Ashford himself, walked into the offices of *The Hawk's Eye* on a Wednesday afternoon, blocking the gray light as the door opened and closed, it was both shocking and inevitable that he should do so. Unsurprisingly, he clenched several copies of her paper in his hand.

Lord Ashford marched through the cramped warren of rooms, and writers, bent over their desks, lifted their heads to watch in openmouthed amazement as he passed. Eleanor's private office lay at the end of the corridor, giving her an ample view of the scene as it played out before her.

The earl stopped in front of Harry Welker's desk. The young writer stared up at Lord Ashford, the men separated not just by the expanse of battered oak but by circumstance and birth as well.

"H-how might I help you, my lord?" Harry asked, his voice cracking.

"Tell me where Mister E. Hawke is." Lord Ashford had a deep voice, rounded by generations of excellent breeding and *noblesse oblige*.

"Mister Hawke, my lord?" There was patent confusion in the young man's voice.

Lord Ashford pointed to one of the papers he carried. "It says here that *The Hawk's Eye* is owned and published by one E. Hawke. Where will I find him?"

"Nowhere, my lord," Harry answered. "There's no *Mister* Hawke here."

The earl scowled, clearly not used to being denied. "This scurrilous rag cannot publish itself."

"It doesn't," Eleanor announced, setting aside her quill and standing. "If you're looking for *Miss* Eleanor Hawke, I'm right over here."

Lord Ashford looked directly at her, and for the first time, she had a sense of what a rabbit might feel like when sighted by a wolf. But she wasn't the only one at a disadvantage. The earl couldn't hide the shock in his expression when he discovered that the publisher and owner of the paper was, in truth, a woman—which gave her a small measure of gratification.

He turned from Harry without another word and walked straight toward her. And she could only stand, pinned by his gaze, as he approached.

The closer he got, the more she realized how dangerous the earl was. Perhaps not in the traditional sense—though she'd heard and written about the duels he'd fought and won—but certainly in the realm of masculine allure. Her few times seeing him had been from a distance: the theater, the races, at a public assembly.

She knew him by sight, but he didn't know her, and they'd never met. And in those instances, her vision had been good enough to recognize that he was a fine specimen, well-formed, handsome—everything a rich and notorious nobleman should be.

But Lord Ashford up close was rather . . . appalling. It didn't seem right that a man so blessed by fortune and title should also be so attractive.

His dark brown hair was fashionably cut and artfully tousled, as if he'd recently risen from a lover's bed. Given his reputation, that was most likely possible. He had a broad forehead, a coin-clean jawline, thick brows, and eyes that, even with yards between her and him, stunned her with their blue clarity. Naturally, he had a mouth that looked very adept at kissing and . . . other things.

He moved with a long-limbed ease that betrayed his skill as a sportsman. His ink-blue coat fit the broad width of his shoulders, and his cream waistcoat, embroidered in gold, defined the shape of his torso—his tailor on Jermyn Street produced excellent work. Snug doeskin breeches were tucked into polished Hessians that came from Bond Street.

Truly, he was quite alarming.

"Miss Hawke?" he asked sharply, coming to stand in front of her paper-cluttered desk. "I wasn't expecting a female."

"Neither were my parents," she answered, sitting, "but they learned to adapt. How might I help you, my lord?"

Though she felt an obligation to ask the question, she braced herself for what was sure to be a scorching lecture.

He removed his hat and set it aside. Then he held up an issue of *The Hawk's Eye* and began to read.

" 'Lord A—d, a figure well-known to our assiduous and genteel readers, was lately seen in the company of a certain Mrs. F—e, whose late husband made his considerable fortune through the manufacture and sale of a woman's garment we blush to mention in these virtuous pages.' " He tossed one of the issues to the ground. "Wrong."

"You cannot deny—"

But he wasn't done. Holding up another issue of the paper, he read again. " 'It may or may not stun our honorable readers to learn that the notorious Lord A—d has not amended his ways following the duel over Lady L., from Y—shire, and has been espied with another married lady of questionable character, at the late-night revels hosted by the equally rakish Mr. S—n. Yet it was noted by our keen-eyed intelligence that this married lady was not the only female vying for the earl's favors.' " This paper he also cast to the floor. "Wrong."

She herself had written those pieces, and while they weren't matchless examples of English prose, she was still rather proud of them, as she was of all her labors. To have her hard work thrown to the ground like so much garbage was rankling.

"I assure you, my lord," she said bitingly, *"The Hawk's Eye* strives for the greatest of accuracy." She had a network of sources, which she used regularly to provide information. Many members of the aristocracy were in dire need of funds, and they gladly turned on each other in order to maintain the pretense of effortless wealth. Eleanor always paid her informants to keep them returning.

Whether or not they lied to her just to collect payment wasn't her concern, but she always preferred it if she could validate their statements. Sometimes that meant going out and conducting a few investigations. But she was a very busy woman—writing articles, editing countless others, managing the paper's finances—and didn't always have the time.

She had to earn a living, after all. And men like the earl didn't.

Continuing, she said, "That's exceptionally conceited of you, my lord, to assume that *you* are Lord A—d." Leaning back in her chair, she gave a thin smile. "I could be writing about Lord Archland. Or perhaps Lord Admond."

"Lord Archland hasn't left his country estate in a decade," the earl answered, "and Lord Admond's days of scandal happened when red heels and powdered wigs were in fashion. The man written about is undoubtedly, nauseatingly, me."

So much for that defense. "Oh, but you're far from nauseating, my lord. In fact, you're enthralling—to my readers," she hastened to add.

Lord Ashford shook his head. "It amazes me that the citizens of London have such paltry lives that they'd care a groat what I did."

"The provinces, too," she added. "I have a thousand subscribers throughout the country."

He threw up his hands. "Ah, that improves the situation immeasurably. I cannot fathom what my concern was."

"As my paper states," she said, "you are London's most notorious rake. Of course people care what you do."

He crossed his arms over his chest, a movement that

emphasized that the width of his shoulders didn't come from the work of a tailor's artful needle.

"One might think that your readers would be far more interested in the food shortages that have resulted from recent crop failures," he fired back. "Or perhaps they might be intrigued by the East Indian volcanic explosion. Maybe, just maybe, they'd be concerned with Argentina declaring its independence from Spain. Did none of that ever cross your mind, Miss Hawke, rather than reporting spurious gossip about a figure as inconsequential as myself?"

Though she was momentarily shocked that a man as infamously dissolute as Lord Ashford would be so well informed, she quickly recovered.

"I'd hardly call you inconsequential, my lord," she countered. "Your family name goes back to the time of Queen Elizabeth. If memory serves, your ancestor Thomas Balfour won himself an earldom as a privateer to the queen—though others merely called him a pirate with a government charter. It seems as though scandal runs in your blood. How could the public not be fascinated?"

It was his turn to look surprised. He likely didn't expect her to be so knowledgeable of his ancestry. But Eleanor was nothing if not thorough. She had *Debrett's* memorized the way others knew their Bible verses.

"Because I am merely one man," he answered. "Granted, a man with a somewhat extensive wardrobe—"

Of mistresses, she silently added.

"But hardly worth page after page of precious paper and ink," he concluded.

"You belong to a gentleman's club, do you not?" she

asked pointedly. "White's, if memory serves. And what do you do there?"

"Drink."

"You appear quite sober now," she said, "and you always take your luncheon there. Given the hour, you likely were at White's, then came here. As I cannot smell the reek of alcohol on your breath or person, I highly doubt that drinking is the only activity in which you engage at your club."

"Ah, you have me figured out. In fact," he said, lowering his voice conspiratorially, "I spend most of my time there plotting how to live off the blood of the lower classes."

"I strongly suspect that if that had been your ambition, I and my commoner brethren would be drained dry by now."

"Perhaps I need to strengthen my motivation," he replied. "You're doing a rather bang-up job of it."

"What a proud day for me," she said. "To have driven an earl toward thoughts of vampirism. But come now, you're being deliberately obtuse. What else—besides imbibe and plot the agony of the lesser classes—do you do at your club?"

"Read the newspaper," he answered.

Ah! Finally. "And for those gentlemen who haven't the connections or wealth to be members of a club, there are always the coffee houses. They stock newspapers for their customers, too."

"Perhaps it's time to get a quill sharpener," he said acidly, "because I fail to see your point."

She came around her desk and leaned against it, so that a distance of only a few feet separated them. "My point, Lord Ashford, is that there are countless sources for the news you cited. Most of their offices can be found within a quarter mile of here. Those papers are for *news*. But *The Hawk's Eye* provides something that the *Times* and other papers do not."

"Paper for lining birdcages," he said.

"Moral guidance."

He gave one single, harsh laugh. "I ought to fetch the attendants from Bedlam, because you're clearly in the grips of a powerful delusion. Like our own dear monarch, God save him. Shall I bring you a mitre and crook and declare you pope?"

She pressed her lips together. This wasn't the first time she'd come under attack for her paper's practices, but seldom by someone as articulate and intelligent as the earl. It didn't help that he had a most distracting physical appearance. How could a man possess such a pair of spectacularly blue eyes? Like the glint of sapphires washed in autumn sunlight.

"It's right here beneath the paper's name," she said, picking up an issue lying on her desk. "*Consilium per stadium.* 'Guidance through observation.' If you led a more moral life, you wouldn't appear in my paper at all."

He looked at her with patent disbelief. "What unbounded cheek, for you to judge me. You, who profit from feeding on carrion, like some quill-wielding hyena."

Eleanor considered herself someone with a thick skin and a decent amount of composure, but for some reason, the earl's words struck her with a strange sensation she hadn't experienced in a long while. If she had to guess, it was a mixture of pain and . . . shame.

She quickly shook the feeling off. Shame was for those who could afford it. And she couldn't.

"I don't judge," she fired back, "only report the facts as I know them."

He snorted. "They aren't facts. Just half-truths buried in terrible prose."

"My writing is *not* terrible," she muttered. "Have you read the *Examiner* lately? *That* is some execrable hack work."

"And yet here I stand," he said flatly, "in *your* office."

"So you do. But, my lord, you may rail and complain and whine like a petulant child—"

He sputtered.

"—but you're a public figure. As such, that makes you fair game. The rest of the world lead fairly dull lives. We get up—"

"As do I."

"Eat our breakfasts."

"I do the same."

"Go to work."

Here, he was silent.

She continued, "Most of us cannot afford to go to the theater or gaming hells or have the social connections to attend private assemblies. But you can, and you do. You are what we all aspire to be, my lord."

He laughed ruefully. "Perhaps you and your readers ought to set your sights higher. There are people of, how would you put it, far greater *moral* character worth mirroring."

"Maybe so," she answered candidly. "I can list dozens of men and women, all of greater purpose and ambition than yourself, that I would much rather see held up as an example to emulate. Teachers or philanthropists."

He looked insulted. "I donate generously to orphanages and veterans' assistance organizations right here in London."

"Do you?" She should make a note of that later. None of her sources had ever uncovered that aspect of the earl's life, but it would make for a surprising and rather delicious counterpoint to his rakish public behavior. It also spoke well of Lord Ashford that he did not attempt to make public his charitable endeavors. But it was rather easier to do her job if she didn't think *too* highly of him.

"Regardless of the content of your character, my lord," she went on, "you live a life only a minute fraction can ever hope to attain. As such, that makes you an object of fascination. And the truth of it is, you cannot stop me or anyone on my staff from writing about you."

"A miserable fact of which I'm well aware," he answered.

She strode back around her desk. "Then I believe we've said all we can to one another, delightful as this exchange has been. Good day, my lord." She started to sit. "I'm rather busy, but I can have Harry show you to the door if you require."

But Lord Ashford didn't move. Stood exactly where he was, with his arms still folded over his chest. "If you are going to use me as your subject, the least you can do is proper research."

She hovered over her chair. "Forgive me for not being Cambridge-educated, but I'm not certain what you are suggesting."

Unfolding his arms, he braced his hands on the edge of her desk, leaning slightly forward. Despite the expanse of the desk separating them, she felt compelled to lean away.

"What I am suggesting, Miss Hawke," he murmured, "is that you accompany me. Day and night. That way, you can see exactly what I do with my time. You see," he continued, a slow smile unfolding, "I don't want you to stop writing about me at all. I want you to get it right."

Daniel still hadn't quite recovered from his shock at learning that E. Hawke was, in fact, *Eleanor* Hawke. She also wasn't the sort of slattern he might expect in this Grub Street milieu. Miss Hawke resembled a prosperous shopkeeper's wife—granted, a pretty shopkeeper's wife, with her wheat-blonde hair, bright hazel eyes, strong but feminine features, and nicely curved figure. She looked to be about his age of thirty-two years, as would befit someone who owned and operated their own business.

A female in a field almost entirely dominated by males. If there were any other women in her line of work, he'd never heard of them. She must have inherited the paper from some male relative—a father or husband, perhaps. Maybe a deceased husband. Certainly she hadn't founded the periodical herself.

Still, here she was, surprising in her respectability. She wore a modest peach-colored dress, and her hair was neatly pinned back. The only sign she worked for a living was the ink staining her fingers.

He hadn't counted on a woman being E. Hawke. But it was actually perfect. His suggestion would be all the more enticing to her. A journalist and a woman were the two most inquisitive creatures on earth. Combine them together, and only a cat could rival her for curiosity.

He'd turn her attention away from the activities that had been consuming him these past two weeks and distract her from his true purpose. While he had her gaze focused elsewhere, he could continue on with his true goal—finding Jonathan.

His proposition clearly intrigued Miss Hawke. She continued to hover over her chair.

Despite her interest, she asked suspiciously, "Why would you *want* me to write about you?"

"As you said," he explained, "I cannot stop you from penning these absurd articles about my life. And if I can't stop you, the very least you can do is be accurate. What better way than to have you come with me each day and night and record my activities? Unless you don't feel up to the task of late-night revelry and observing firsthand how the elite of Society fill their wicked hours."

This was most assuredly not the truth. But he wasn't about to explain that Jonathan Lawson, his closest friend since childhood, had been missing for nearly a month. The situation was even more dire, because soon after Jonathan's disappearance, his elder brother had died. Now Jonathan was the heir to one of England's oldest and most esteemed dukedoms—and no one could find him. Before his disappearance, he'd been seen with low, rough company. Men who slunk around the alleys of the East End and lived like rats. If the truth ever got out about Jonathan's vanishing—especially in the newspapers—the family could be utterly ruined.

But Daniel, as Miss Hawke had so thoroughly argued, was a public figure. She documented his every movement. He had to turn her shrewd gaze away from the hunt for Jonathan. Providing specifically engineered distractions was exactly the strategy that was needed. So he'd open himself up to her scrutiny—because he owed it to Jonathan. A minor inconvenience was nothing compared to the failure to honor the unspoken promises of friendship.

And Daniel had failed Jonathan's friendship spectacularly.

Miss Hawke dropped into her chair, swiveling the seat back and forth as she mulled over his offer. Her brow furrowed, and she steepled her fingers, pressing them to her bottom lip. Were he a painter—which he assuredly was not—he'd paint the scene and title it *Study in Wary Contemplation*.

Finally, the swiveling of her chair stopped, and she faced him. "I don't trust you," she stated baldly.

No one except Jonathan and his friend Marwood spoke to him so candidly. Yet Miss Hawke addressed him as if she had every right to be so blunt. As though they were equals. On every level.

He waited to feel a hot wave of outrage or anger. None came. It was . . . refreshing. To be talked to like he was . . . himself. Not the Earl of Ashford, a nobleman that required flattery or coddling or toadying deference. But an ordinary man.

"Why should you?" he answered frankly.

His own candor seemed to catch her by surprise, which felt like a small victory. She wasn't the only one capable of shocking someone.

"I've no reason to," she replied. "We've clearly established ourselves at cross purposes. You've already observed two salient facts about me. I'm the owner of this enterprise. And I'm a woman."

"Both facts have been noted by me, yes." The unfortunate truth was that had he seen Miss Hawke on the other side of a ballroom, he would have sought to claim a dance—if not more. She was distractingly attractive. Worldly, clever. Slim and curved. But his intent was too important to let something like her prettiness throw him off his course.

She couldn't know his motivations for being here, or what prompted him to offer up such an outrageous proposition. And if she rejected his offer . . . No, she had to accept. The reputation of an influential family depended on it. Even more important, Jonathan's life lay on the line.

Miss Hawke continued, "Neither condition has inclined me to have faith in others, particularly men."

That caught his attention.

Before he could press her on that interesting admission, she continued, "And yet . . ." She steepled her fingers together again. "I'd be a fool to refuse your proposition. After all, what's to stop you from going to one of my competitors with the same offer?"

He didn't mention that none of the other scandal sheets reported on him as regularly and with such underlying glee as *The Hawk's Eye*.

"Nothing," he said. "Only my own inclination."

Her brow still lowered in thought, she stood and began to pace the length of her office—which wasn't very far, so she caromed back and forth like a snooker ball.

"We could make it a regular feature," she murmured, mostly to herself. "Advertise it in upcoming issues leading up to the series. Drive up sales. And we'll call it . . . we can call it . . ."

"The Adventures of Lord A.," he suggested.

She threw him an exasperated look, as if disappointed with his efforts. "Not nearly titillating enough."

"Forgive me if I'm not familiar with the ways of lurid prose."

"You'll never make it as a journalist," she fired back.

"Thank the heavens," he replied.

As she paced her tiny office, she continually brushed past him. He caught her scent of ink, oil from printing presses, and cinnamon. Daniel had no desire to press himself into the corner like a frightened dog, so he remained where he stood, despite the disconcerting proximity of Miss Hawke.

Suddenly, she stopped, and her face lit up. Inspiration had struck, and it turned her from pretty to extraordinary in an instant.

"To Ride with a Rake," she pronounced.

He winced. Of all the names he'd been called in his life—"rogue," "prodigal," "libertine"—*rake* had always been one of his least favorite. It implied a certain leering, cheap smuttiness. "We don't need to use that word."

"Oh, but we do," she answered, face shining. "Other than the word *duke,* nothing intrigues potential readers more than *rake.* You do want people to read the columns, don't you?"

Given his preferences, his natural inclination was to say no. But these were extraordinary circumstances, and he needed as many eyes fixed on his activities as possible. "Yes," he said through gritted teeth.

She beamed at him. "Excellent. *To Ride with a Rake* it shall be."

A sudden thought bloomed in his mind. "My exceptionally keen powers of observation have noted that you are, in fact, female. Keeping company with me will harm your reputation."

Her laugh was husky, honey over polished stones. "I'm a writer, my lord. I *have* no reputation."

Most of the women of his acquaintance guarded their names assiduously, fearfully. They lived in a world where a woman's social standing meant everything. But this strange Miss Hawke seemed to dwell in a fringe realm, unconcerned about what anyone thought about her. As if she were a man. Or, at the least, a man's equal.

How very intriguing.

"Then we're agreed, my lord?" she pressed. "I'm to accompany you on your sundry activities, and write about them for *The Hawk's Eye*?"

This was it. His last chance before throwing wide the doors of his life and making himself the object of public examination. He'd been scrutinized before, but never to the extent that he proposed now. The very thought made his chest tighten and his fists clench, ready to defend himself and his privacy. Gentlemen never did anything for notoriety's sake. They were discreet, elegant, reserved.

There was nothing discreet, elegant, or reserved about appearing like a circus attraction in the pages of Miss Hawke's scandal sheet. Yet he had to. For Jonathan's family. More importantly, for Jonathan himself.

"We're agreed," he said.

She stuck out her hand. Offering it to shake. He stared at it for a moment. Ladies didn't shake hands— they presented them to be bowed over, or else the women curtsied. But here was more proof that Miss Hawke was unlike any other female he'd ever known.

His handshake was his bond. This final gesture would seal his fate.

Finally, he took her hand in his. He still wore his gloves, but through the delicate kidskin he could feel calluses lining her fingers—she worked for a living. Her hand was warm, too, even through the thin leather of his gloves. A tropic current pulsed through him. What would it feel like to have their bare palms press against each other, skin to skin? He'd known the feel of many women, but none like her.

She gazed down at their joined hands, a faint frown nestled between her eyebrows. As if trying to puzzle out an enigma.

He'd have to be on his guard around her. She was the kind of person who would never give up on a mystery until every aspect of it was uncovered. If she unearthed his true motive for this proposition, the consequences would be ruinous.

Abruptly, she broke the grip between them. Her hand pressed against her skirts. She cleared her throat. "We should fix a schedule. When shall we begin?"

"As soon as possible."

She narrowed her eyes. "In a hurry, my lord?"

Using years of a nobleman's training, he made his voice smooth and unaffected. "Don't want to keep your readers in the dark for too long." Which wasn't an answer, but he wasn't about to give her one.

"Tomorrow will suffice," she answered, "if that suits you."

"It does," he answered. "I'd been planning on spending our evening at Donnegan's."

"I'm not familiar with it."

"This gaming hell isn't exactly sanctioned."

"A gaming hell." She practically bounced on her feet in eagerness, then stilled. "Do they allow women?"

"No—so I might have to come up with a new plan."
All this time, he'd been planning that E. Hawke was a
man.

"I can get my hands on some masculine attire," she
said. "A disguise." Far from looking daunted by the
prospect of wearing men's clothing and infiltrating a
haven of male vice, Miss Hawke looked as excited as
a child given free rein in a toy shop. A very immoral
toy shop.

"How?"

"I have friends in the theater," she answered.

"Naturally—one employment of disrepute gravi-
tates toward another."

"And yet titled men lead lives of such incomparable
virtue."

"We *are* fond of the theater," he said drily. "Feeds
our appetite for dissipation."

"Well, my dissipated friends at the Imperial Theater
will give me access to their costumes and wigs."

He lifted his brows. "The Imperial. They're known
for their rather . . . unconventional theatrical offerings."
His friend Marwood almost never missed a night at the
Imperial. Marwood especially loved the burlettas of
Mrs. Delamere, which inevitably skewered the upper
classes.

Miss Hawke's quick, wide smile caught him between the ribs. "When one doesn't have a patent, one
has to be a bit inventive in order to bring in patrons."

He set his hat on his head. "Tomorrow night, then.
I'll pick you up at the Imperial."

"Tomorrow night."

After a pause, he turned and left, all the while aware
of her gaze on his back as he strode from the office.

He'd no choice—this had to be done. He'd have to see this through, whatever it might bring. Yet he couldn't forget the feel of her hand in his. Slim and warm and strong. As he stepped out onto the street, where his carriage waited for him, a thought whispered that he'd just agreed to a bargain with a very pretty devil.

The Casebook of Barnaby Adair novels from
#1 *New York Times* bestselling author

Stephanie
LAURENS

WHERE THE HEART LEADS
978-0-06-124338-7

Handsome, enigmatic, and deliciously dangerous, Barnaby Adair has made his name by solving crimes within the *ton*. When Penelope Ashford appeals for his aid in solving the mystery of the disappearing orphans in her care, he is moved by her plight—and captivated by her beauty.

THE MASTERFUL MR. MONTAGUE
978-0-06-206866-8

When Lady Halstead is murdered, Barnaby Adair helps her devoted lady-companion, Miss Violet Matcham, and her financial adviser, Montague, expose a cunning killer. But will Montague and Violet learn the shocking truth too late to seize their chance at enduring love?

LOVING ROSE
978-0-06-206867-5

Rose has a plausible explanation for why she and her children are residing in Thomas Glendower's secluded manor. Revealing the truth would be impossibly dangerous, yet day by day he wins her trust, and then her heart. But when her enemy closes in, Rose must turn to Thomas to protect her and her children.

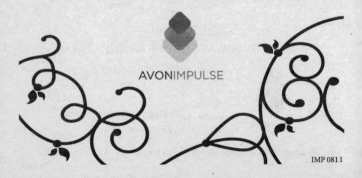